CHAPTER

23

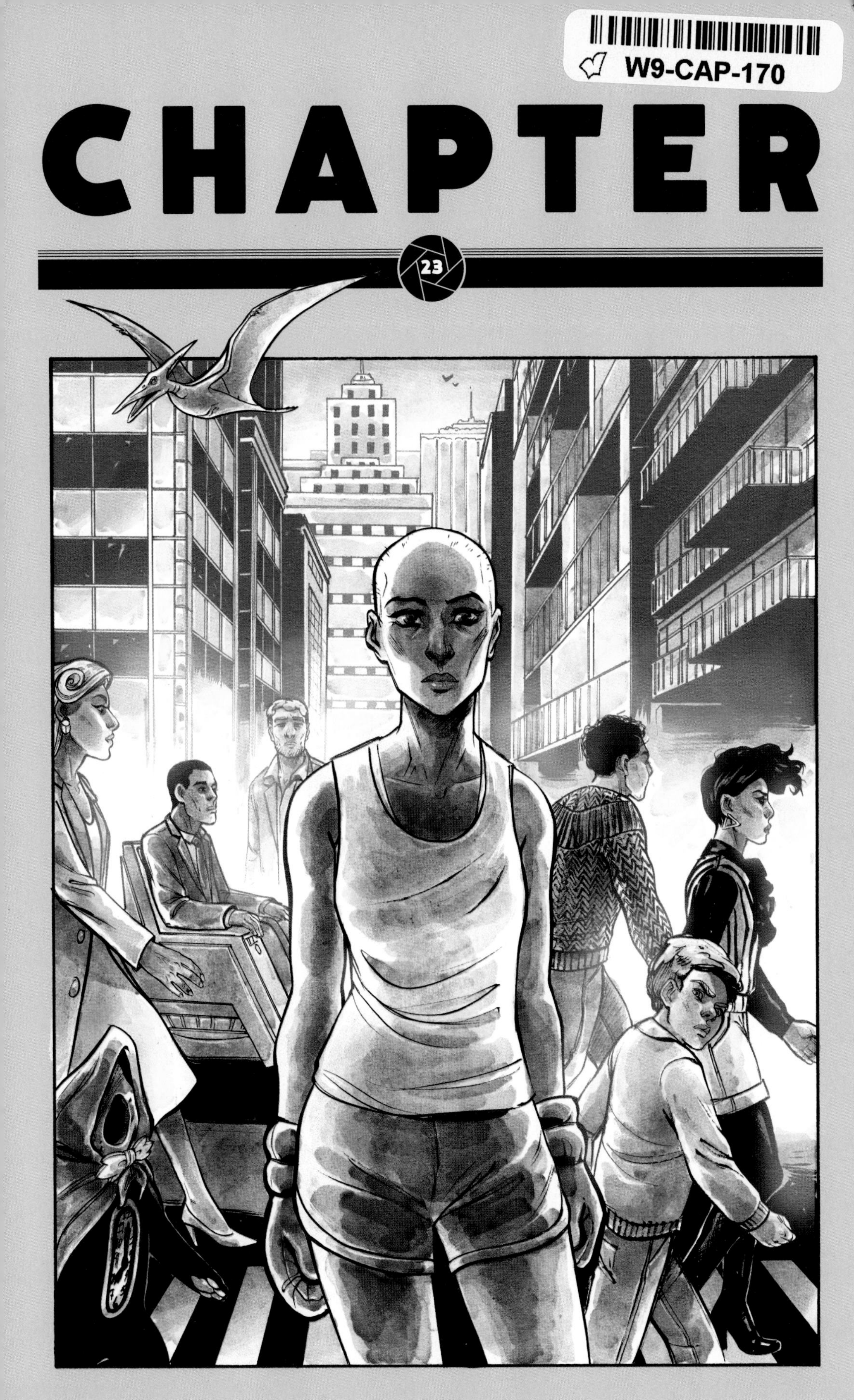

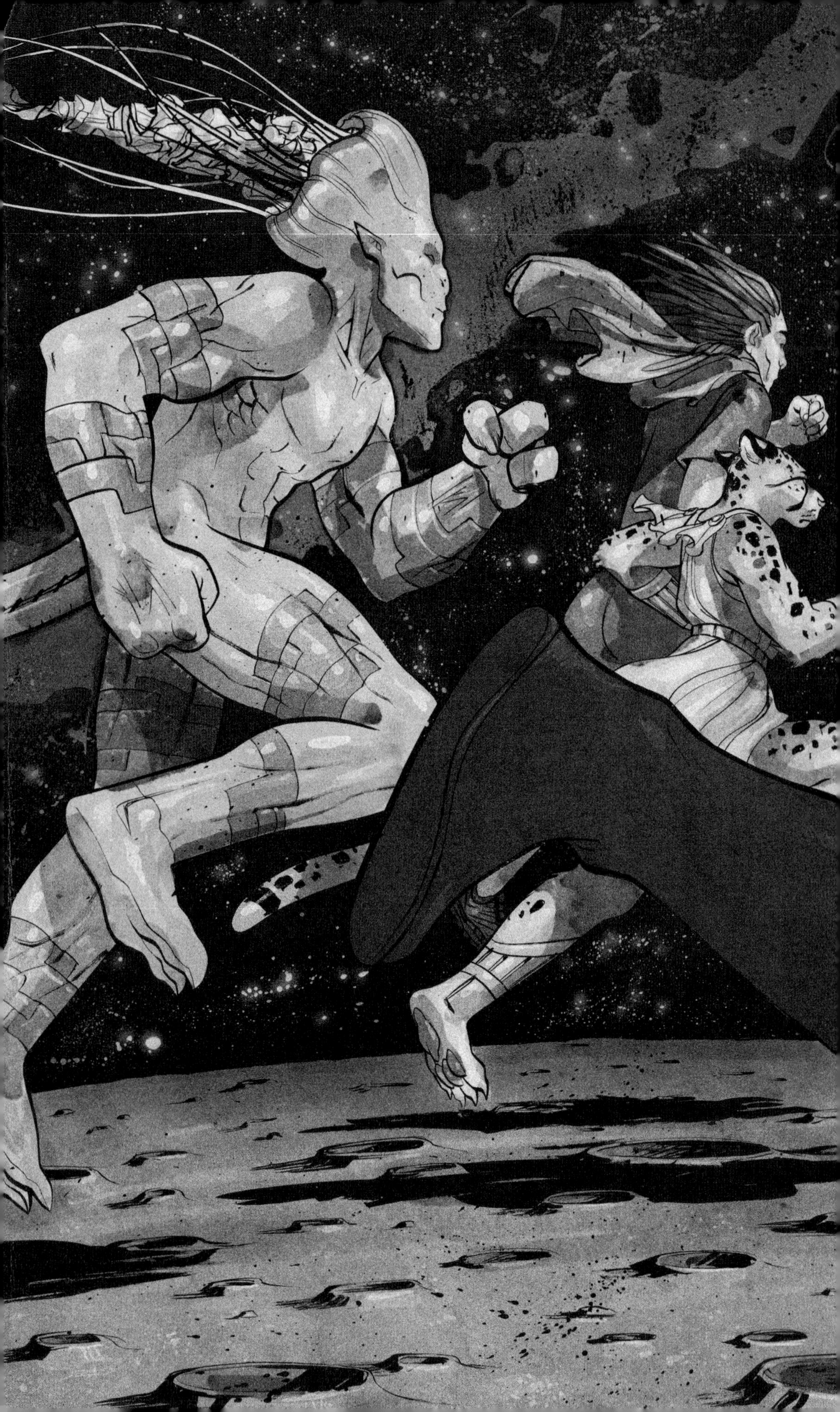

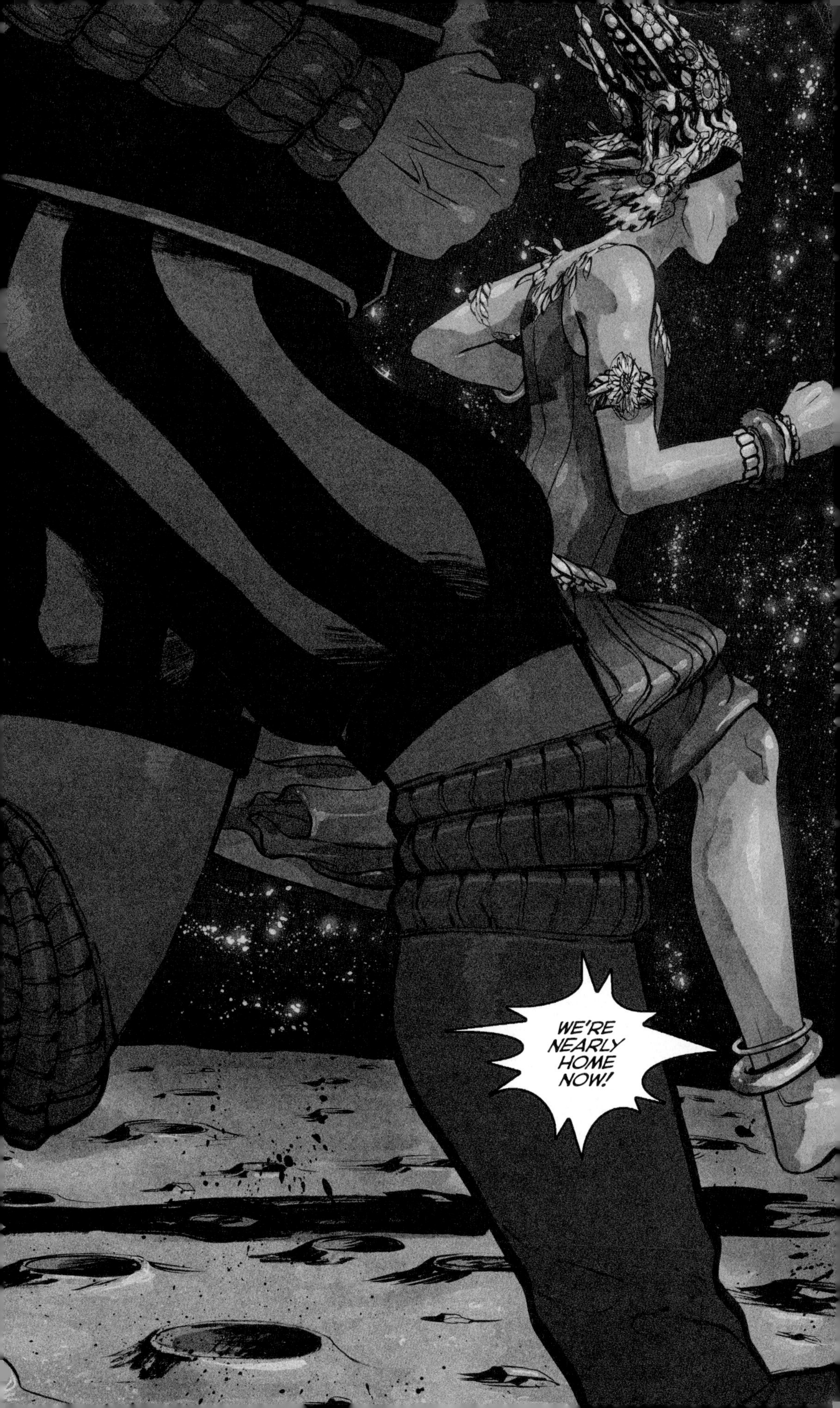
WE'RE NEARLY HOME NOW!

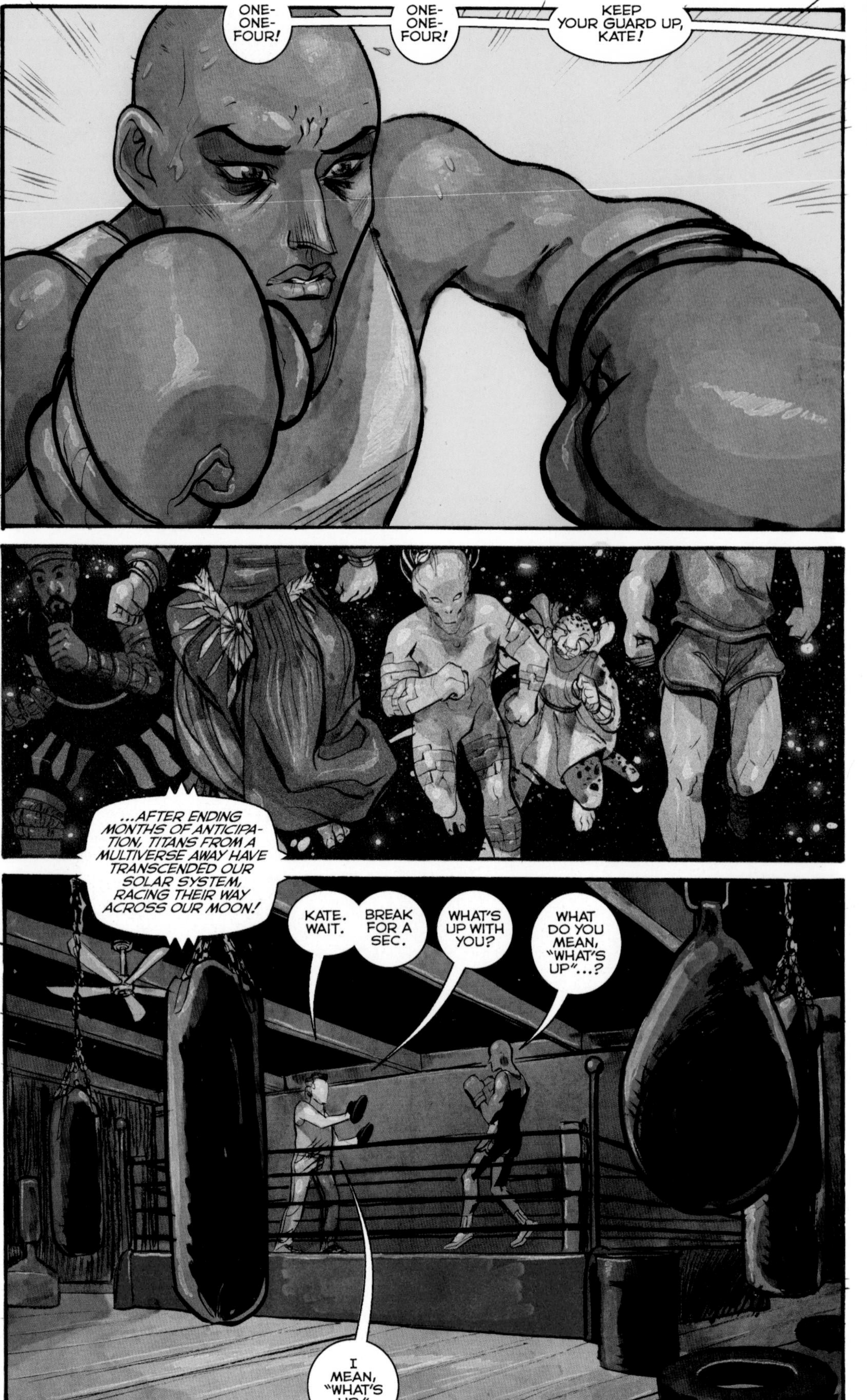
ONE-
ONE-
FOUR!
ONE-
ONE-
FOUR!
KEEP YOUR GUARD UP, KATE!
...AFTER ENDING MONTHS OF ANTICIPATION, TITANS FROM A MULTIVERSE AWAY HAVE TRANSCENDED OUR SOLAR SYSTEM, RACING THEIR WAY ACROSS OUR MOON!
KATE. WAIT.
BREAK FOR A SEC.
WHAT'S UP WITH YOU?
WHAT DO YOU MEAN, "WHAT'S UP"...?
I MEAN, "WHAT'S UP."

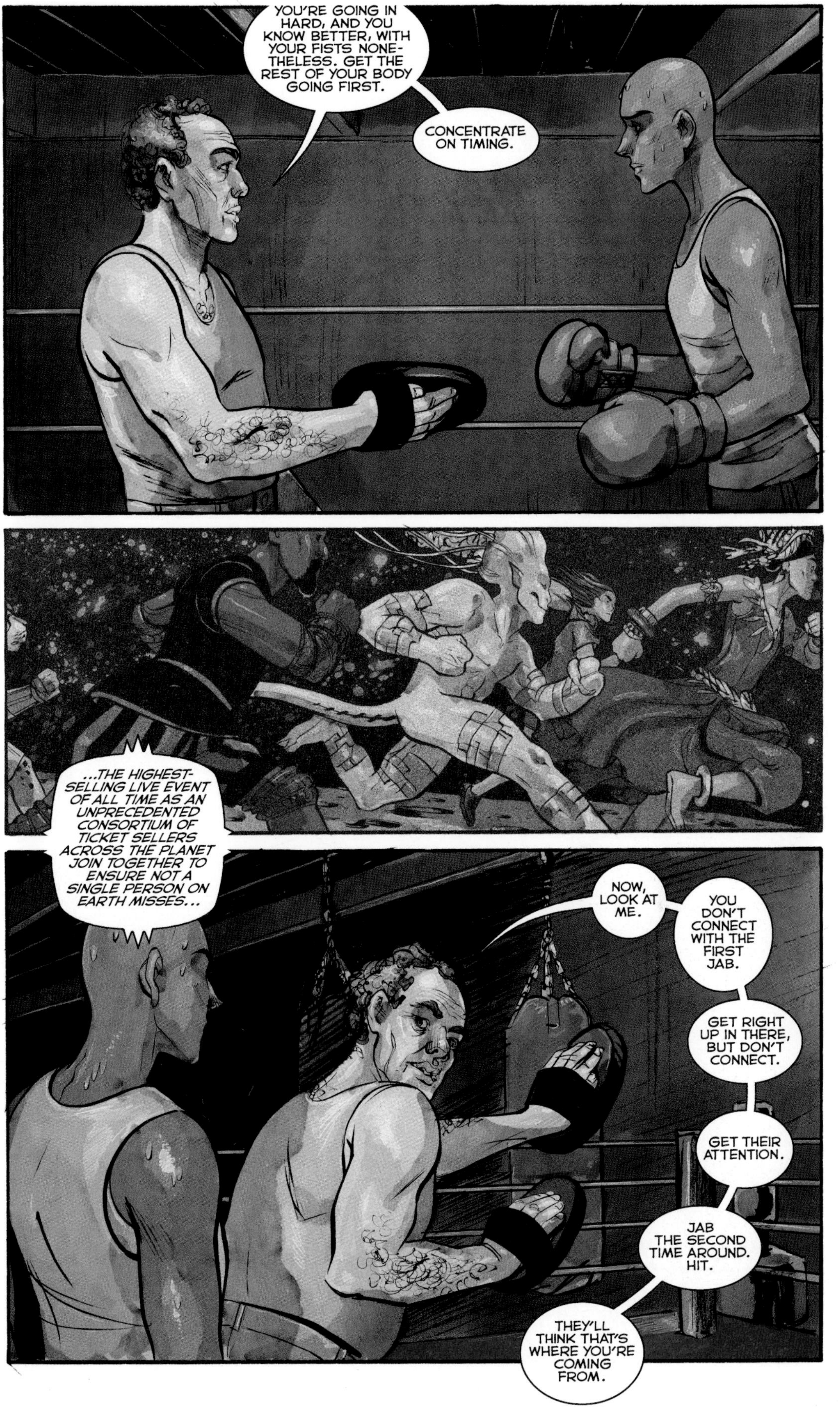
YOU'RE GOING IN HARD, AND YOU KNOW BETTER, WITH YOUR FISTS NONE-THELESS. GET THE REST OF YOUR BODY GOING FIRST.
CONCENTRATE ON TIMING.
...THE HIGHEST-SELLING LIVE EVENT OF ALL TIME AS AN UNPRECEDENTED CONSORTIUM OF TICKET SELLERS ACROSS THE PLANET JOIN TOGETHER TO ENSURE NOT A SINGLE PERSON ON EARTH MISSES...
NOW, LOOK AT ME.
YOU DON'T CONNECT WITH THE FIRST JAB.
GET RIGHT UP IN THERE, BUT DON'T CONNECT.
GET THEIR ATTENTION.
JAB THE SECOND TIME AROUND. HIT.
THEY'LL THINK THAT'S WHERE YOU'RE COMING FROM.

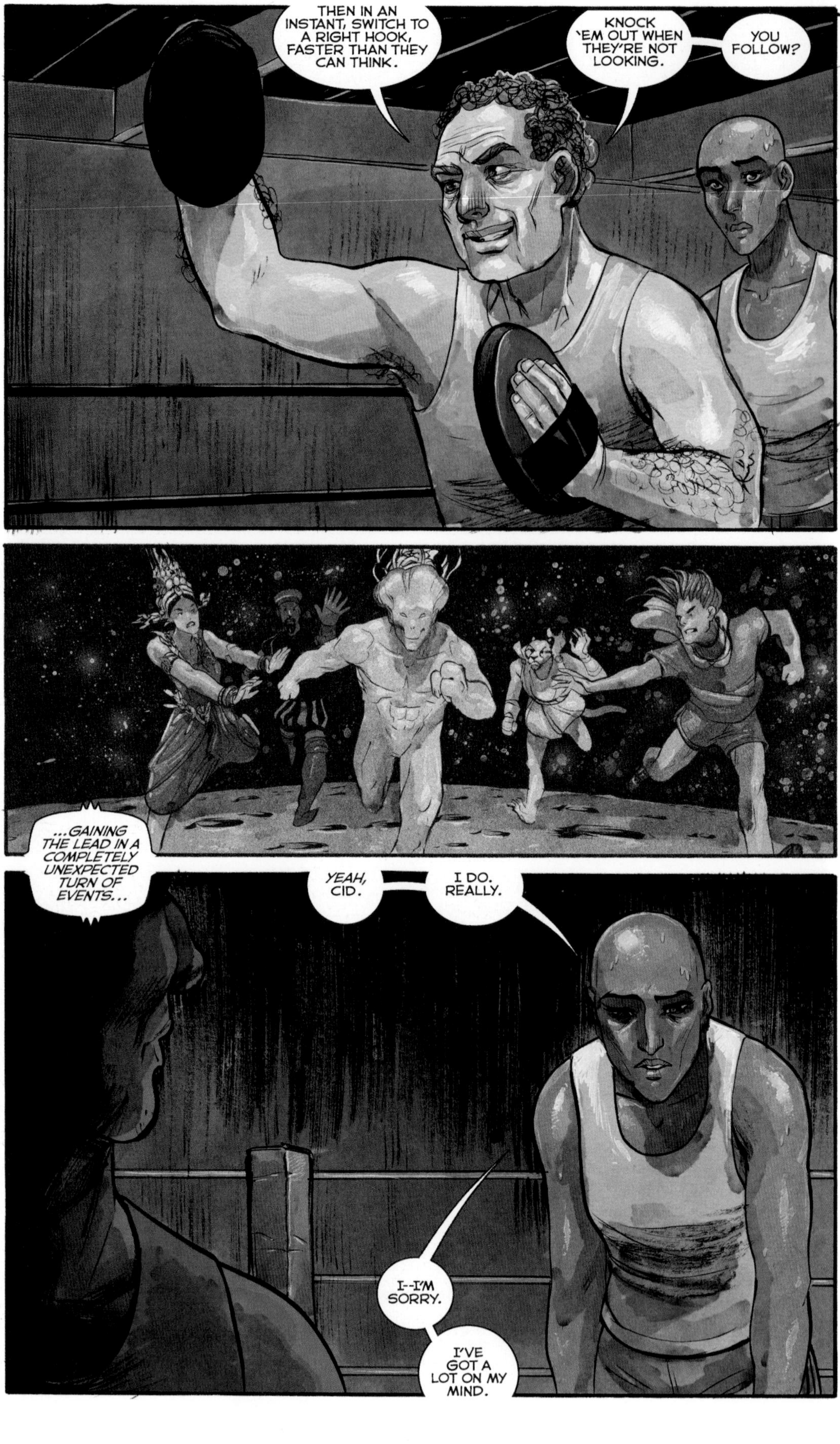
THEN IN AN INSTANT, SWITCH TO A RIGHT HOOK, FASTER THAN THEY CAN THINK.
KNOCK 'EM OUT WHEN THEY'RE NOT LOOKING.
YOU FOLLOW?
...GAINING THE LEAD IN A COMPLETELY UNEXPECTED TURN OF EVENTS...
YEAH, CID.
I DO. REALLY.
I--I'M SORRY.
I'VE GOT A LOT ON MY MIND.

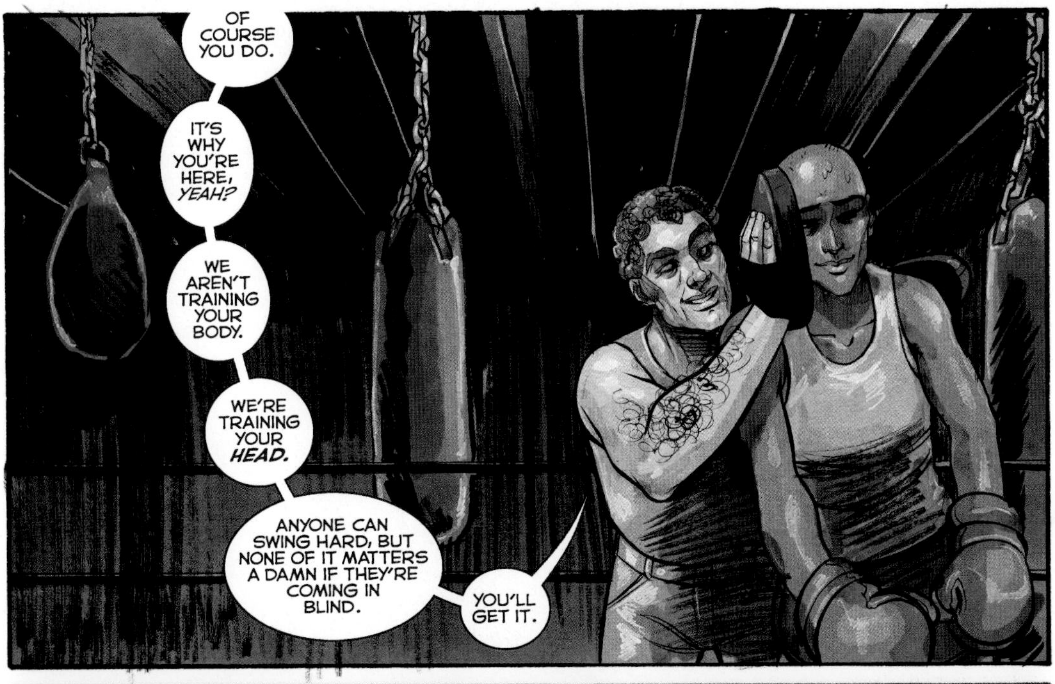
OF COURSE YOU DO.
IT'S WHY YOU'RE HERE, *YEAH?*
WE AREN'T TRAINING YOUR BODY.
WE'RE TRAINING YOUR ***HEAD.***
ANYONE CAN SWING HARD, BUT NONE OF IT MATTERS A DAMN IF THEY'RE COMING IN BLIND.
YOU'LL GET IT.

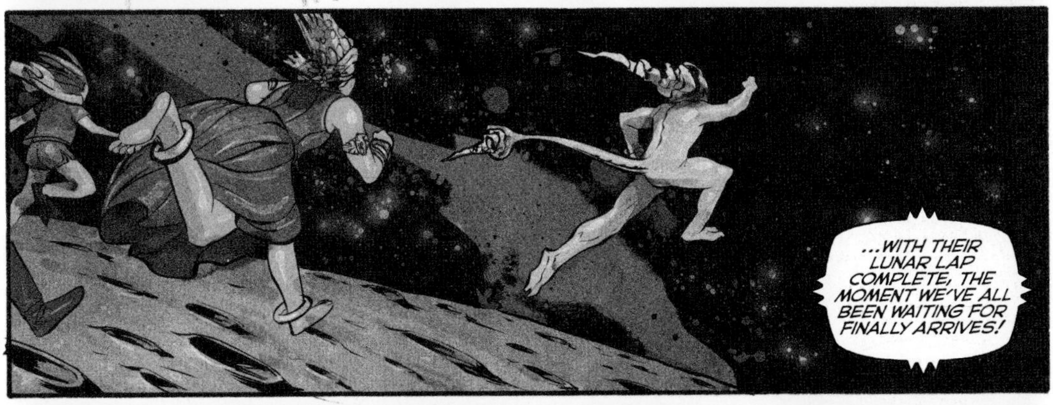
...WITH THEIR LUNAR LAP COMPLETE, THE MOMENT WE'VE ALL BEEN WAITING FOR FINALLY ARRIVES!

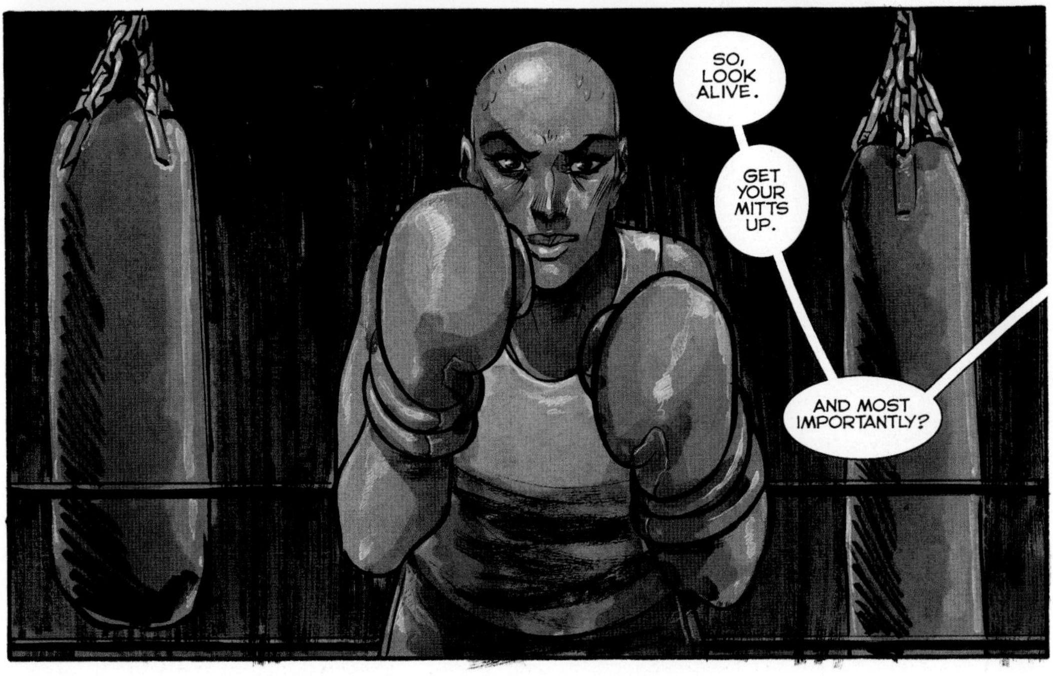
SO, LOOK ALIVE.
GET YOUR MITTS UP.
AND MOST IMPORTANTLY?

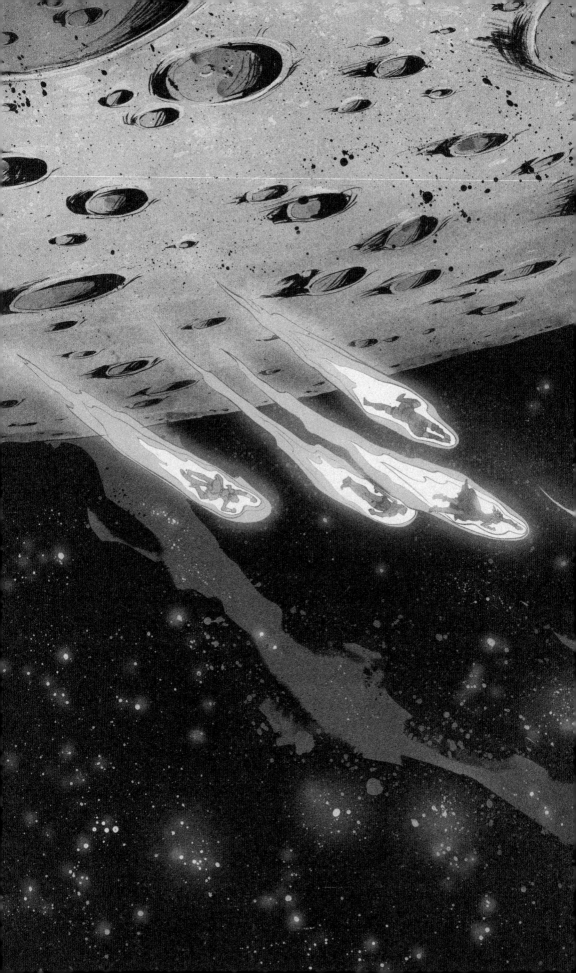

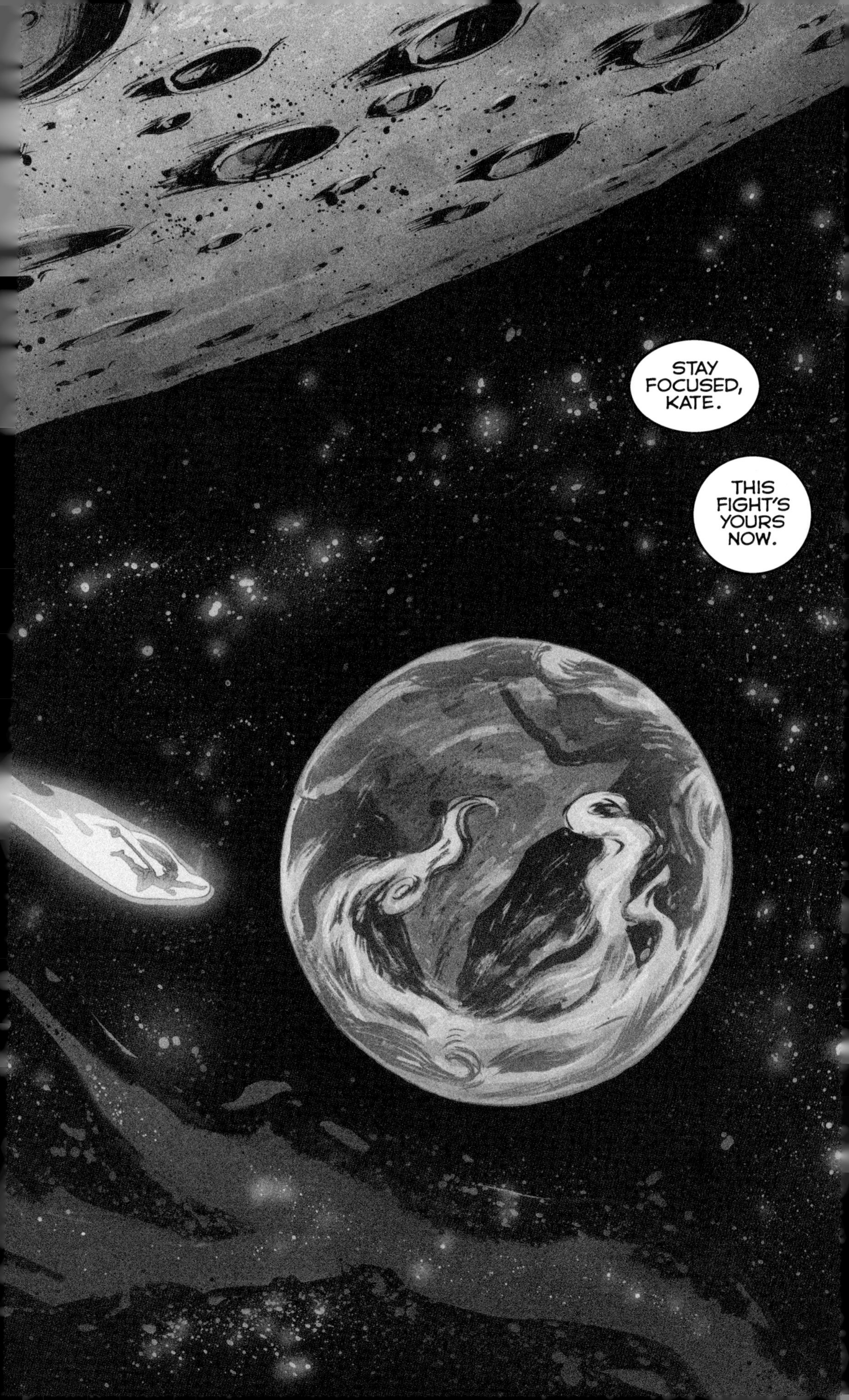
STAY FOCUSED, KATE.
THIS FIGHT'S YOURS NOW.

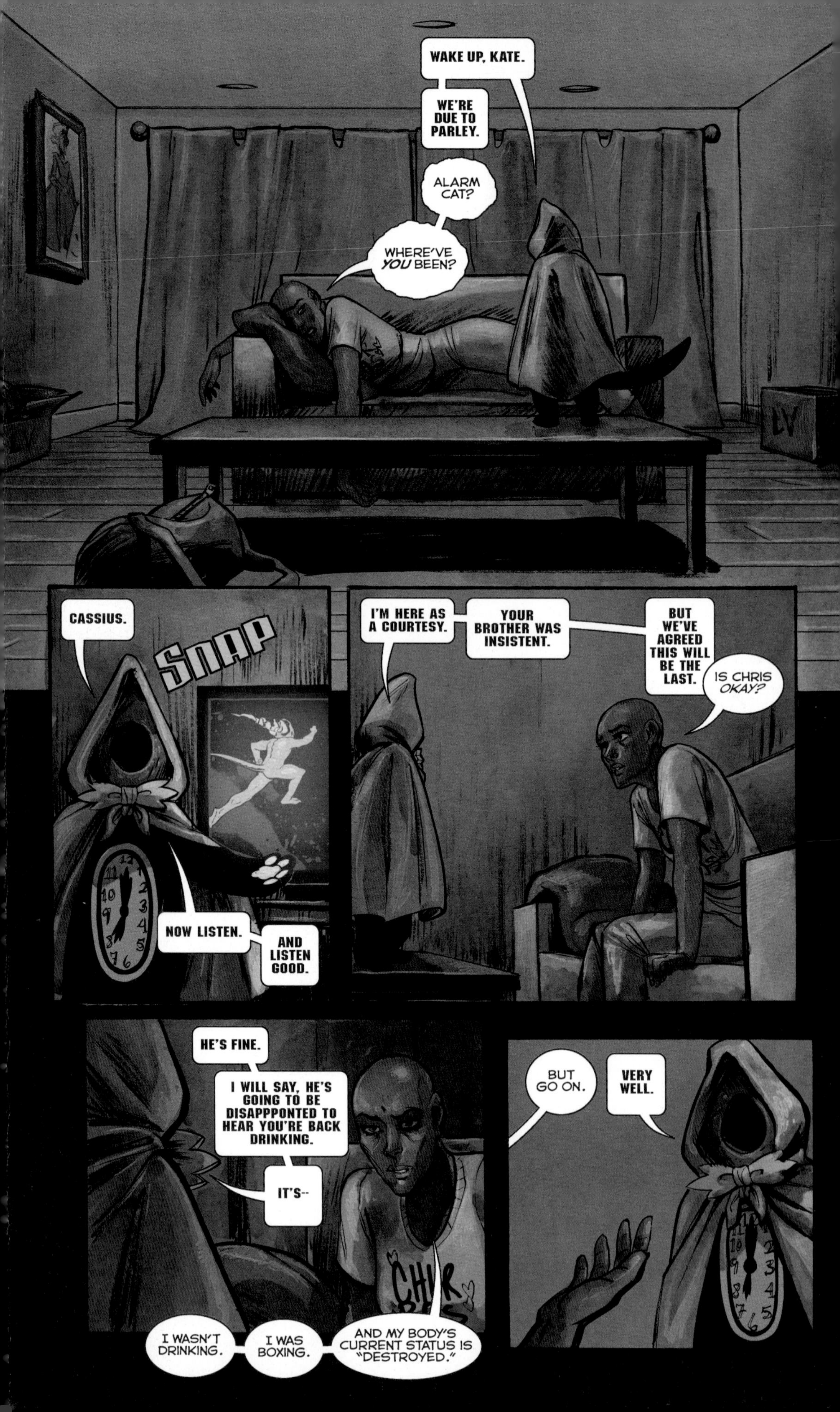
WAKE UP, KATE.
WE'RE DUE TO PARLEY.
ALARM CAT?
WHERE'VE *YOU* BEEN?
CASSIUS.
SNAP
NOW LISTEN.
AND LISTEN GOOD.
I'M HERE AS A COURTESY.
YOUR BROTHER WAS INSISTENT.
BUT WE'VE AGREED THIS WILL BE THE LAST.
IS CHRIS *OKAY?*
HE'S FINE.
I WILL SAY, HE'S GOING TO BE DISAPPPONTED TO HEAR YOU'RE BACK DRINKING.
IT'S--
I WASN'T DRINKING.
I WAS BOXING.
AND MY BODY'S CURRENT STATUS IS "DESTROYED."
VERY WELL.
BUT GO ON.

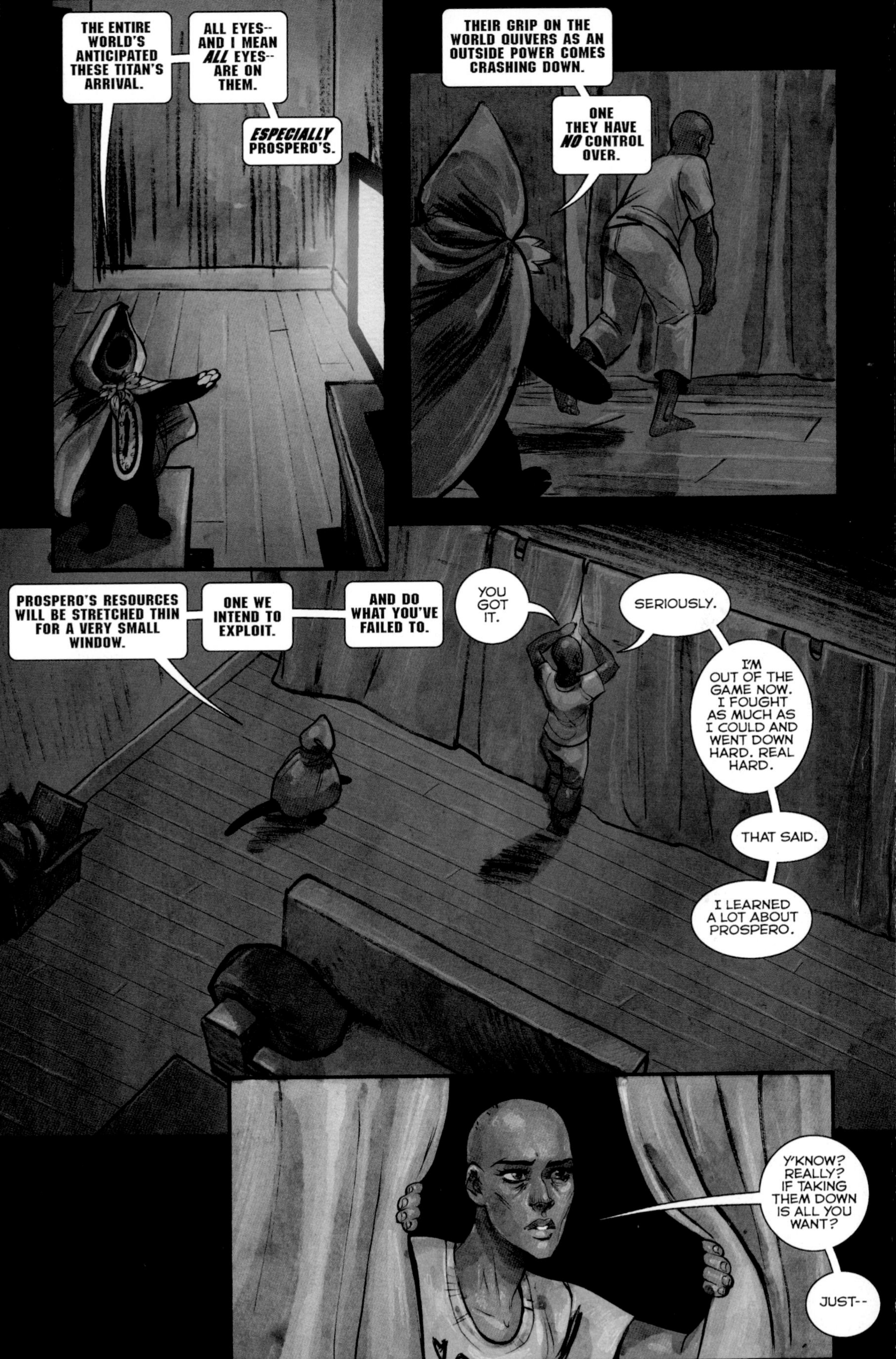
THE ENTIRE WORLD'S ANTICIPATED THESE TITAN'S ARRIVAL.
ALL EYES-- AND I MEAN *ALL* EYES-- ARE ON THEM.
ESPECIALLY PROSPERO'S.
THEIR GRIP ON THE WORLD QUIVERS AS AN OUTSIDE POWER COMES CRASHING DOWN.
ONE THEY HAVE *NO* CONTROL OVER.
PROSPERO'S RESOURCES WILL BE STRETCHED THIN FOR A VERY SMALL WINDOW.
ONE WE INTEND TO EXPLOIT.
AND DO WHAT YOU'VE FAILED TO.
YOU GOT IT.
SERIOUSLY.
I'M OUT OF THE GAME NOW. I FOUGHT AS MUCH AS I COULD AND WENT DOWN HARD. REAL HARD.
THAT SAID.
I LEARNED A LOT ABOUT PROSPERO.
Y'KNOW? REALLY? IF TAKING THEM DOWN IS ALL YOU WANT?
JUST--

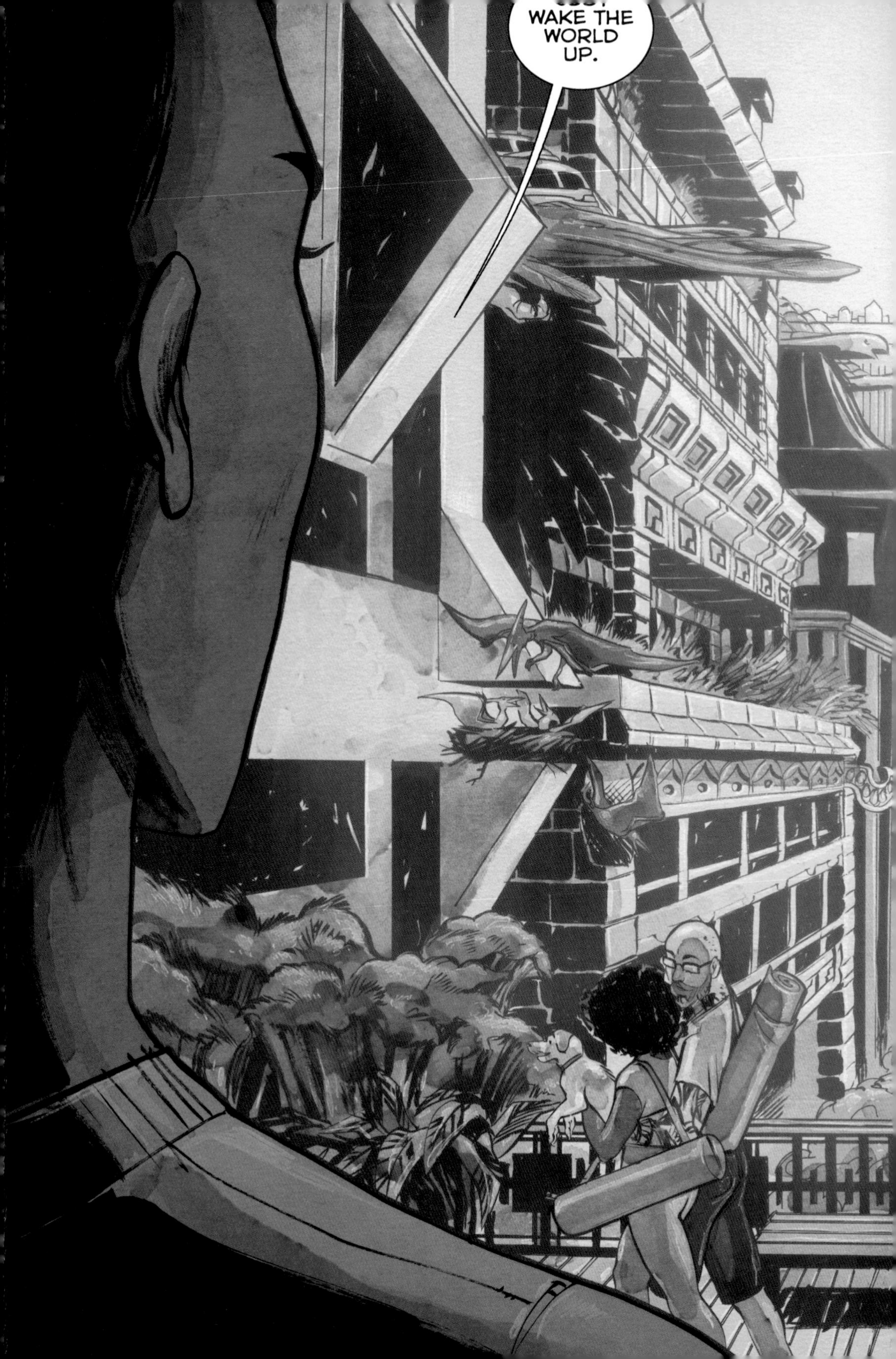
WAKE THE WORLD UP.

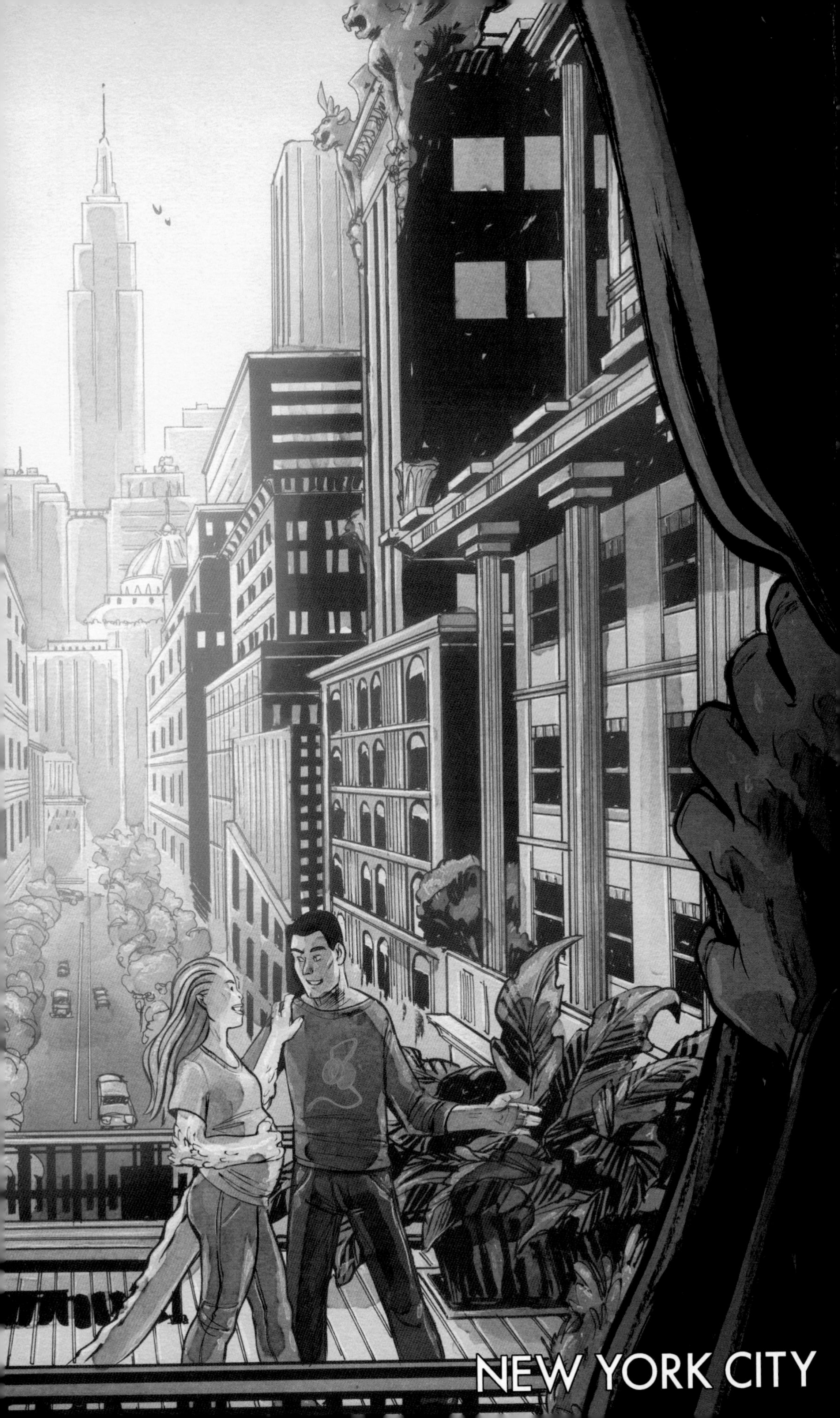
NEW YORK CITY

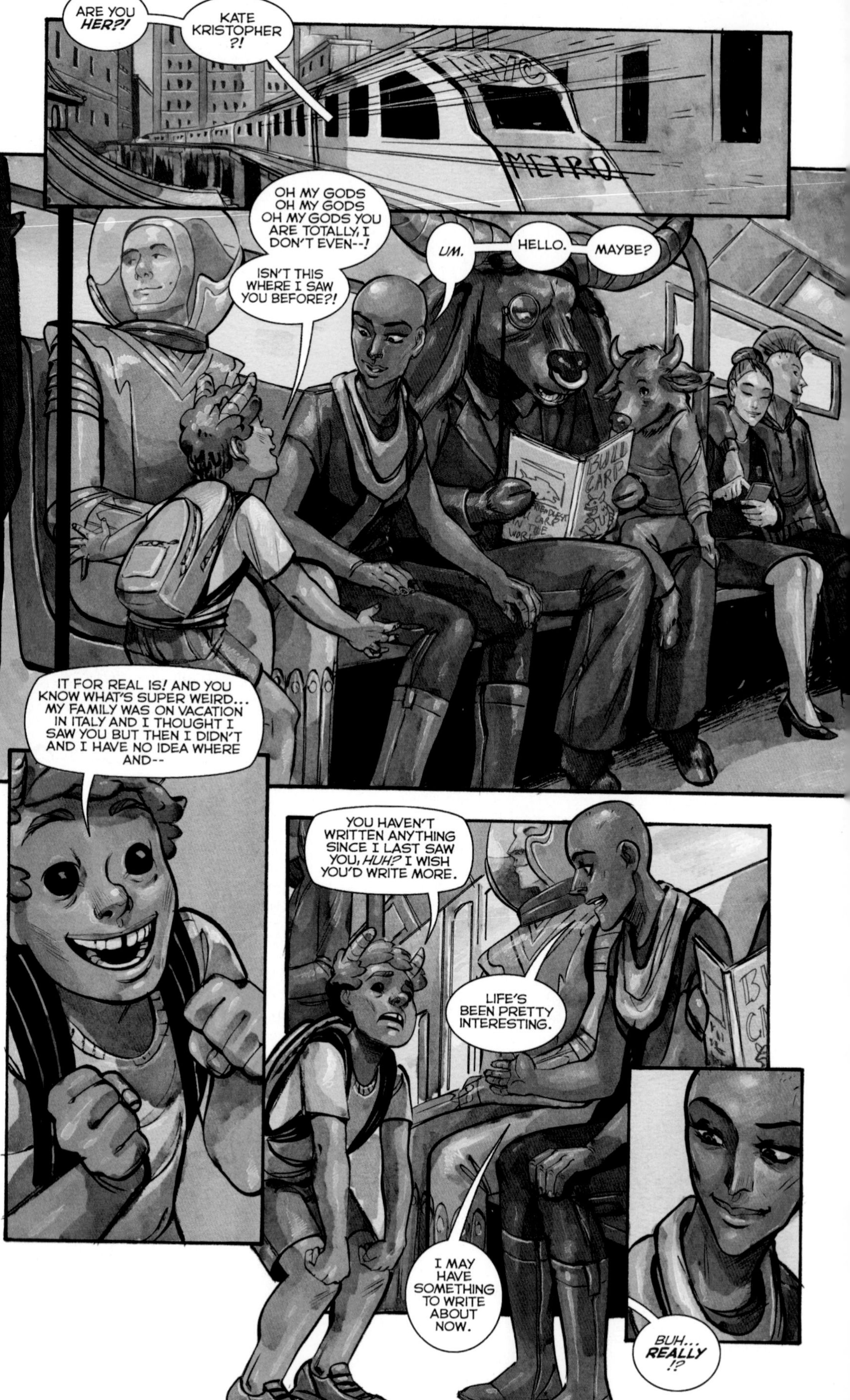
ARE YOU *HER?!*
KATE KRISTOPHER ?!
METRO
OH MY GODS OH MY GODS OH MY GODS YOU ARE TOTALLY, I DON'T EVEN--!
ISN'T THIS WHERE I SAW YOU BEFORE?!
UM.
HELLO.
MAYBE?
IT FOR REAL IS! AND YOU KNOW WHAT'S SUPER WEIRD... MY FAMILY WAS ON VACATION IN ITALY AND I THOUGHT I SAW YOU BUT THEN I DIDN'T AND I HAVE NO IDEA WHERE AND--
YOU HAVEN'T WRITTEN ANYTHING SINCE I LAST SAW YOU, *HUH?* I WISH YOU'D WRITE MORE.
LIFE'S BEEN PRETTY INTERESTING.
I MAY HAVE SOMETHING TO WRITE ABOUT NOW.
*BUH... **REALLY** !?*

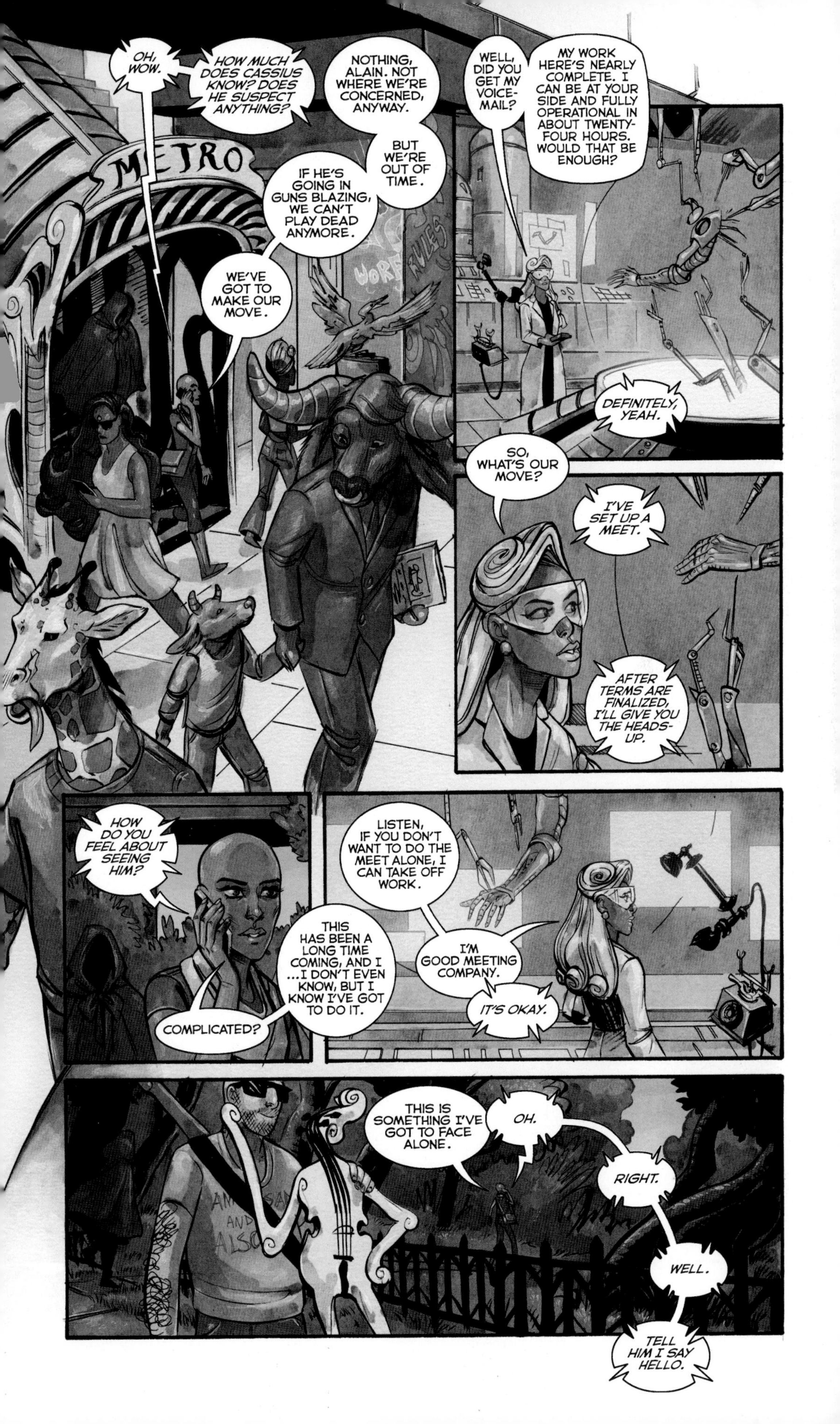
METRO
OH, WOW.
HOW MUCH DOES CASSIUS KNOW? DOES HE SUSPECT ANYTHING?
NOTHING, ALAIN. NOT WHERE WE'RE CONCERNED, ANYWAY.
BUT WE'RE OUT OF TIME.
IF HE'S GOING IN GUNS BLAZING, WE CAN'T PLAY DEAD ANYMORE.
WE'VE GOT TO MAKE OUR MOVE.
WELL, DID YOU GET MY VOICE-MAIL?
MY WORK HERE'S NEARLY COMPLETE. I CAN BE AT YOUR SIDE AND FULLY OPERATIONAL IN ABOUT TWENTY-FOUR HOURS. WOULD THAT BE ENOUGH?
DEFINITELY, YEAH.
SO, WHAT'S OUR MOVE?
I'VE SET UP A MEET.
AFTER TERMS ARE FINALIZED, I'LL GIVE YOU THE HEADS-UP.
HOW DO YOU FEEL ABOUT SEEING HIM?
COMPLICATED?
THIS HAS BEEN A LONG TIME COMING, AND I ...I DON'T EVEN KNOW, BUT I KNOW I'VE GOT TO DO IT.
LISTEN, IF YOU DON'T WANT TO DO THE MEET ALONE, I CAN TAKE OFF WORK.
I'M GOOD MEETING COMPANY.
IT'S OKAY.
THIS IS SOMETHING I'VE GOT TO FACE ALONE.
OH.
RIGHT.
WELL.
TELL HIM I SAY HELLO.

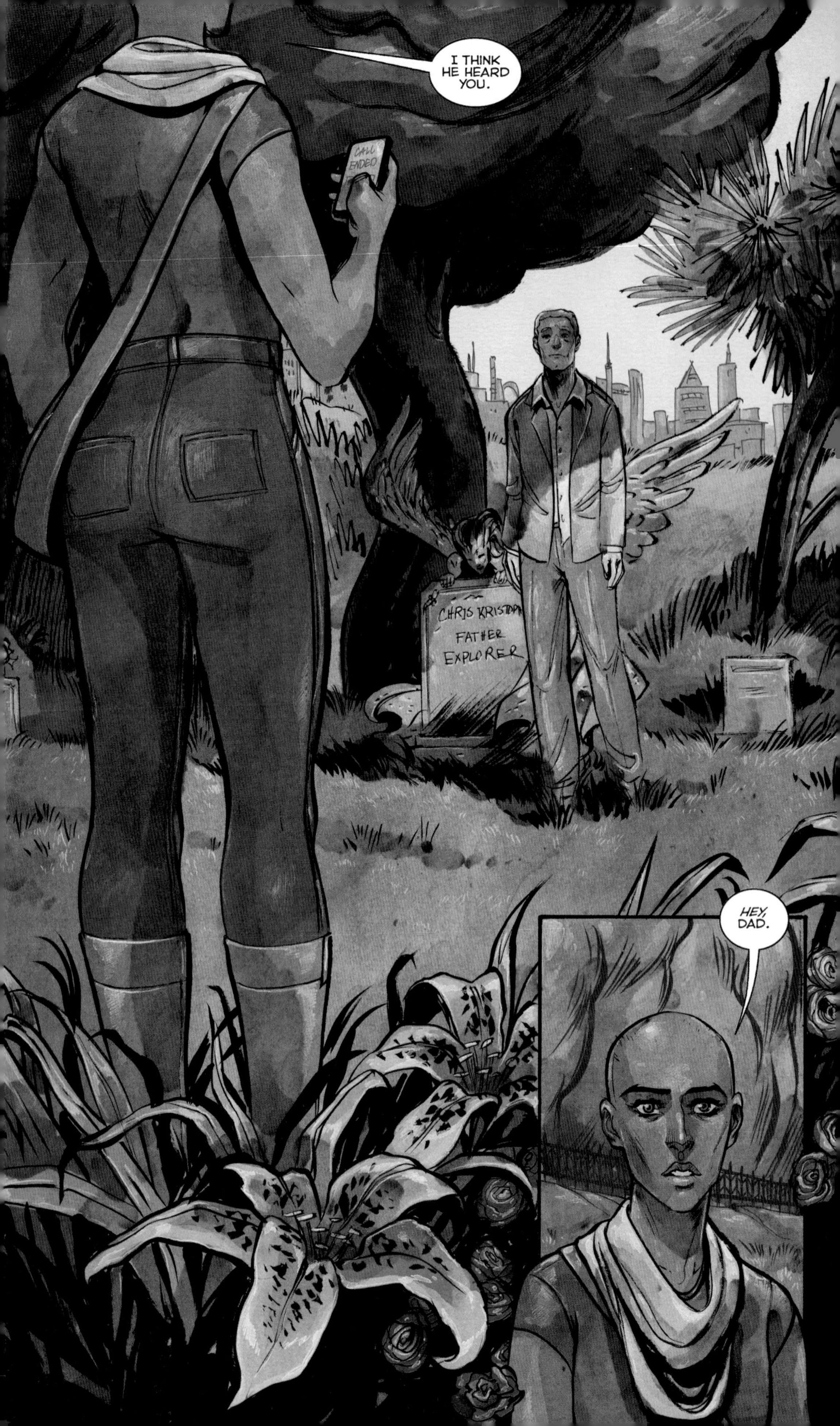
I THINK HE HEARD YOU.
CALL ENDED
CHRIS KRISTOPH
FATHER
EXPLORER
HEY, DAD.

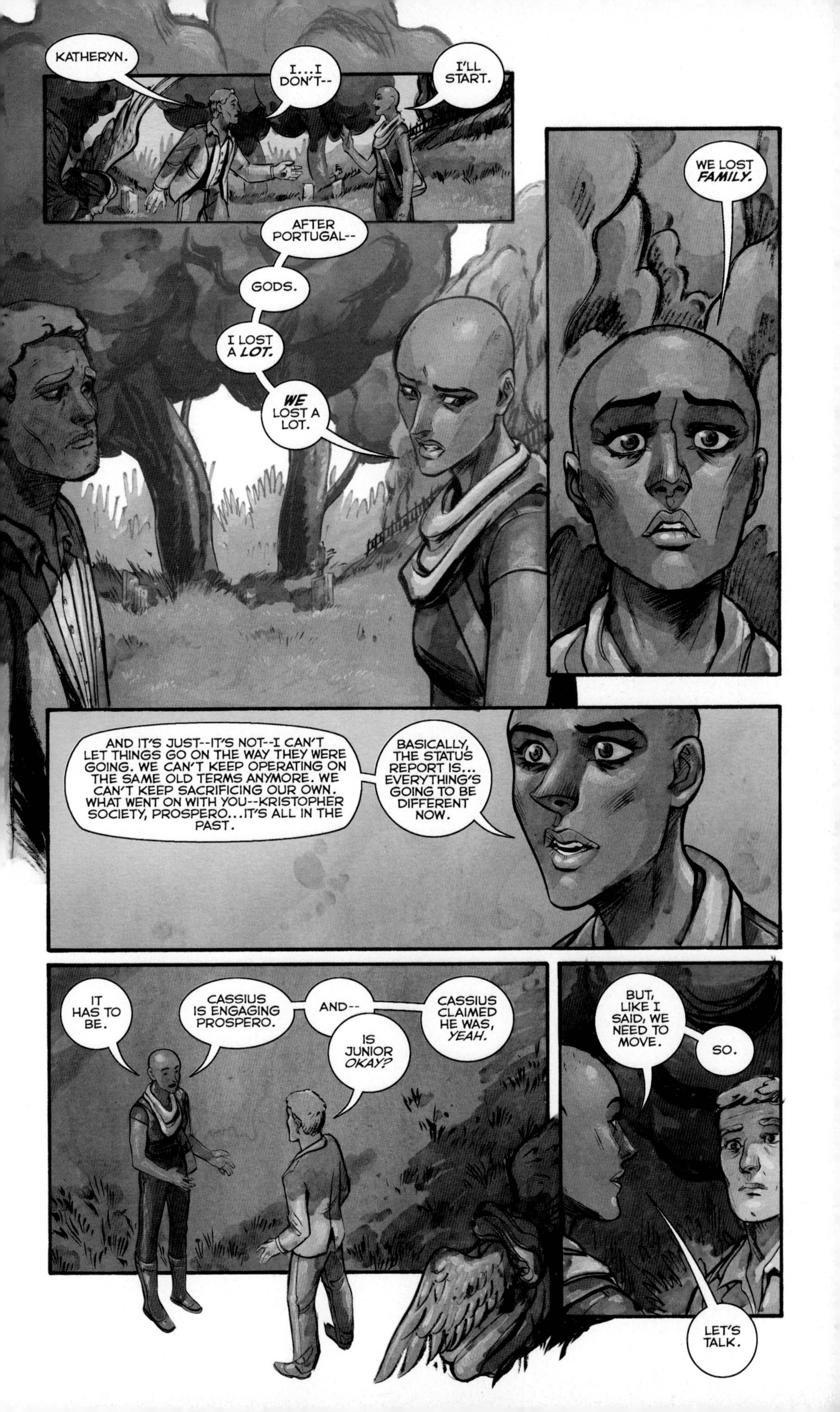
KATHERYN.
I...I DON'T--
I'LL START.
WE LOST *FAMILY.*
AFTER PORTUGAL--
GODS.
I LOST A *LOT.*
WE LOST A LOT.
AND IT'S JUST--IT'S NOT--I CAN'T LET THINGS GO ON THE WAY THEY WERE GOING. WE CAN'T KEEP OPERATING ON THE SAME OLD TERMS ANYMORE. WE CAN'T KEEP SACRIFICING OUR OWN. WHAT WENT ON WITH YOU--KRISTOPHER SOCIETY, PROSPERO...IT'S ALL IN THE PAST.
BASICALLY, THE STATUS REPORT IS... EVERYTHING'S GOING TO BE DIFFERENT NOW.
IT HAS TO BE.
CASSIUS IS ENGAGING PROSPERO.
AND--
IS JUNIOR *OKAY?*
CASSIUS CLAIMED HE WAS, *YEAH.*
BUT, LIKE I SAID, WE NEED TO MOVE.
SO.
LET'S TALK.

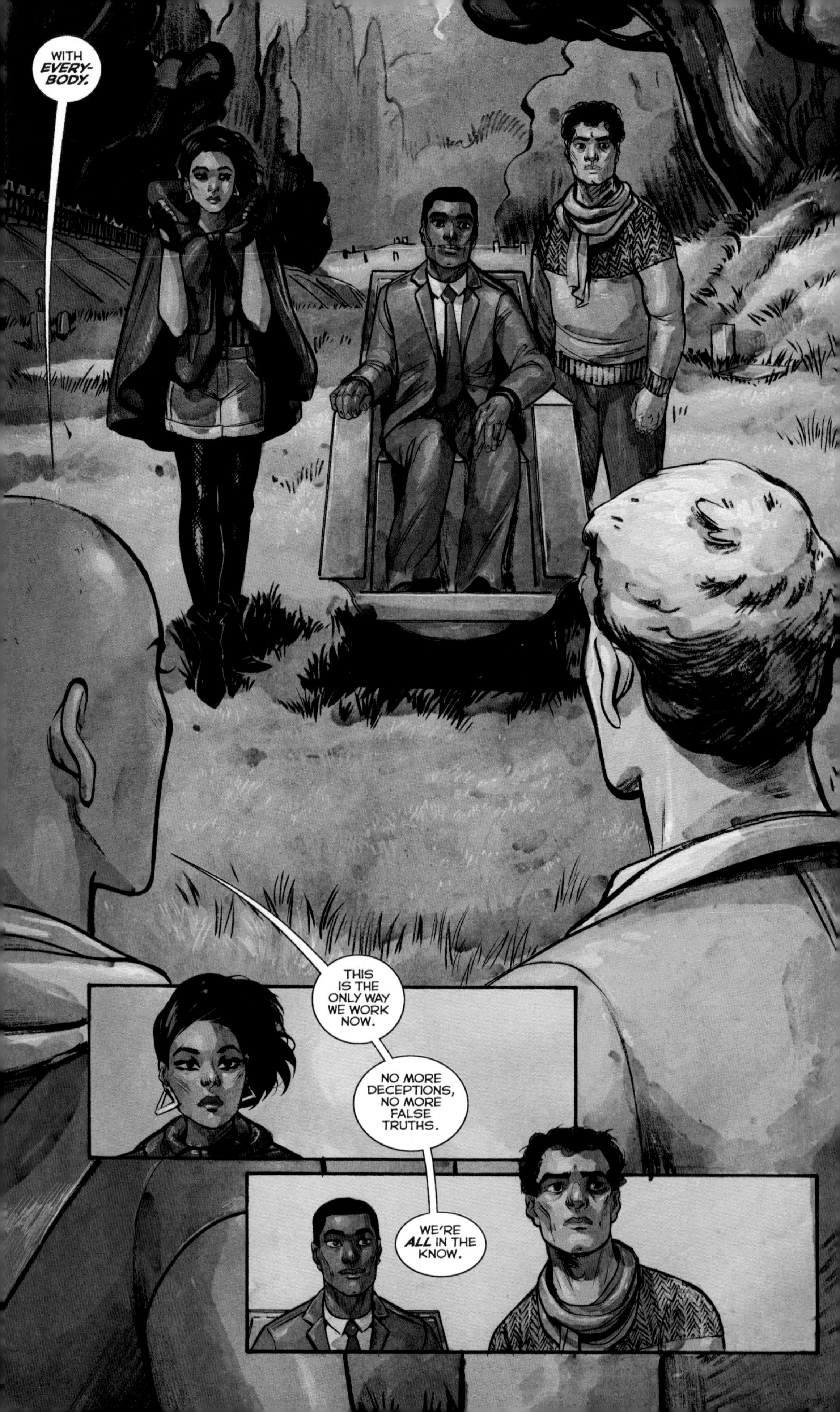
WITH EVERY-BODY.
THIS IS THE ONLY WAY WE WORK NOW.
NO MORE DECEPTIONS, NO MORE FALSE TRUTHS.
WE'RE ALL IN THE KNOW.

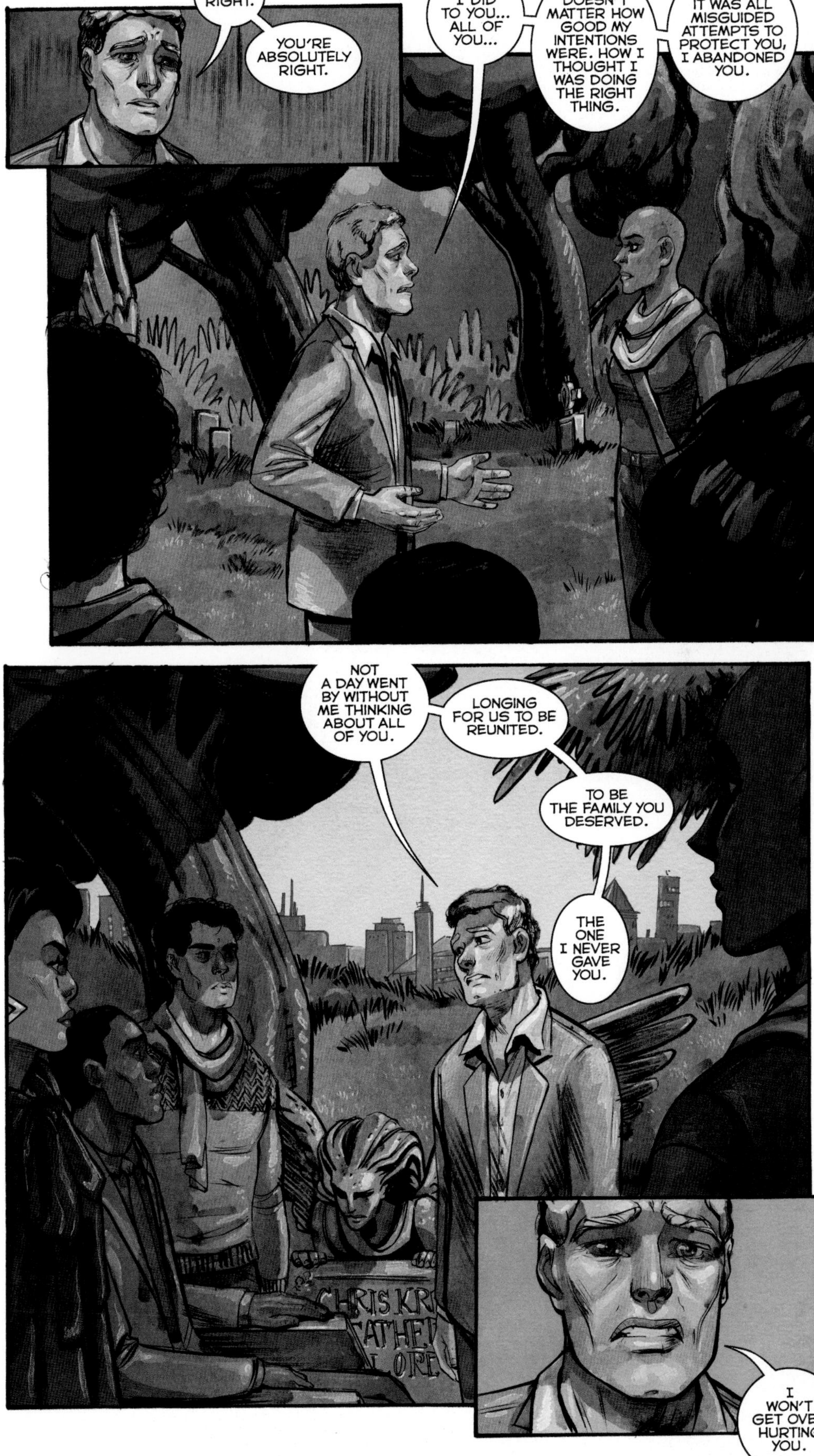
YOU'RE RIGHT.
YOU'RE ABSOLUTELY RIGHT.
WHAT I DID TO YOU... ALL OF YOU...
...IT DOESN'T MATTER HOW GOOD MY INTENTIONS WERE. HOW I THOUGHT I WAS DOING THE RIGHT THING.
EVEN IF IT WAS ALL MISGUIDED ATTEMPTS TO PROTECT YOU, I ABANDONED YOU.
NOT A DAY WENT BY WITHOUT ME THINKING ABOUT ALL OF YOU.
LONGING FOR US TO BE REUNITED.
TO BE THE FAMILY YOU DESERVED.
THE ONE I NEVER GAVE YOU.
I WON'T GET OVER HURTING YOU.

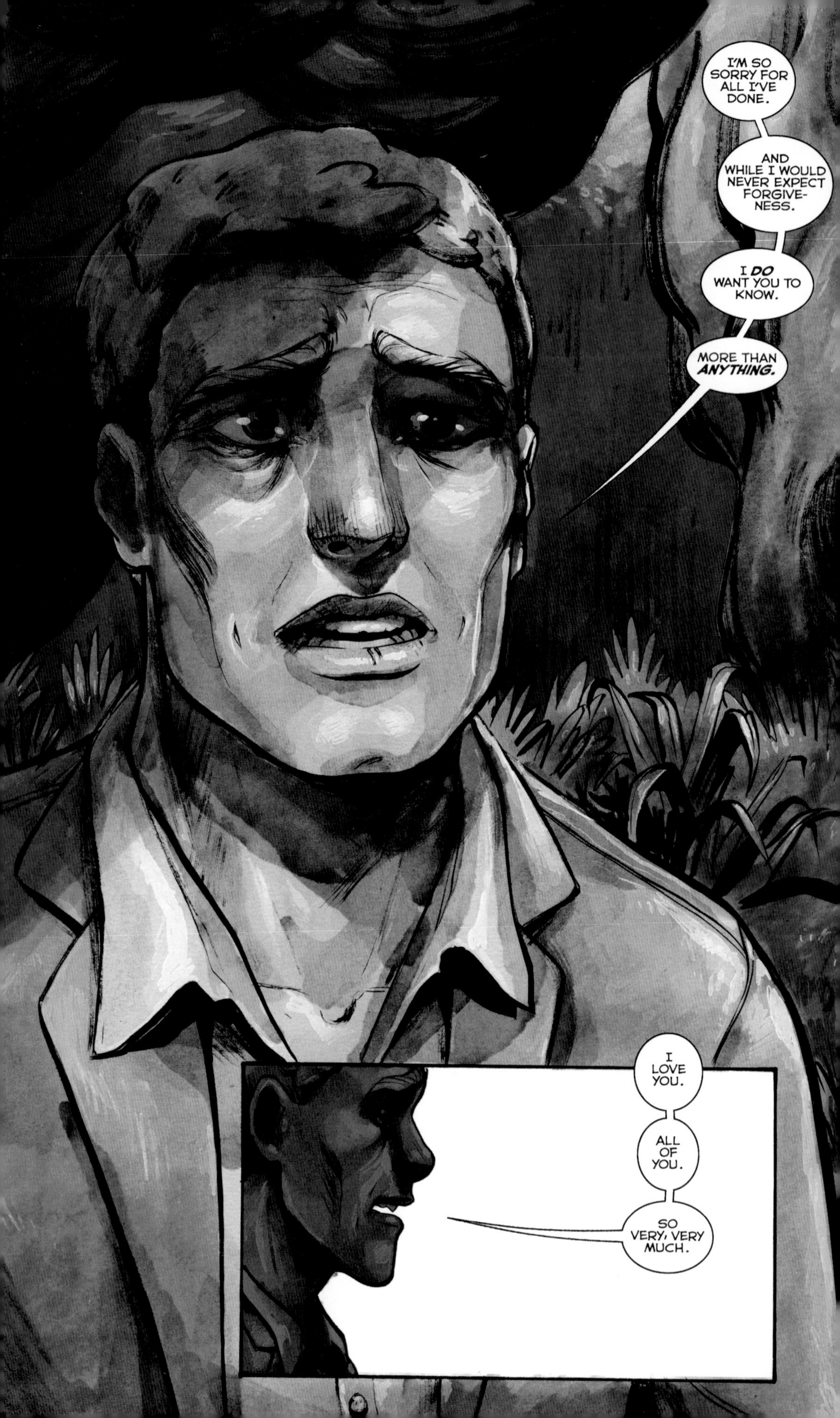
I'M SO SORRY FOR ALL I'VE DONE.
AND WHILE I WOULD NEVER EXPECT FORGIVE-NESS.
I *DO* WANT YOU TO KNOW.
MORE THAN ***ANYTHING.***
I LOVE YOU.
ALL OF YOU.
SO VERY, VERY MUCH.

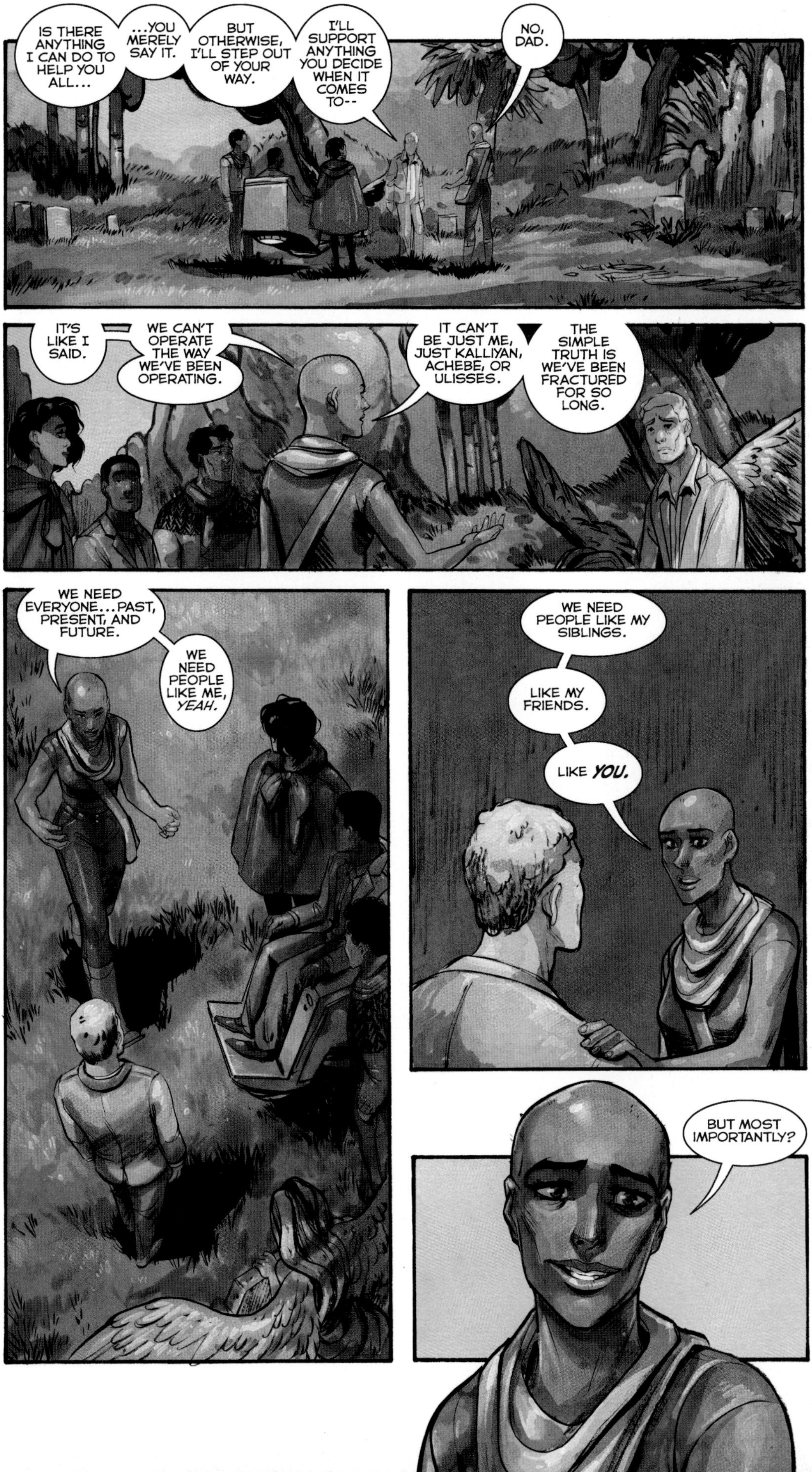

IS THERE ANYTHING I CAN DO TO HELP YOU ALL...
...YOU MERELY SAY IT.
BUT OTHERWISE, I'LL STEP OUT OF YOUR WAY.
I'LL SUPPORT ANYTHING YOU DECIDE WHEN IT COMES TO--
NO, DAD.
IT'S LIKE I SAID.
WE CAN'T OPERATE THE WAY WE'VE BEEN OPERATING.
IT CAN'T BE JUST ME, JUST KALLIYAN, ACHEBE, OR ULISSES.
THE SIMPLE TRUTH IS WE'VE BEEN FRACTURED FOR SO LONG.
WE NEED EVERYONE...PAST, PRESENT, AND FUTURE.
WE NEED PEOPLE LIKE ME, *YEAH.*
WE NEED PEOPLE LIKE MY SIBLINGS.
LIKE MY FRIENDS.
LIKE ***YOU.***
BUT MOST IMPORTANTLY?

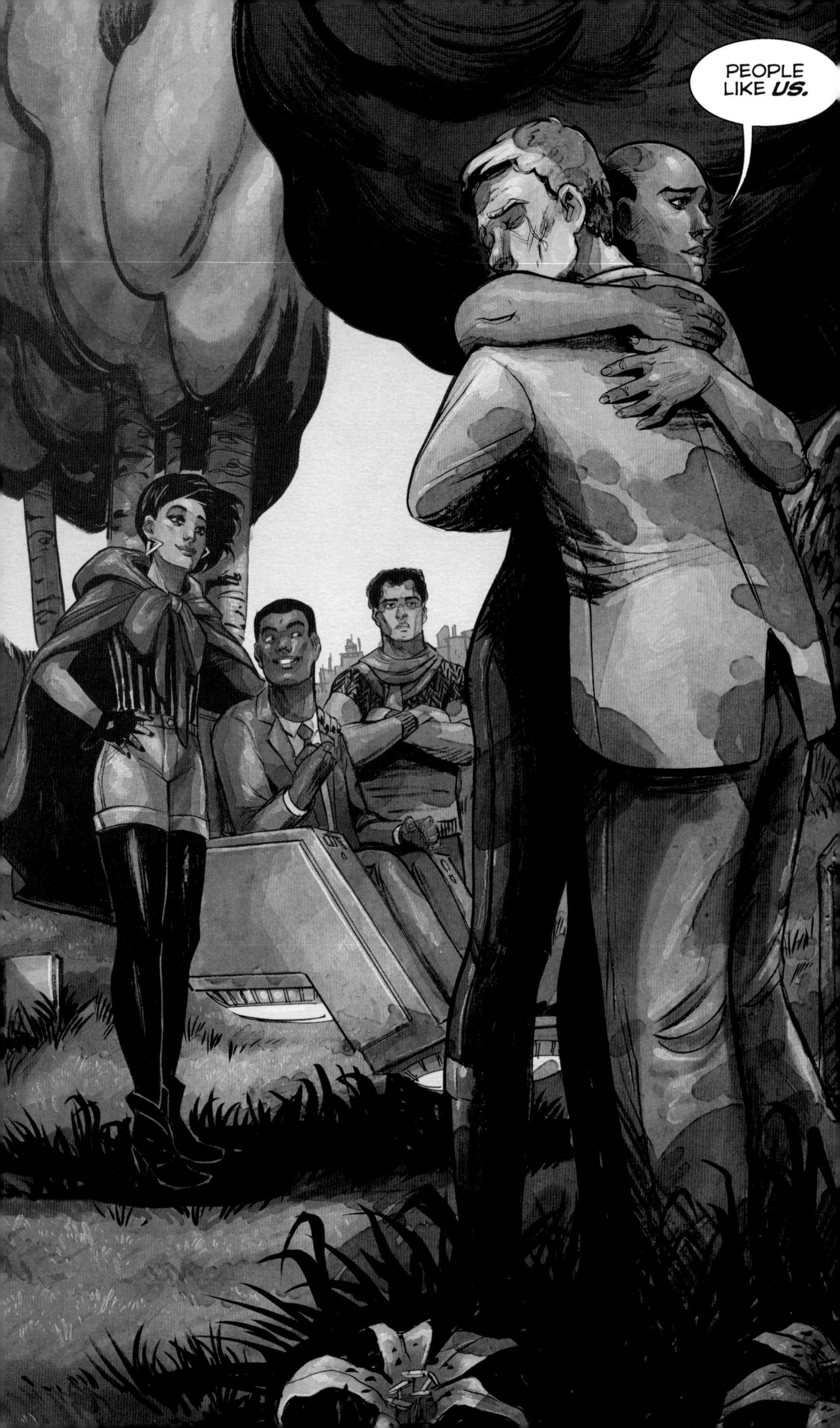
PEOPLE LIKE *US.*

CHAPTER 24

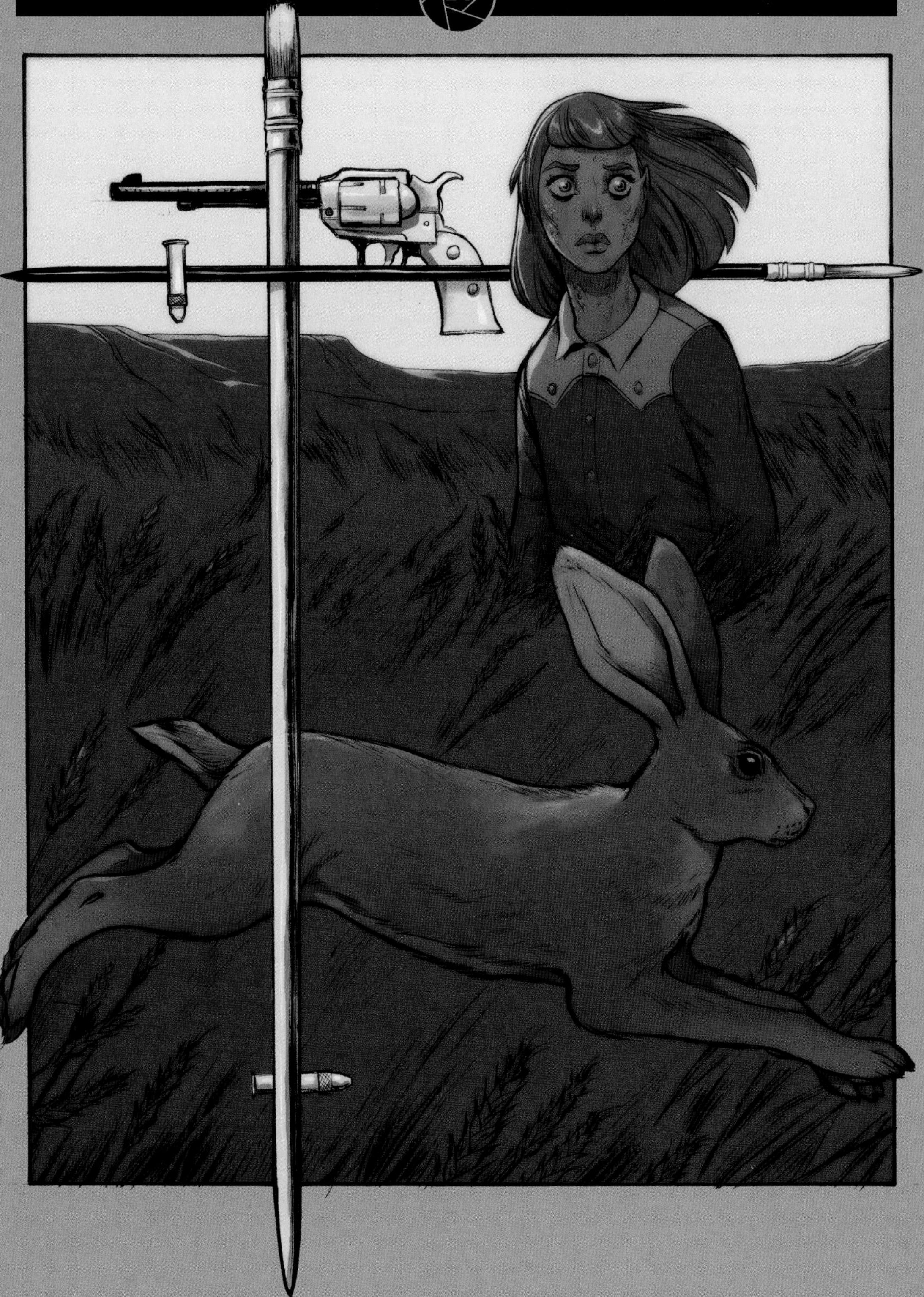

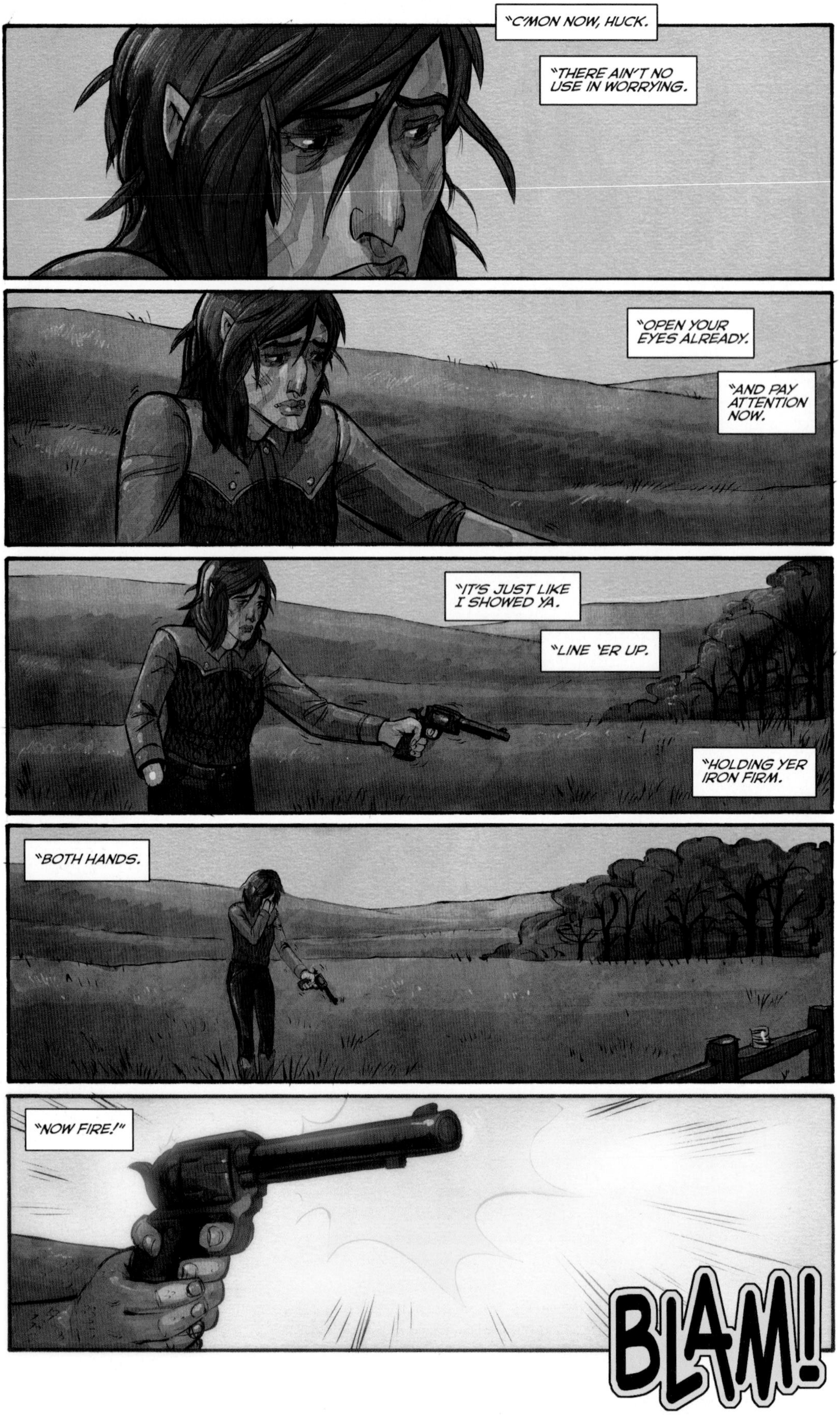
"C'MON NOW, HUCK.
"THERE AIN'T NO USE IN WORRYING.
"OPEN YOUR EYES ALREADY.
"AND PAY ATTENTION NOW.
"IT'S JUST LIKE I SHOWED YA.
"LINE 'ER UP.
"HOLDING YER IRON FIRM.
"BOTH HANDS.
"NOW FIRE!"
BLAM!

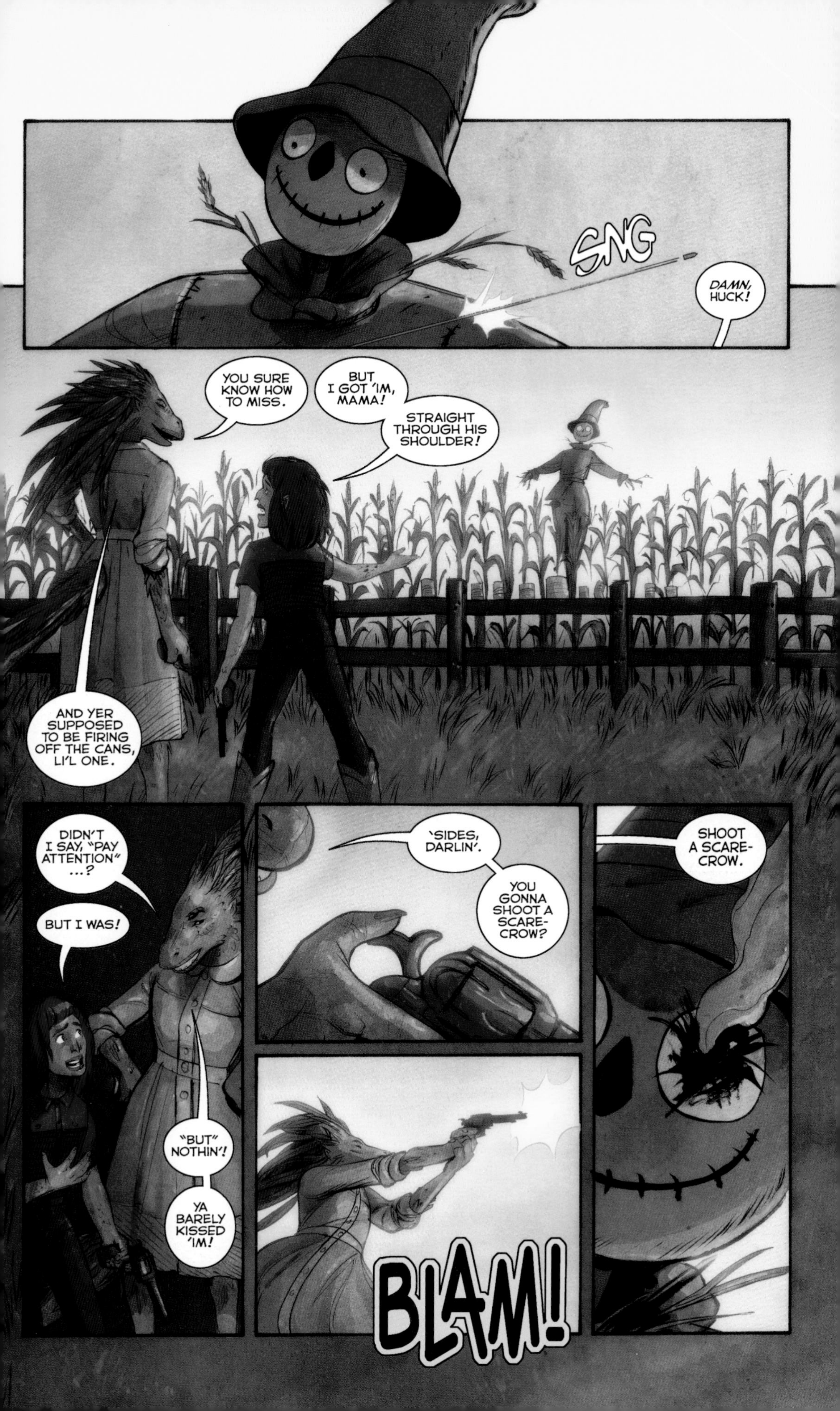
SNG
DAMN, HUCK!
YOU SURE KNOW HOW TO MISS.
BUT I GOT 'IM, MAMA!
STRAIGHT THROUGH HIS SHOULDER!
AND YER SUPPOSED TO BE FIRING OFF THE CANS, LI'L ONE.
DIDN'T I SAY, "PAY ATTENTION" ...?
BUT I WAS!
"BUT" NOTHIN'!
YA BARELY KISSED 'IM!
'SIDES, DARLIN'.
YOU GONNA SHOOT A SCARE-CROW?
BLAM!
SHOOT A SCARE-CROW.

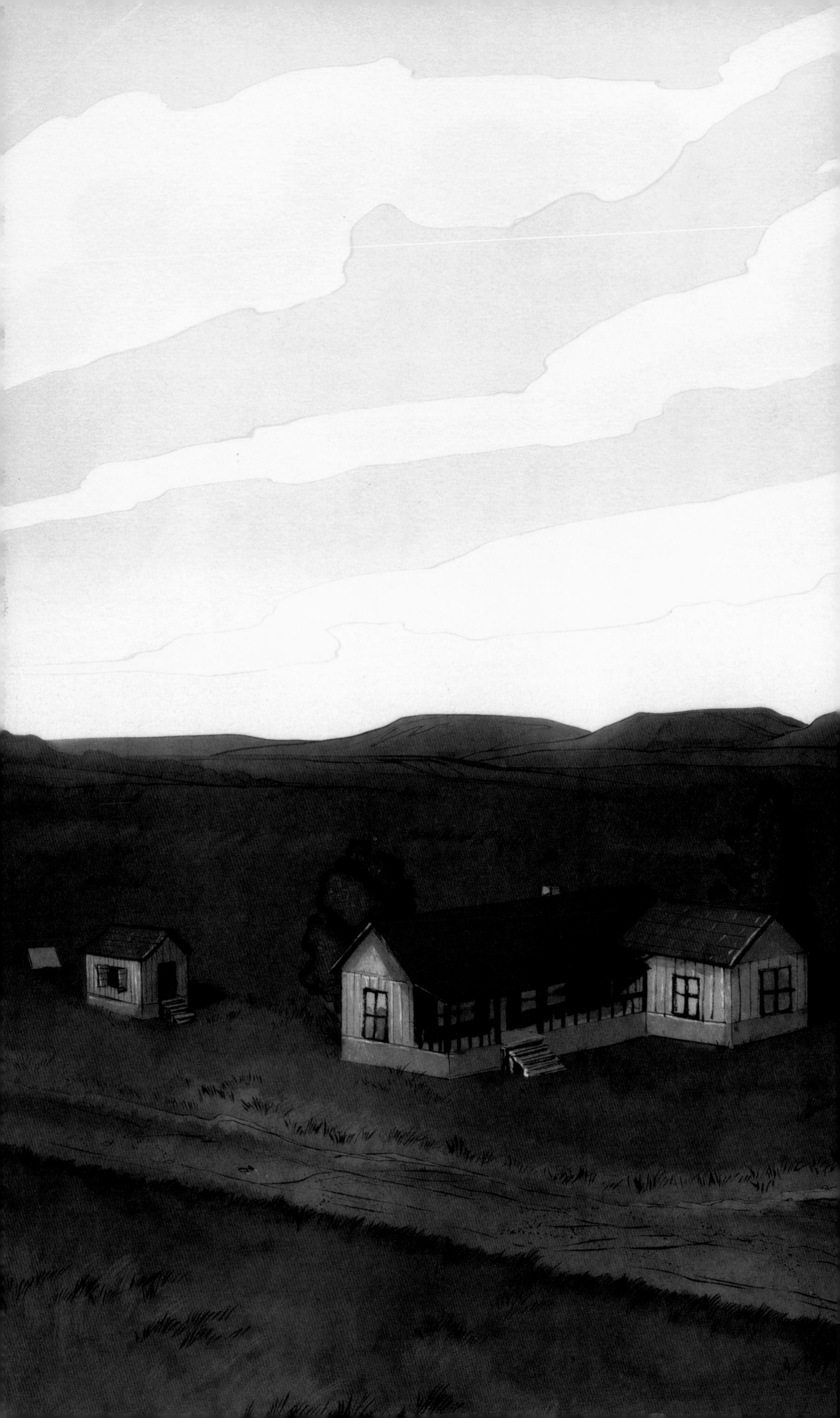

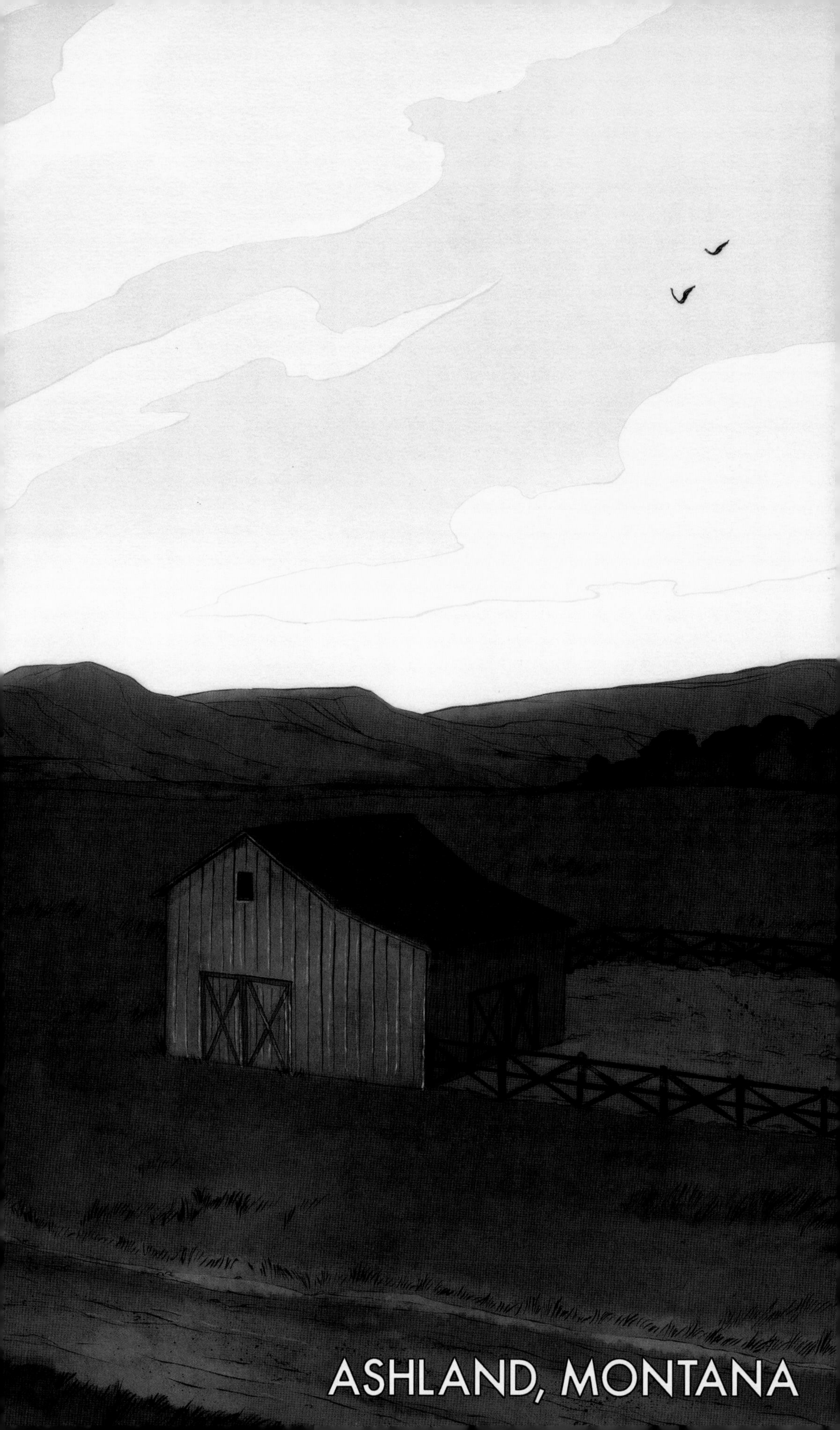
ASHLAND, MONTANA

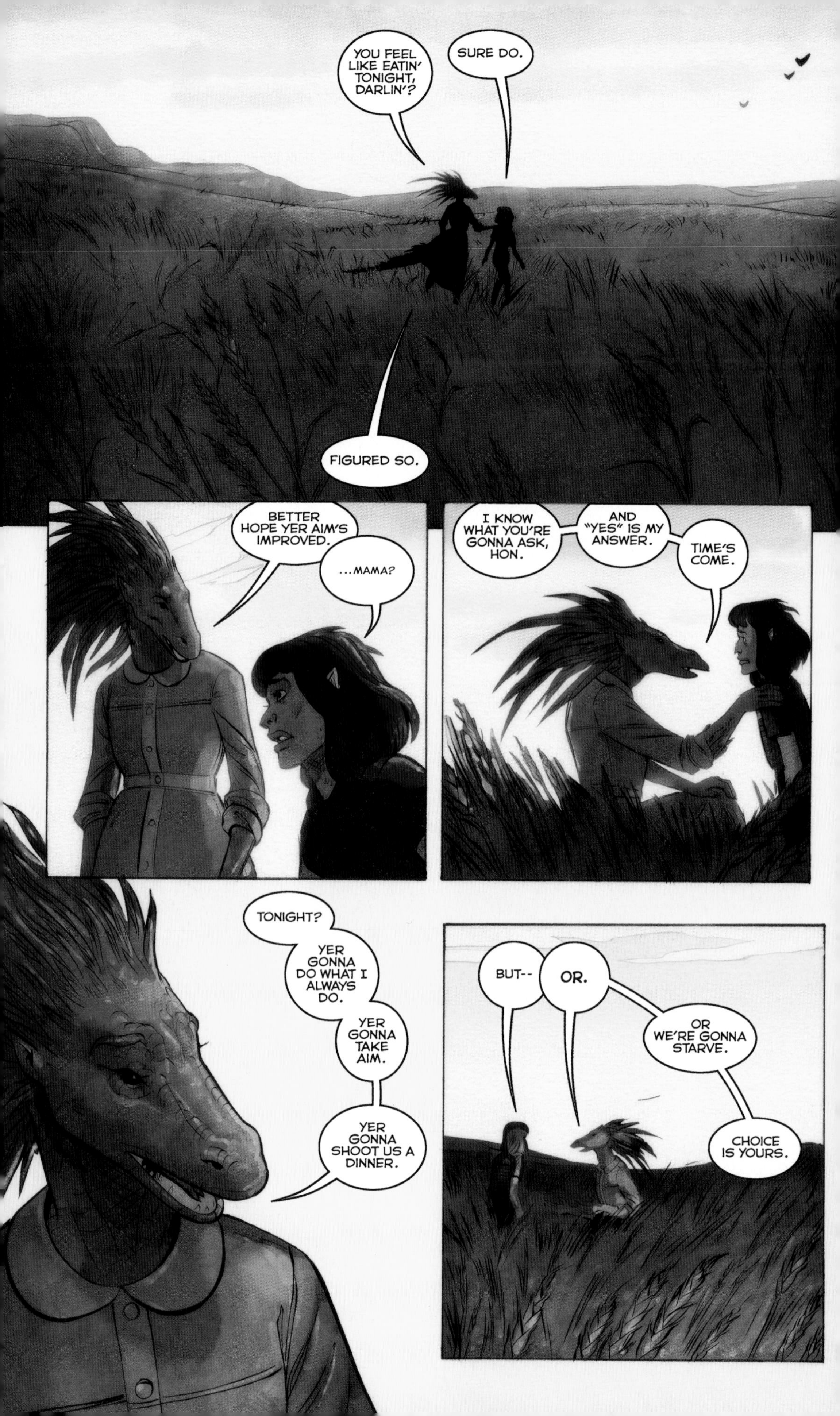
YOU FEEL LIKE EATIN' TONIGHT, DARLIN'?
SURE DO.
FIGURED SO.
BETTER HOPE YER AIM'S IMPROVED.
...MAMA?
I KNOW WHAT YOU'RE GONNA ASK, HON.
AND "YES" IS MY ANSWER.
TIME'S COME.
TONIGHT?
YER GONNA DO WHAT I ALWAYS DO.
YER GONNA TAKE AIM.
YER GONNA SHOOT US A DINNER.
BUT--
OR.
OR WE'RE GONNA STARVE.
CHOICE IS YOURS.

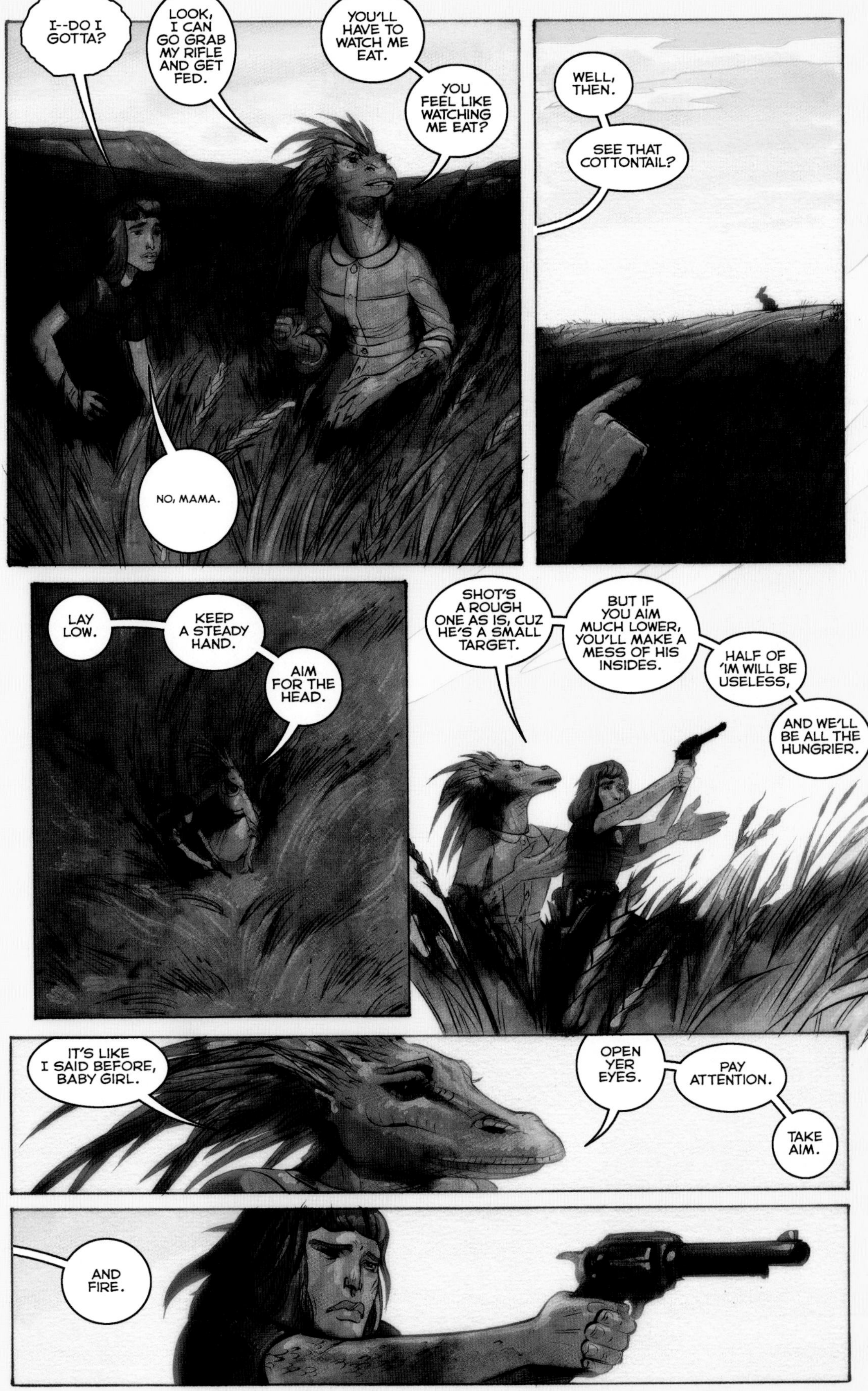
I--DO I GOTTA?
LOOK, I CAN GO GRAB MY RIFLE AND GET FED.
YOU'LL HAVE TO WATCH ME EAT.
YOU FEEL LIKE WATCHING ME EAT?
NO, MAMA.
WELL, THEN.
SEE THAT COTTONTAIL?
LAY LOW.
KEEP A STEADY HAND.
AIM FOR THE HEAD.
SHOT'S A ROUGH ONE AS IS, CUZ HE'S A SMALL TARGET.
BUT IF YOU AIM MUCH LOWER, YOU'LL MAKE A MESS OF HIS INSIDES.
HALF OF 'IM WILL BE USELESS,
AND WE'LL BE ALL THE HUNGRIER.
IT'S LIKE I SAID BEFORE, BABY GIRL.
OPEN YER EYES.
PAY ATTENTION.
TAKE AIM.
AND FIRE.

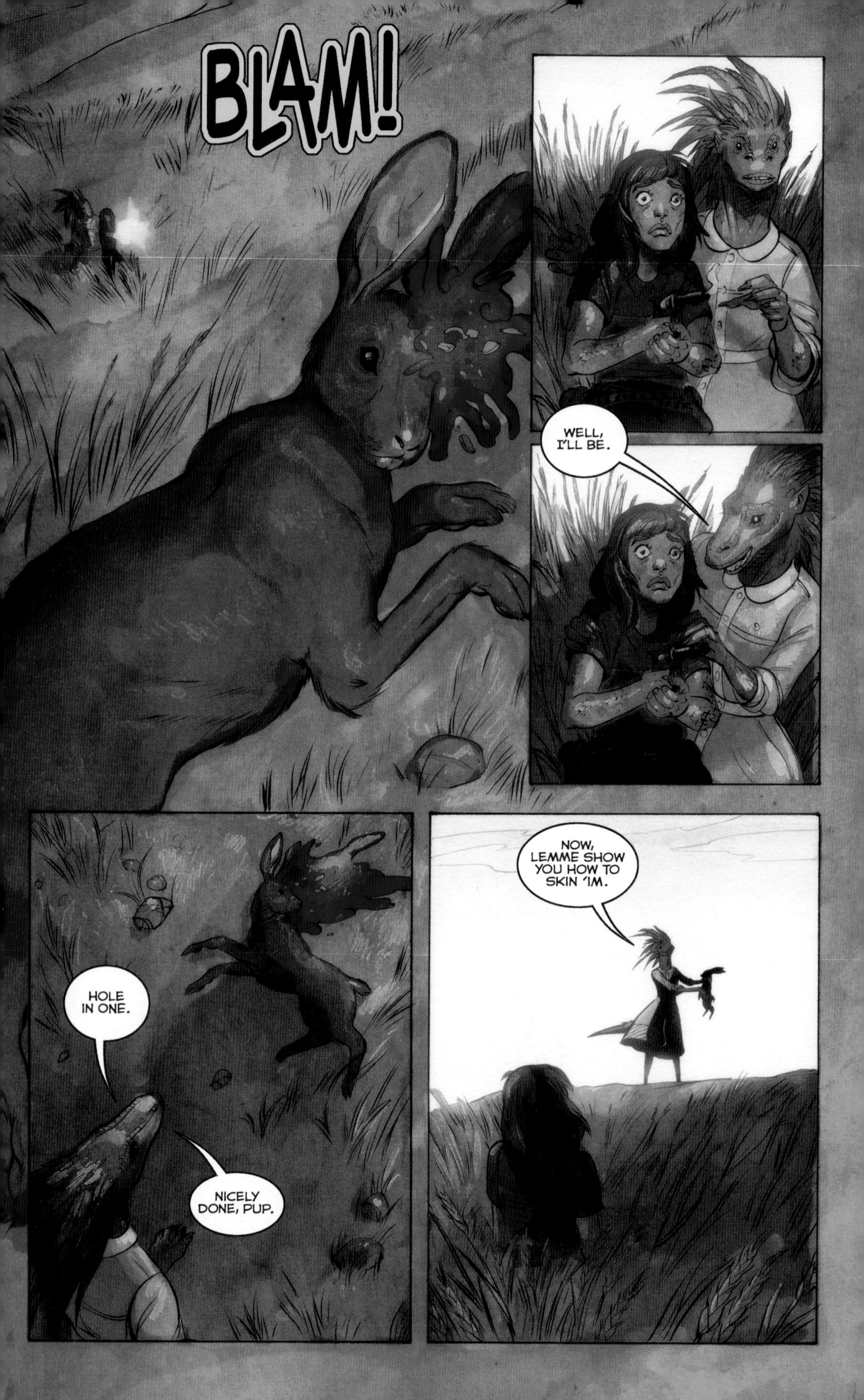
BLAM!
WELL, I'LL BE.
HOLE IN ONE.
NICELY DONE, PUP.
NOW, LEMME SHOW YOU HOW TO SKIN 'IM.

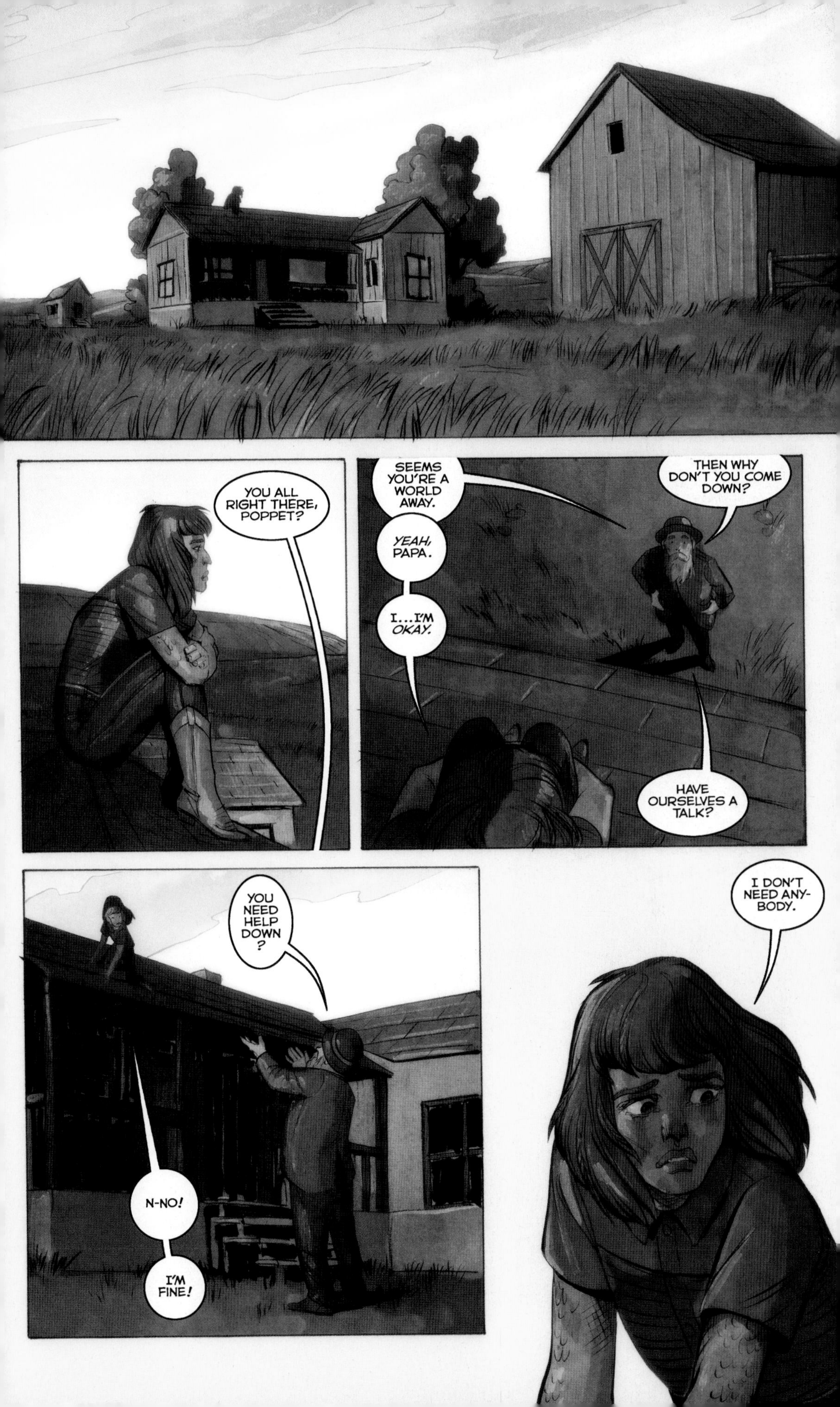
YOU ALL RIGHT THERE, POPPET?
SEEMS YOU'RE A WORLD AWAY.
YEAH, PAPA.
I...I'M OKAY.
THEN WHY DON'T YOU COME DOWN?
HAVE OURSELVES A TALK?
YOU NEED HELP DOWN?
N-NO!
I'M FINE!
I DON'T NEED ANY-BODY.

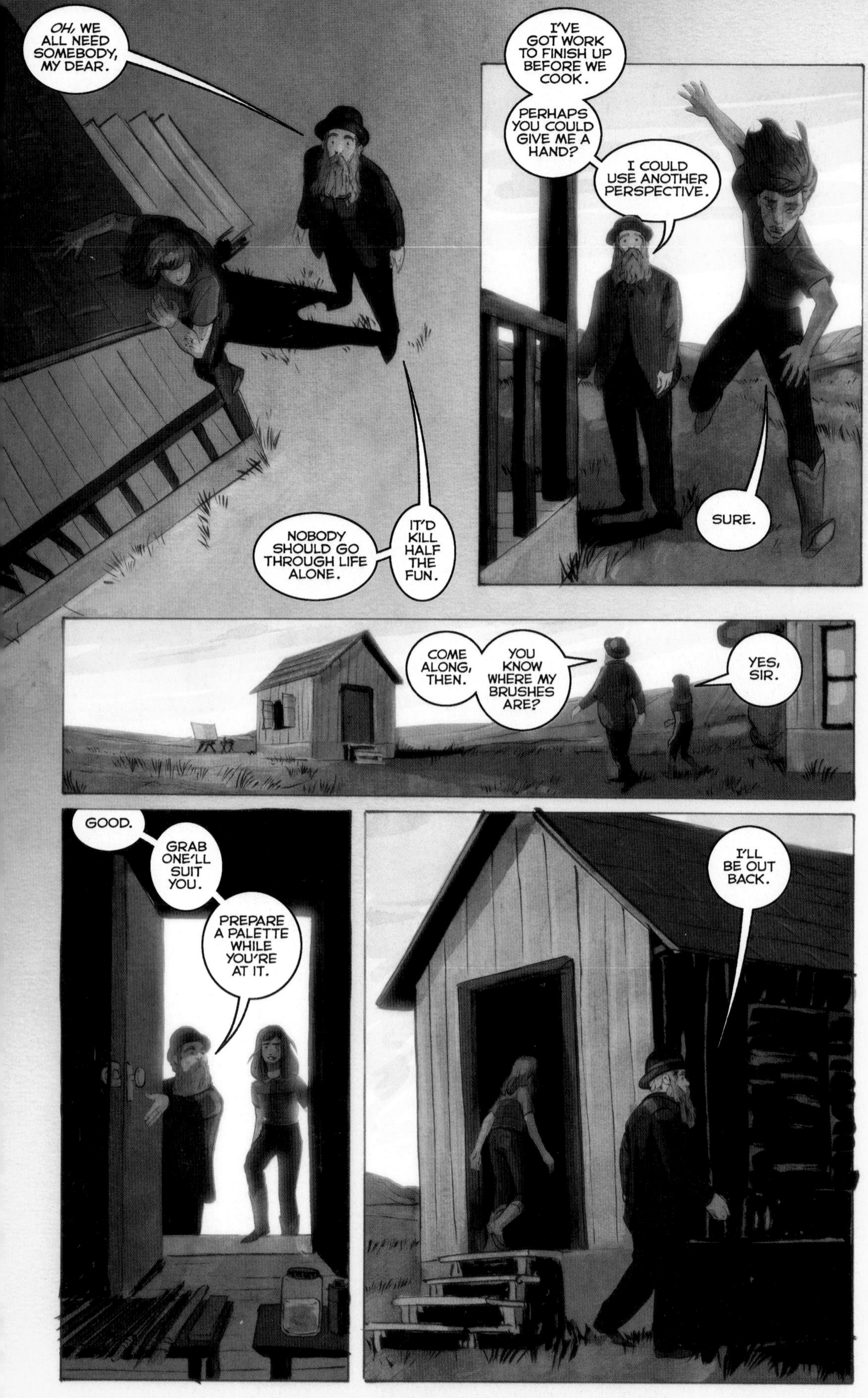
OH, WE ALL NEED SOMEBODY, MY DEAR.
NOBODY SHOULD GO THROUGH LIFE ALONE.
IT'D KILL HALF THE FUN.
I'VE GOT WORK TO FINISH UP BEFORE WE COOK.
PERHAPS YOU COULD GIVE ME A HAND?
I COULD USE ANOTHER PERSPECTIVE.
SURE.
COME ALONG, THEN.
YOU KNOW WHERE MY BRUSHES ARE?
YES, SIR.
GOOD.
GRAB ONE'LL SUIT YOU.
PREPARE A PALETTE WHILE YOU'RE AT IT.
I'LL BE OUT BACK.

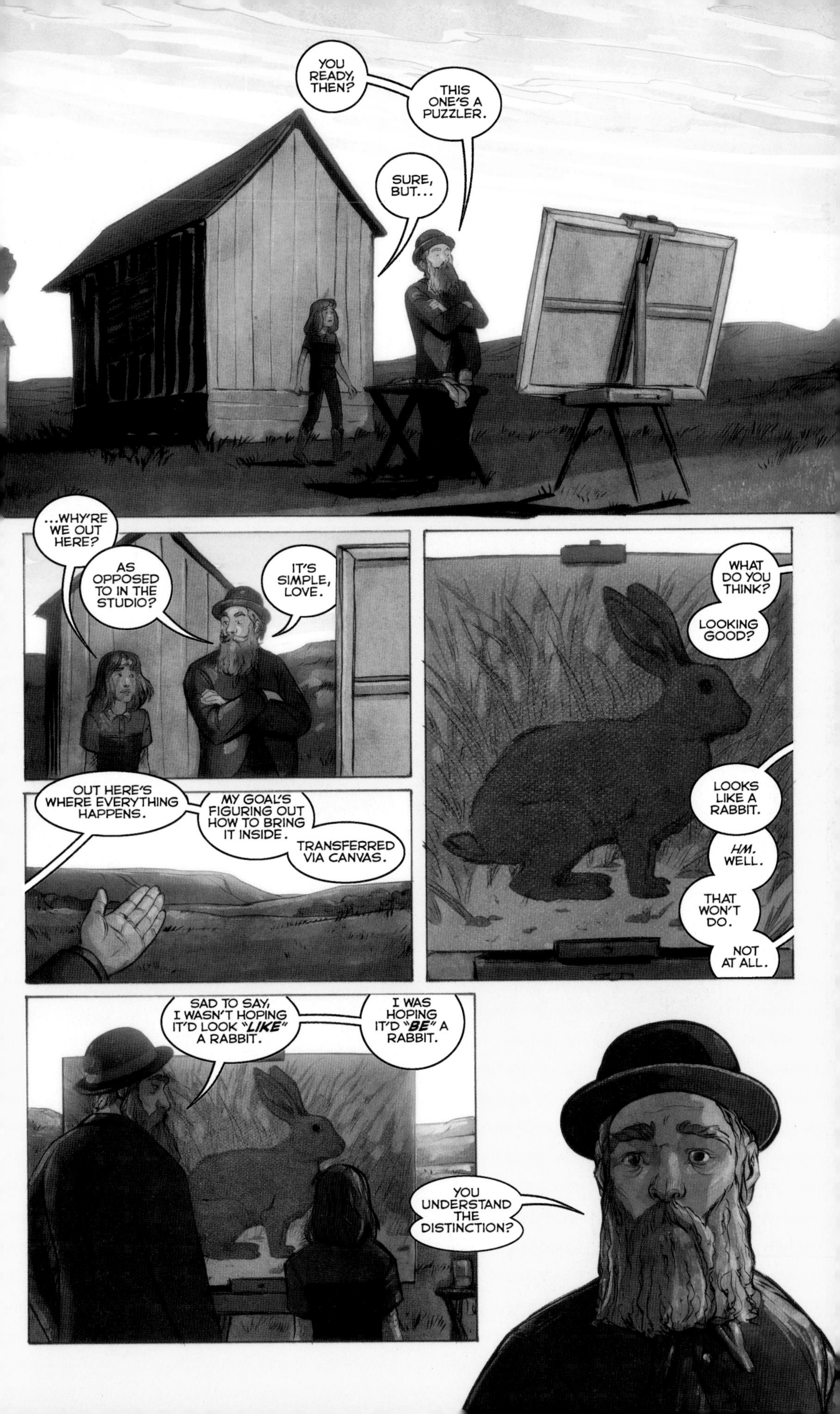
YOU READY, THEN?
THIS ONE'S A PUZZLER.
SURE, BUT...
...WHY'RE WE OUT HERE?
AS OPPOSED TO IN THE STUDIO?
IT'S SIMPLE, LOVE.
OUT HERE'S WHERE EVERYTHING HAPPENS.
MY GOAL'S FIGURING OUT HOW TO BRING IT INSIDE.
TRANSFERRED VIA CANVAS.
WHAT DO YOU THINK?
LOOKING GOOD?
LOOKS LIKE A RABBIT.
HM. WELL.
THAT WON'T DO.
NOT AT ALL.
SAD TO SAY, I WASN'T HOPING IT'D LOOK "*LIKE*" A RABBIT.
I WAS HOPING IT'D "*BE*" A RABBIT.
YOU UNDERSTAND THE DISTINCTION?

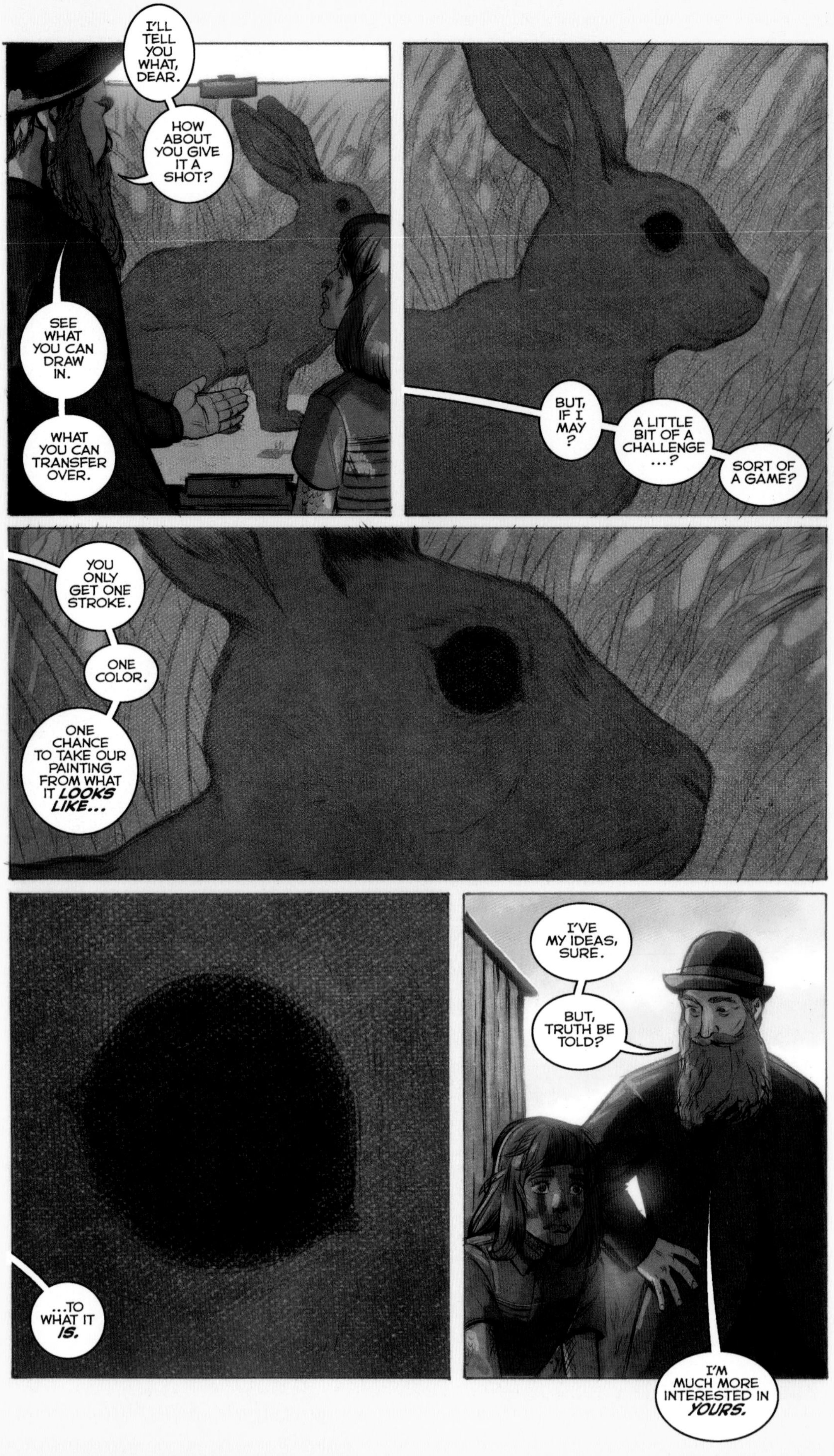
I'LL TELL YOU WHAT, DEAR.
HOW ABOUT YOU GIVE IT A SHOT?
SEE WHAT YOU CAN DRAW IN.
WHAT YOU CAN TRANSFER OVER.
BUT, IF I MAY?
A LITTLE BIT OF A CHALLENGE ...?
SORT OF A GAME?
YOU ONLY GET ONE STROKE.
ONE COLOR.
ONE CHANCE TO TAKE OUR PAINTING FROM WHAT IT *LOOKS LIKE...*
...TO WHAT IT *IS.*
I'VE MY IDEAS, SURE.
BUT, TRUTH BE TOLD?
I'M MUCH MORE INTERESTED IN *YOURS.*

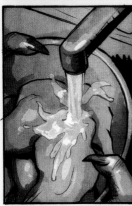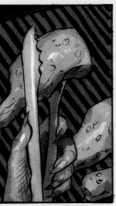

BLAM!

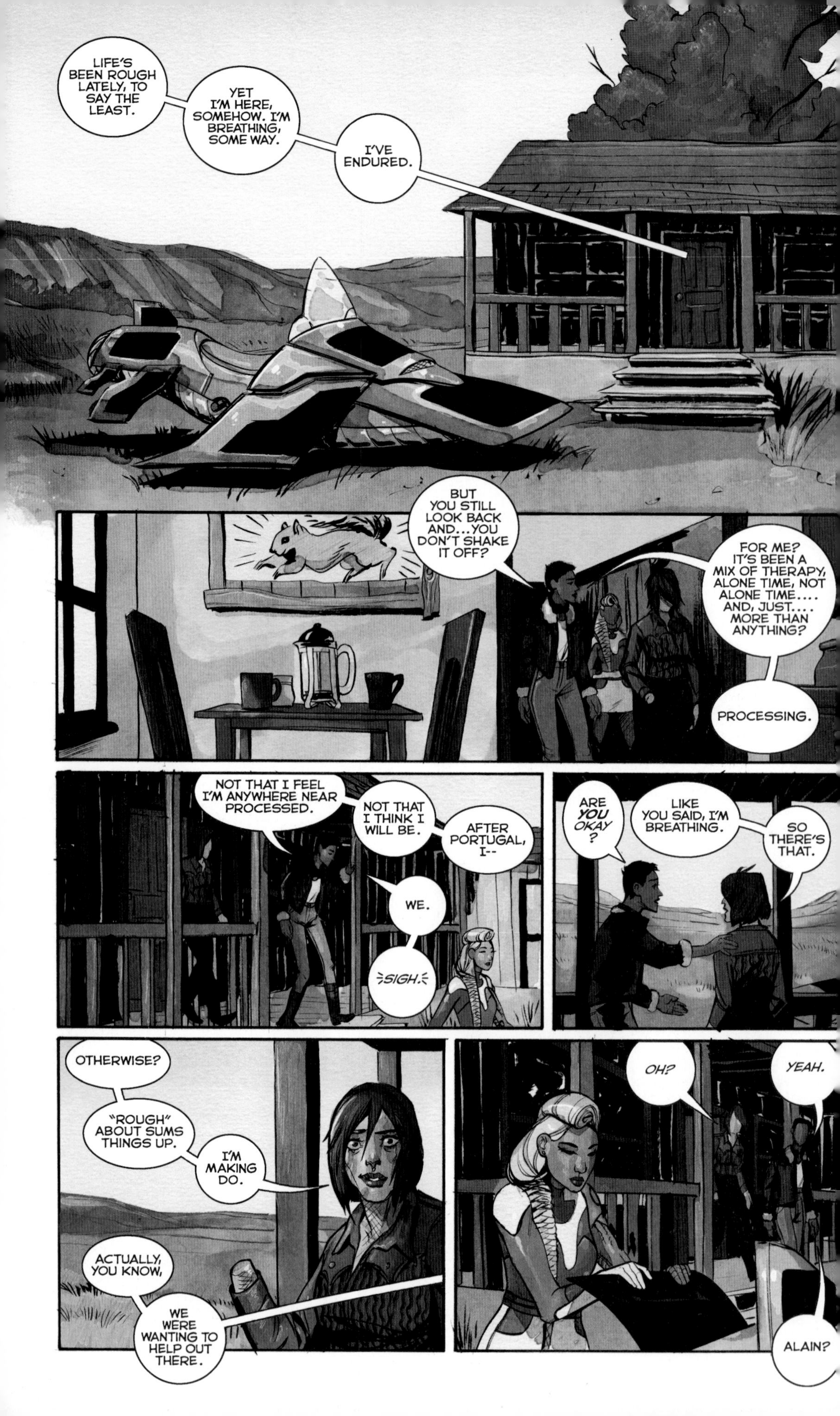

LIFE'S BEEN ROUGH LATELY, TO SAY THE LEAST.
YET I'M HERE, SOMEHOW. I'M BREATHING, SOME WAY.
I'VE ENDURED.
BUT YOU STILL LOOK BACK AND...YOU DON'T SHAKE IT OFF?
FOR ME? IT'S BEEN A MIX OF THERAPY, ALONE TIME, NOT ALONE TIME.... AND, JUST.... MORE THAN ANYTHING?
PROCESSING.
NOT THAT I FEEL I'M ANYWHERE NEAR PROCESSED.
NOT THAT I THINK I WILL BE.
AFTER PORTUGAL, I--
WE.
SIGH.
ARE YOU OKAY?
LIKE YOU SAID, I'M BREATHING.
SO THERE'S THAT.
OTHERWISE?
"ROUGH" ABOUT SUMS THINGS UP.
I'M MAKING DO.
ACTUALLY, YOU KNOW,
WE WERE WANTING TO HELP OUT THERE.
OH?
YEAH.
ALAIN?

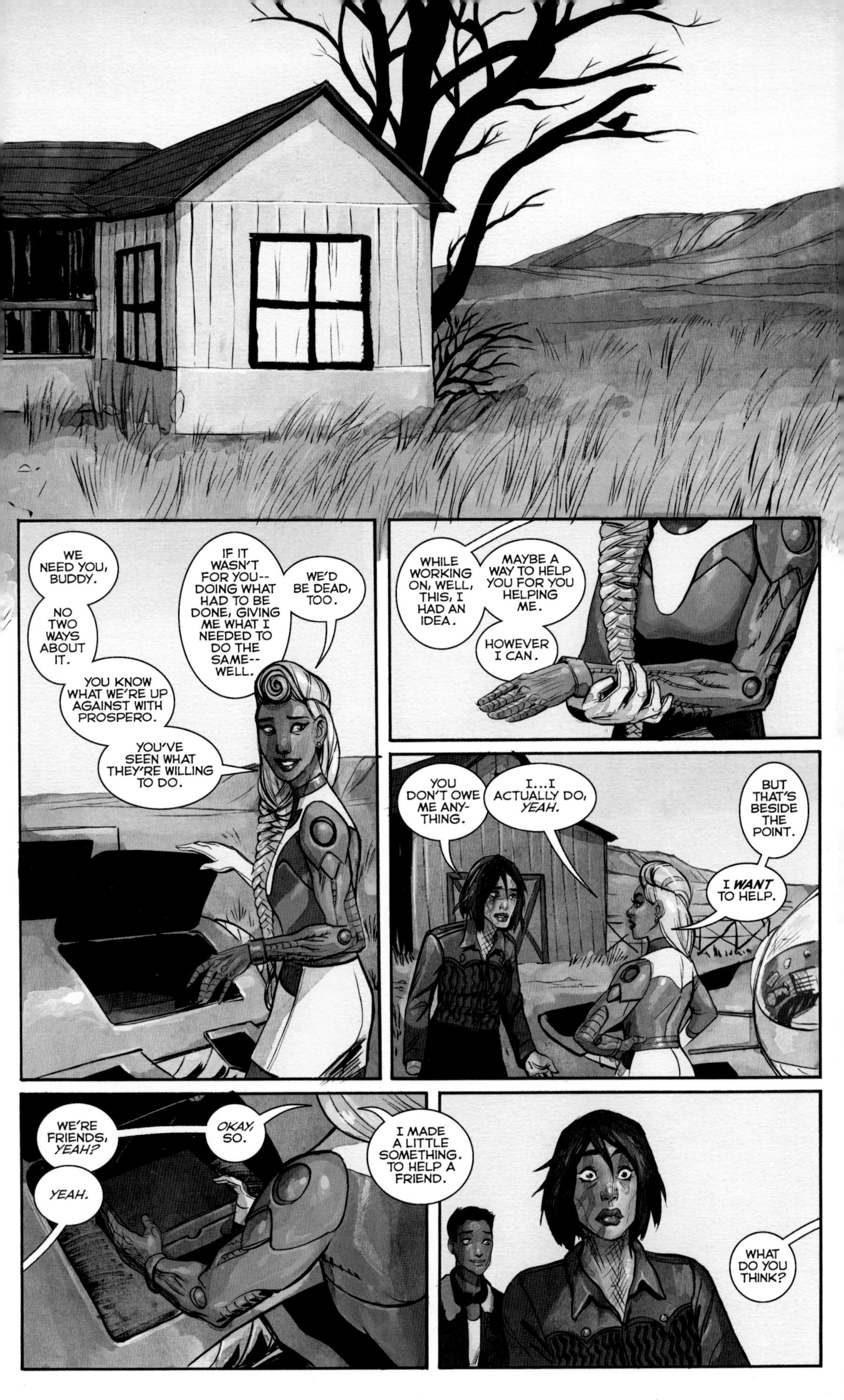
WE NEED YOU, BUDDY.
NO TWO WAYS ABOUT IT.
YOU KNOW WHAT WE'RE UP AGAINST WITH PROSPERO.
YOU'VE SEEN WHAT THEY'RE WILLING TO DO.
IF IT WASN'T FOR YOU-- DOING WHAT HAD TO BE DONE, GIVING ME WHAT I NEEDED TO DO THE SAME-- WELL.
WE'D BE DEAD, TOO.
WHILE WORKING ON, WELL, THIS, I HAD AN IDEA.
MAYBE A WAY TO HELP YOU FOR YOU HELPING ME.
HOWEVER I CAN.
YOU DON'T OWE ME ANY-THING.
I...I ACTUALLY DO, *YEAH.*
BUT THAT'S BESIDE THE POINT.
I ***WANT*** TO HELP.
WE'RE FRIENDS, *YEAH?*
YEAH.
OKAY, SO.
I MADE A LITTLE SOMETHING. TO HELP A FRIEND.
WHAT DO YOU THINK?

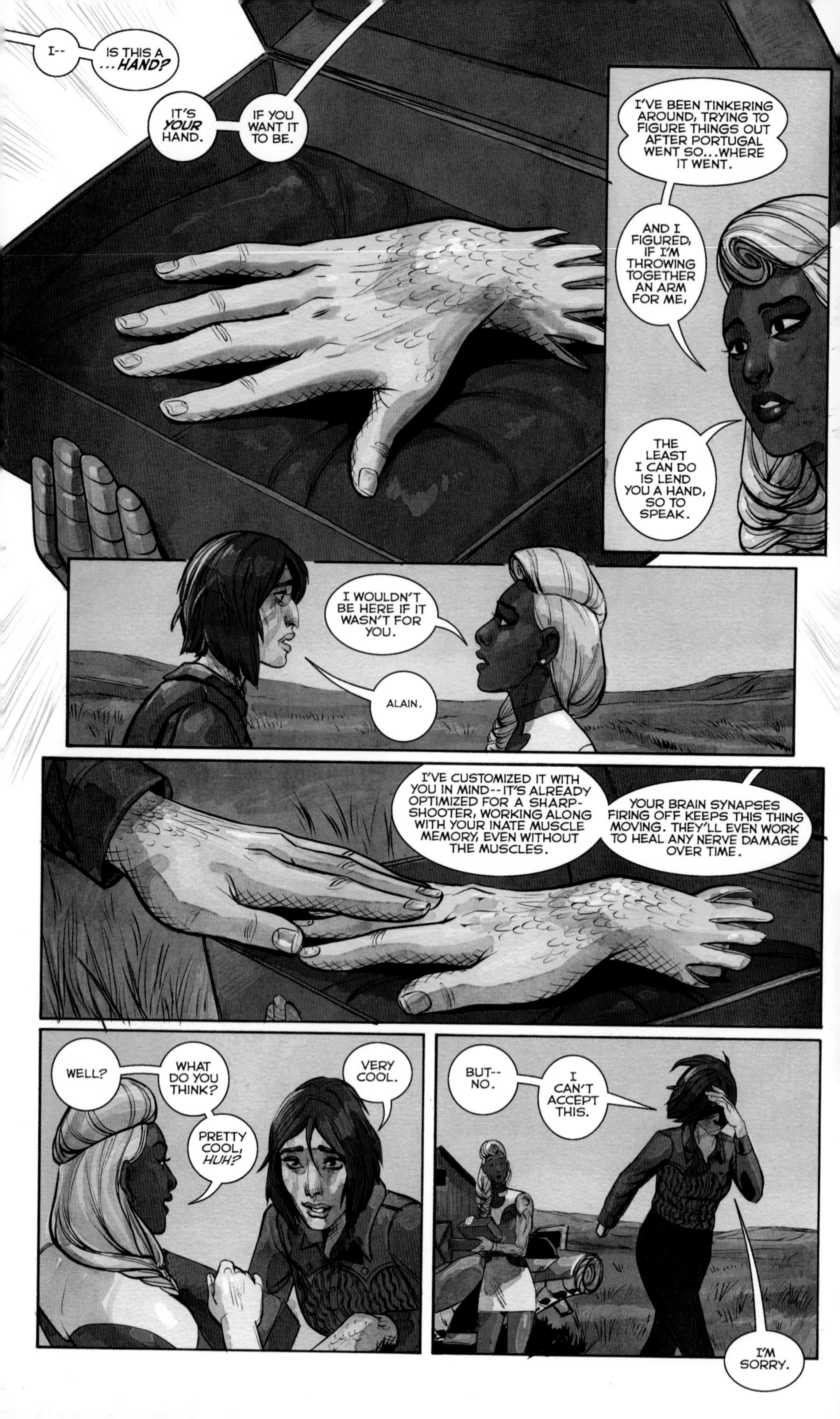
I--
IS THIS A ...HAND?
IT'S YOUR HAND.
IF YOU WANT IT TO BE.
I'VE BEEN TINKERING AROUND, TRYING TO FIGURE THINGS OUT AFTER PORTUGAL WENT SO...WHERE IT WENT.
AND I FIGURED, IF I'M THROWING TOGETHER AN ARM FOR ME,
THE LEAST I CAN DO IS LEND YOU A HAND, SO TO SPEAK.
I WOULDN'T BE HERE IF IT WASN'T FOR YOU.
ALAIN.
I'VE CUSTOMIZED IT WITH YOU IN MIND--IT'S ALREADY OPTIMIZED FOR A SHARP-SHOOTER, WORKING ALONG WITH YOUR INATE MUSCLE MEMORY, EVEN WITHOUT THE MUSCLES.
YOUR BRAIN SYNAPSES FIRING OFF KEEPS THIS THING MOVING. THEY'LL EVEN WORK TO HEAL ANY NERVE DAMAGE OVER TIME.
WELL?
WHAT DO YOU THINK?
PRETTY COOL, HUH?
VERY COOL.
BUT-- NO.
I CAN'T ACCEPT THIS.
I'M SORRY.

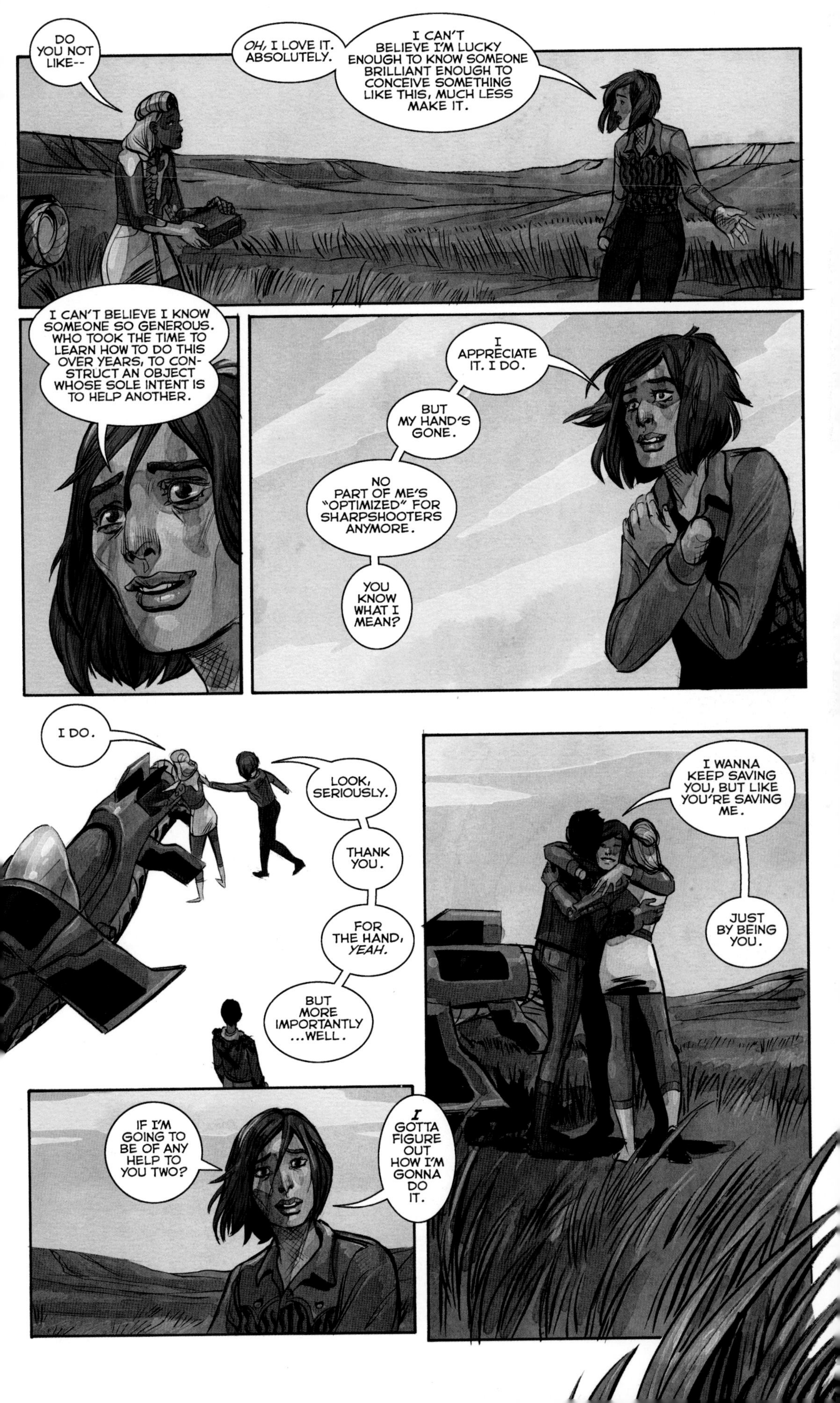
DO YOU NOT LIKE--
OH, I LOVE IT. ABSOLUTELY.
I CAN'T BELIEVE I'M LUCKY ENOUGH TO KNOW SOMEONE BRILLIANT ENOUGH TO CONCEIVE SOMETHING LIKE THIS, MUCH LESS MAKE IT.
I CAN'T BELIEVE I KNOW SOMEONE SO GENEROUS. WHO TOOK THE TIME TO LEARN HOW TO DO THIS OVER YEARS, TO CON- STRUCT AN OBJECT WHOSE SOLE INTENT IS TO HELP ANOTHER.
I APPRECIATE IT. I DO.
BUT MY HAND'S GONE.
NO PART OF ME'S "OPTIMIZED" FOR SHARPSHOOTERS ANYMORE.
YOU KNOW WHAT I MEAN?
I DO.
LOOK, SERIOUSLY.
THANK YOU.
FOR THE HAND, *YEAH.*
BUT MORE IMPORTANTLY ...WELL.
IF I'M GOING TO BE OF ANY HELP TO YOU TWO?
I GOTTA FIGURE OUT HOW I'M GONNA DO IT.
I WANNA KEEP SAVING YOU, BUT LIKE YOU'RE SAVING ME.
JUST BY BEING YOU.

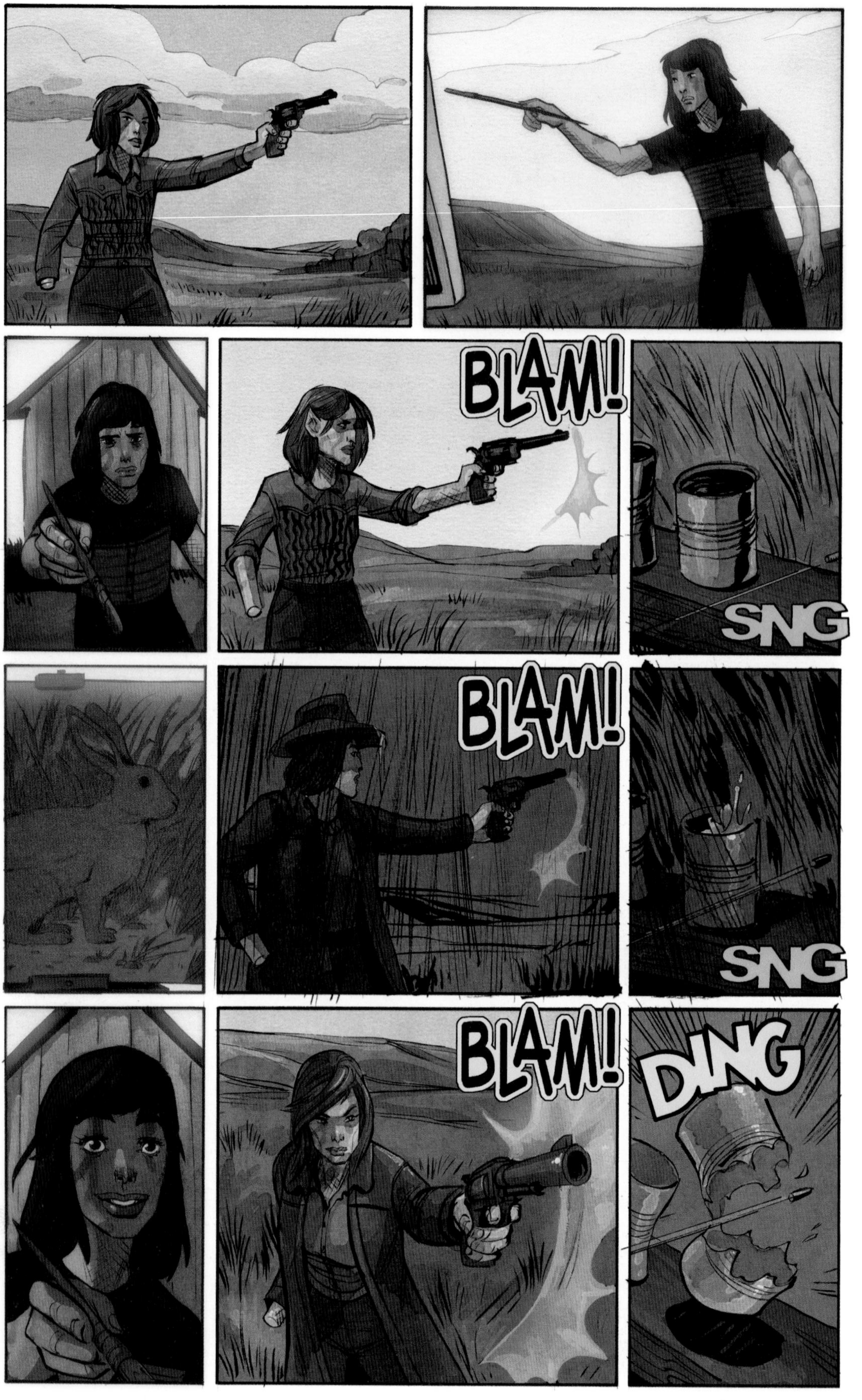
BLAM!
SNG
BLAM!
SNG
BLAM!
DING

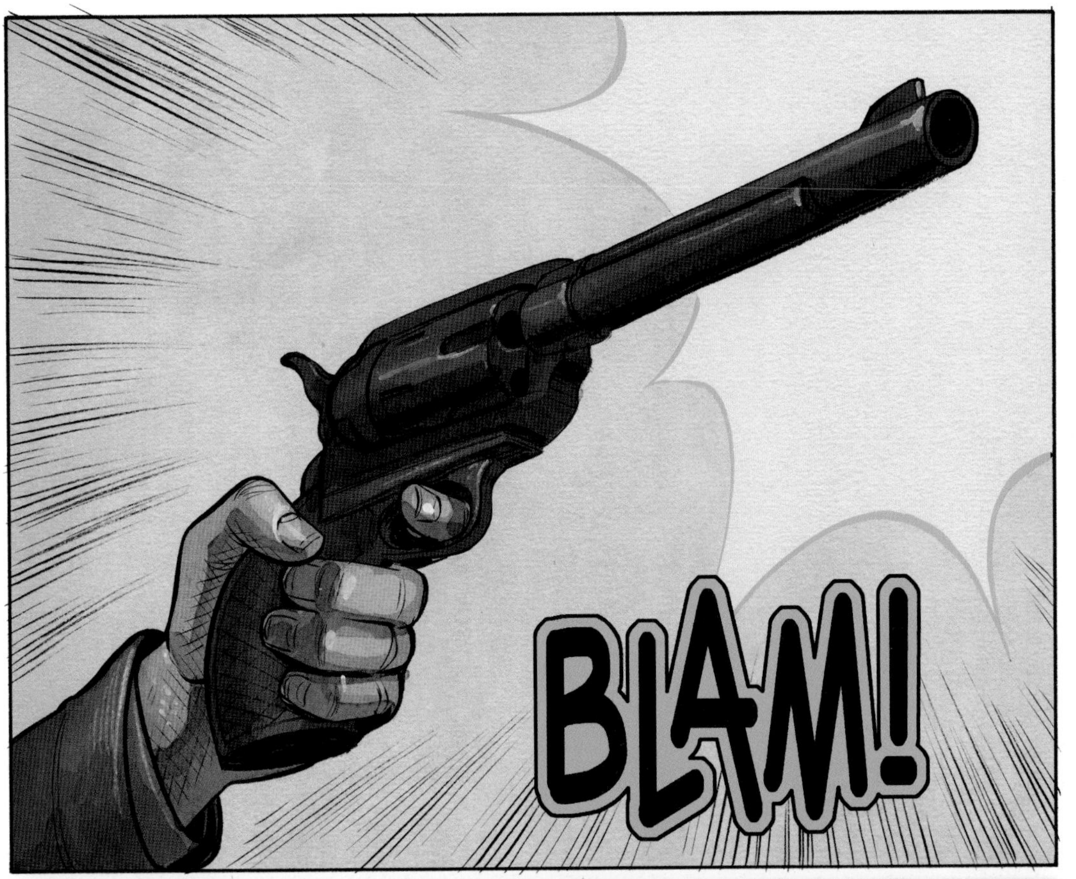
BLAM!
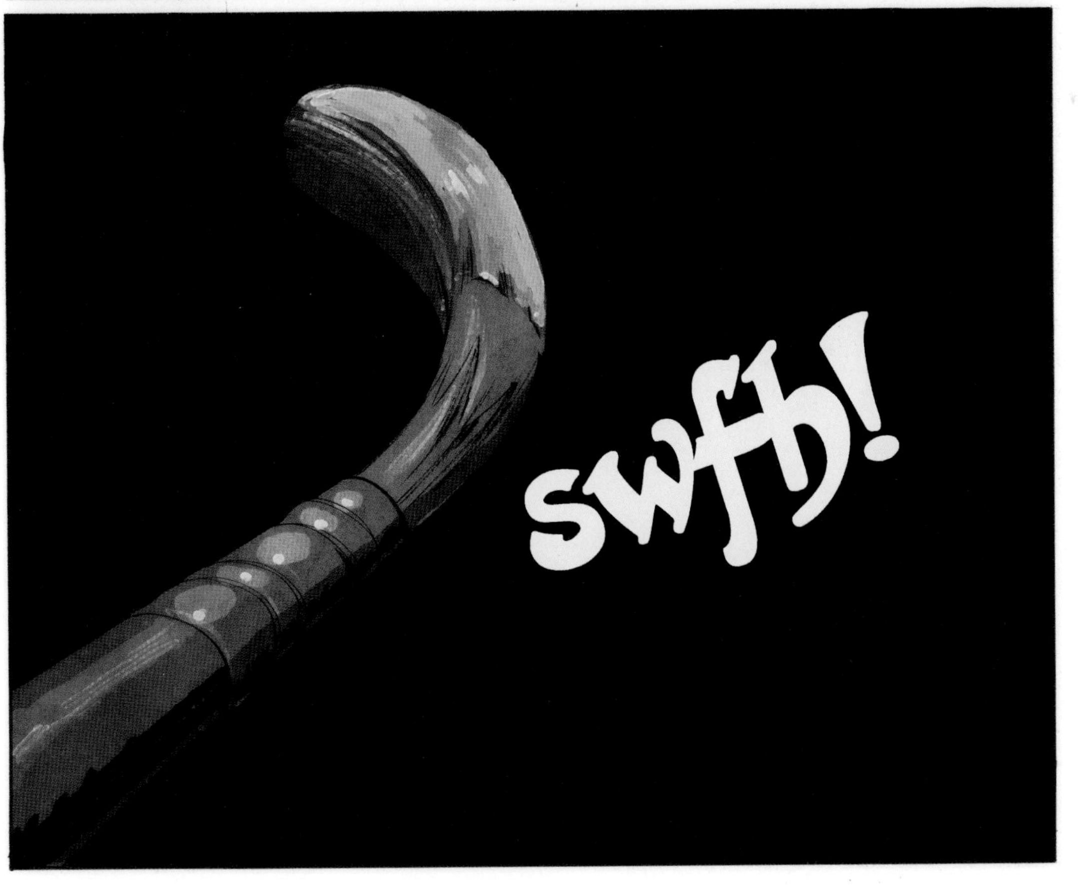
swfh!

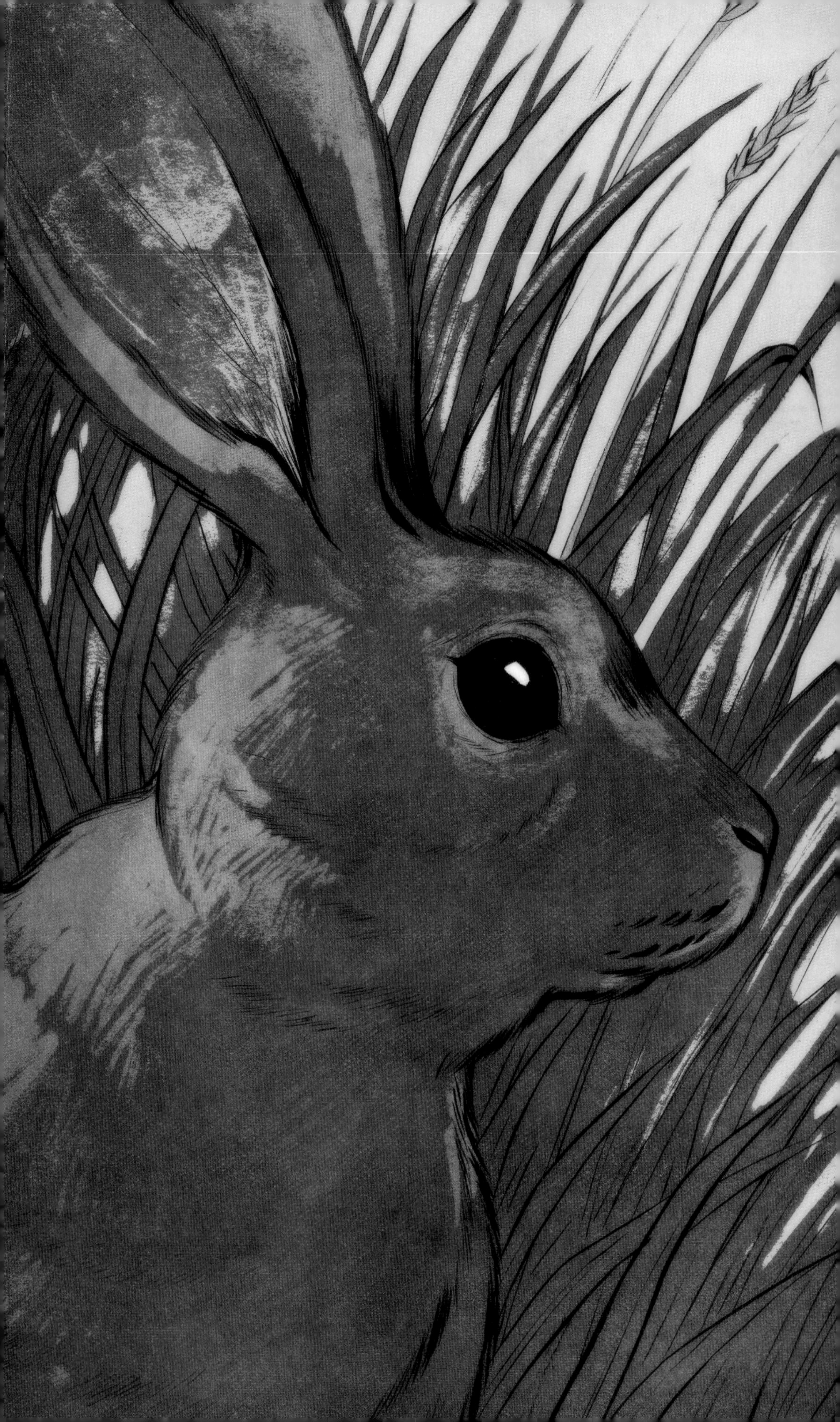

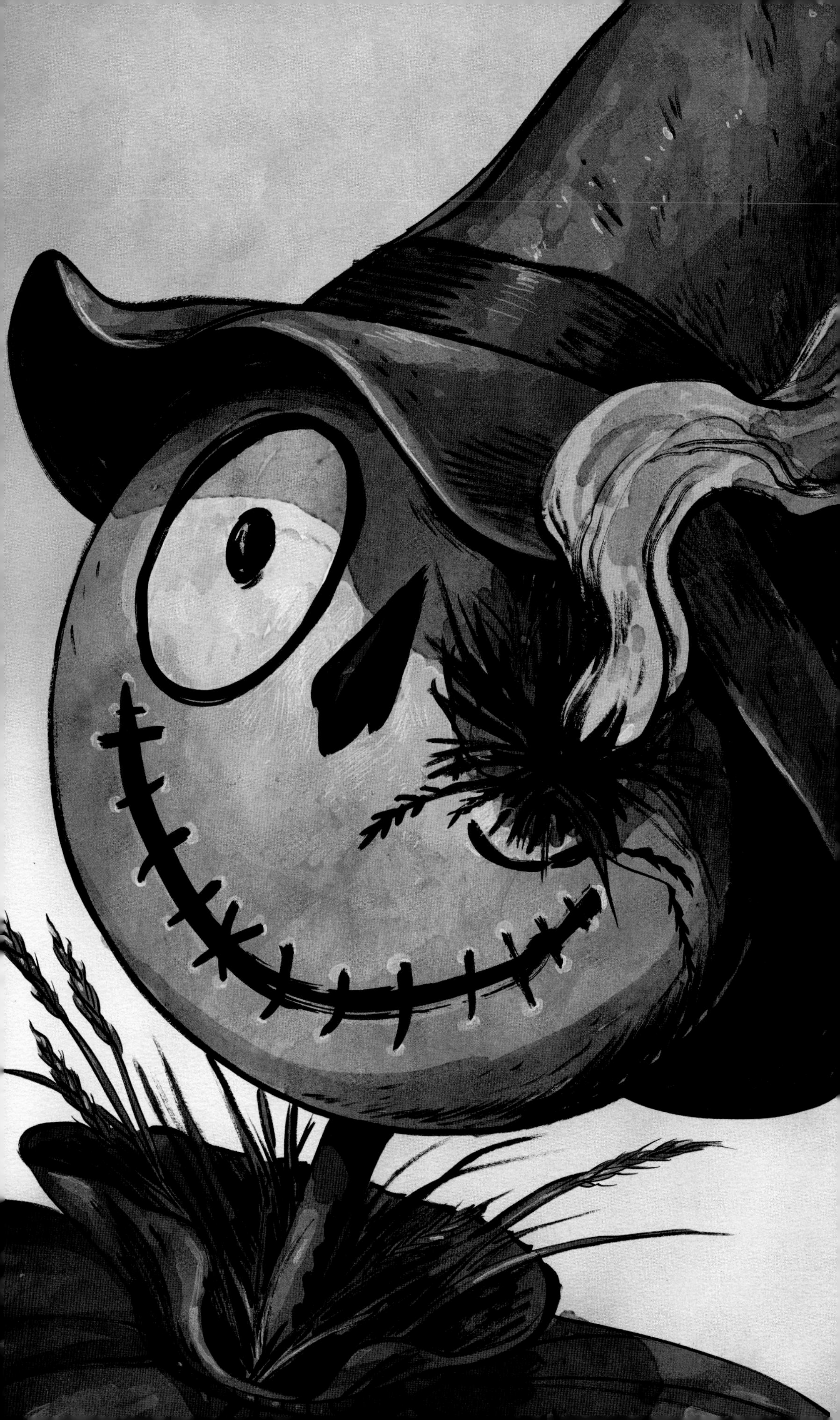

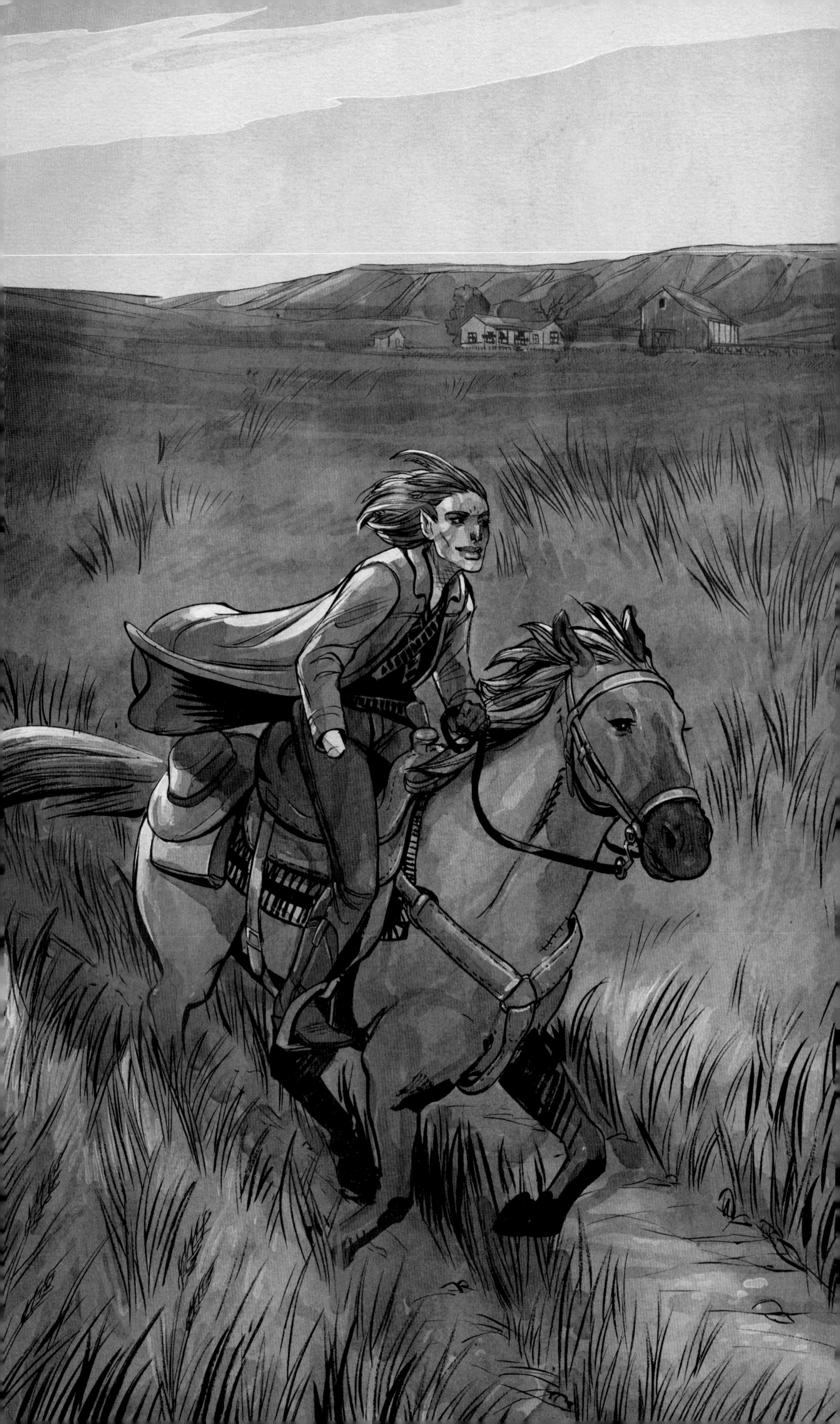

CHAPTER

25

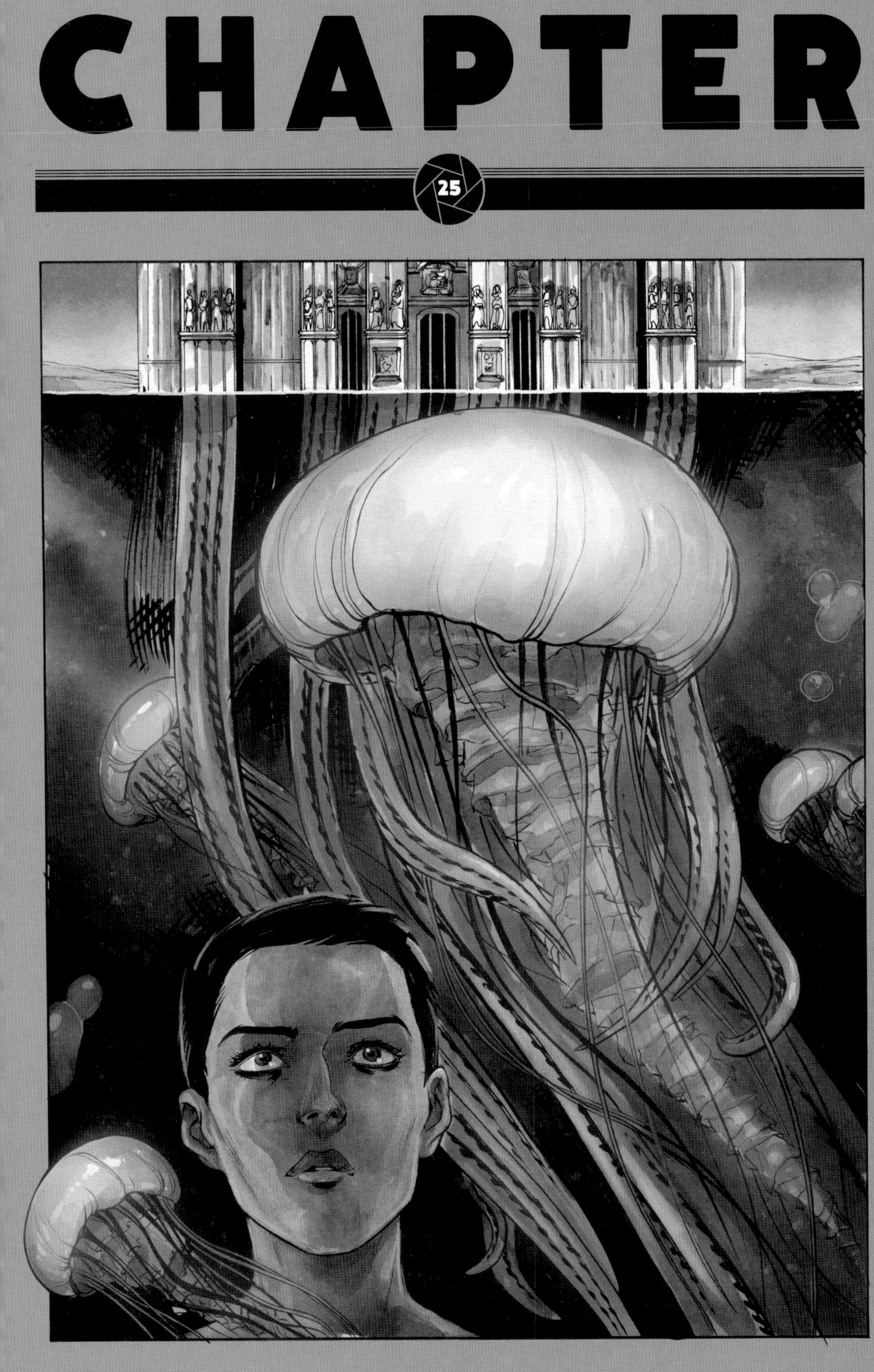

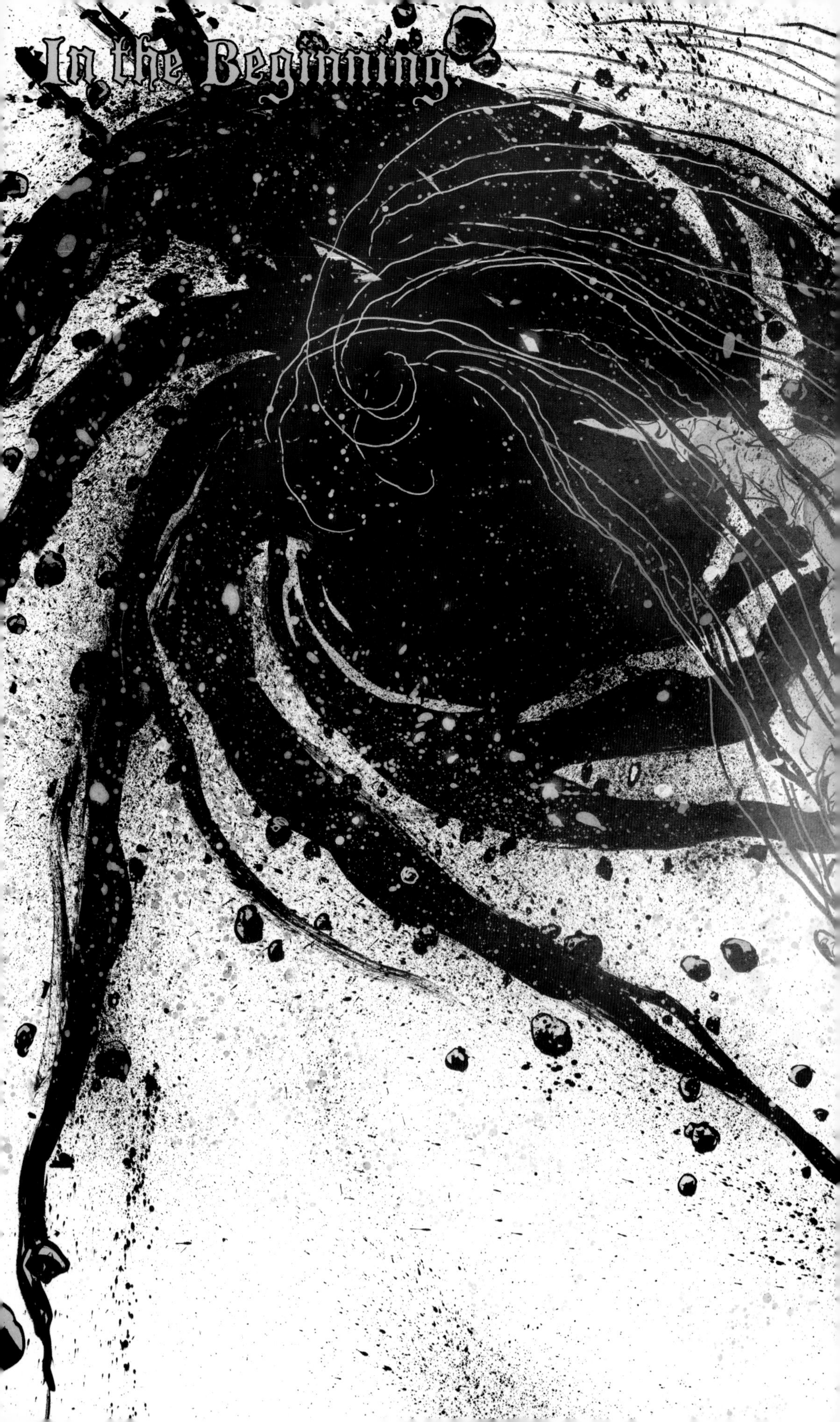
In the Beginning.

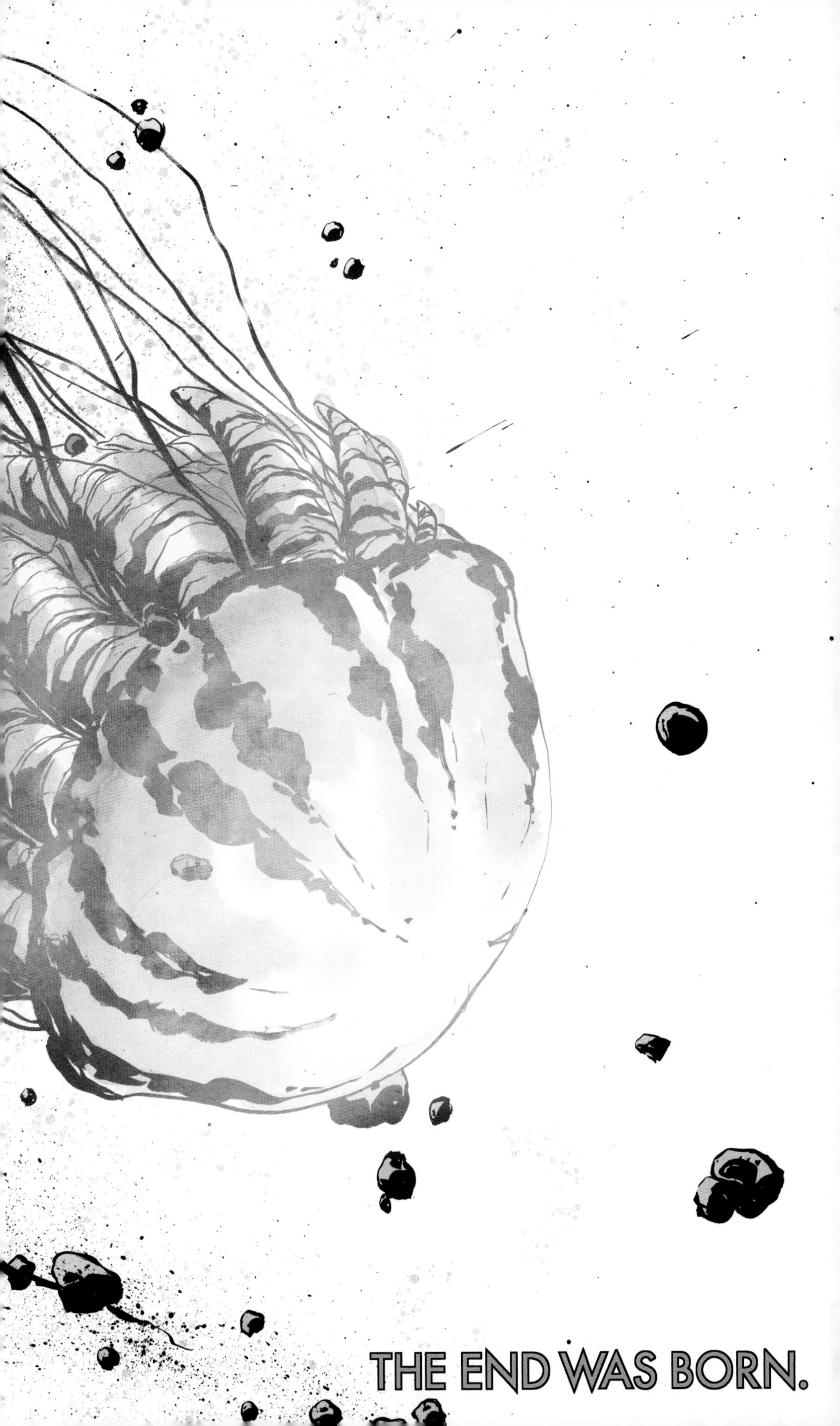
THE END WAS BORN.

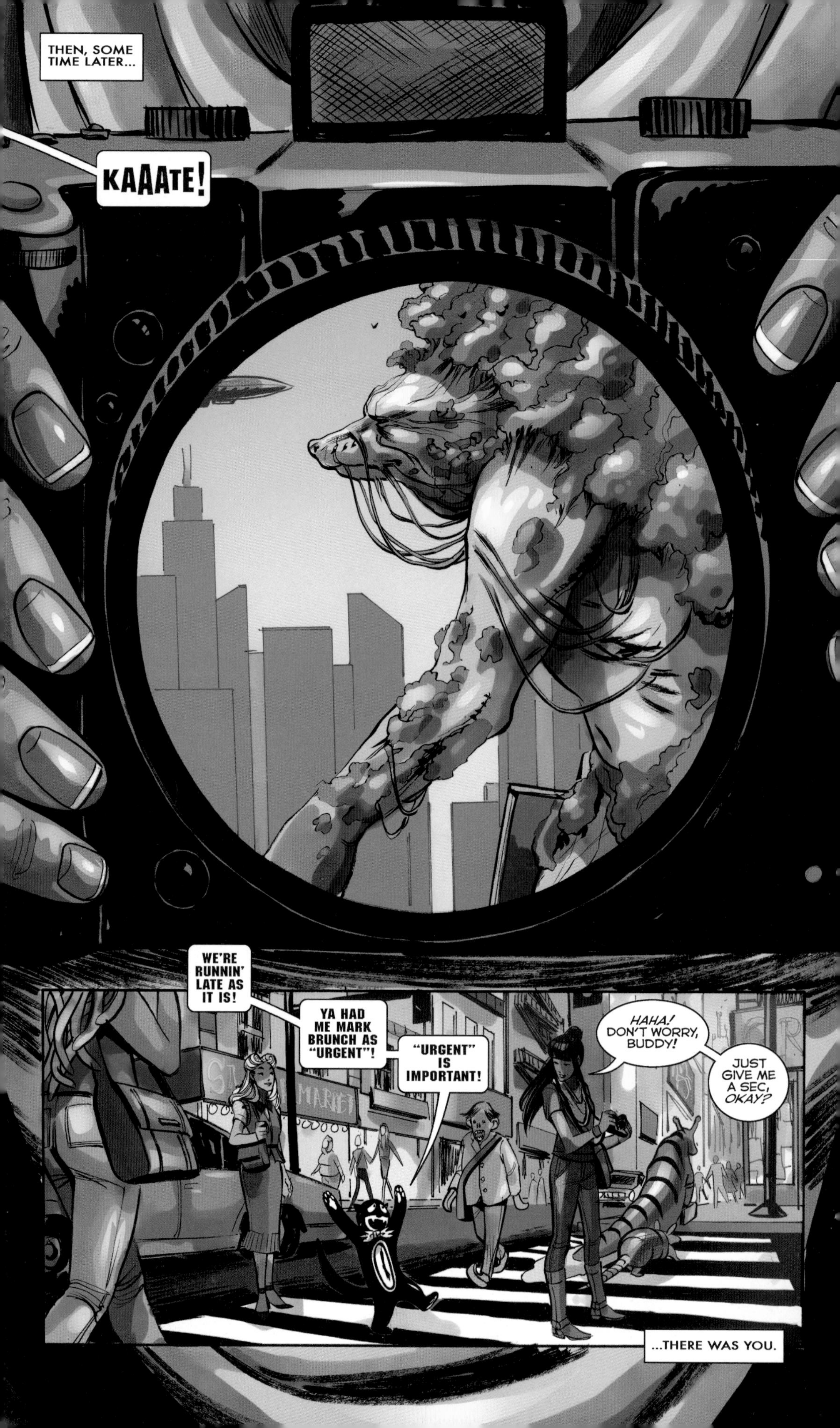
THEN, SOME TIME LATER...
KAAATE!
WE'RE RUNNIN' LATE AS IT IS!
YA HAD ME MARK BRUNCH AS "URGENT"!
"URGENT" IS IMPORTANT!
HAHA! DON'T WORRY, BUDDY!
JUST GIVE ME A SEC, OKAY?
...THERE WAS YOU.

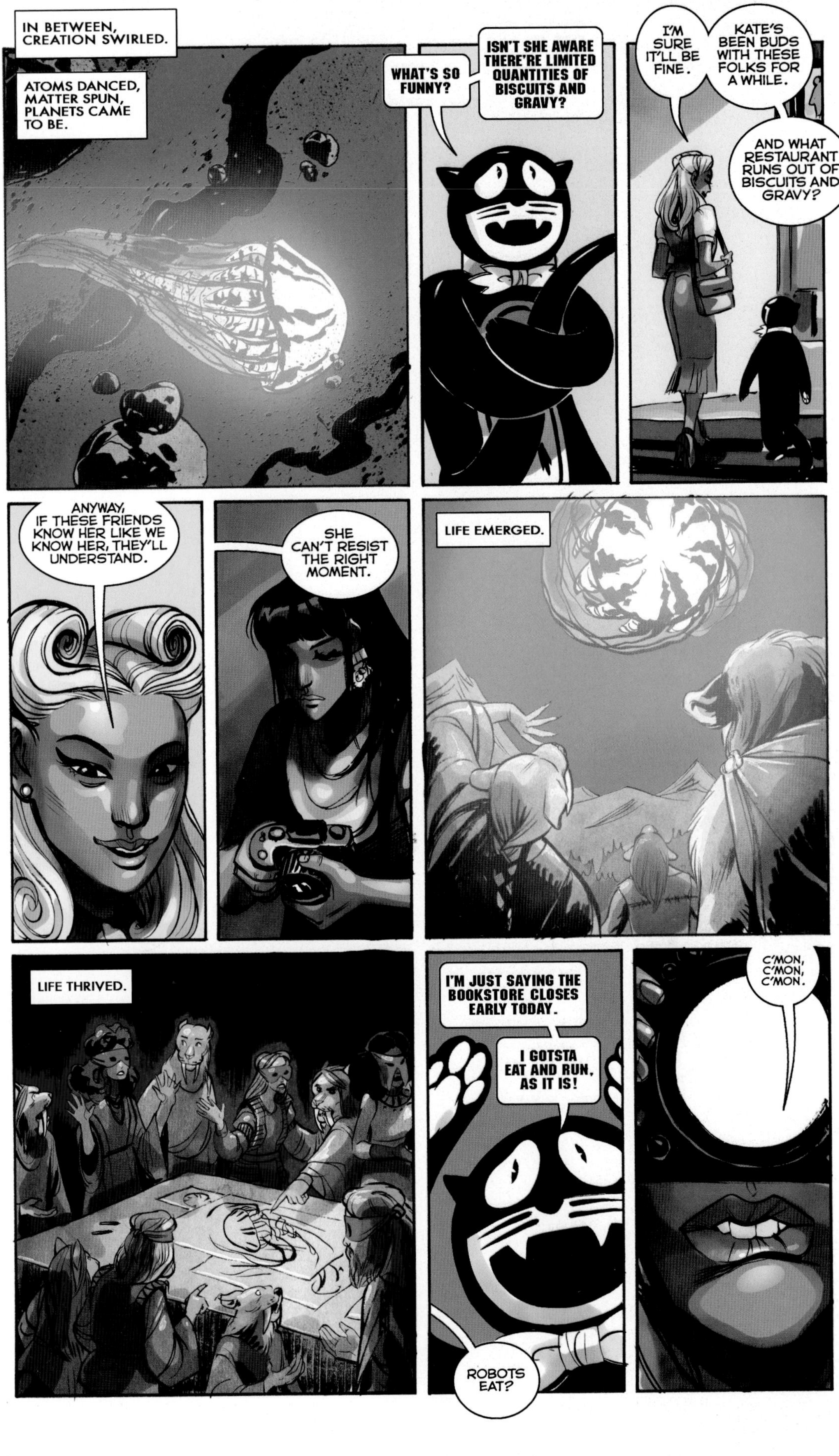
IN BETWEEN, CREATION SWIRLED.
ATOMS DANCED, MATTER SPUN, PLANETS CAME TO BE.
WHAT'S SO FUNNY?
ISN'T SHE AWARE THERE'RE LIMITED QUANTITIES OF BISCUITS AND GRAVY?
I'M SURE IT'LL BE FINE.
KATE'S BEEN BUDS WITH THESE FOLKS FOR A WHILE.
AND WHAT RESTAURANT RUNS OUT OF BISCUITS AND GRAVY?
ANYWAY, IF THESE FRIENDS KNOW HER LIKE WE KNOW HER, THEY'LL UNDERSTAND.
SHE CAN'T RESIST THE RIGHT MOMENT.
LIFE EMERGED.
LIFE THRIVED.
I'M JUST SAYING THE BOOKSTORE CLOSES EARLY TODAY.
I GOTSTA EAT AND RUN, AS IT IS!
ROBOTS EAT?
C'MON, C'MON, C'MON.

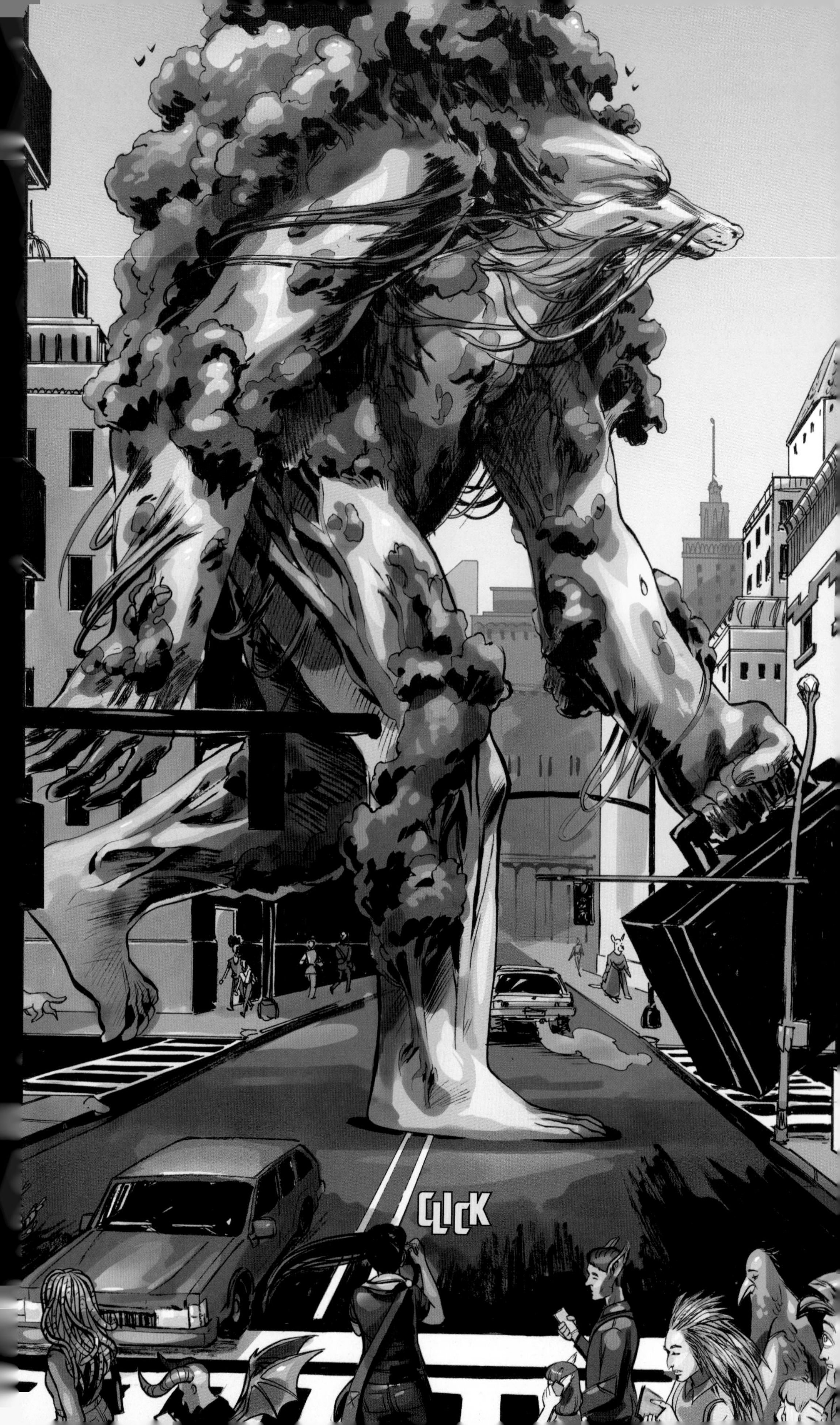
CLICK

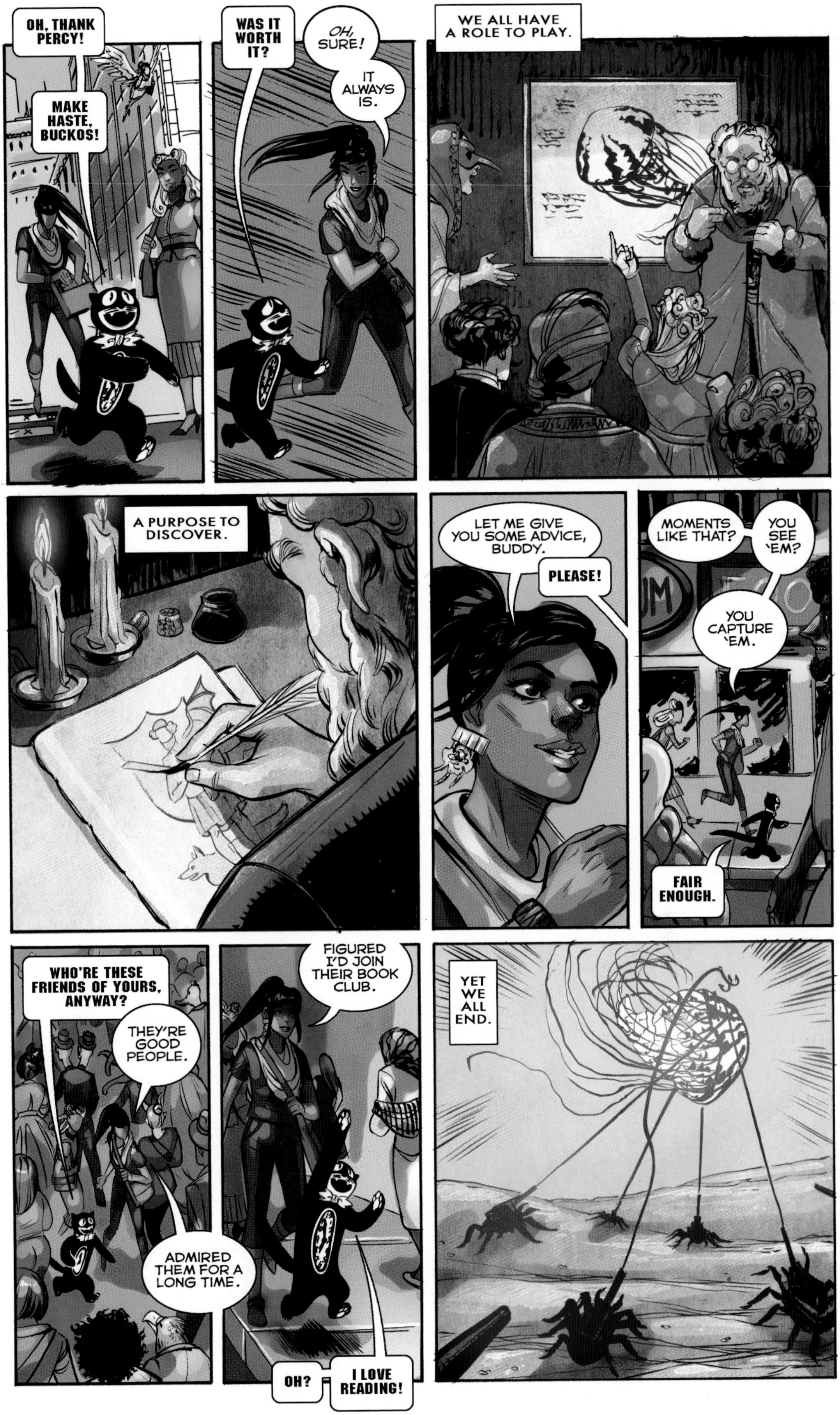

OH, THANK PERCY!
MAKE HASTE, BUCKOS!
WAS IT WORTH IT?
OH, SURE!
IT ALWAYS IS.
WE ALL HAVE A ROLE TO PLAY.
A PURPOSE TO DISCOVER.
LET ME GIVE YOU SOME ADVICE, BUDDY.
PLEASE!
MOMENTS LIKE THAT?
YOU SEE 'EM?
YOU CAPTURE 'EM.
FAIR ENOUGH.
WHO'RE THESE FRIENDS OF YOURS, ANYWAY?
THEY'RE GOOD PEOPLE.
ADMIRED THEM FOR A LONG TIME.
FIGURED I'D JOIN THEIR BOOK CLUB.
OH?
I LOVE READING!
YET WE ALL END.

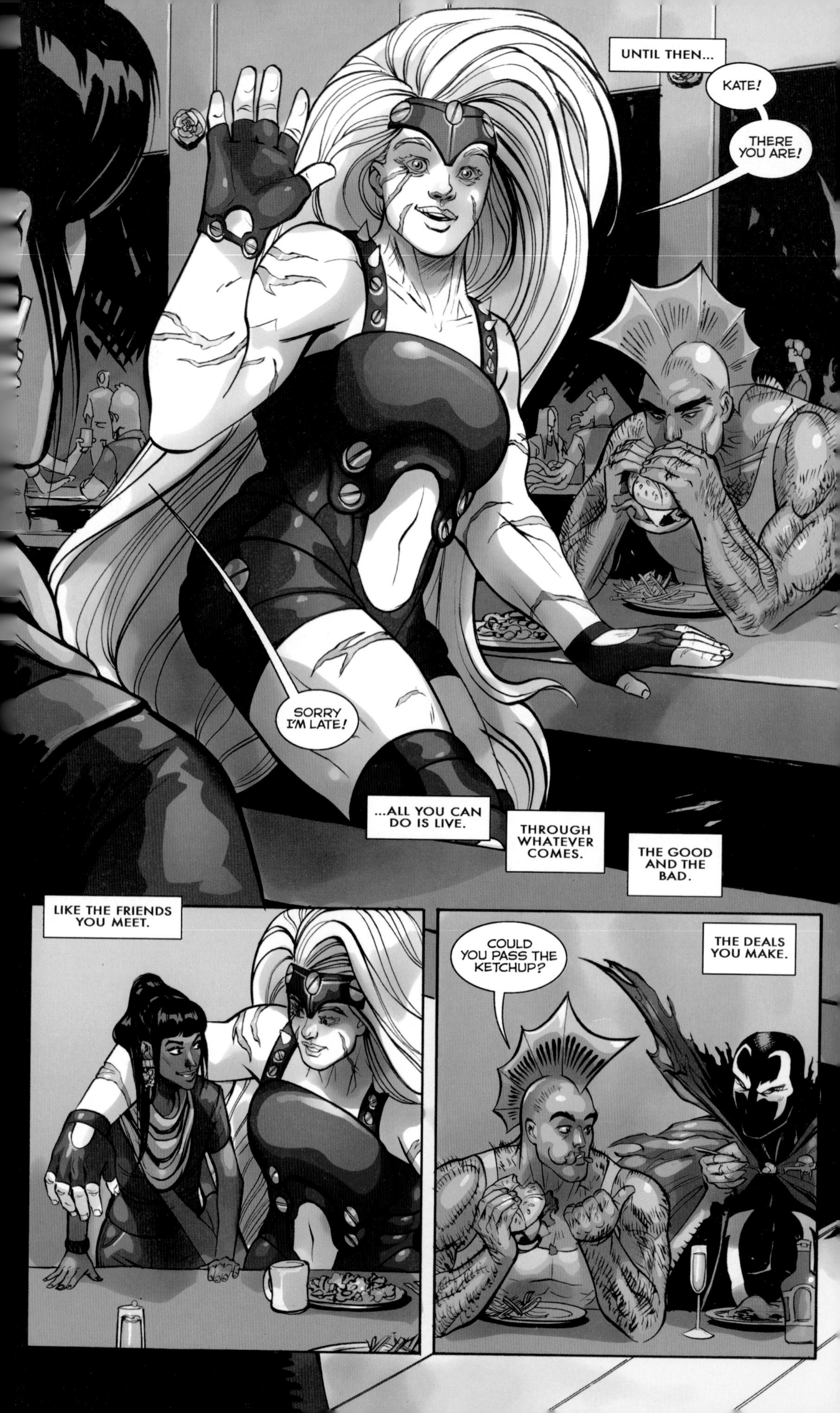
UNTIL THEN...
KATE!
THERE YOU ARE!
SORRY I'M LATE!
...ALL YOU CAN DO IS LIVE.
THROUGH WHATEVER COMES.
THE GOOD AND THE BAD.
LIKE THE FRIENDS YOU MEET.
COULD YOU PASS THE KETCHUP?
THE DEALS YOU MAKE.

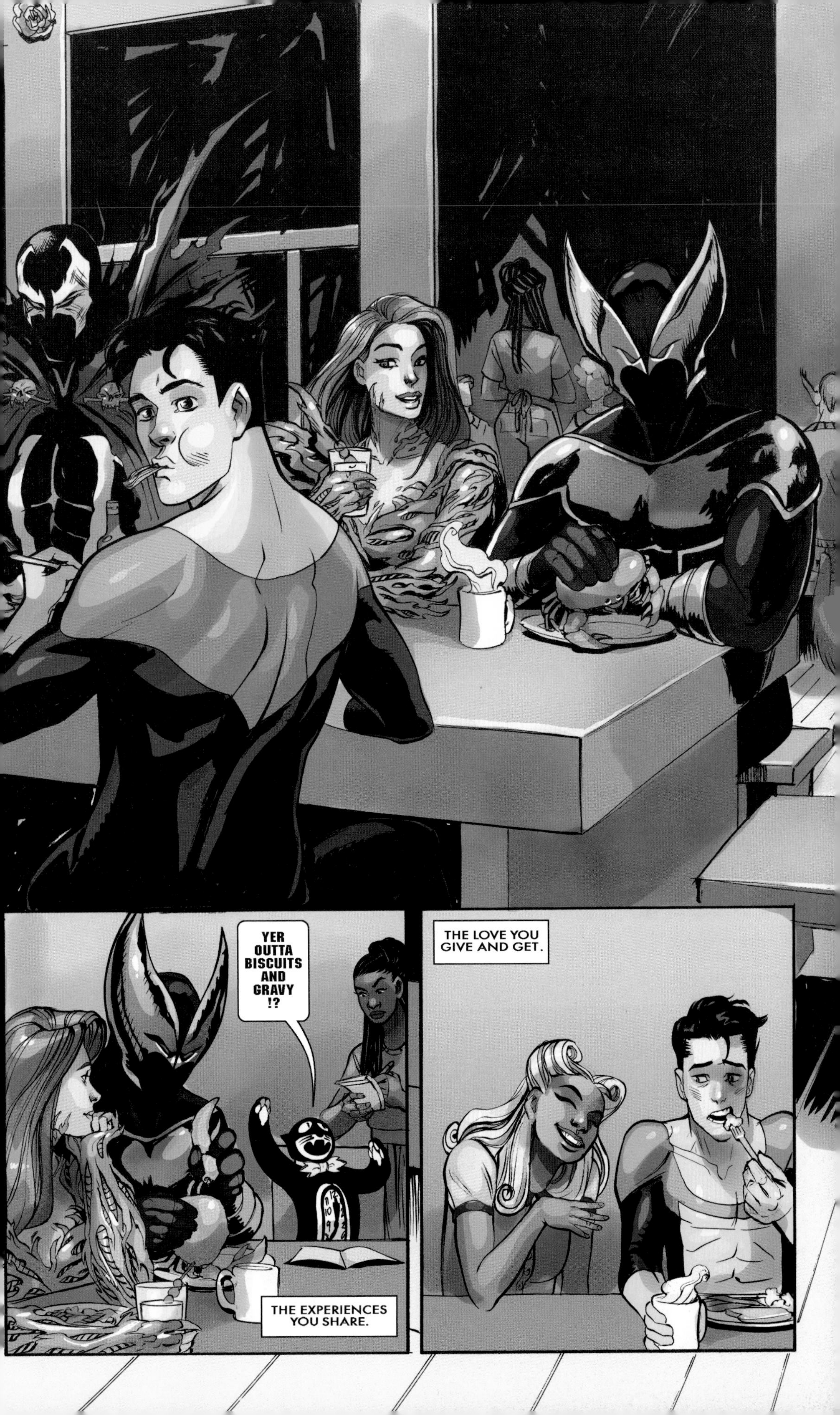
YER OUTTA BISCUITS AND GRAVY !?
THE EXPERIENCES YOU SHARE.
THE LOVE YOU GIVE AND GET.

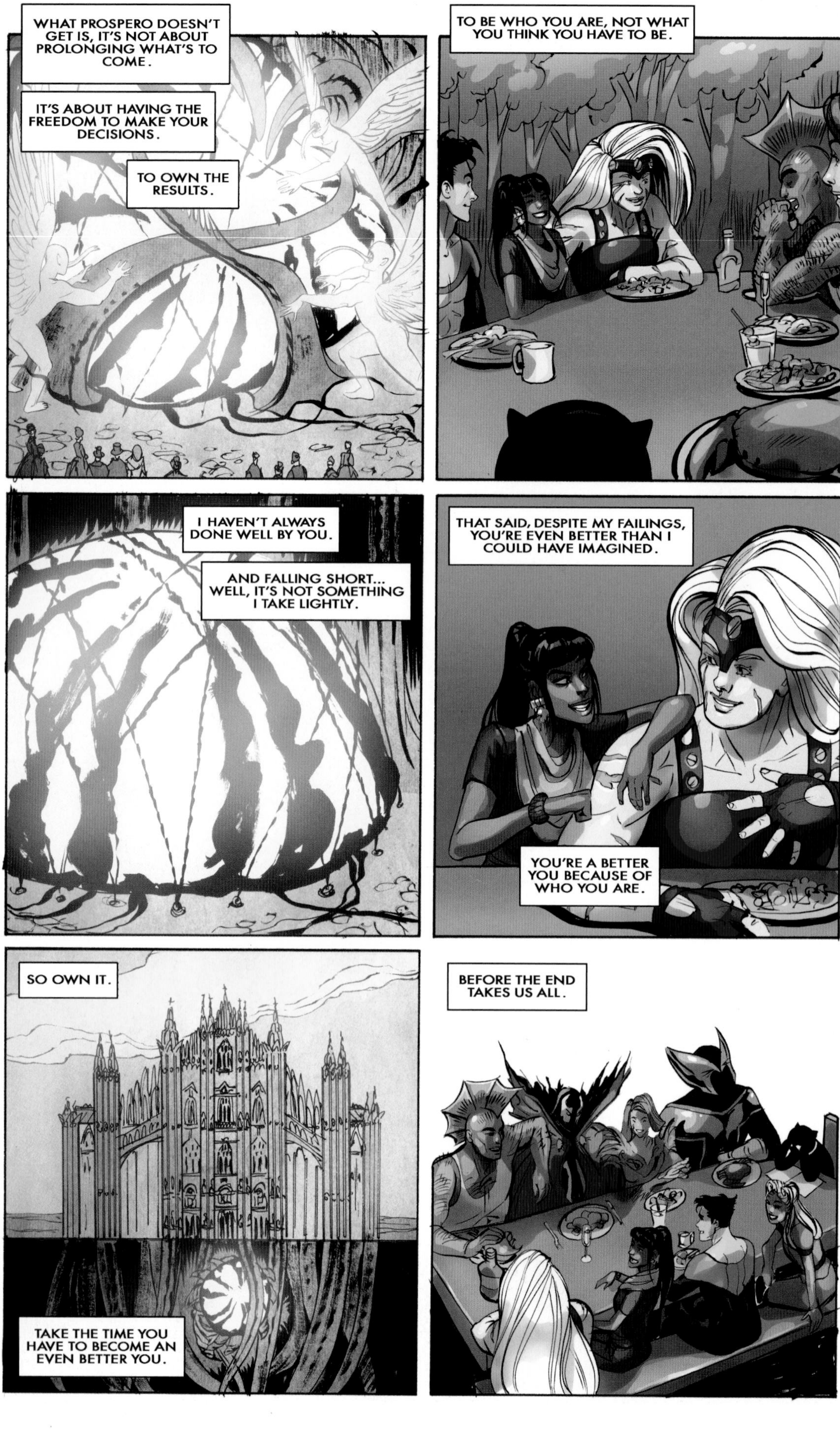
WHAT PROSPERO DOESN'T GET IS, IT'S NOT ABOUT PROLONGING WHAT'S TO COME.
IT'S ABOUT HAVING THE FREEDOM TO MAKE YOUR DECISIONS.
TO OWN THE RESULTS.
TO BE WHO YOU ARE, NOT WHAT YOU THINK YOU HAVE TO BE.
I HAVEN'T ALWAYS DONE WELL BY YOU.
AND FALLING SHORT... WELL, IT'S NOT SOMETHING I TAKE LIGHTLY.
THAT SAID, DESPITE MY FAILINGS, YOU'RE EVEN BETTER THAN I COULD HAVE IMAGINED.
YOU'RE A BETTER YOU BECAUSE OF WHO YOU ARE.
SO OWN IT.
TAKE THE TIME YOU HAVE TO BECOME AN EVEN BETTER YOU.
BEFORE THE END TAKES US ALL.

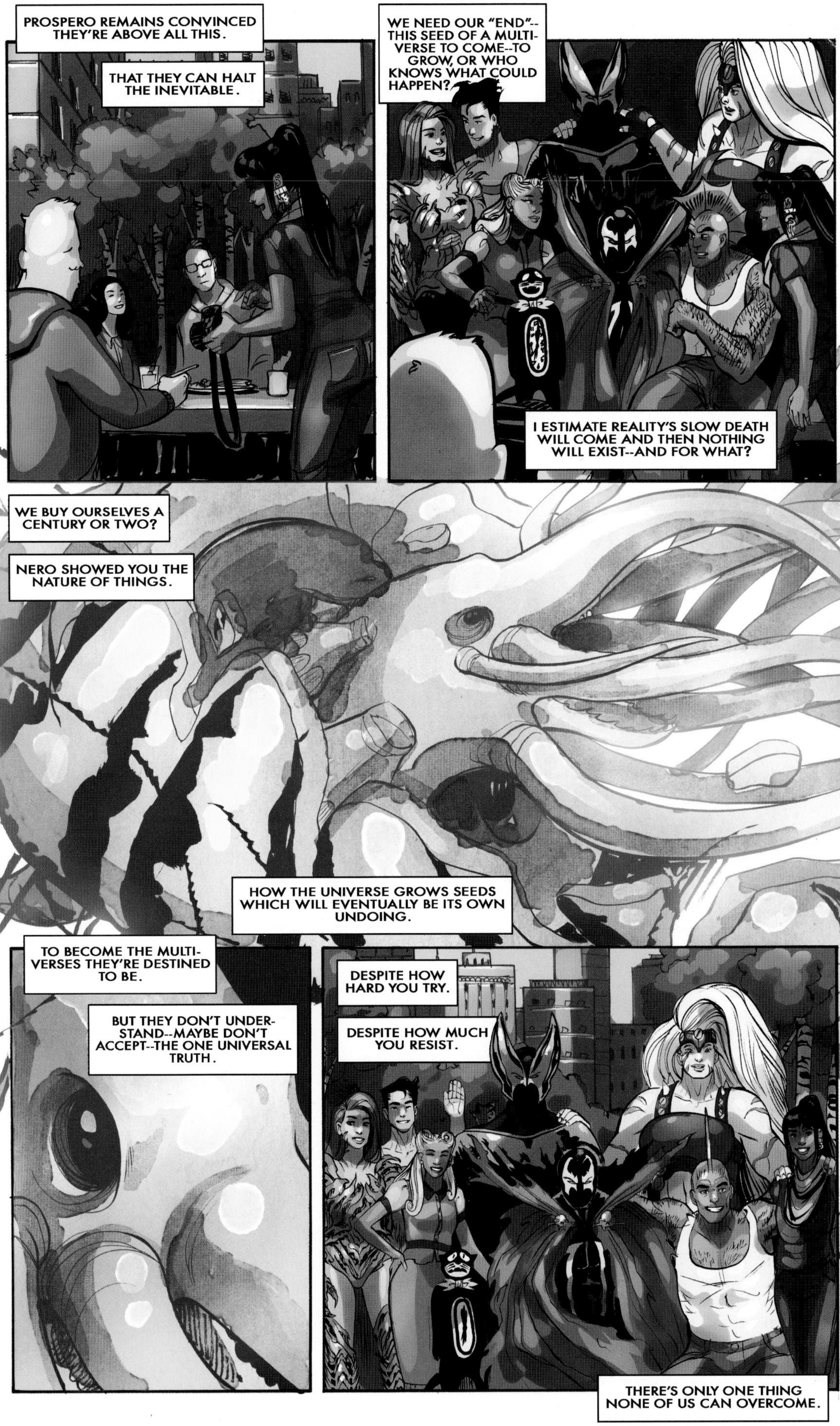
PROSPERO REMAINS CONVINCED THEY'RE ABOVE ALL THIS.
THAT THEY CAN HALT THE INEVITABLE.
WE NEED OUR "END"--THIS SEED OF A MULTI-VERSE TO COME--TO GROW, OR WHO KNOWS WHAT COULD HAPPEN?
I ESTIMATE REALITY'S SLOW DEATH WILL COME AND THEN NOTHING WILL EXIST--AND FOR WHAT?
WE BUY OURSELVES A CENTURY OR TWO?
NERO SHOWED YOU THE NATURE OF THINGS.
HOW THE UNIVERSE GROWS SEEDS WHICH WILL EVENTUALLY BE ITS OWN UNDOING.
TO BECOME THE MULTI-VERSES THEY'RE DESTINED TO BE.
BUT THEY DON'T UNDER-STAND--MAYBE DON'T ACCEPT--THE ONE UNIVERSAL TRUTH.
DESPITE HOW HARD YOU TRY.
DESPITE HOW MUCH YOU RESIST.
THERE'S ONLY ONE THING NONE OF US CAN OVERCOME.

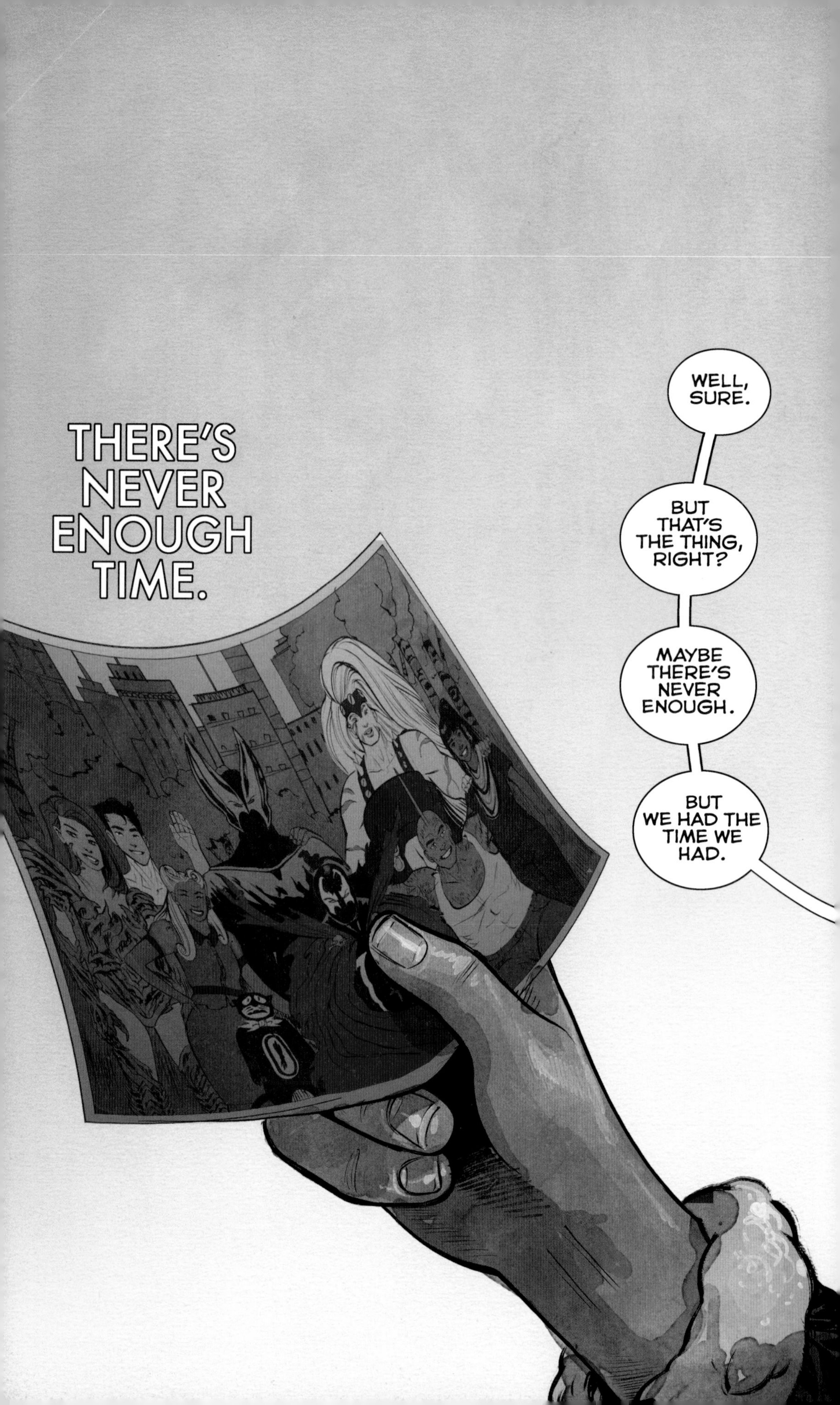
THERE'S NEVER ENOUGH TIME.
WELL, SURE.
BUT THAT'S THE THING, RIGHT?
MAYBE THERE'S NEVER ENOUGH.
BUT WE HAD THE TIME WE HAD.

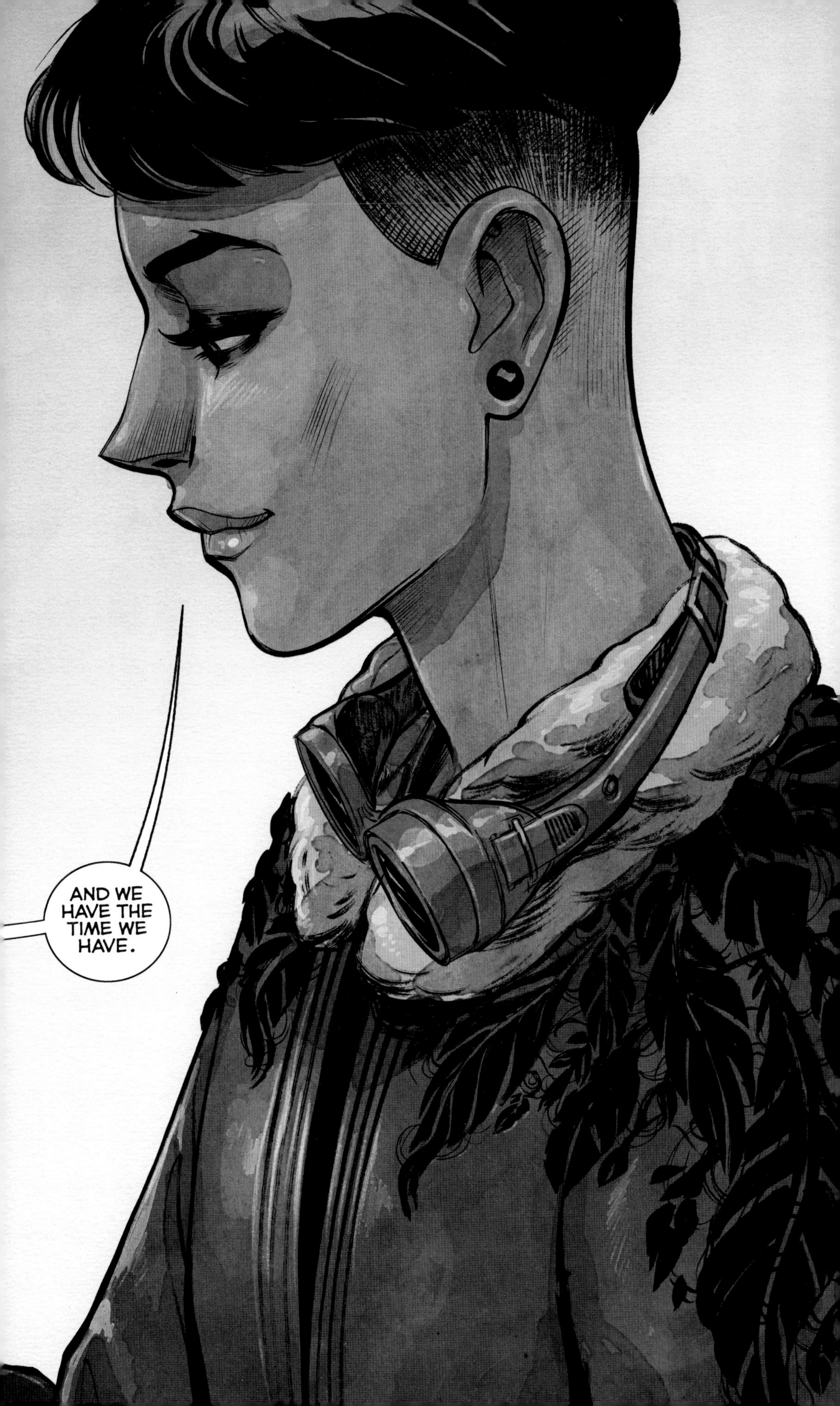
AND WE HAVE THE TIME WE HAVE.

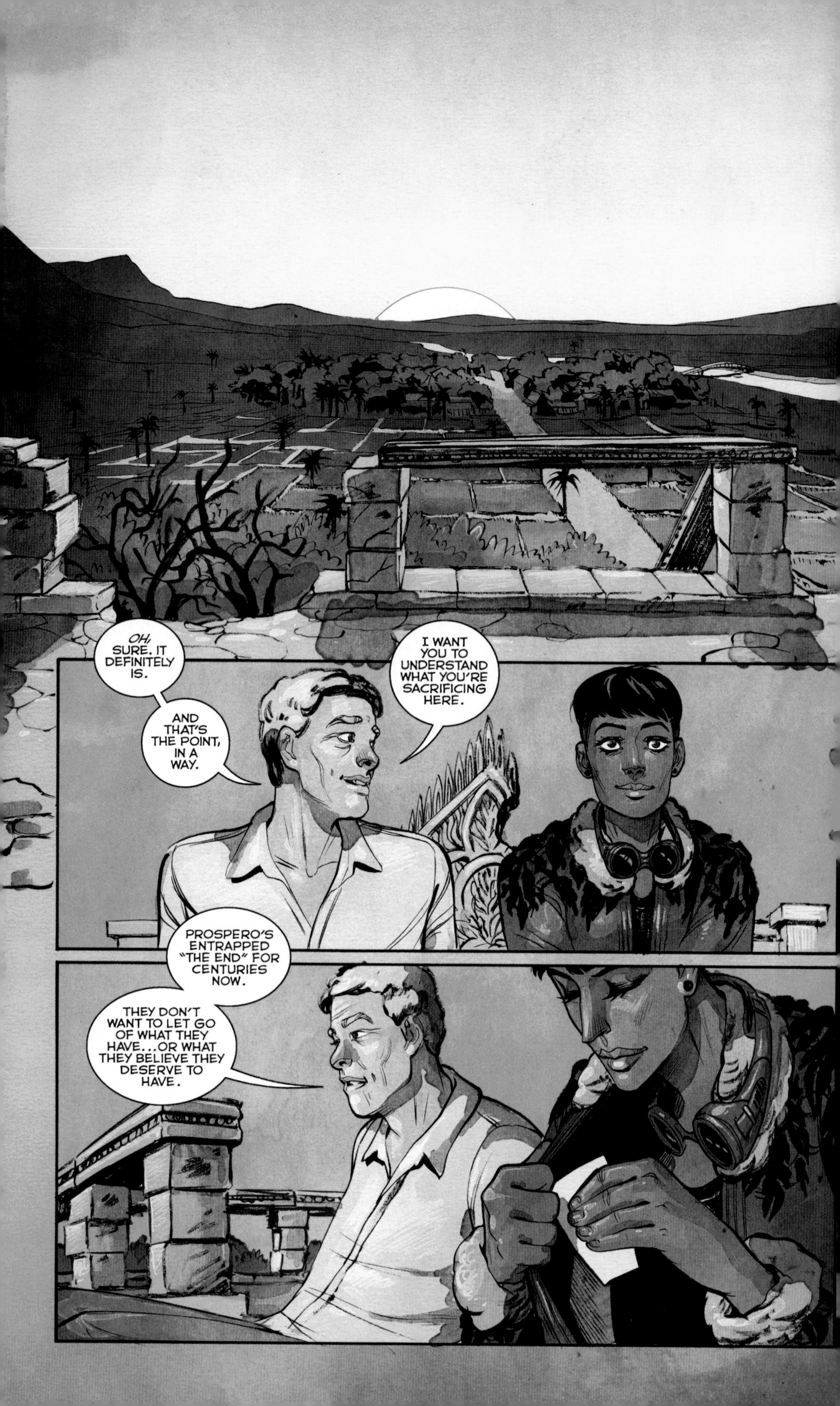
OH, SURE. IT DEFINITELY IS.
AND THAT'S THE POINT, IN A WAY.
I WANT YOU TO UNDERSTAND WHAT YOU'RE SACRIFICING HERE.
PROSPERO'S ENTRAPPED "THE END" FOR CENTURIES NOW.
THEY DON'T WANT TO LET GO OF WHAT THEY HAVE...OR WHAT THEY BELIEVE THEY DESERVE TO HAVE.

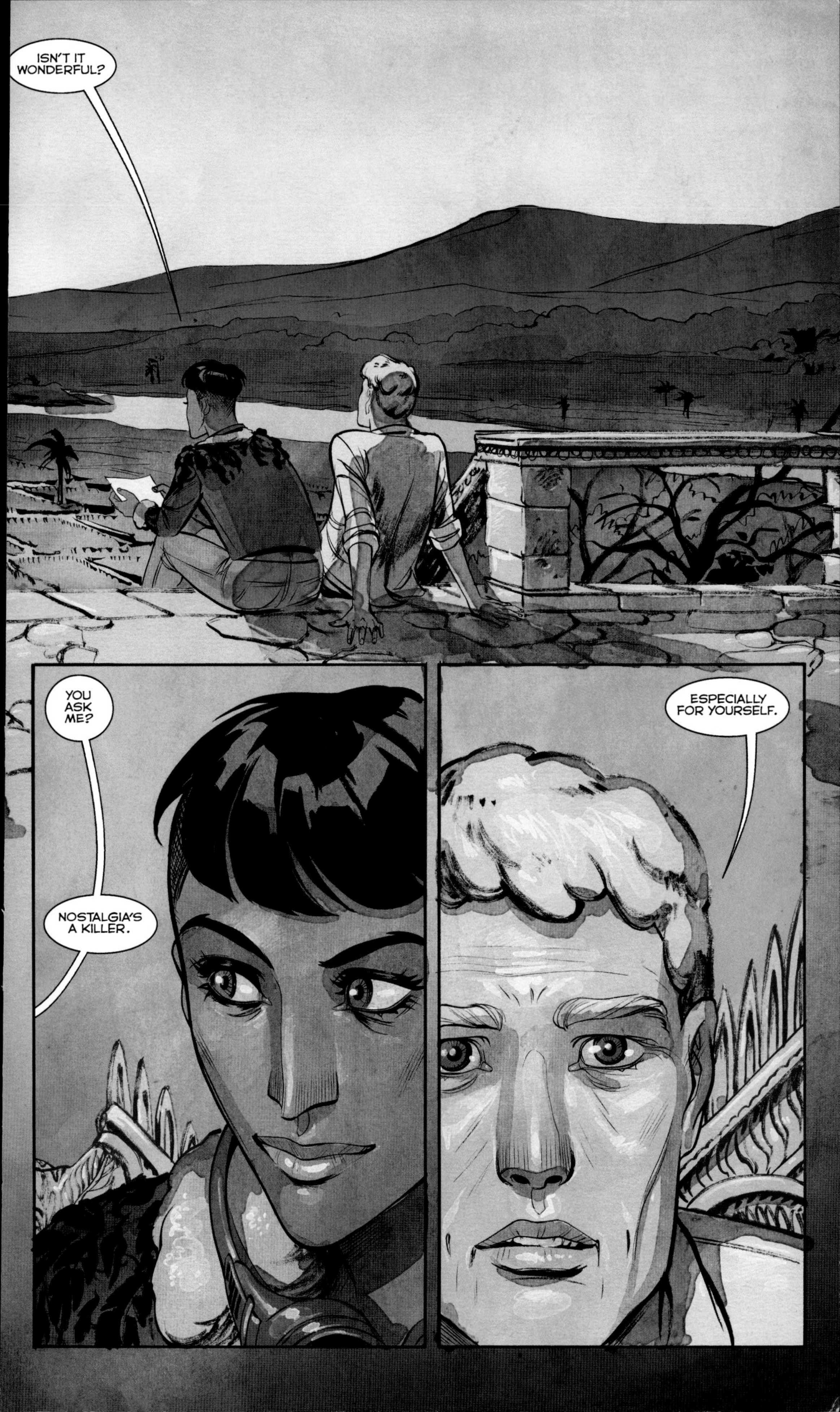
ISN'T IT WONDERFUL?
YOU ASK ME?
NOSTALGIA'S A KILLER.
ESPECIALLY FOR YOURSELF.

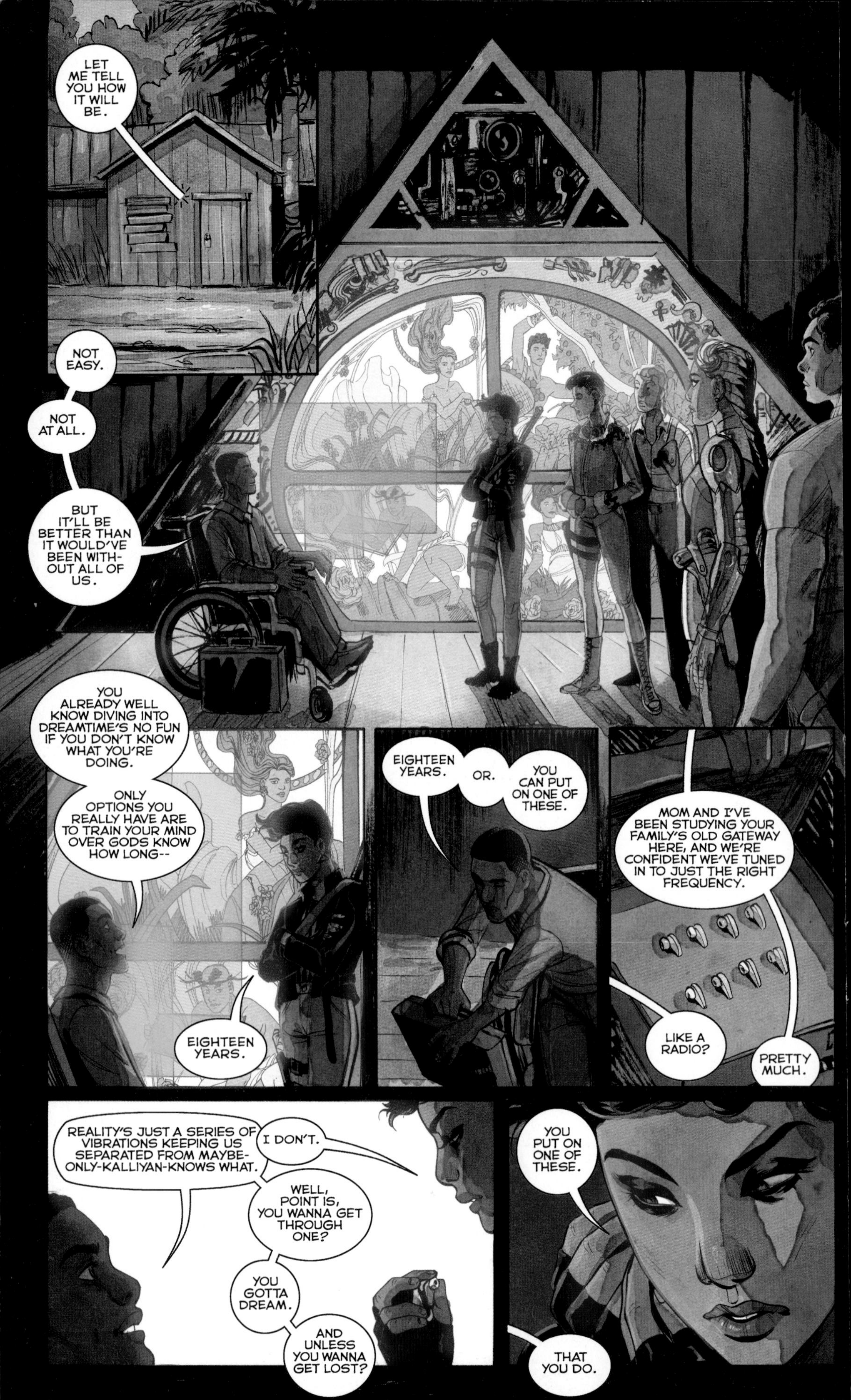
LET ME TELL YOU HOW IT WILL BE.
NOT EASY.
NOT AT ALL.
BUT IT'LL BE BETTER THAN IT WOULD'VE BEEN WITHOUT ALL OF US.
YOU ALREADY WELL KNOW DIVING INTO DREAMTIME'S NO FUN IF YOU DON'T KNOW WHAT YOU'RE DOING.
ONLY OPTIONS YOU REALLY HAVE ARE TO TRAIN YOUR MIND OVER GODS KNOW HOW LONG--
EIGHTEEN YEARS.
EIGHTEEN YEARS.
OR.
YOU CAN PUT ON ONE OF THESE.
MOM AND I'VE BEEN STUDYING YOUR FAMILY'S OLD GATEWAY HERE, AND WE'RE CONFIDENT WE'VE TUNED IN TO JUST THE RIGHT FREQUENCY.
LIKE A RADIO?
PRETTY MUCH.
REALITY'S JUST A SERIES OF VIBRATIONS KEEPING US SEPARATED FROM MAYBE-ONLY-KALLIYAN-KNOWS WHAT.
I DON'T.
WELL, POINT IS, YOU WANNA GET THROUGH ONE?
YOU GOTTA DREAM.
AND UNLESS YOU WANNA GET LOST?
YOU PUT ON ONE OF THESE.
THAT YOU DO.

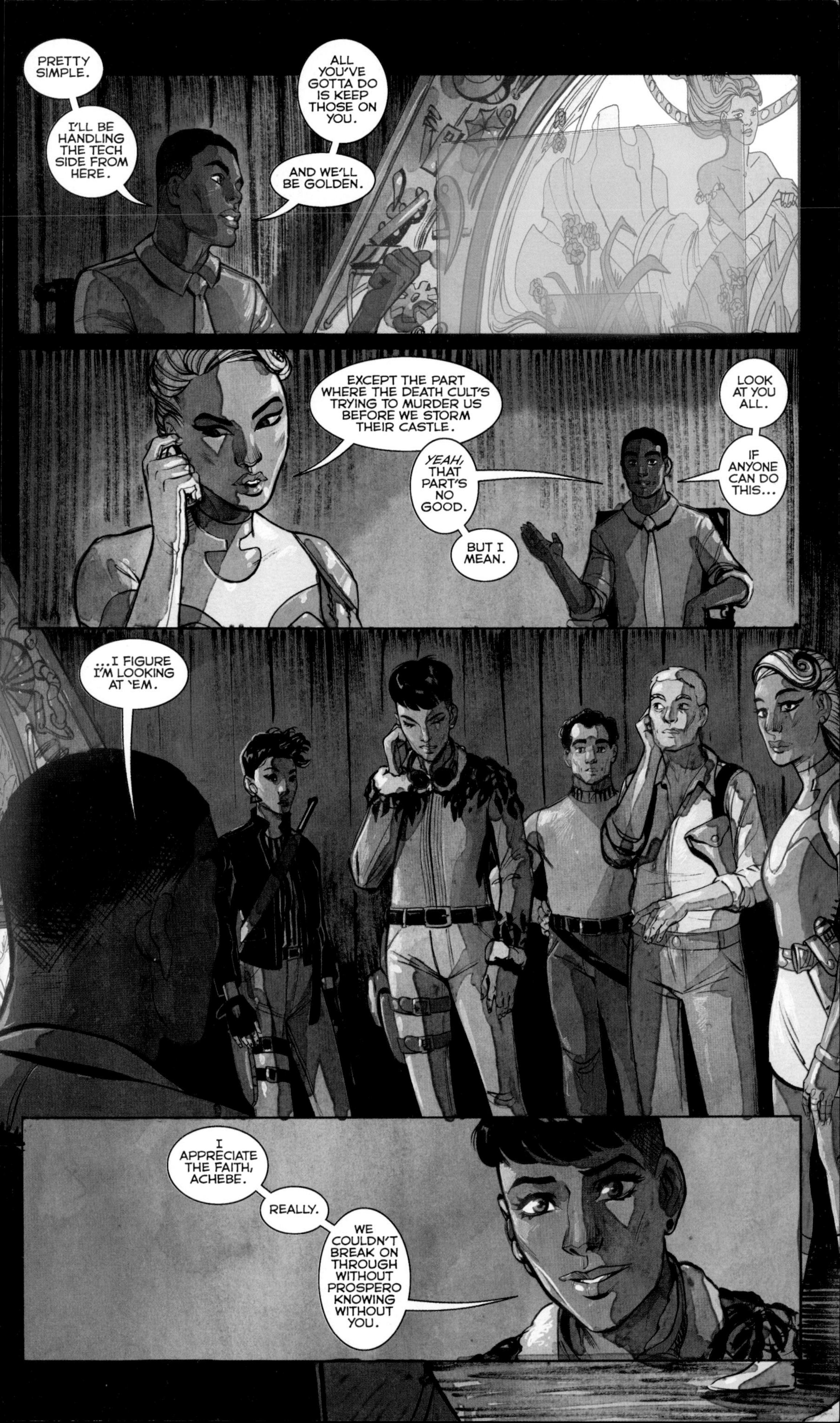
PRETTY SIMPLE.
I'LL BE HANDLING THE TECH SIDE FROM HERE.
ALL YOU'VE GOTTA DO IS KEEP THOSE ON YOU.
AND WE'LL BE GOLDEN.
EXCEPT THE PART WHERE THE DEATH CULT'S TRYING TO MURDER US BEFORE WE STORM THEIR CASTLE.
YEAH, THAT PART'S NO GOOD.
BUT I MEAN.
LOOK AT YOU ALL.
IF ANYONE CAN DO THIS...
...I FIGURE I'M LOOKING AT 'EM.
I APPRECIATE THE FAITH, ACHEBE.
REALLY.
WE COULDN'T BREAK ON THROUGH WITHOUT PROSPERO KNOWING WITHOUT YOU.

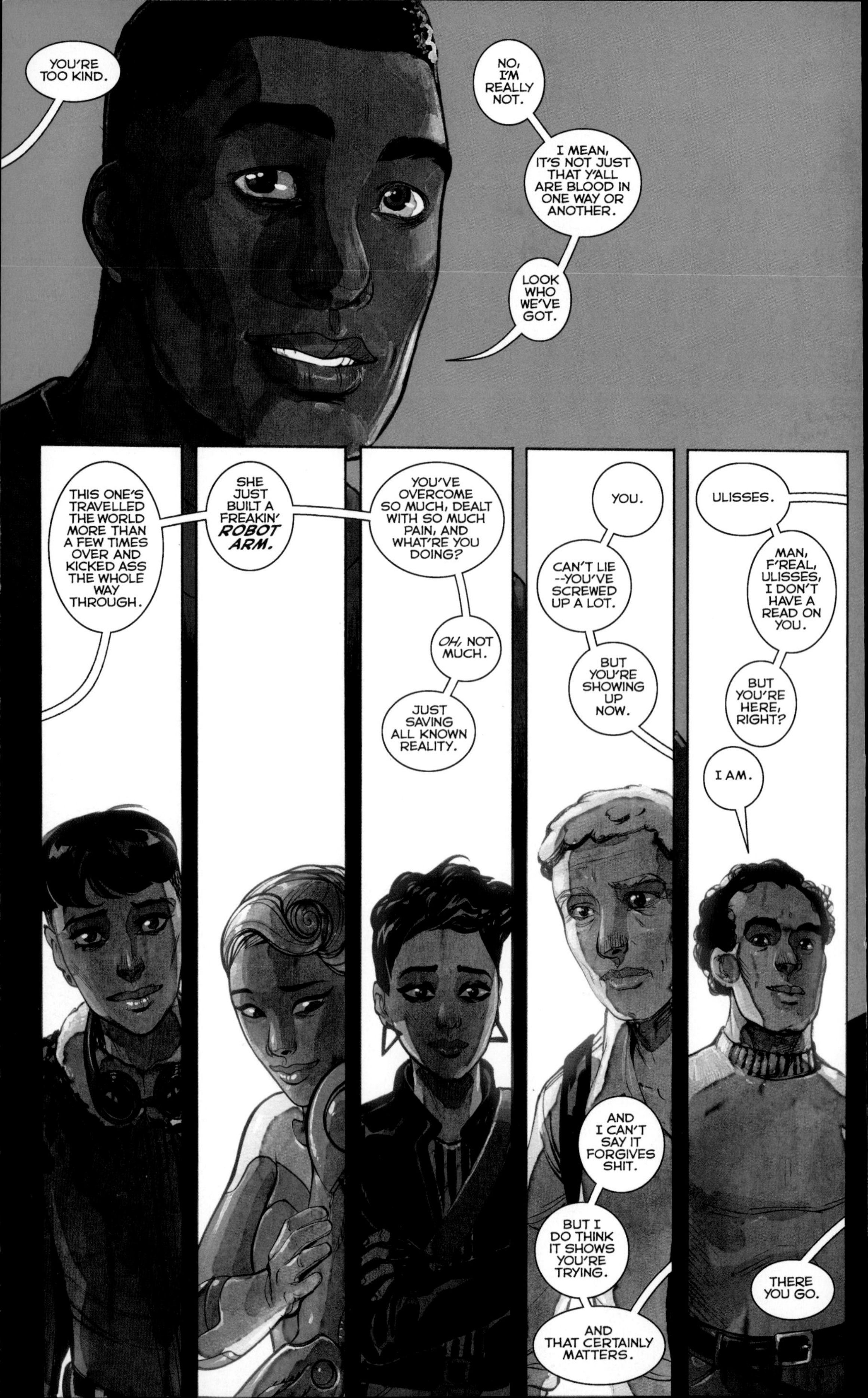
YOU'RE TOO KIND.
NO, I'M REALLY NOT.
I MEAN, IT'S NOT JUST THAT Y'ALL ARE BLOOD IN ONE WAY OR ANOTHER.
LOOK WHO WE'VE GOT.
THIS ONE'S TRAVELLED THE WORLD MORE THAN A FEW TIMES OVER AND KICKED ASS THE WHOLE WAY THROUGH.
SHE JUST BUILT A FREAKIN' *ROBOT ARM.*
YOU'VE OVERCOME SO MUCH, DEALT WITH SO MUCH PAIN, AND WHAT'RE YOU DOING?
OH, NOT MUCH.
JUST SAVING ALL KNOWN REALITY.
YOU.
CAN'T LIE --YOU'VE SCREWED UP A LOT.
BUT YOU'RE SHOWING UP NOW.
AND I CAN'T SAY IT FORGIVES SHIT.
BUT I DO THINK IT SHOWS YOU'RE TRYING.
AND THAT CERTAINLY MATTERS.
ULISSES.
MAN, F'REAL, ULISSES, I DON'T HAVE A READ ON YOU.
BUT YOU'RE HERE, RIGHT?
I AM.
THERE YOU GO.

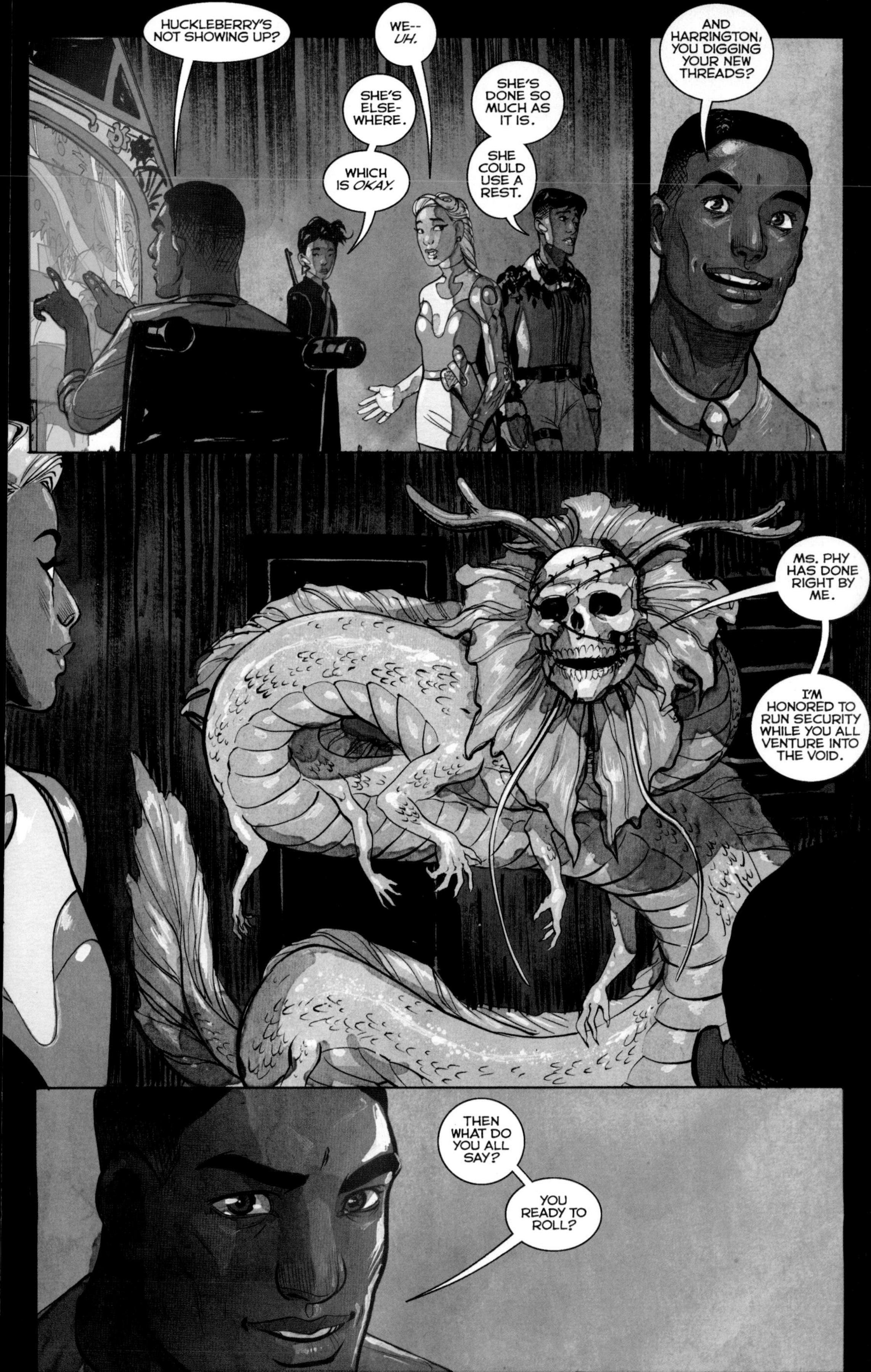
HUCKLEBERRY'S NOT SHOWING UP?
WE-- UH.
SHE'S ELSE-WHERE.
WHICH IS OKAY.
SHE'S DONE SO MUCH AS IT IS.
SHE COULD USE A REST.
AND HARRINGTON, YOU DIGGING YOUR NEW THREADS?
Ms. PHY HAS DONE RIGHT BY ME.
I'M HONORED TO RUN SECURITY WHILE YOU ALL VENTURE INTO THE VOID.
THEN WHAT DO YOU ALL SAY?
YOU READY TO ROLL?

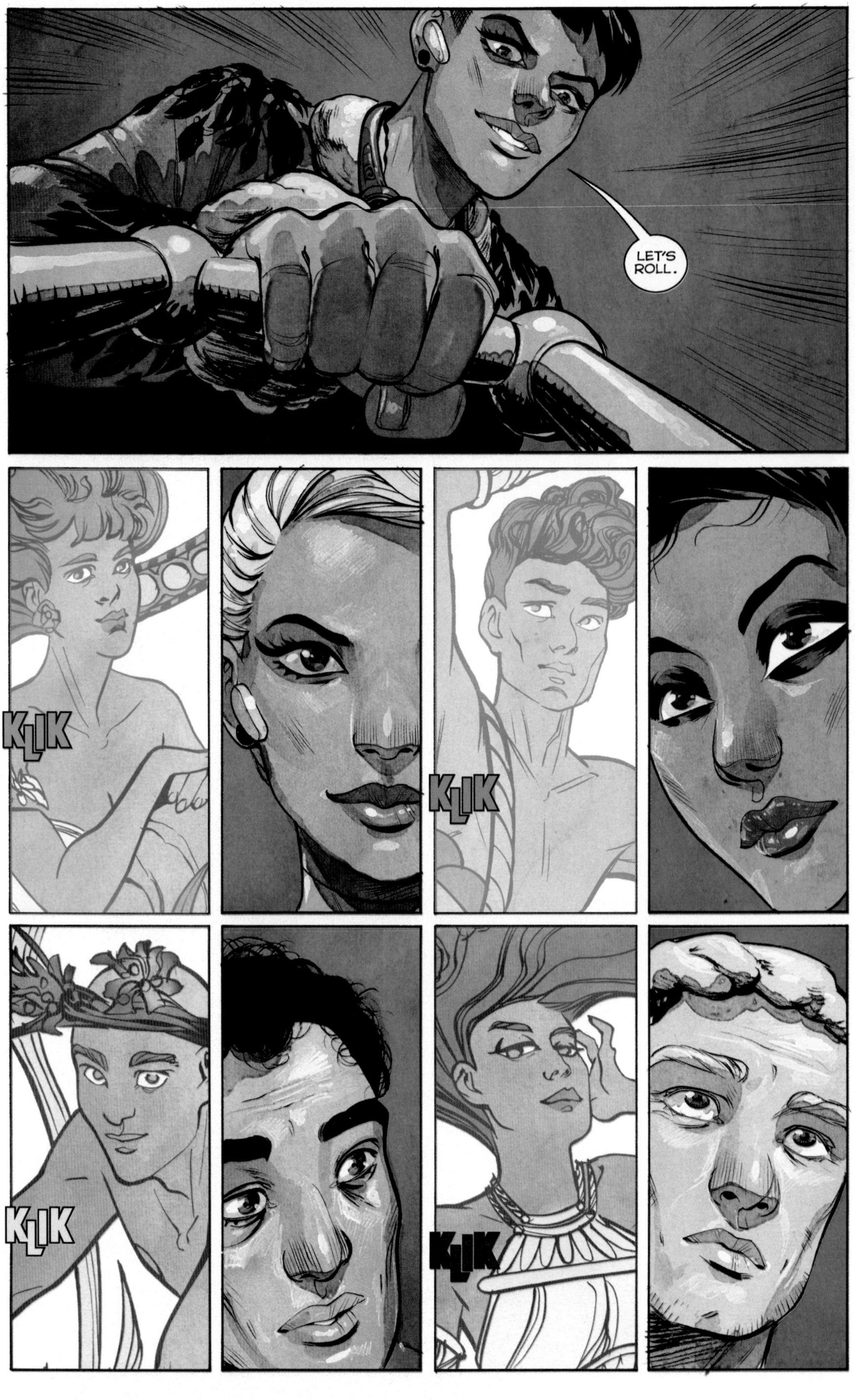
LET'S ROLL.
KLIK
KLIK
KLIK
KLIK

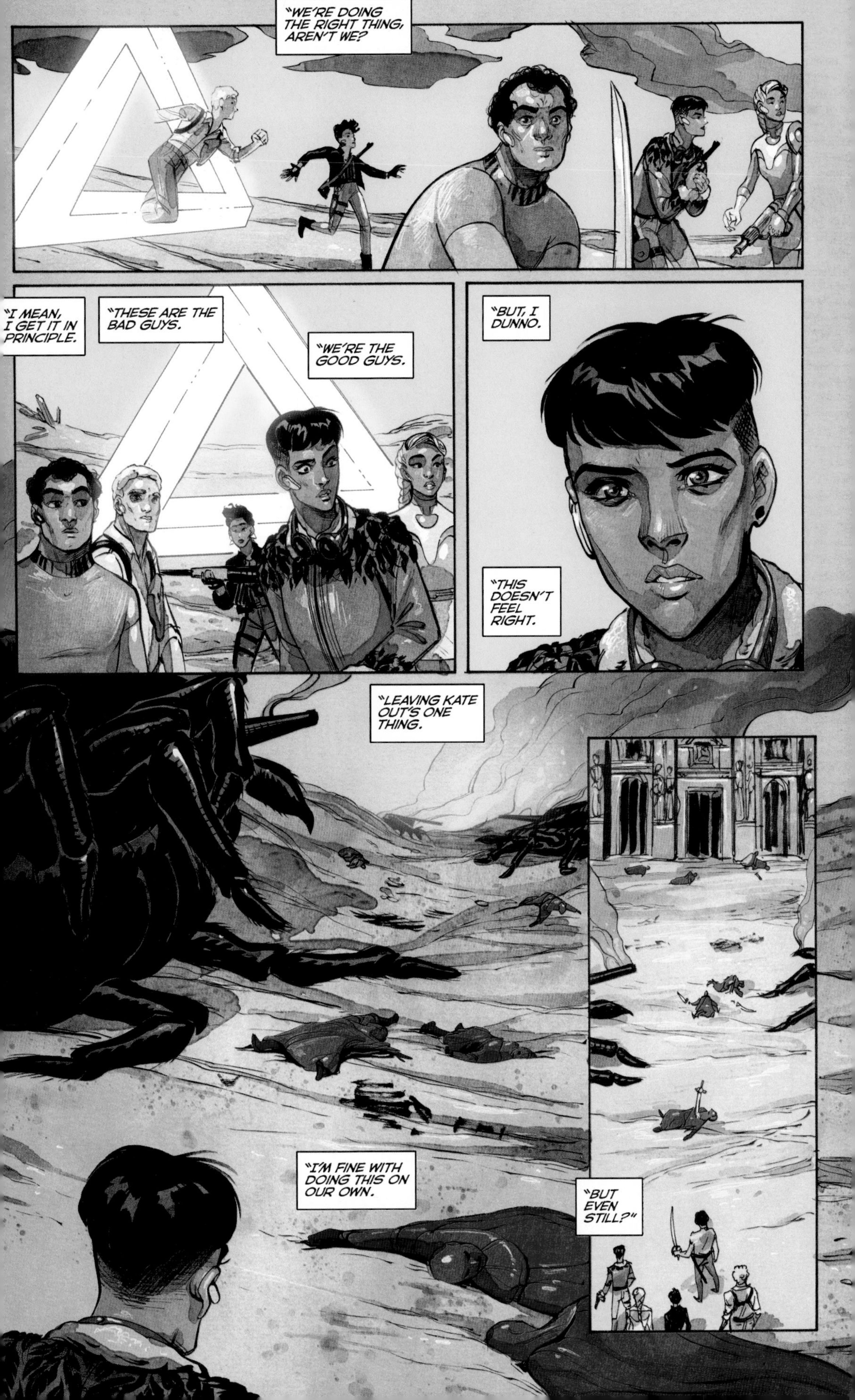
"WE'RE DOING THE RIGHT THING, AREN'T WE?
"I MEAN, I GET IT IN PRINCIPLE.
"THESE ARE THE BAD GUYS.
"WE'RE THE GOOD GUYS.
"BUT, I DUNNO.
"THIS DOESN'T FEEL RIGHT.
"LEAVING KATE OUT'S ONE THING.
"I'M FINE WITH DOING THIS ON OUR OWN.
"BUT EVEN STILL?"

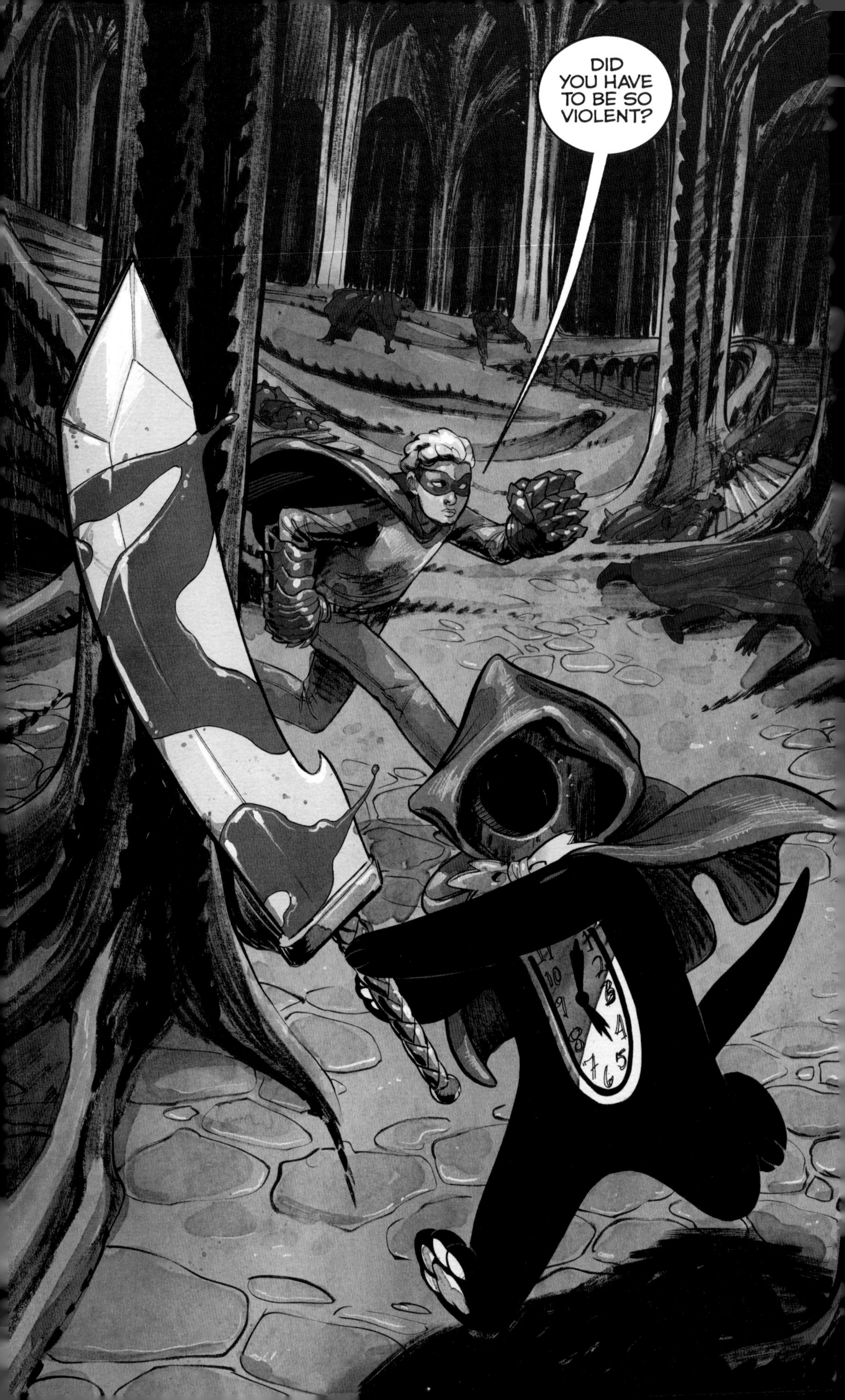
DID YOU HAVE TO BE SO VIOLENT?

CHAPTER 26

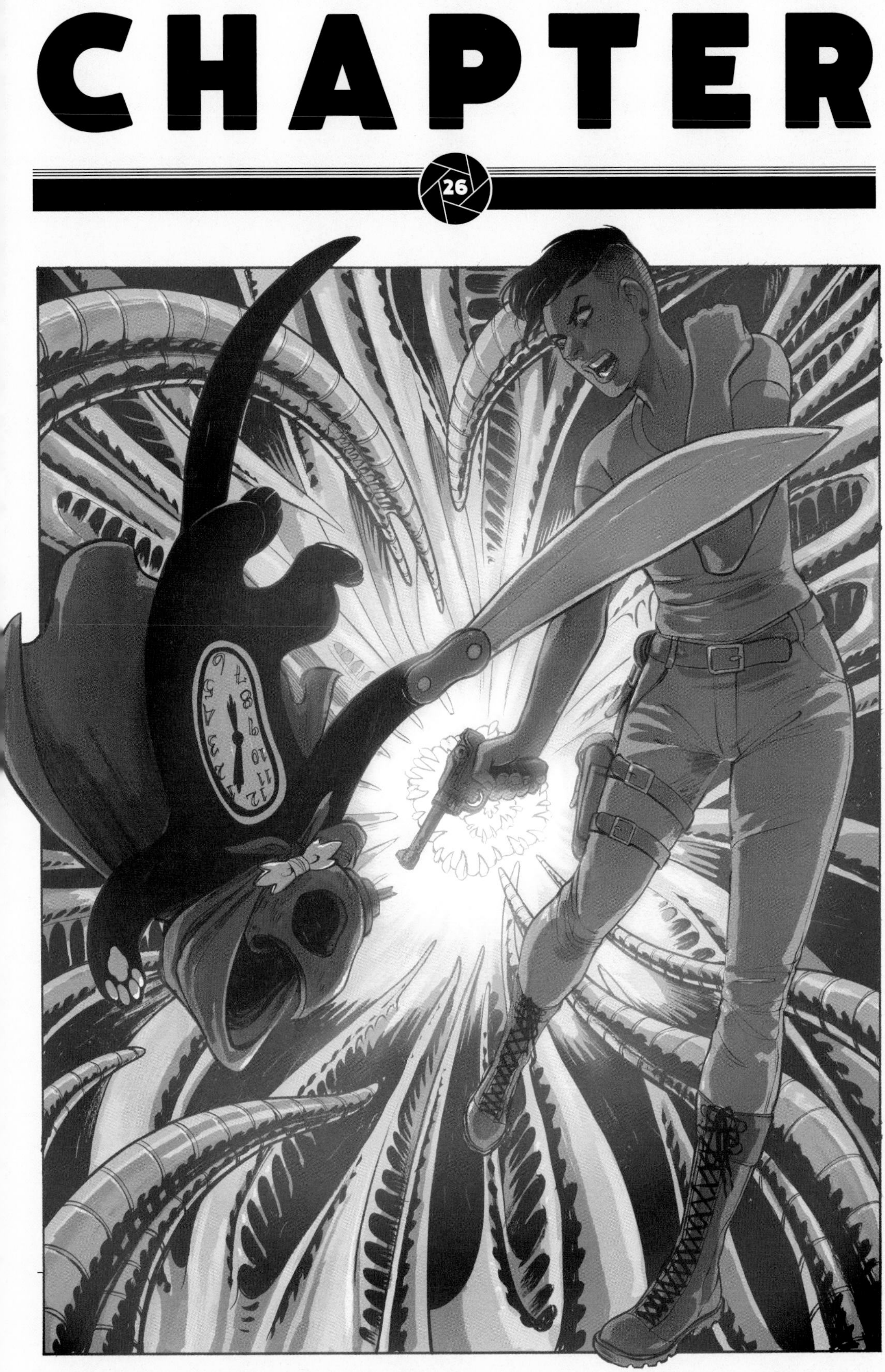

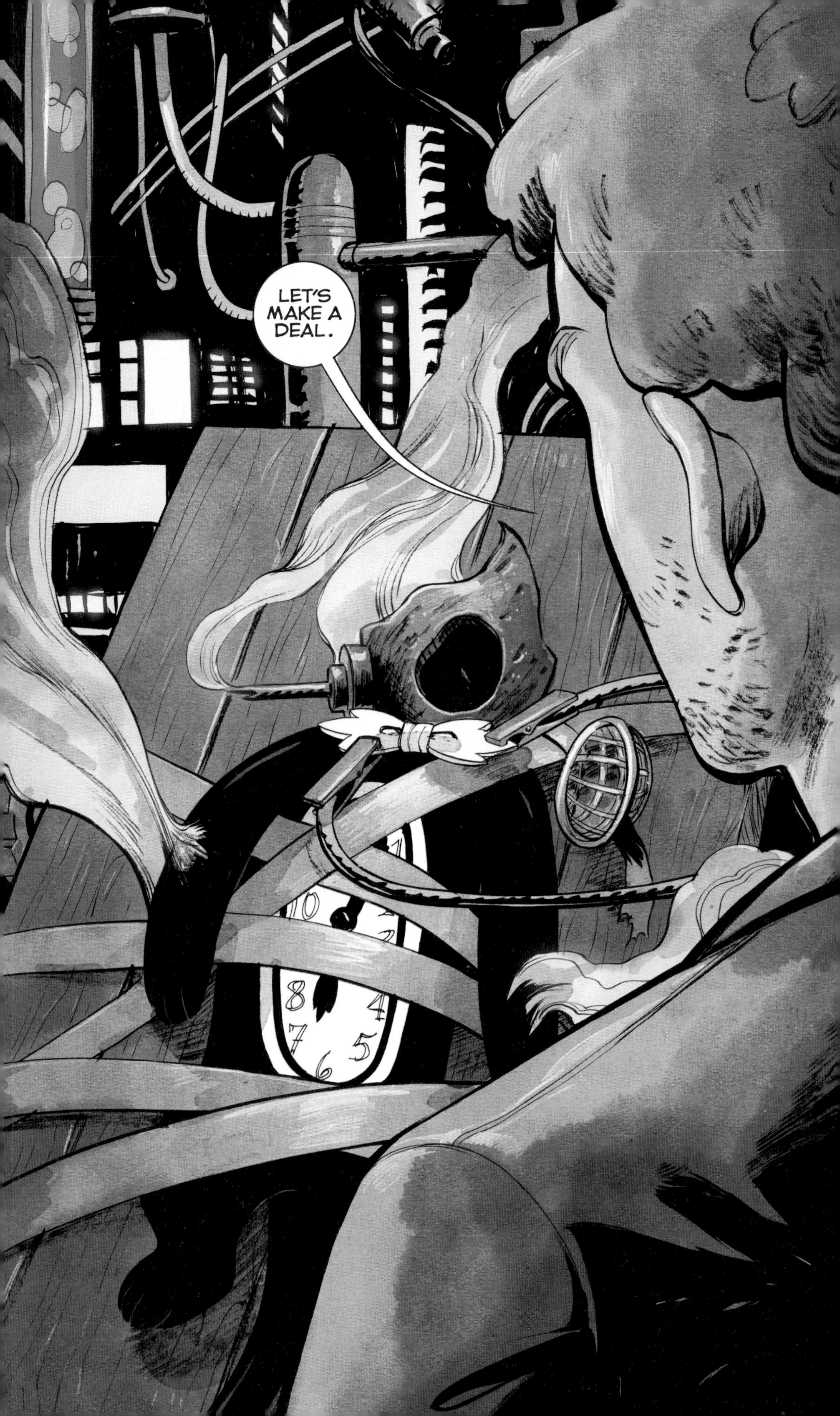
LET'S MAKE A DEAL.

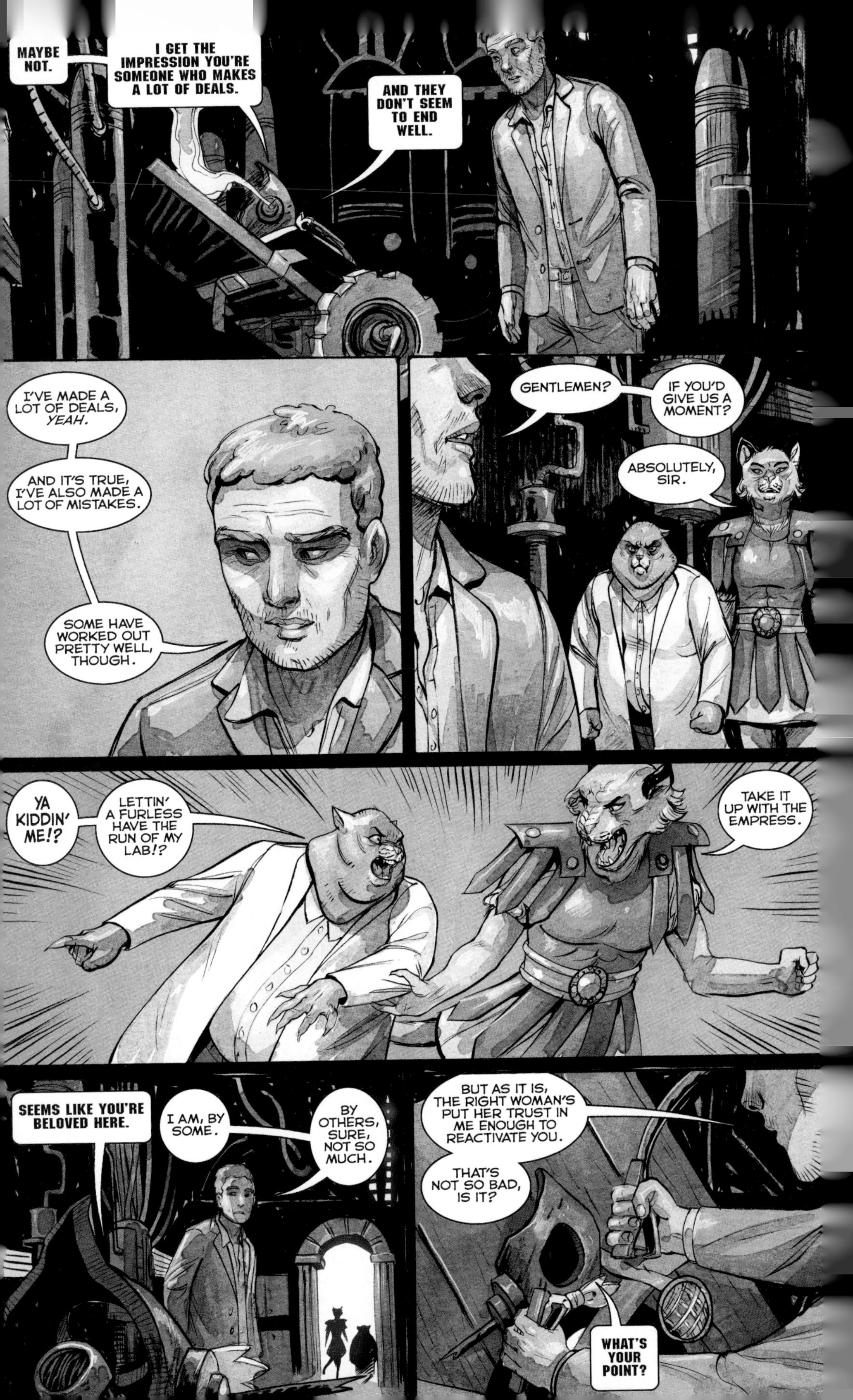
MAYBE NOT.
I GET THE IMPRESSION YOU'RE SOMEONE WHO MAKES A LOT OF DEALS.
AND THEY DON'T SEEM TO END WELL.
I'VE MADE A LOT OF DEALS, *YEAH.*
AND IT'S TRUE, I'VE ALSO MADE A LOT OF MISTAKES.
SOME HAVE WORKED OUT PRETTY WELL, THOUGH.
GENTLEMEN?
IF YOU'D GIVE US A MOMENT?
ABSOLUTELY, SIR.
YA KIDDIN' ME!?
LETTIN' A FURLESS HAVE THE RUN OF MY LAB!?
TAKE IT UP WITH THE EMPRESS.
SEEMS LIKE YOU'RE BELOVED HERE.
I AM, BY SOME.
BY OTHERS, SURE, NOT SO MUCH.
BUT AS IT IS, THE RIGHT WOMAN'S PUT HER TRUST IN ME ENOUGH TO REACTIVATE YOU.
THAT'S NOT SO BAD, IS IT?
WHAT'S YOUR POINT?

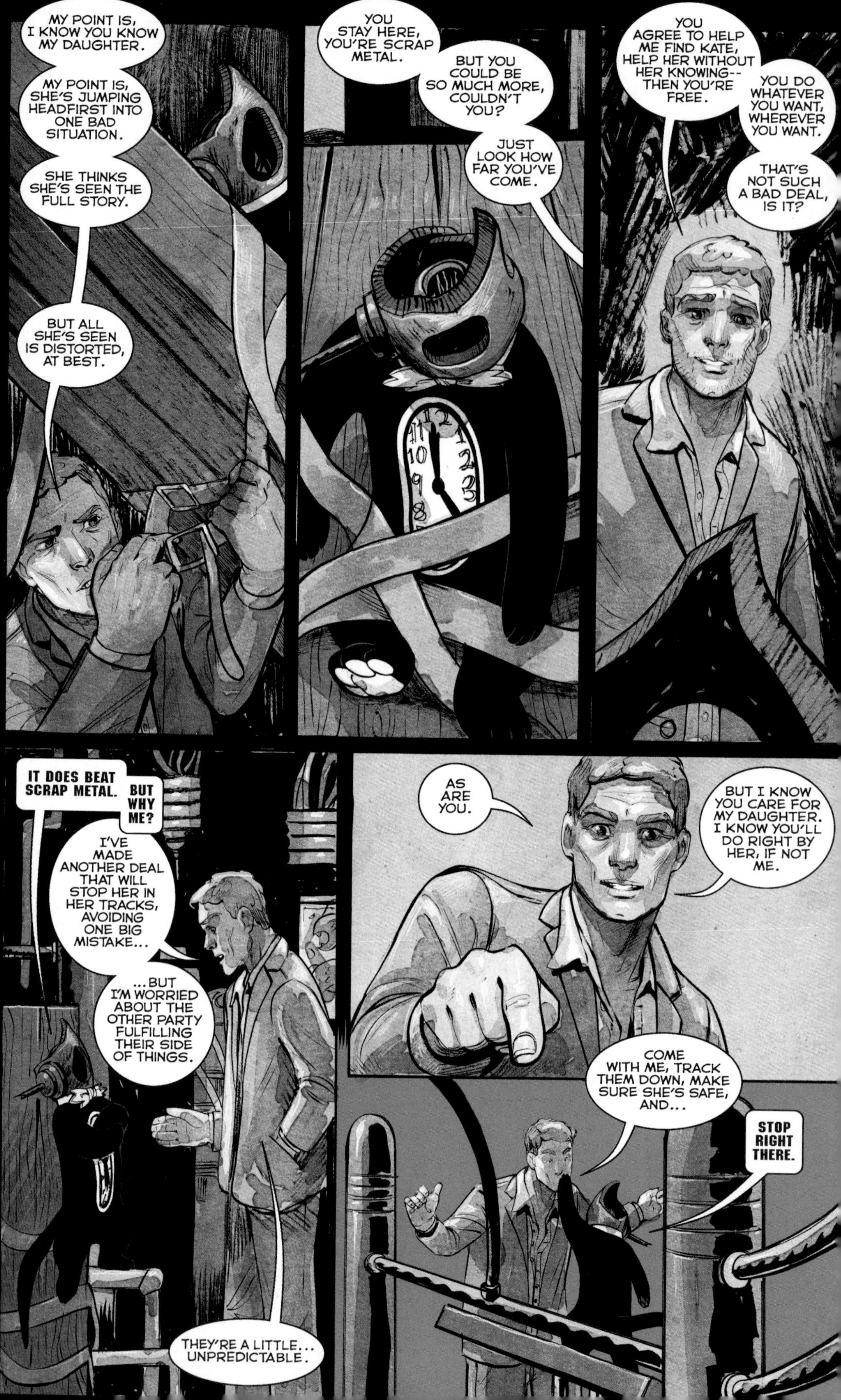
MY POINT IS, I KNOW YOU KNOW MY DAUGHTER.
MY POINT IS, SHE'S JUMPING HEADFIRST INTO ONE BAD SITUATION.
SHE THINKS SHE'S SEEN THE FULL STORY.
BUT ALL SHE'S SEEN IS DISTORTED, AT BEST.
YOU STAY HERE, YOU'RE SCRAP METAL.
BUT YOU COULD BE SO MUCH MORE, COULDN'T YOU?
JUST LOOK HOW FAR YOU'VE COME.
YOU AGREE TO HELP ME FIND KATE, HELP HER WITHOUT HER KNOWING-- THEN YOU'RE FREE.
YOU DO WHATEVER YOU WANT, WHEREVER YOU WANT.
THAT'S NOT SUCH A BAD DEAL, IS IT?
IT DOES BEAT SCRAP METAL.
BUT WHY ME?
I'VE MADE ANOTHER DEAL THAT WILL STOP HER IN HER TRACKS, AVOIDING ONE BIG MISTAKE...
...BUT I'M WORRIED ABOUT THE OTHER PARTY FULFILLING THEIR SIDE OF THINGS.
THEY'RE A LITTLE... UNPREDICTABLE.
AS ARE YOU.
BUT I KNOW YOU CARE FOR MY DAUGHTER. I KNOW YOU'LL DO RIGHT BY HER, IF NOT ME.
COME WITH ME, TRACK THEM DOWN, MAKE SURE SHE'S SAFE, AND...
STOP RIGHT THERE.

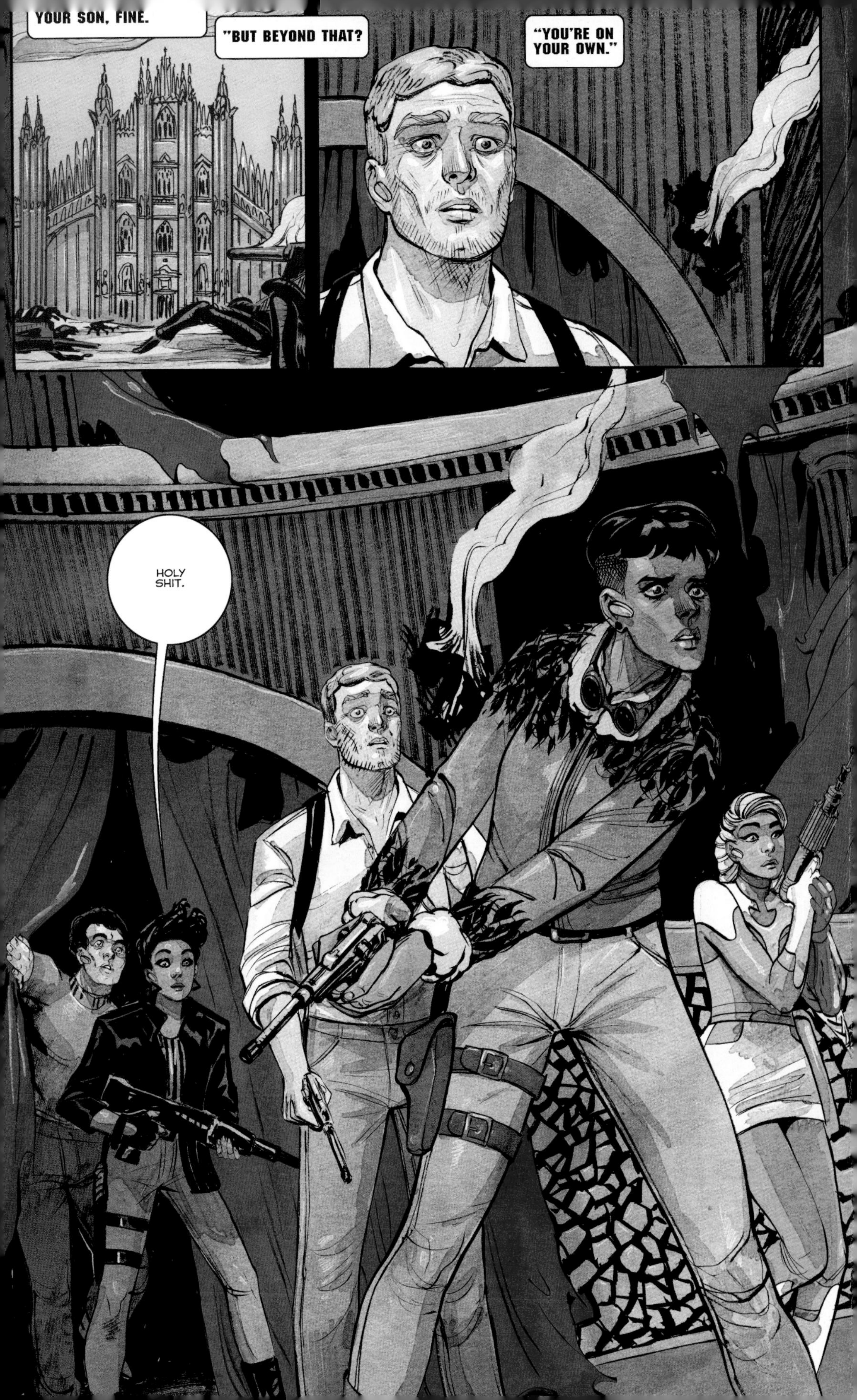
YOUR SON, FINE.
"BUT BEYOND THAT?
"YOU'RE ON YOUR OWN."
HOLY SHIT.

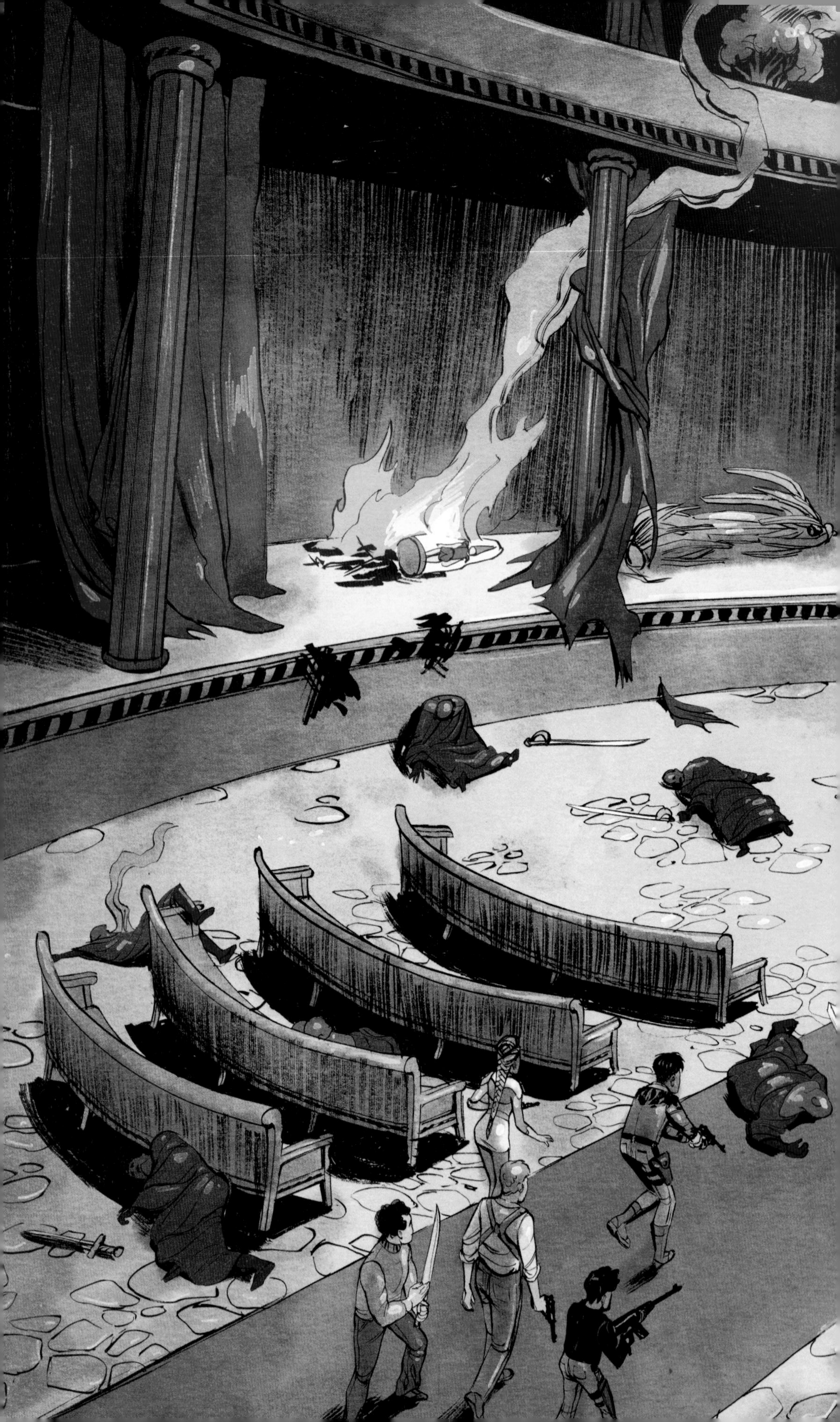

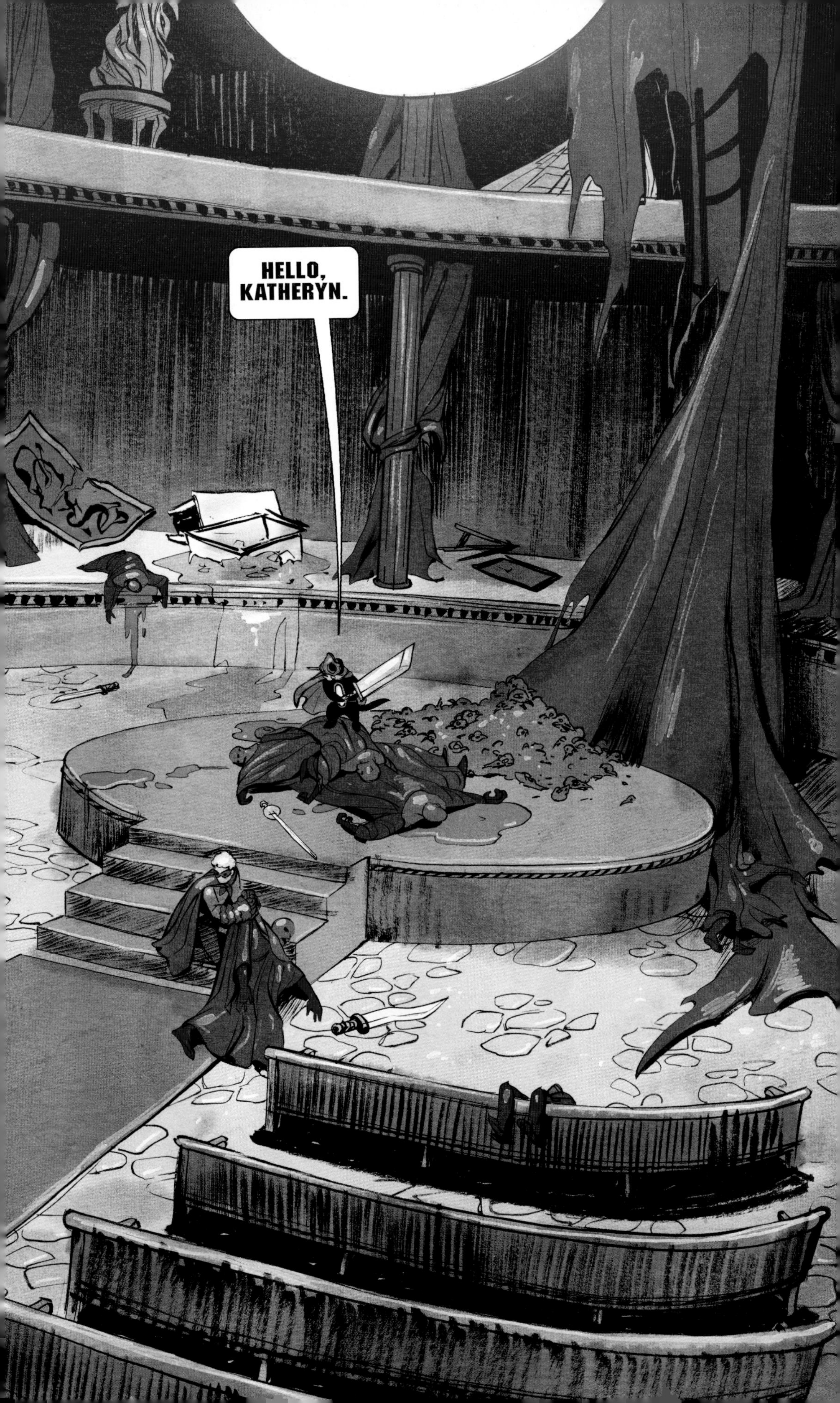
HELLO, KATHERYN.

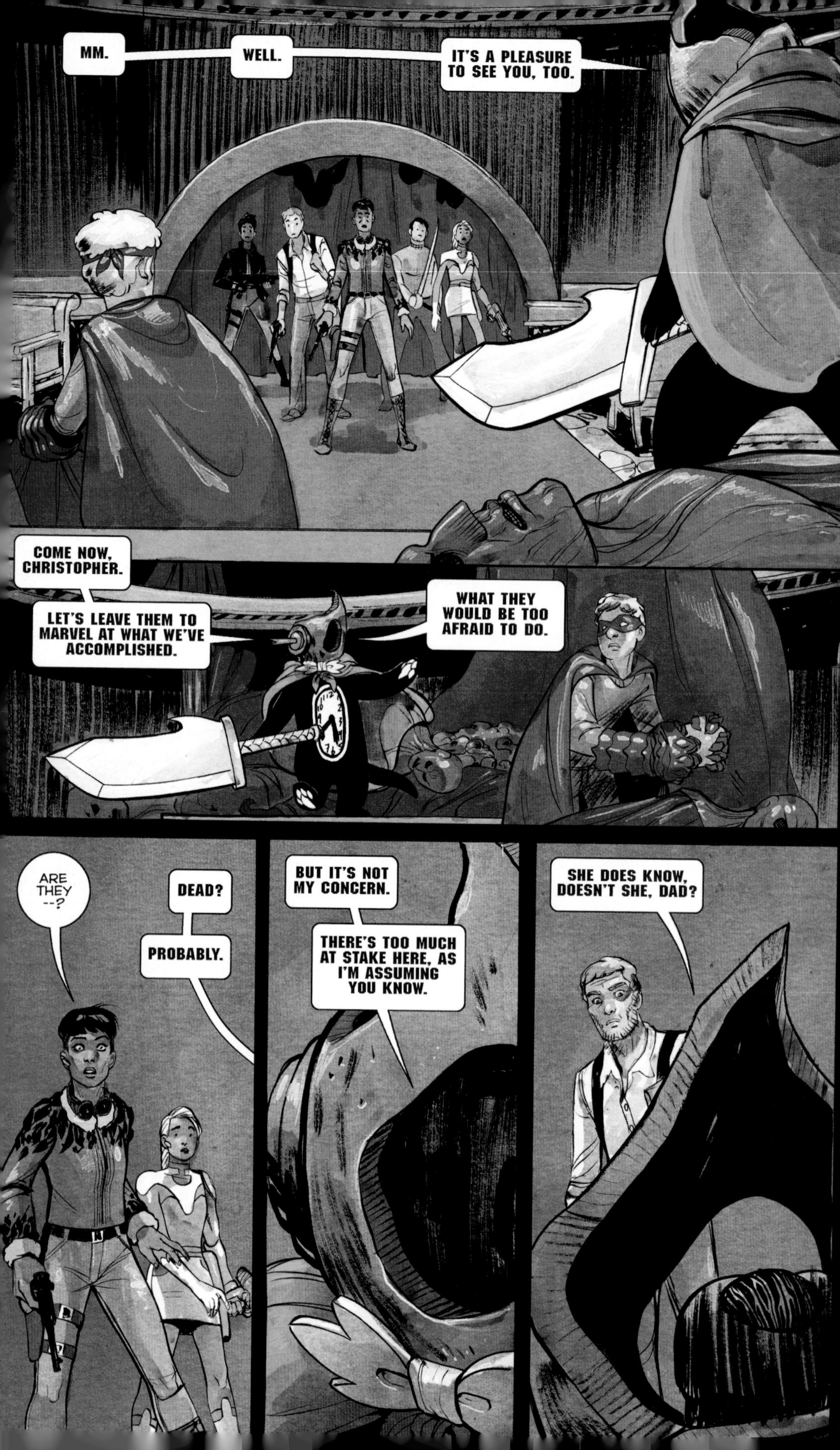
MM.
WELL.
IT'S A PLEASURE TO SEE YOU, TOO.
COME NOW, CHRISTOPHER.
LET'S LEAVE THEM TO MARVEL AT WHAT WE'VE ACCOMPLISHED.
WHAT THEY WOULD BE TOO AFRAID TO DO.
ARE THEY --?
DEAD?
PROBABLY.
BUT IT'S NOT MY CONCERN.
THERE'S TOO MUCH AT STAKE HERE, AS I'M ASSUMING YOU KNOW.
SHE DOES KNOW, DOESN'T SHE, DAD?

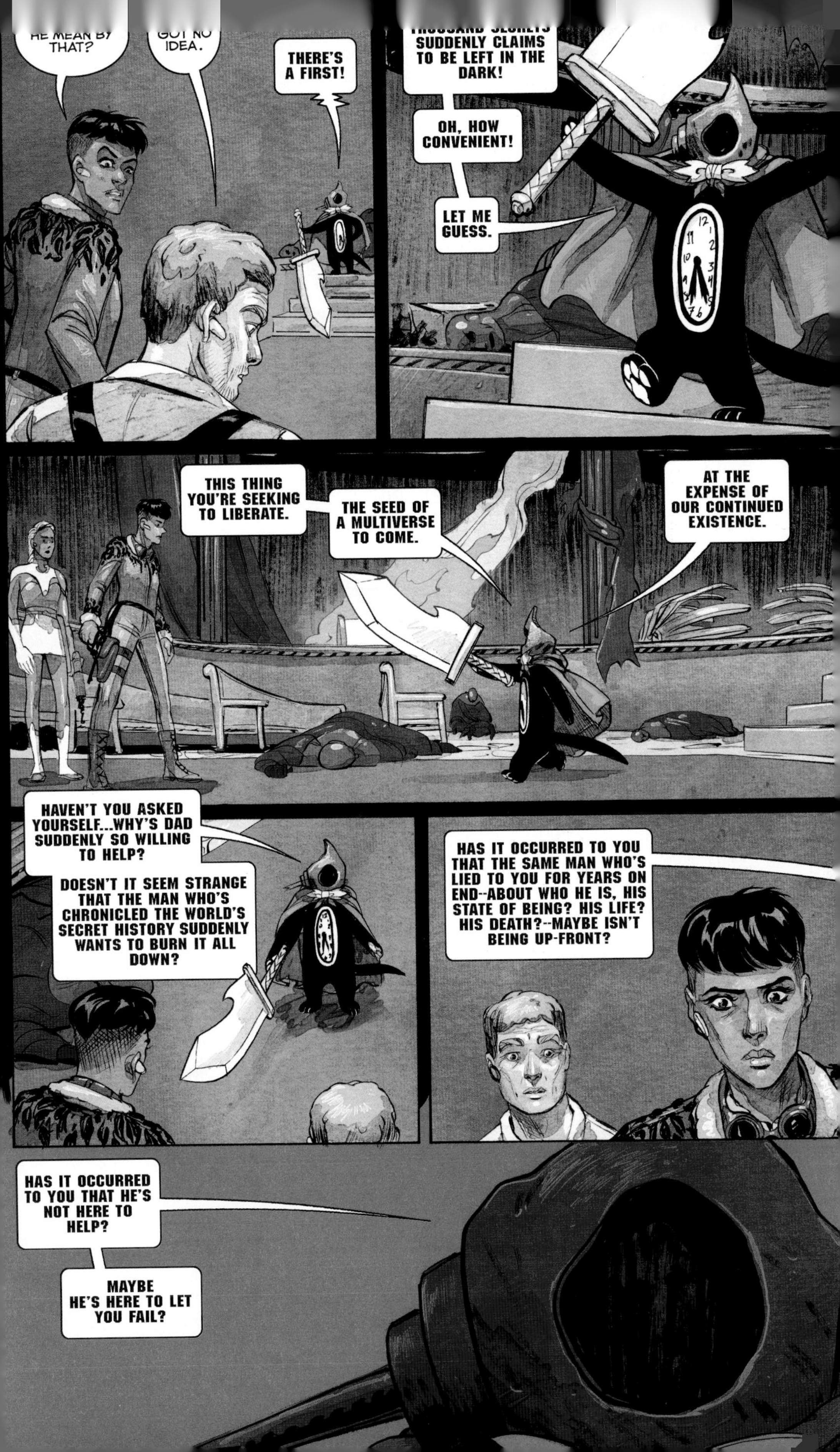
HE MEAN BY THAT?
GOT NO IDEA.
THERE'S A FIRST!
SUDDENLY CLAIMS TO BE LEFT IN THE DARK!
OH, HOW CONVENIENT!
LET ME GUESS.
THIS THING YOU'RE SEEKING TO LIBERATE.
THE SEED OF A MULTIVERSE TO COME.
AT THE EXPENSE OF OUR CONTINUED EXISTENCE.
HAVEN'T YOU ASKED YOURSELF...WHY'S DAD SUDDENLY SO WILLING TO HELP?
DOESN'T IT SEEM STRANGE THAT THE MAN WHO'S CHRONICLED THE WORLD'S SECRET HISTORY SUDDENLY WANTS TO BURN IT ALL DOWN?
HAS IT OCCURRED TO YOU THAT THE SAME MAN WHO'S LIED TO YOU FOR YEARS ON END--ABOUT WHO HE IS, HIS STATE OF BEING? HIS LIFE? HIS DEATH?--MAYBE ISN'T BEING UP-FRONT?
HAS IT OCCURRED TO YOU THAT HE'S NOT HERE TO HELP?
MAYBE HE'S HERE TO LET YOU FAIL?

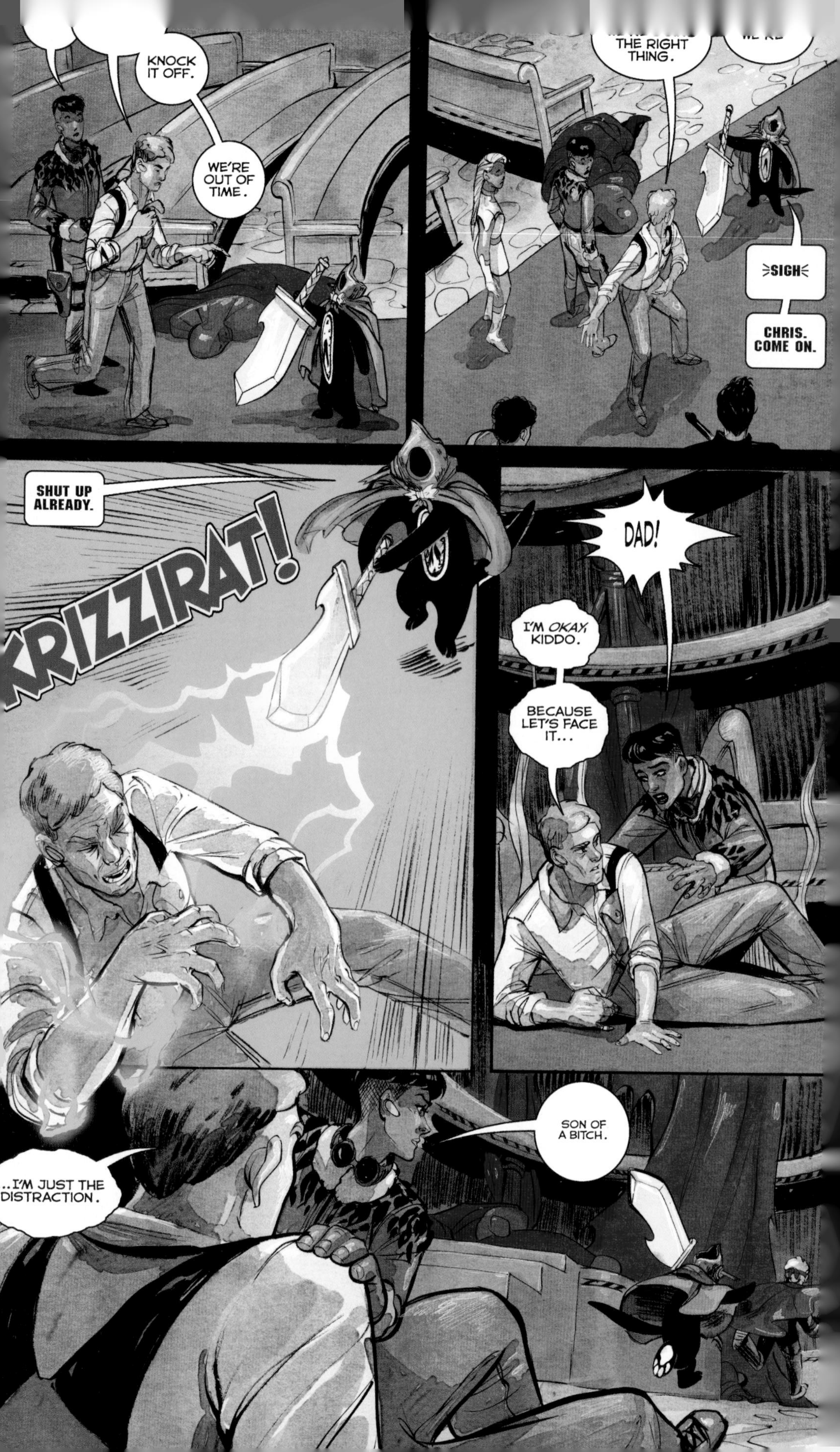
KNOCK IT OFF.
WE'RE OUT OF TIME.
THE RIGHT THING.
⋝SIGH⋜
CHRIS. COME ON.
SHUT UP ALREADY.
KRIZZIRAT!
DAD!
I'M *OKAY*, KIDDO.
BECAUSE LET'S FACE IT...
...I'M JUST THE DISTRACTION.
SON OF A BITCH.

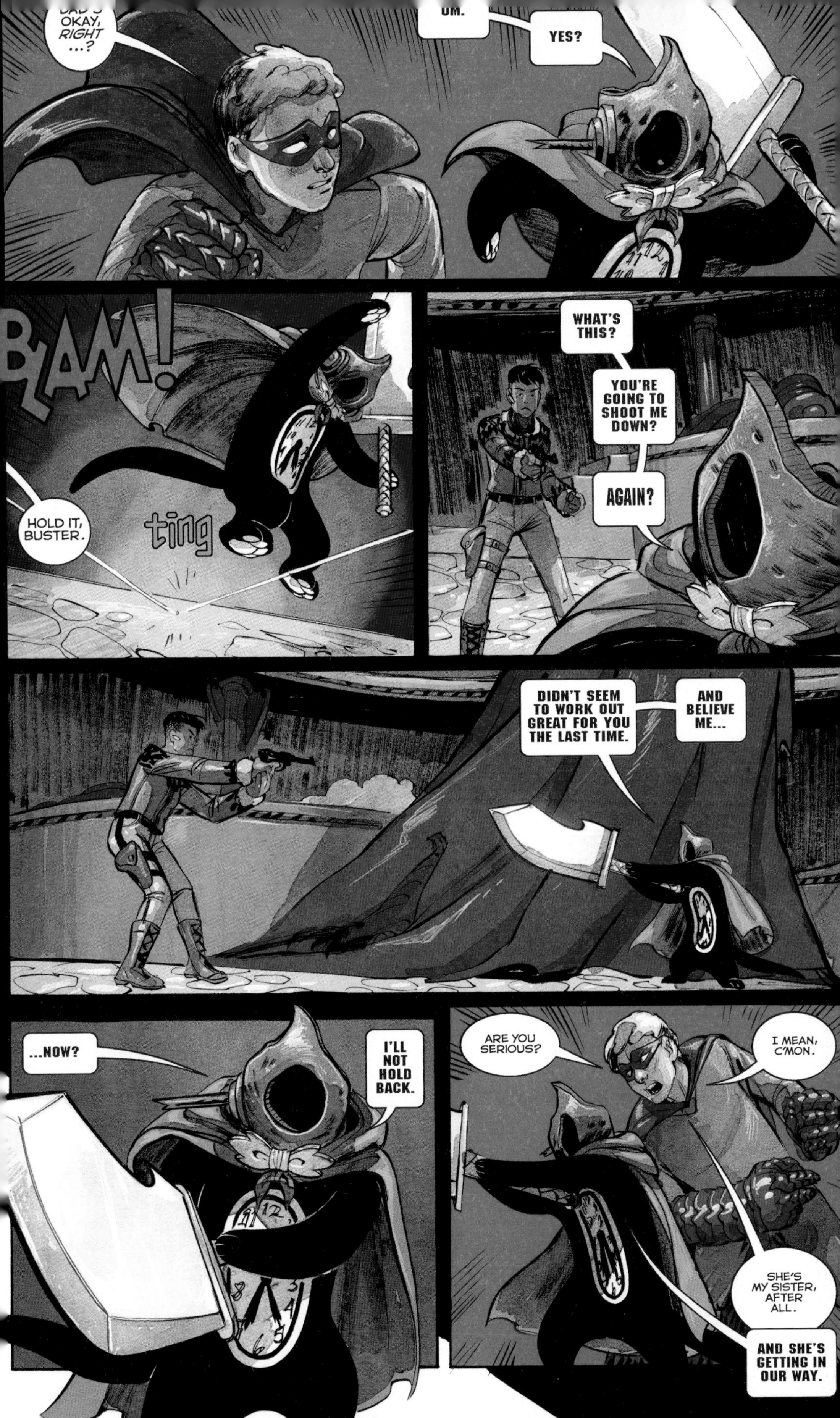

OKAY, RIGHT ...?
UM.
YES?
BAM!
HOLD IT, BUSTER.
ting
WHAT'S THIS?
YOU'RE GOING TO SHOOT ME DOWN?
AGAIN?
DIDN'T SEEM TO WORK OUT GREAT FOR YOU THE LAST TIME.
AND BELIEVE ME...
...NOW?
I'LL NOT HOLD BACK.
ARE YOU SERIOUS?
I MEAN, C'MON.
SHE'S MY SISTER, AFTER ALL.
AND SHE'S GETTING IN OUR WAY.

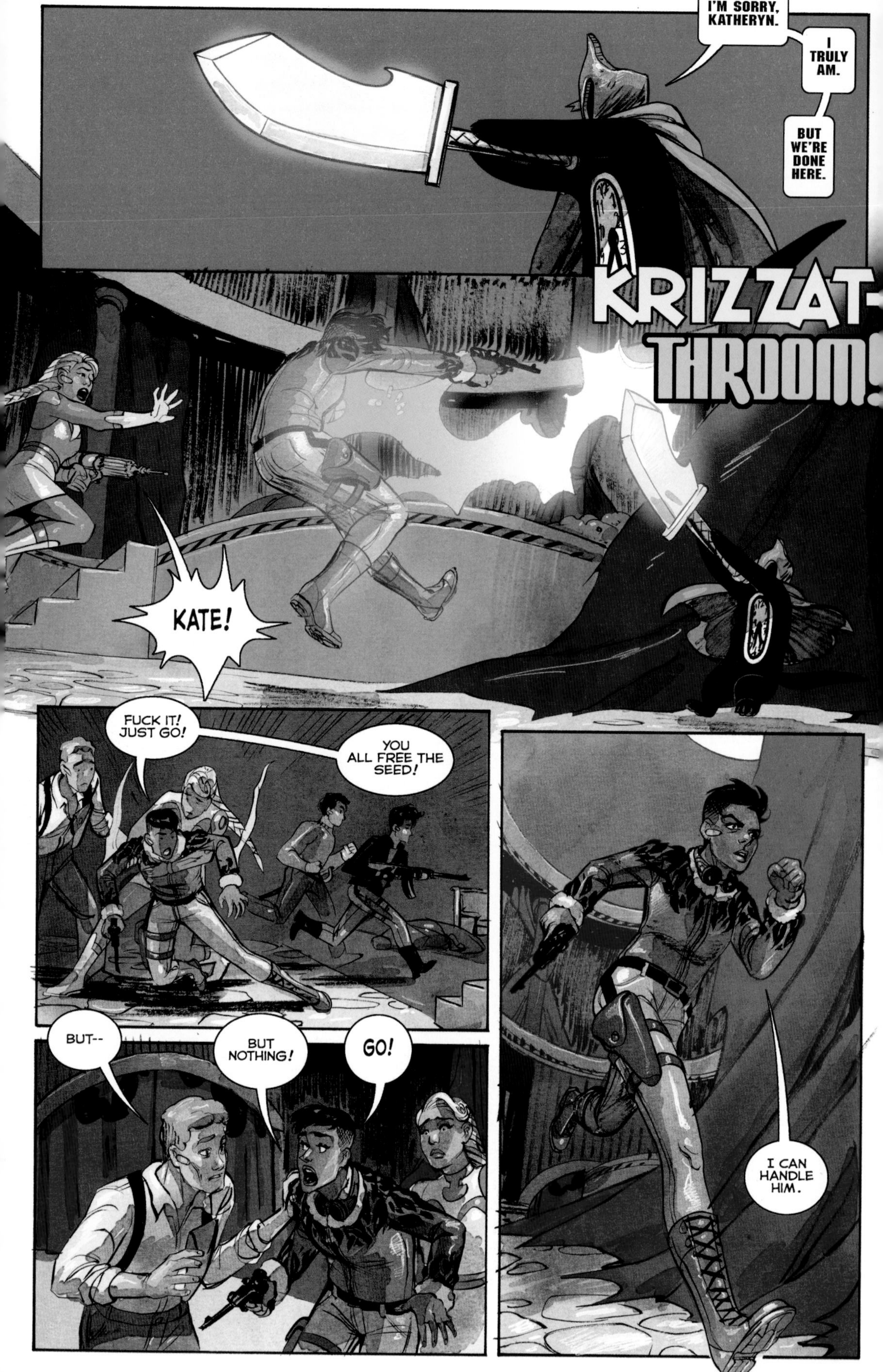
I'M SORRY, KATHERYN.
I TRULY AM.
BUT WE'RE DONE HERE.
KRIZZAT-THROOM!
KATE!
FUCK IT! JUST GO!
YOU ALL FREE THE SEED!
BUT--
BUT NOTHING!
GO!
I CAN HANDLE HIM.

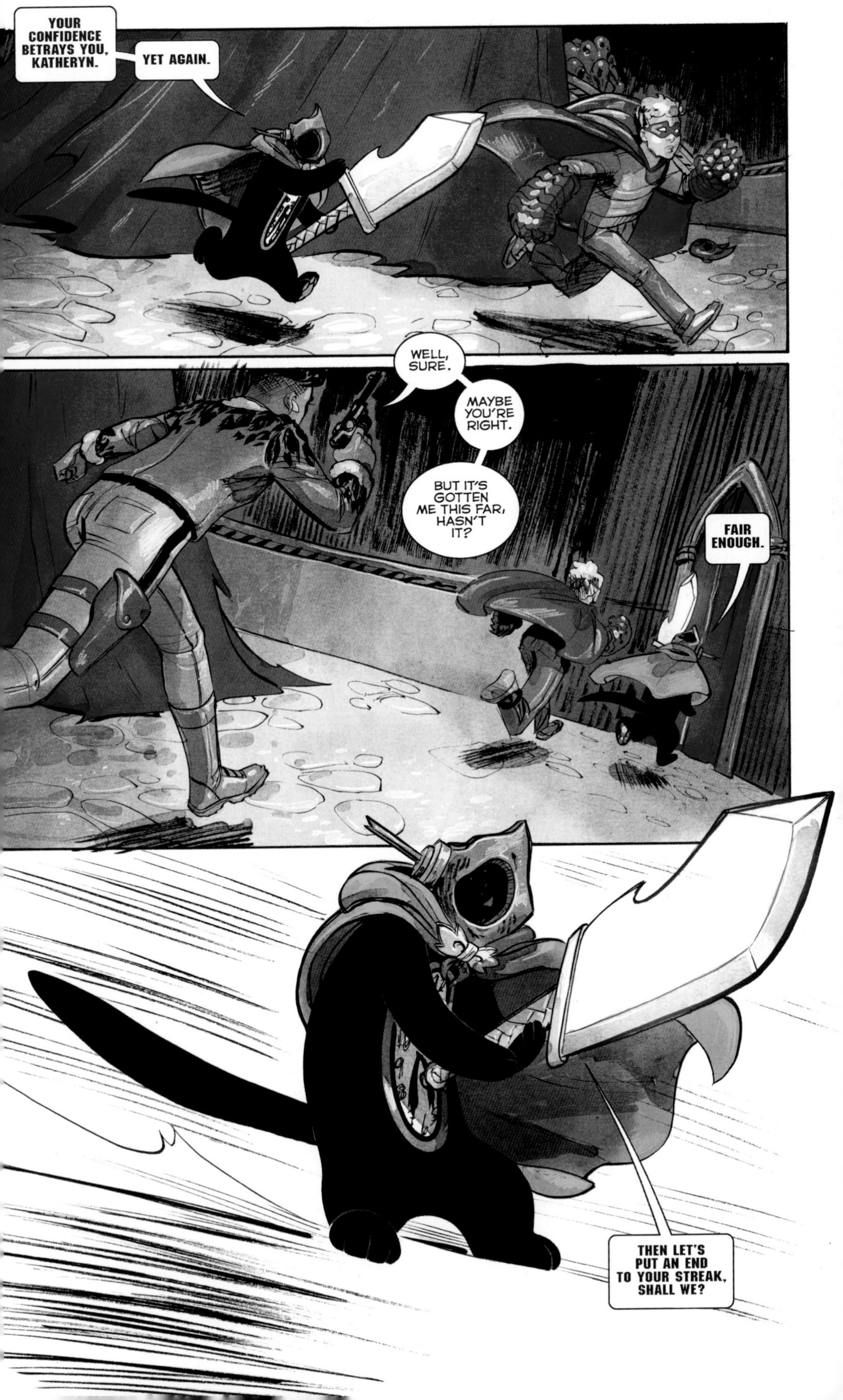
YOUR CONFIDENCE BETRAYS YOU, KATHERYN.
YET AGAIN.
WELL, SURE.
MAYBE YOU'RE RIGHT.
BUT IT'S GOTTEN ME THIS FAR, HASN'T IT?
FAIR ENOUGH.
THEN LET'S PUT AN END TO YOUR STREAK, SHALL WE?

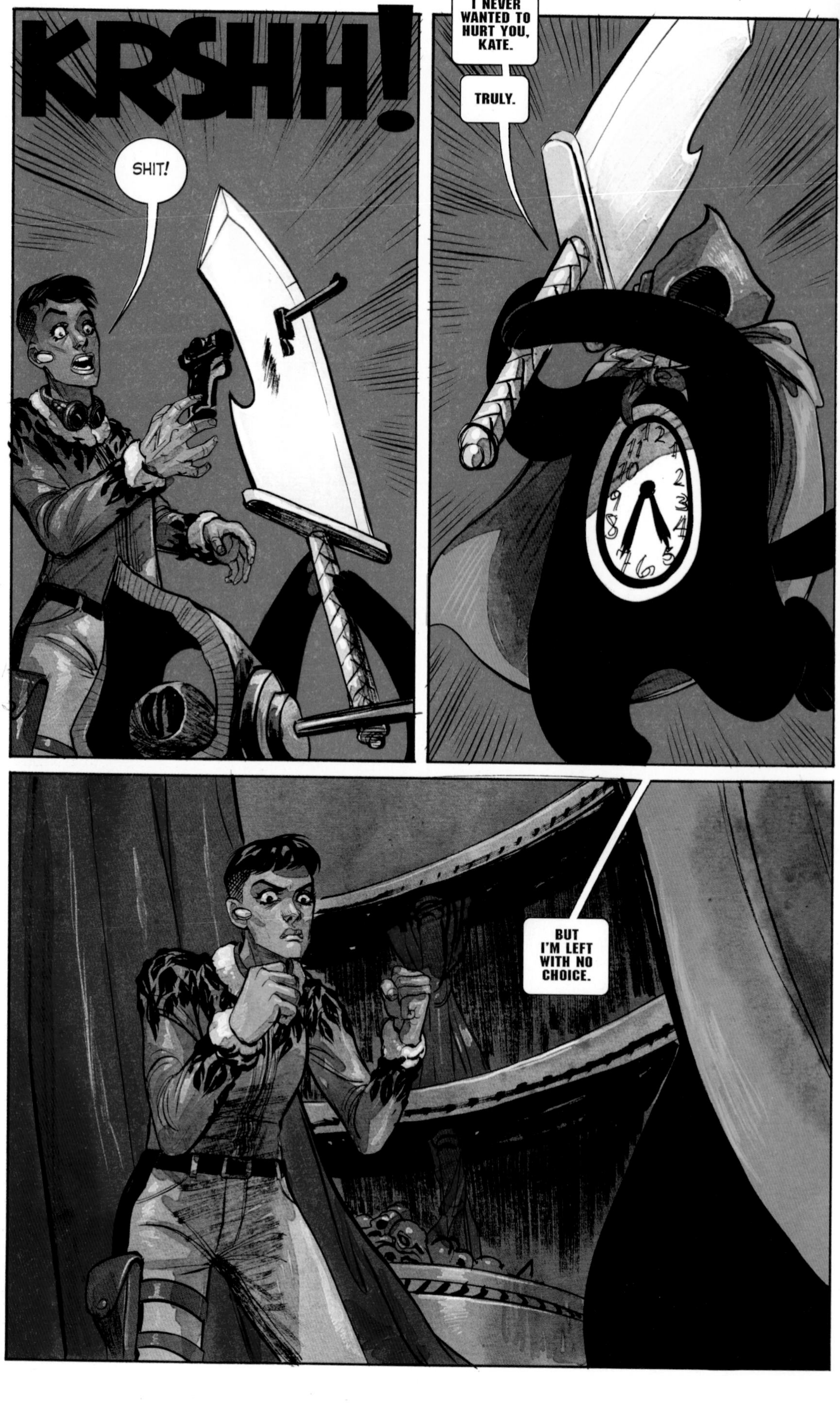
KRSHH!
SHIT!
I NEVER WANTED TO HURT YOU, KATE.
TRULY.
BUT I'M LEFT WITH NO CHOICE.

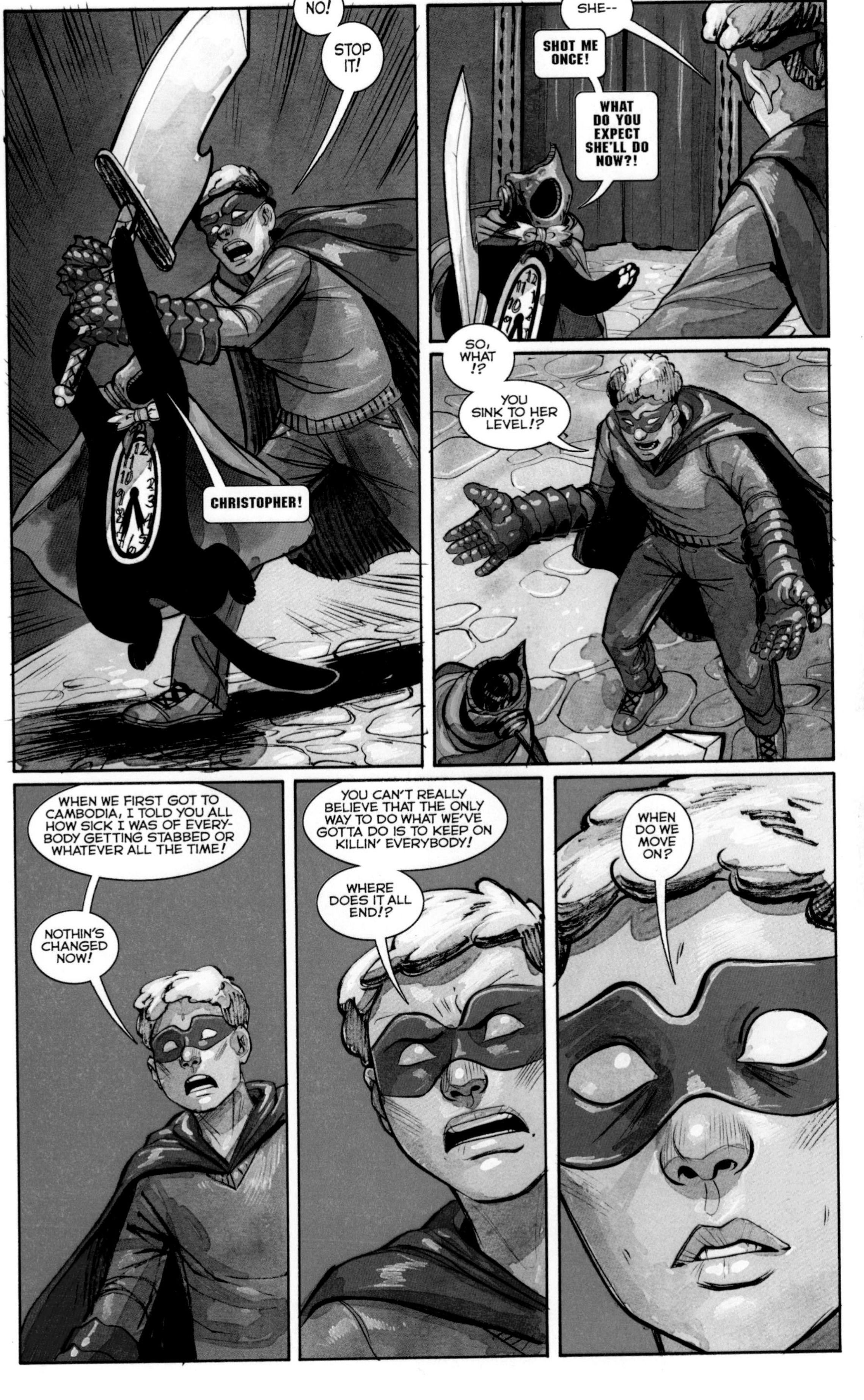
NO!
STOP IT!
CHRISTOPHER!
SHE--
SHOT ME ONCE!
WHAT DO YOU EXPECT SHE'LL DO NOW?!
SO, WHAT!?
YOU SINK TO HER LEVEL!?
WHEN WE FIRST GOT TO CAMBODIA, I TOLD YOU ALL HOW SICK I WAS OF EVERY-BODY GETTING STABBED OR WHATEVER ALL THE TIME!
NOTHIN'S CHANGED NOW!
YOU CAN'T REALLY BELIEVE THAT THE ONLY WAY TO DO WHAT WE'VE GOTTA DO IS TO KEEP ON KILLIN' EVERYBODY!
WHERE DOES IT ALL END!?
WHEN DO WE MOVE ON?

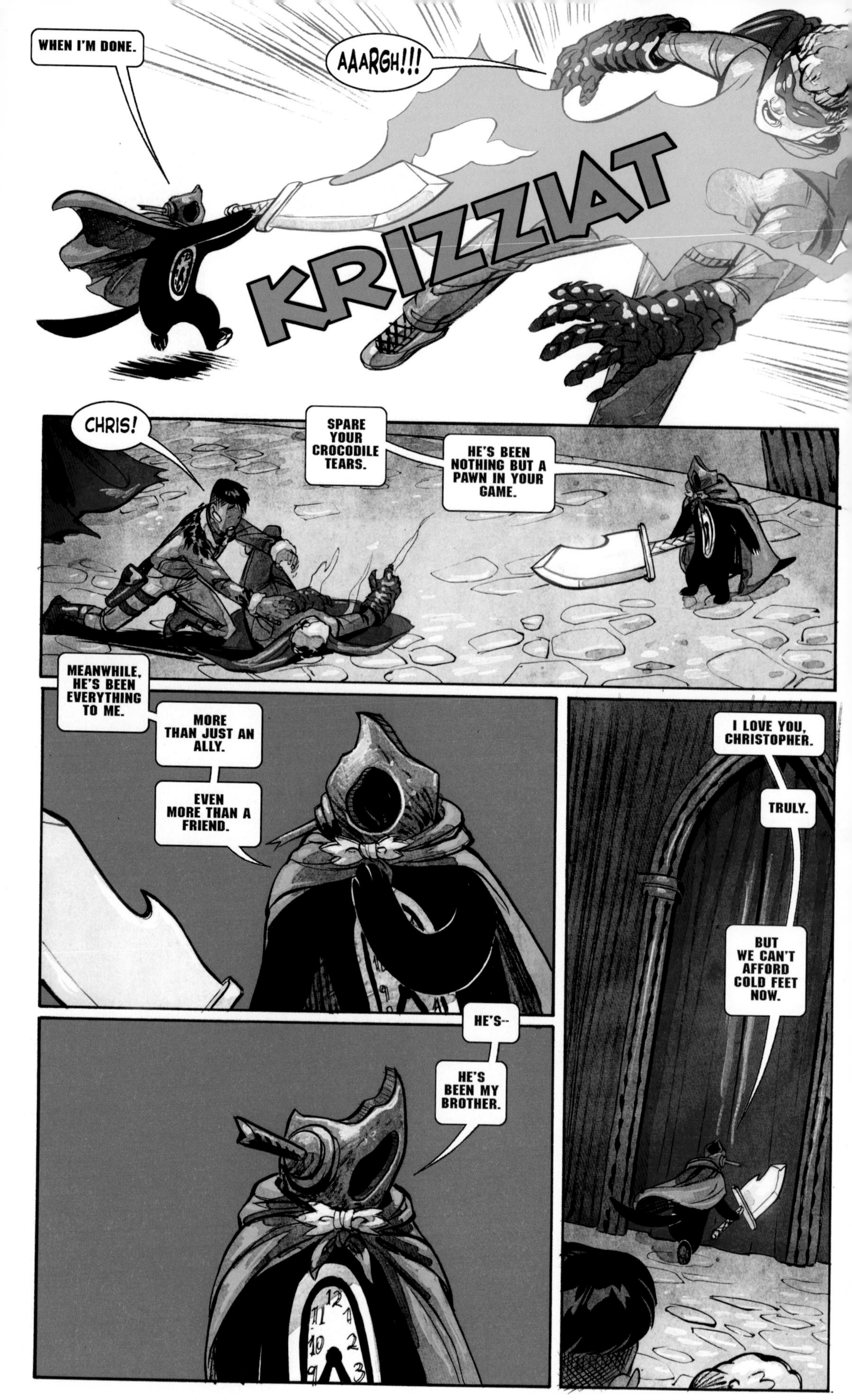
WHEN I'M DONE.
AAARGH!!!
KRIZZIAT
CHRIS!
SPARE YOUR CROCODILE TEARS.
HE'S BEEN NOTHING BUT A PAWN IN YOUR GAME.
MEANWHILE, HE'S BEEN EVERYTHING TO ME.
MORE THAN JUST AN ALLY.
EVEN MORE THAN A FRIEND.
HE'S--
HE'S BEEN MY BROTHER.
I LOVE YOU, CHRISTOPHER.
TRULY.
BUT WE CAN'T AFFORD COLD FEET NOW.

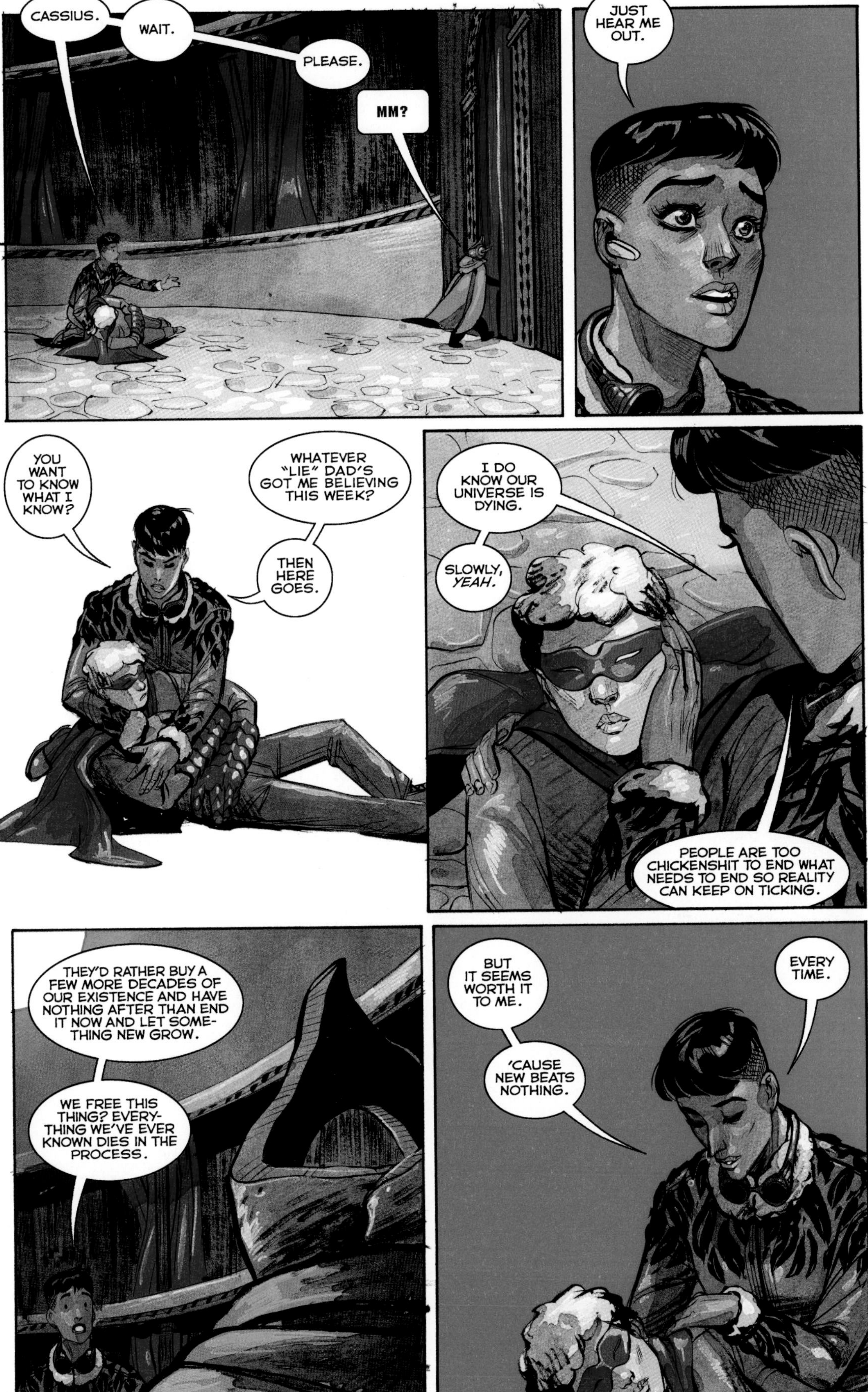
CASSIUS.
WAIT.
PLEASE.
MM?
JUST HEAR ME OUT.
YOU WANT TO KNOW WHAT I KNOW?
WHATEVER "LIE" DAD'S GOT ME BELIEVING THIS WEEK?
THEN HERE GOES.
I DO KNOW OUR UNIVERSE IS DYING.
SLOWLY, *YEAH.*
PEOPLE ARE TOO CHICKENSHIT TO END WHAT NEEDS TO END SO REALITY CAN KEEP ON TICKING.
THEY'D RATHER BUY A FEW MORE DECADES OF OUR EXISTENCE AND HAVE NOTHING AFTER THAN END IT NOW AND LET SOME-THING NEW GROW.
WE FREE THIS THING? EVERY-THING WE'VE EVER KNOWN DIES IN THE PROCESS.
BUT IT SEEMS WORTH IT TO ME.
'CAUSE NEW BEATS NOTHING.
EVERY TIME.

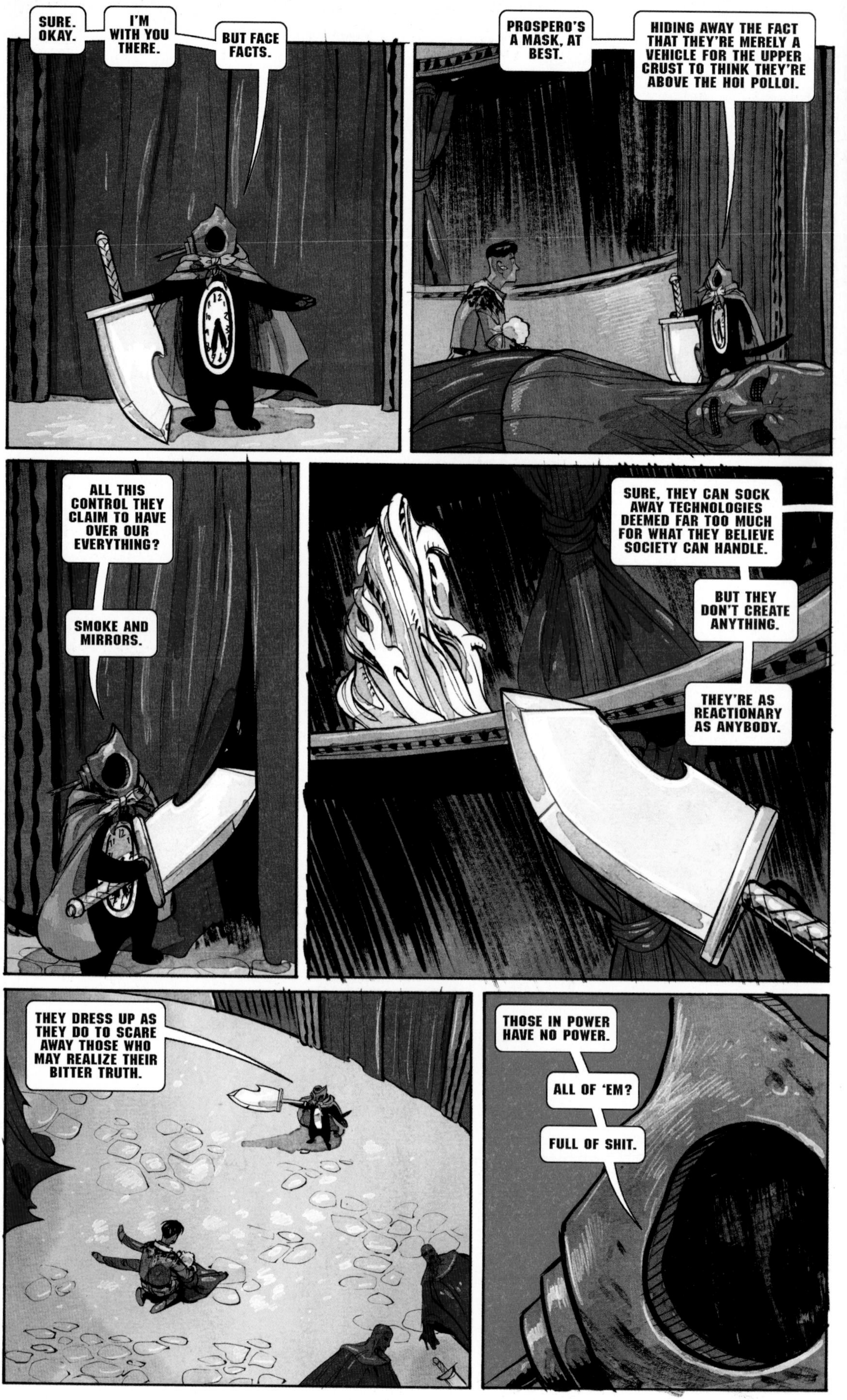
SURE. OKAY.
I'M WITH YOU THERE.
BUT FACE FACTS.
PROSPERO'S A MASK, AT BEST.
HIDING AWAY THE FACT THAT THEY'RE MERELY A VEHICLE FOR THE UPPER CRUST TO THINK THEY'RE ABOVE THE HOI POLLOI.
ALL THIS CONTROL THEY CLAIM TO HAVE OVER OUR EVERYTHING?
SMOKE AND MIRRORS.
SURE, THEY CAN SOCK AWAY TECHNOLOGIES DEEMED FAR TOO MUCH FOR WHAT THEY BELIEVE SOCIETY CAN HANDLE.
BUT THEY DON'T CREATE ANYTHING.
THEY'RE AS REACTIONARY AS ANYBODY.
THEY DRESS UP AS THEY DO TO SCARE AWAY THOSE WHO MAY REALIZE THEIR BITTER TRUTH.
THOSE IN POWER HAVE NO POWER.
ALL OF 'EM?
FULL OF SHIT.

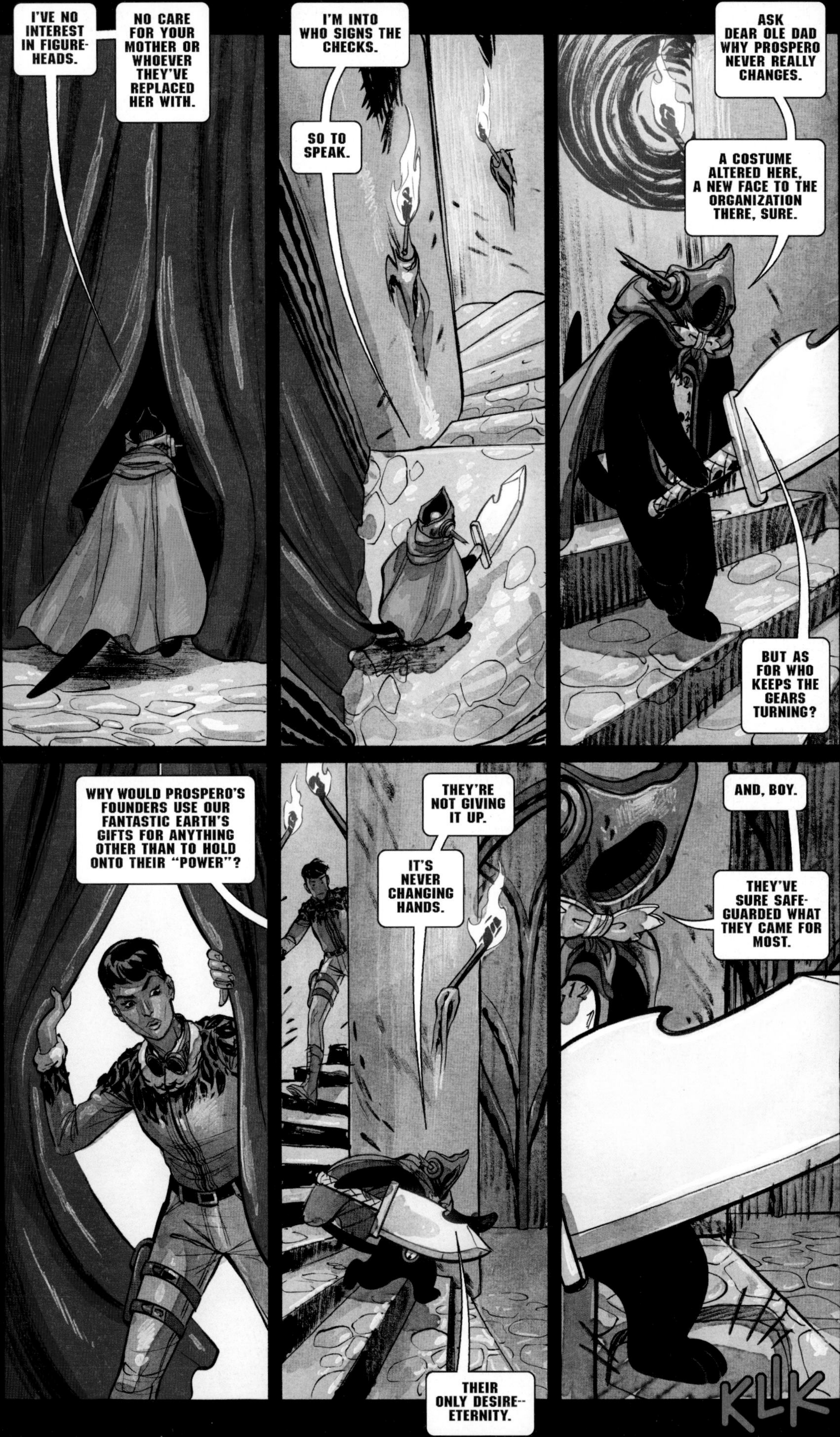

I'VE NO INTEREST IN FIGURE-HEADS.
NO CARE FOR YOUR MOTHER OR WHOEVER THEY'VE REPLACED HER WITH.
I'M INTO WHO SIGNS THE CHECKS.
SO TO SPEAK.
ASK DEAR OLE DAD WHY PROSPERO NEVER REALLY CHANGES.
A COSTUME ALTERED HERE, A NEW FACE TO THE ORGANIZATION THERE, SURE.
BUT AS FOR WHO KEEPS THE GEARS TURNING?
WHY WOULD PROSPERO'S FOUNDERS USE OUR FANTASTIC EARTH'S GIFTS FOR ANYTHING OTHER THAN TO HOLD ONTO THEIR "POWER"?
THEY'RE NOT GIVING IT UP.
IT'S NEVER CHANGING HANDS.
THEIR ONLY DESIRE-- ETERNITY.
AND, BOY.
THEY'VE SURE SAFE-GUARDED WHAT THEY CAME FOR MOST.
KLIK

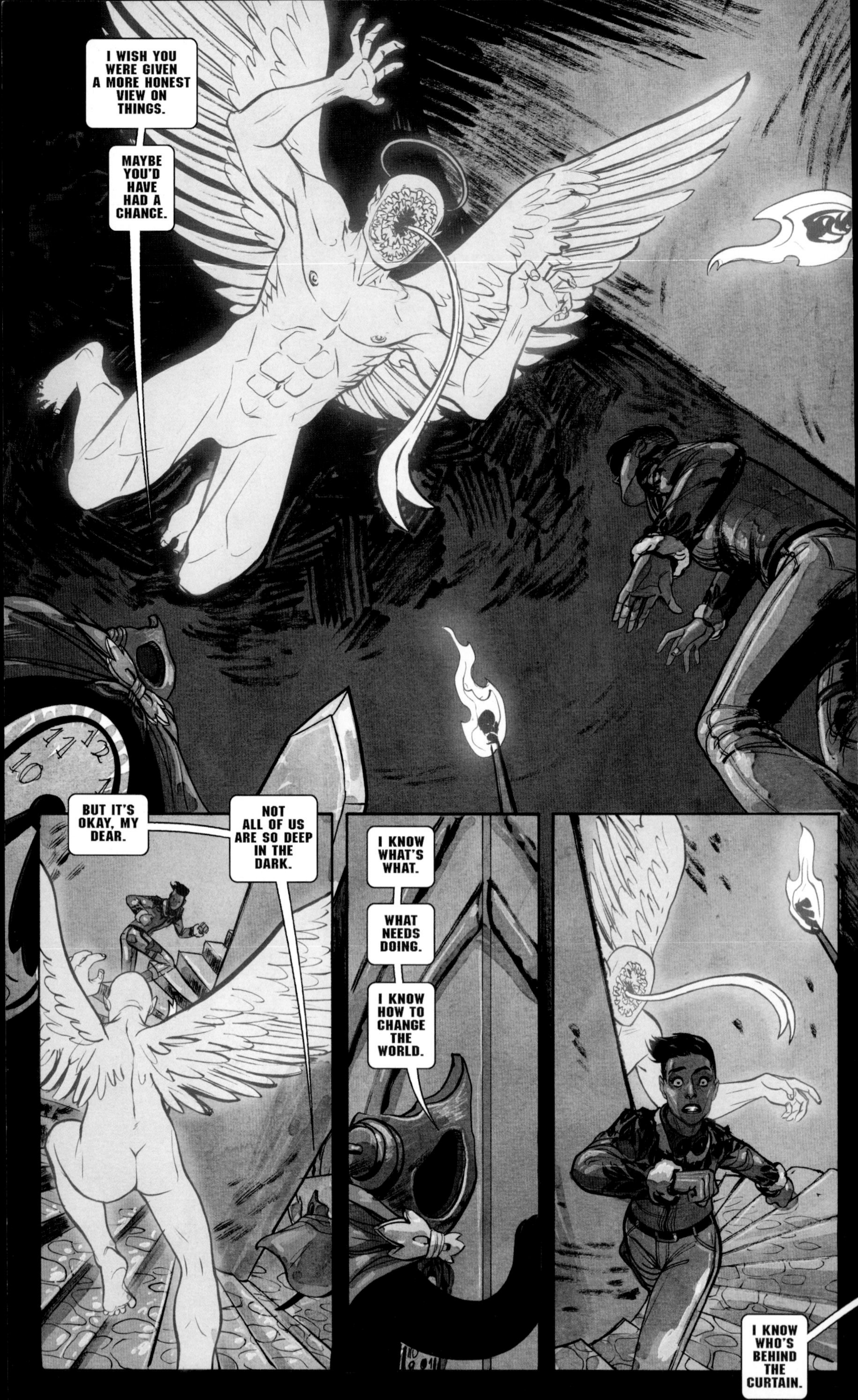
I WISH YOU WERE GIVEN A MORE HONEST VIEW ON THINGS.
MAYBE YOU'D HAVE HAD A CHANCE.
BUT IT'S OKAY, MY DEAR.
NOT ALL OF US ARE SO DEEP IN THE DARK.
I KNOW WHAT'S WHAT.
WHAT NEEDS DOING.
I KNOW HOW TO CHANGE THE WORLD.
I KNOW WHO'S BEHIND THE CURTAIN.

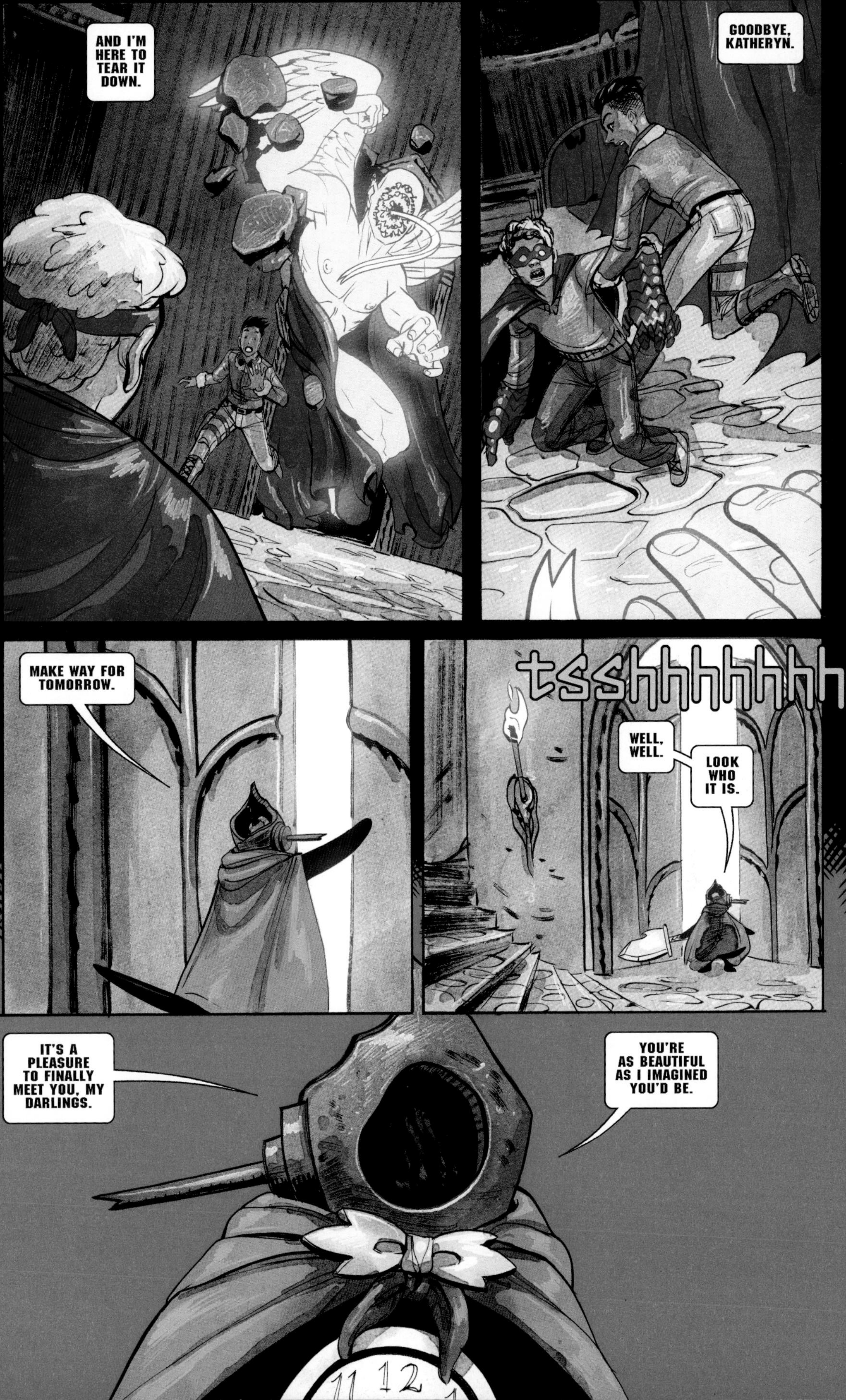
AND I'M HERE TO TEAR IT DOWN.
GOODBYE, KATHERYN.
MAKE WAY FOR TOMORROW.
tsshhhhhhh
WELL, WELL.
LOOK WHO IT IS.
IT'S A PLEASURE TO FINALLY MEET YOU, MY DARLINGS.
YOU'RE AS BEAUTIFUL AS I IMAGINED YOU'D BE.

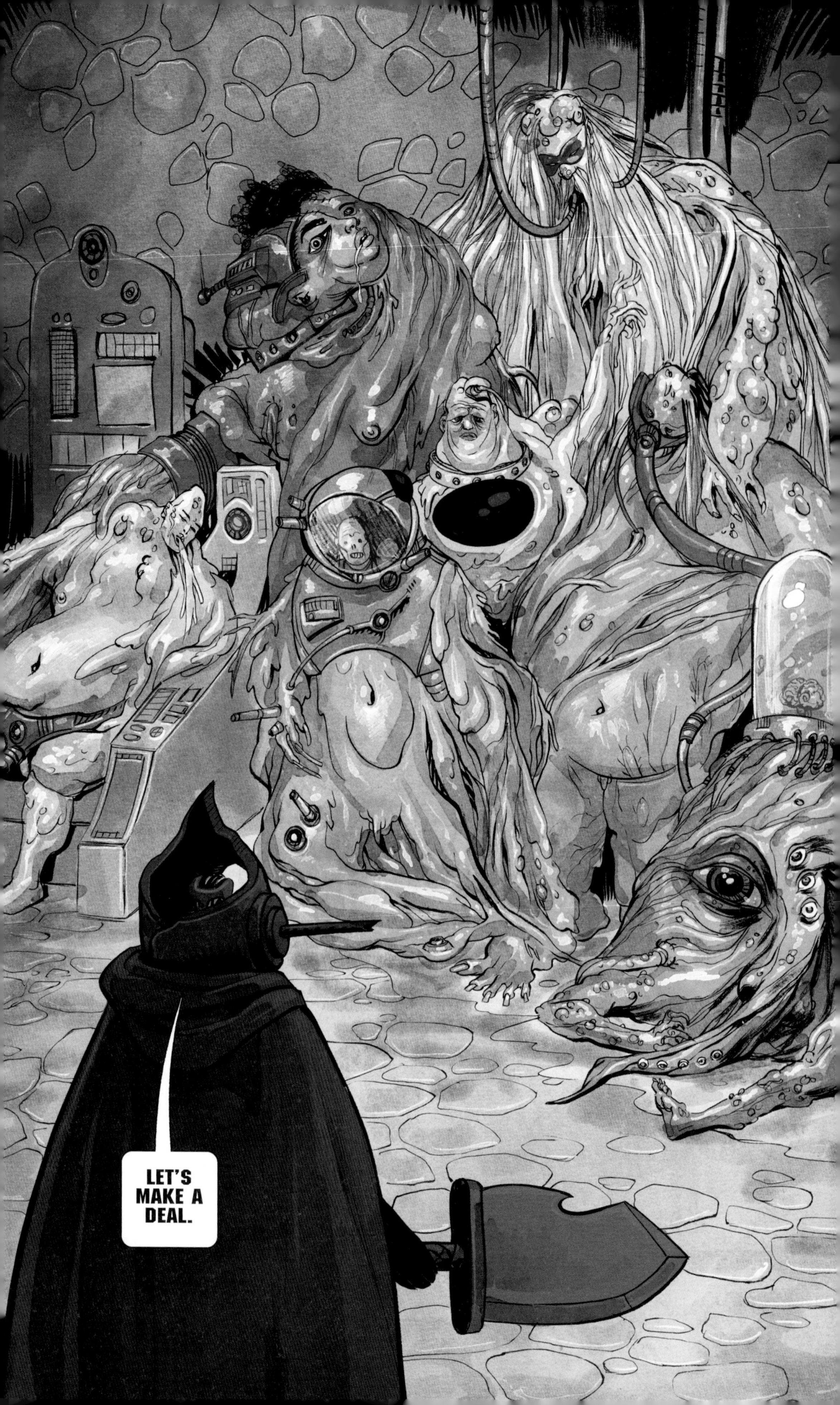
LET'S MAKE A DEAL.

CHAPTER 27

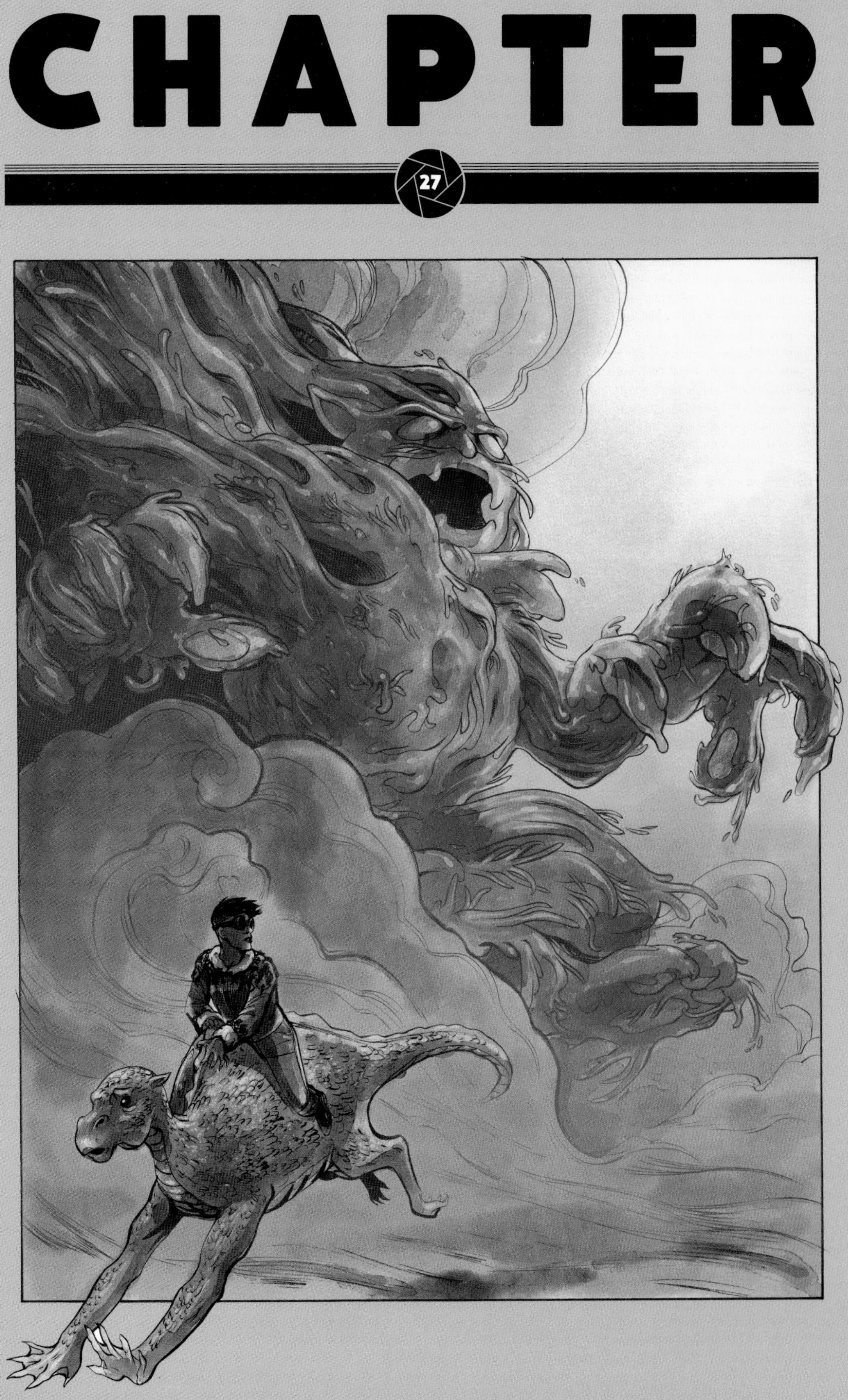

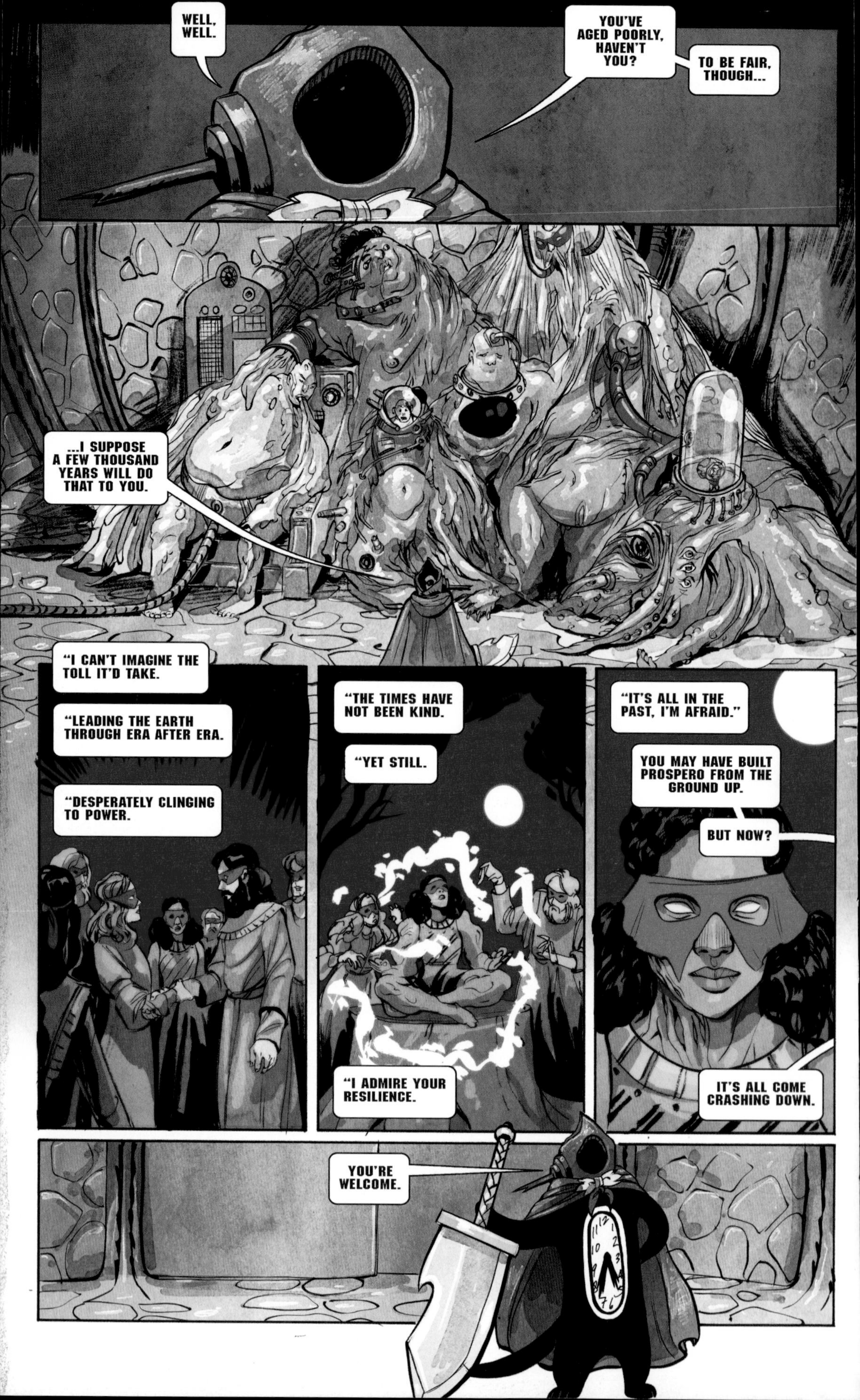
WELL, WELL.
YOU'VE AGED POORLY, HAVEN'T YOU?
TO BE FAIR, THOUGH...
...I SUPPOSE A FEW THOUSAND YEARS WILL DO THAT TO YOU.
"I CAN'T IMAGINE THE TOLL IT'D TAKE.
"LEADING THE EARTH THROUGH ERA AFTER ERA.
"DESPERATELY CLINGING TO POWER.
"THE TIMES HAVE NOT BEEN KIND.
"YET STILL.
"I ADMIRE YOUR RESILIENCE.
"IT'S ALL IN THE PAST, I'M AFRAID."
YOU MAY HAVE BUILT PROSPERO FROM THE GROUND UP.
BUT NOW?
IT'S ALL COME CRASHING DOWN.
YOU'RE WELCOME.

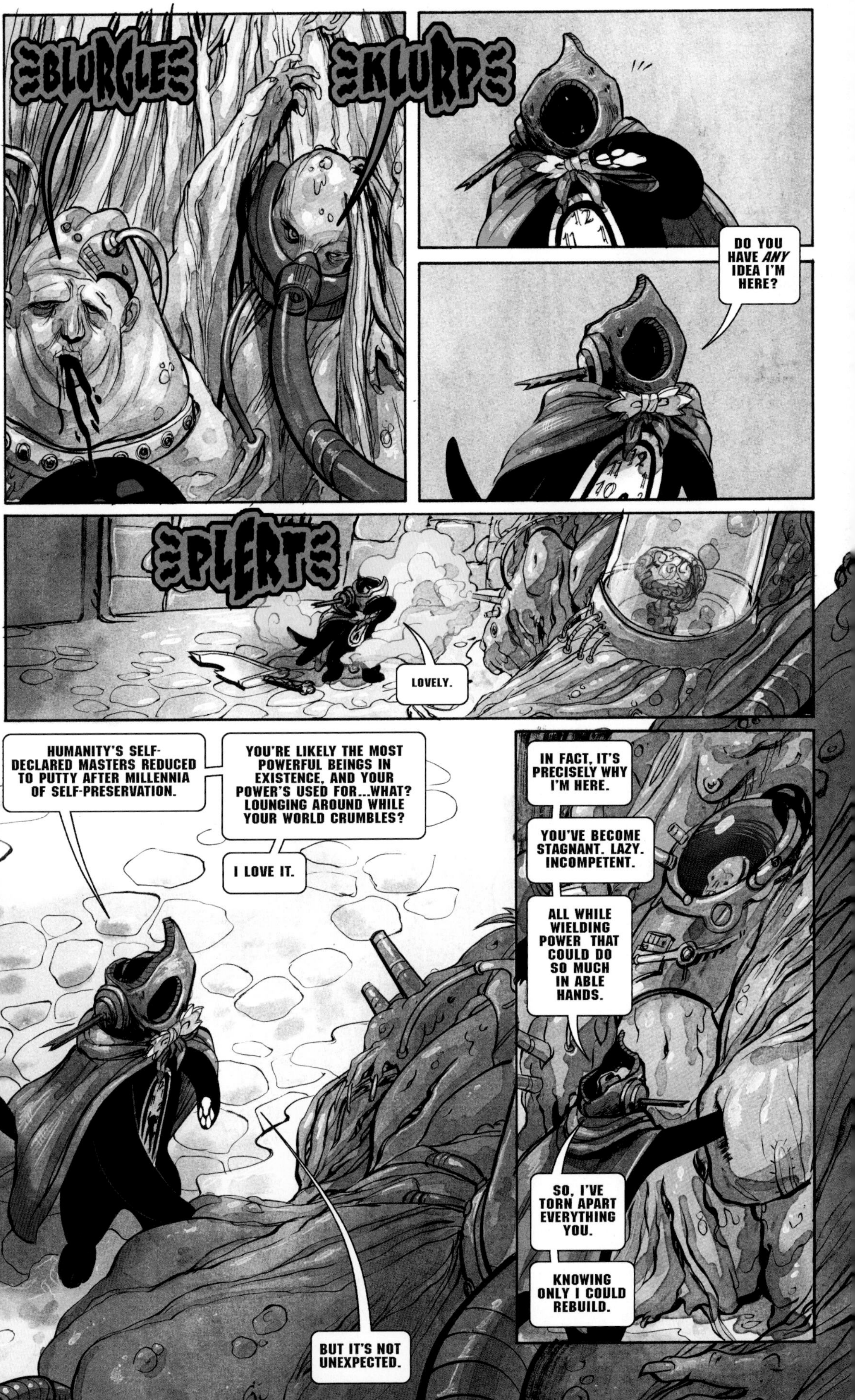
BLURGLE
KLURP
DO YOU HAVE *ANY* IDEA I'M HERE?
PLERT
LOVELY.
HUMANITY'S SELF-DECLARED MASTERS REDUCED TO PUTTY AFTER MILLENNIA OF SELF-PRESERVATION.
YOU'RE LIKELY THE MOST POWERFUL BEINGS IN EXISTENCE, AND YOUR POWER'S USED FOR...WHAT? LOUNGING AROUND WHILE YOUR WORLD CRUMBLES?
I LOVE IT.
BUT IT'S NOT UNEXPECTED.
IN FACT, IT'S PRECISELY WHY I'M HERE.
YOU'VE BECOME STAGNANT. LAZY. INCOMPETENT.
ALL WHILE WIELDING POWER THAT COULD DO SO MUCH IN ABLE HANDS.
SO, I'VE TORN APART EVERYTHING YOU.
KNOWING ONLY I COULD REBUILD.

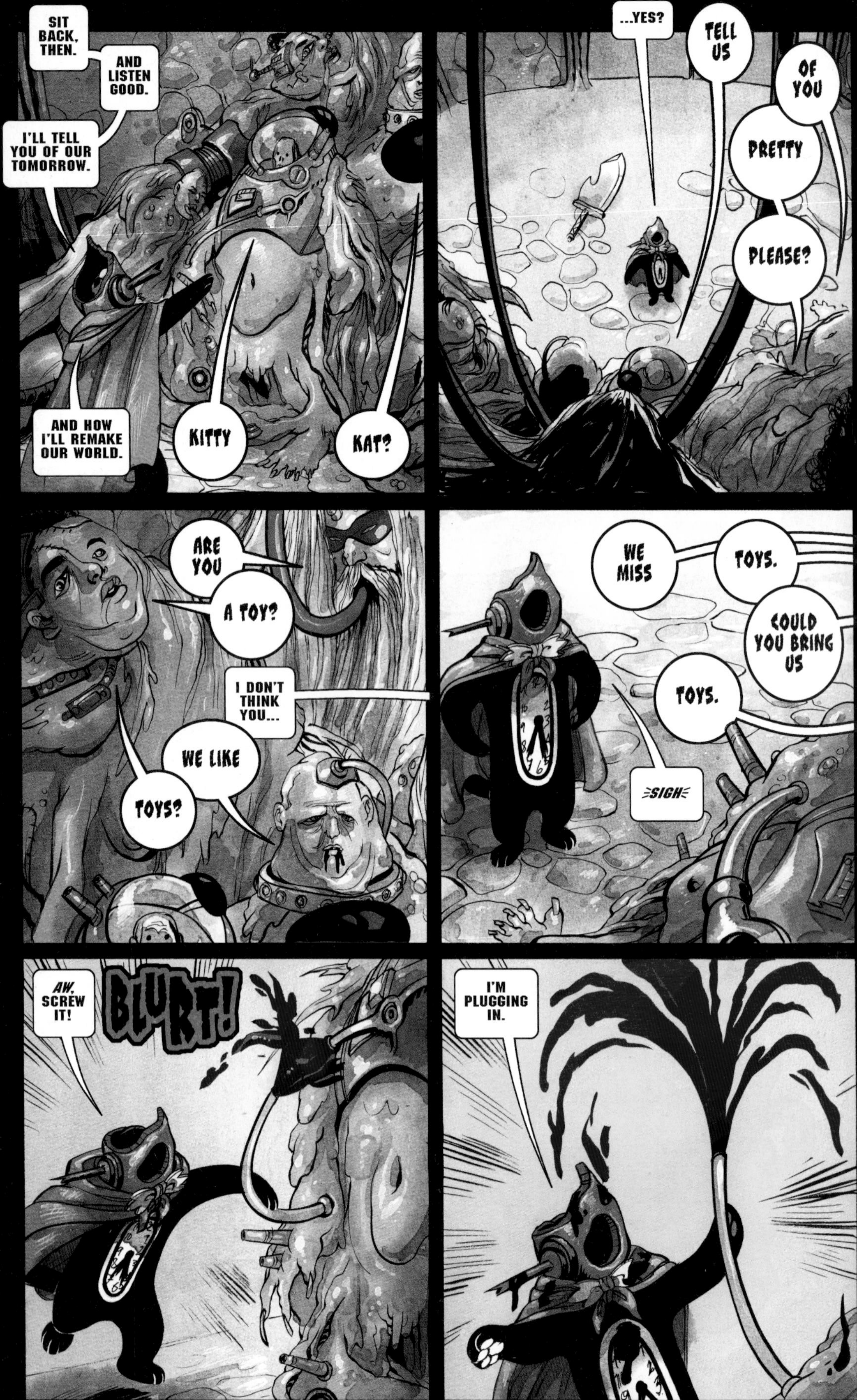
SIT BACK, THEN.
AND LISTEN GOOD.
I'LL TELL YOU OF OUR TOMORROW.
AND HOW I'LL REMAKE OUR WORLD.
KITTY
KAT?
...YES?
TELL US
OF YOU
PRETTY
PLEASE?
ARE YOU
A TOY?
I DON'T THINK YOU...
WE LIKE
TOYS?
WE MISS
TOYS.
COULD YOU BRING US
TOYS.
SIGH
AW, SCREW IT!
BLURT!
I'M PLUGGING IN.

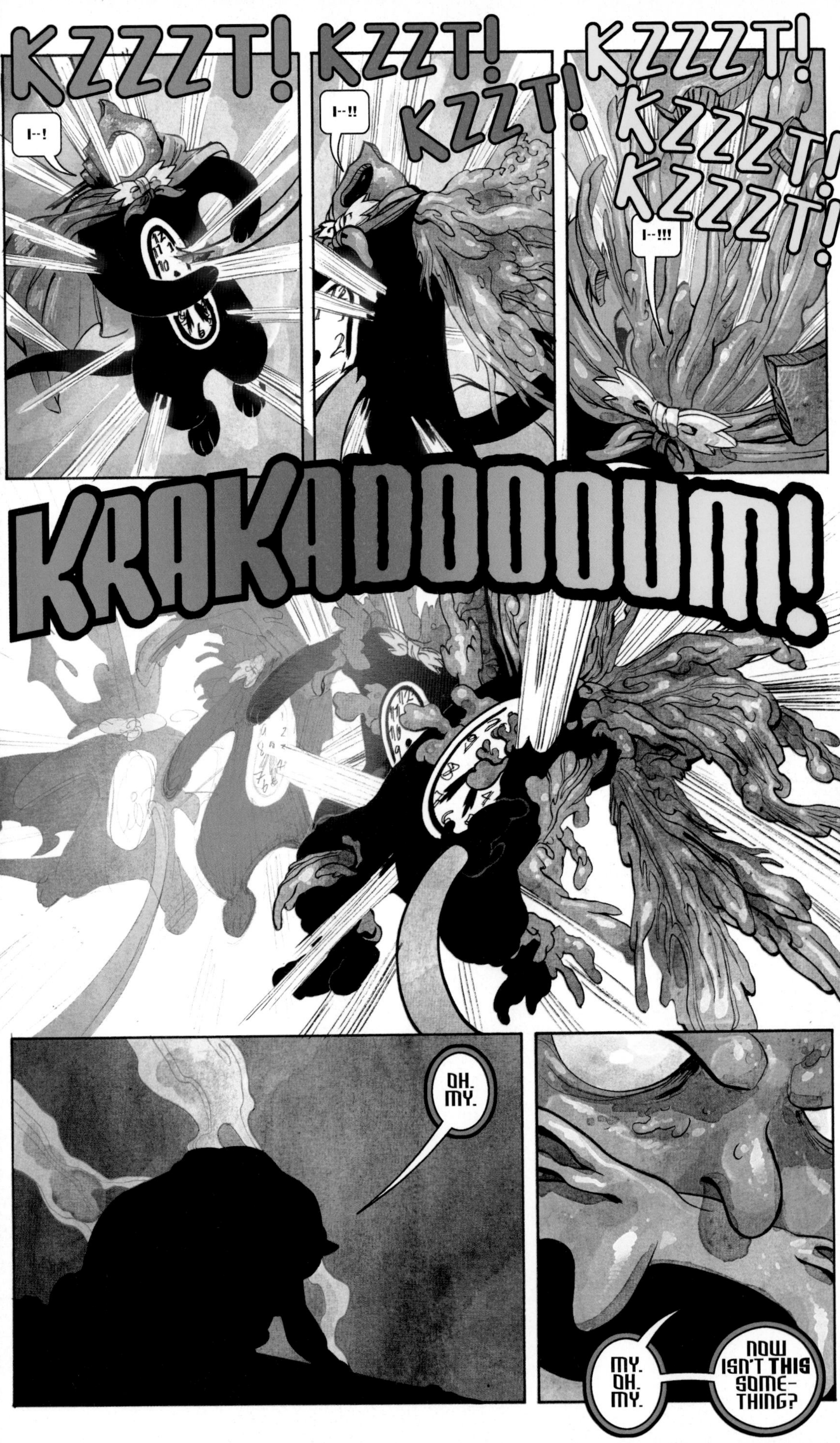
KZZZZT!
I--!
KZZZT!
I--!!
KZZZT!
KZZZZT!
KZZZZT!
KZZZZT!
I--!!!
KRAKADOOOOUM!
OH. MY.
MY. OH. MY.
NOW ISN'T THIS SOME-THING?

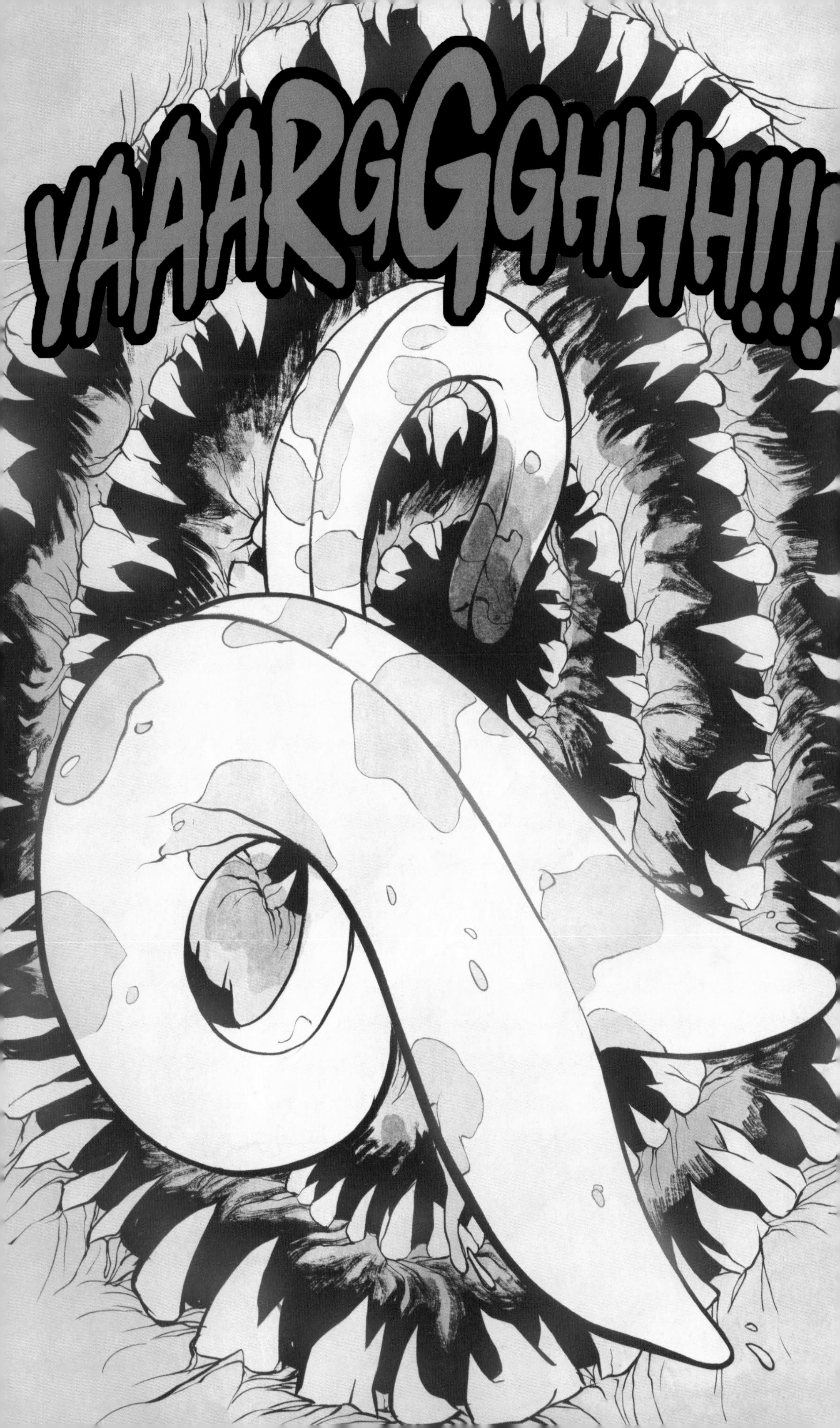
YAAARGGGHHH!!!

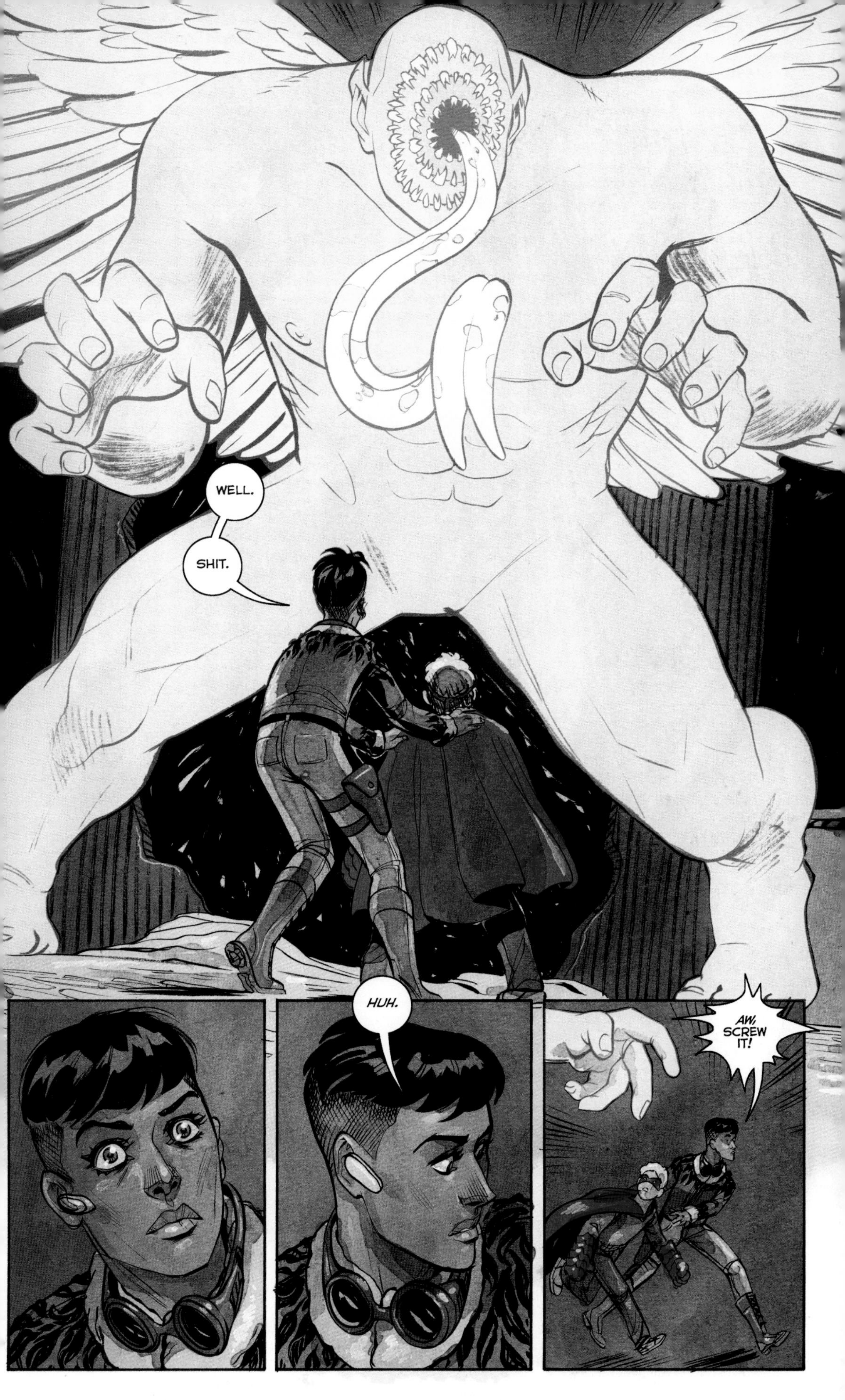

WELL.
SHIT.
HUH.
AW, SCREW IT!

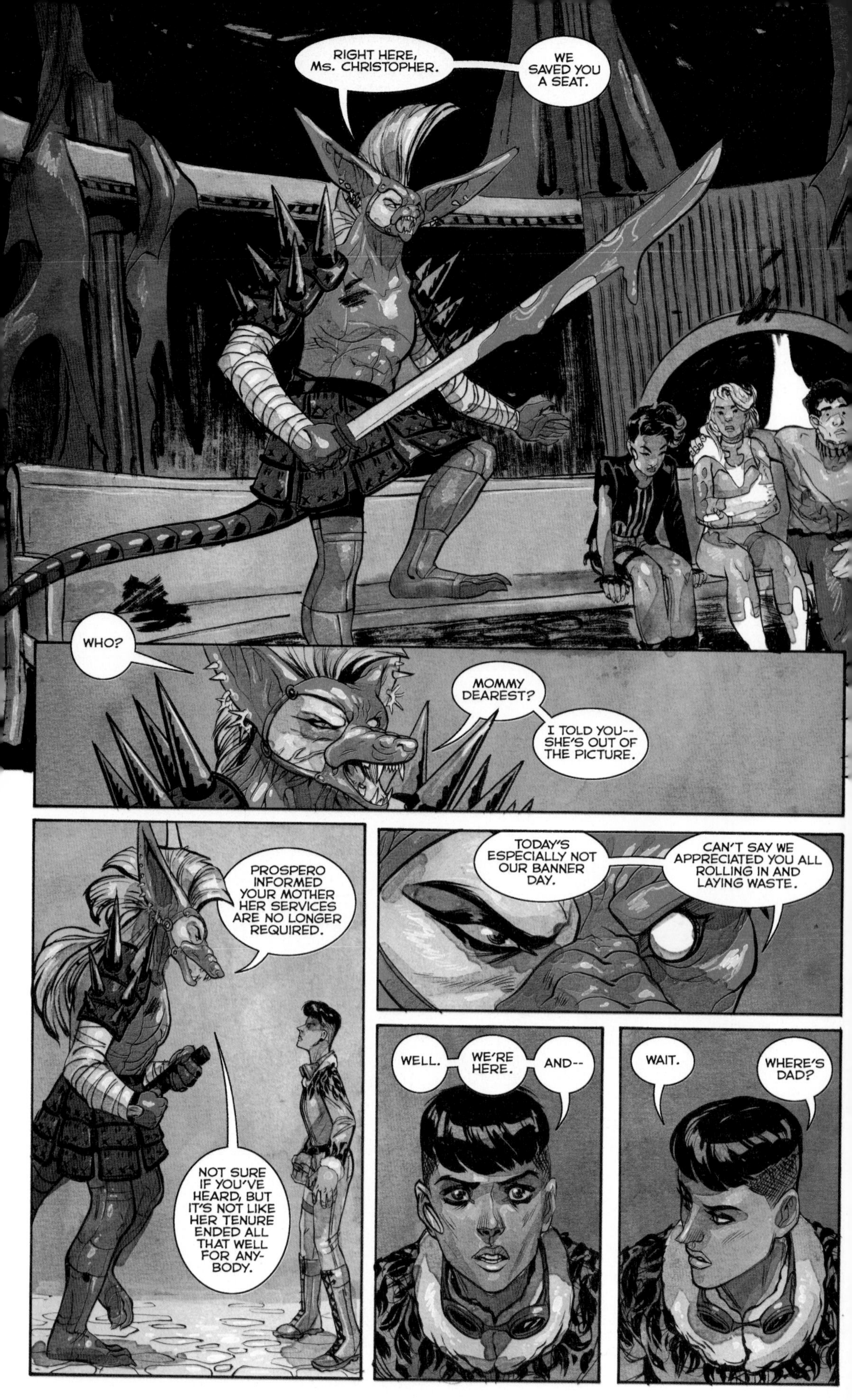
RIGHT HERE, Ms. CHRISTOPHER.
WE SAVED YOU A SEAT.
WHO?
MOMMY DEAREST?
I TOLD YOU-- SHE'S OUT OF THE PICTURE.
PROSPERO INFORMED YOUR MOTHER HER SERVICES ARE NO LONGER REQUIRED.
NOT SURE IF YOU'VE HEARD, BUT IT'S NOT LIKE HER TENURE ENDED ALL THAT WELL FOR ANY-BODY.
TODAY'S ESPECIALLY NOT OUR BANNER DAY.
CAN'T SAY WE APPRECIATED YOU ALL ROLLING IN AND LAYING WASTE.
WELL.
WE'RE HERE.
AND--
WAIT.
WHERE'S DAD?

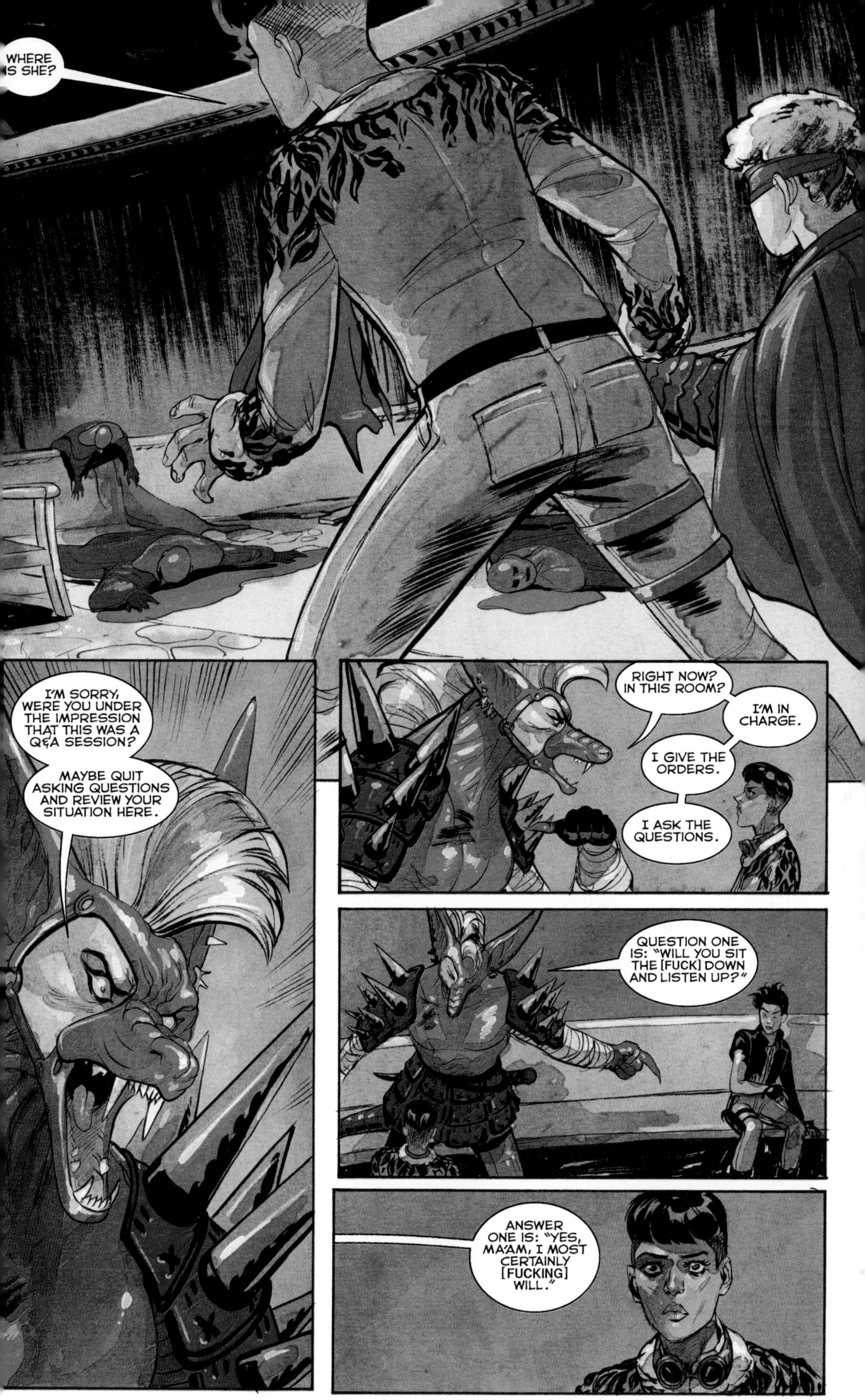
WHERE IS SHE?
I'M SORRY, WERE YOU UNDER THE IMPRESSION THAT THIS WAS A Q&A SESSION?
MAYBE QUIT ASKING QUESTIONS AND REVIEW YOUR SITUATION HERE.
RIGHT NOW? IN THIS ROOM?
I'M IN CHARGE.
I GIVE THE ORDERS.
I ASK THE QUESTIONS.
QUESTION ONE IS: "WILL YOU SIT THE [FUCK] DOWN AND LISTEN UP?"
ANSWER ONE IS: "YES, MA'AM, I MOST CERTAINLY [FUCKING] WILL."

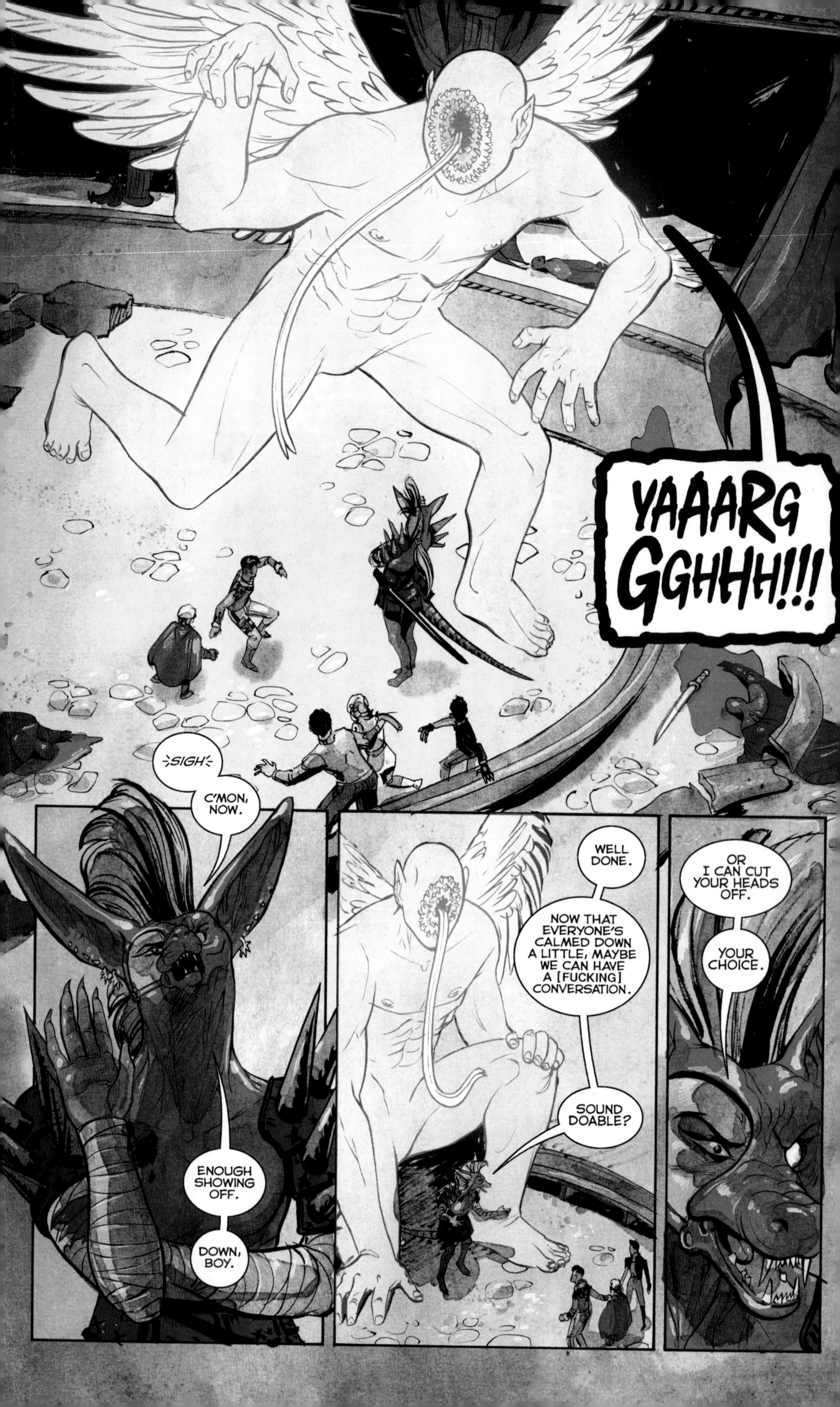
YAAARG GGHHH!!!
SIGH
C'MON, NOW.
ENOUGH SHOWING OFF.
DOWN, BOY.
WELL DONE.
NOW THAT EVERYONE'S CALMED DOWN A LITTLE, MAYBE WE CAN HAVE A [FUCKING] CONVERSATION.
SOUND DOABLE?
OR I CAN CUT YOUR HEADS OFF.
YOUR CHOICE.

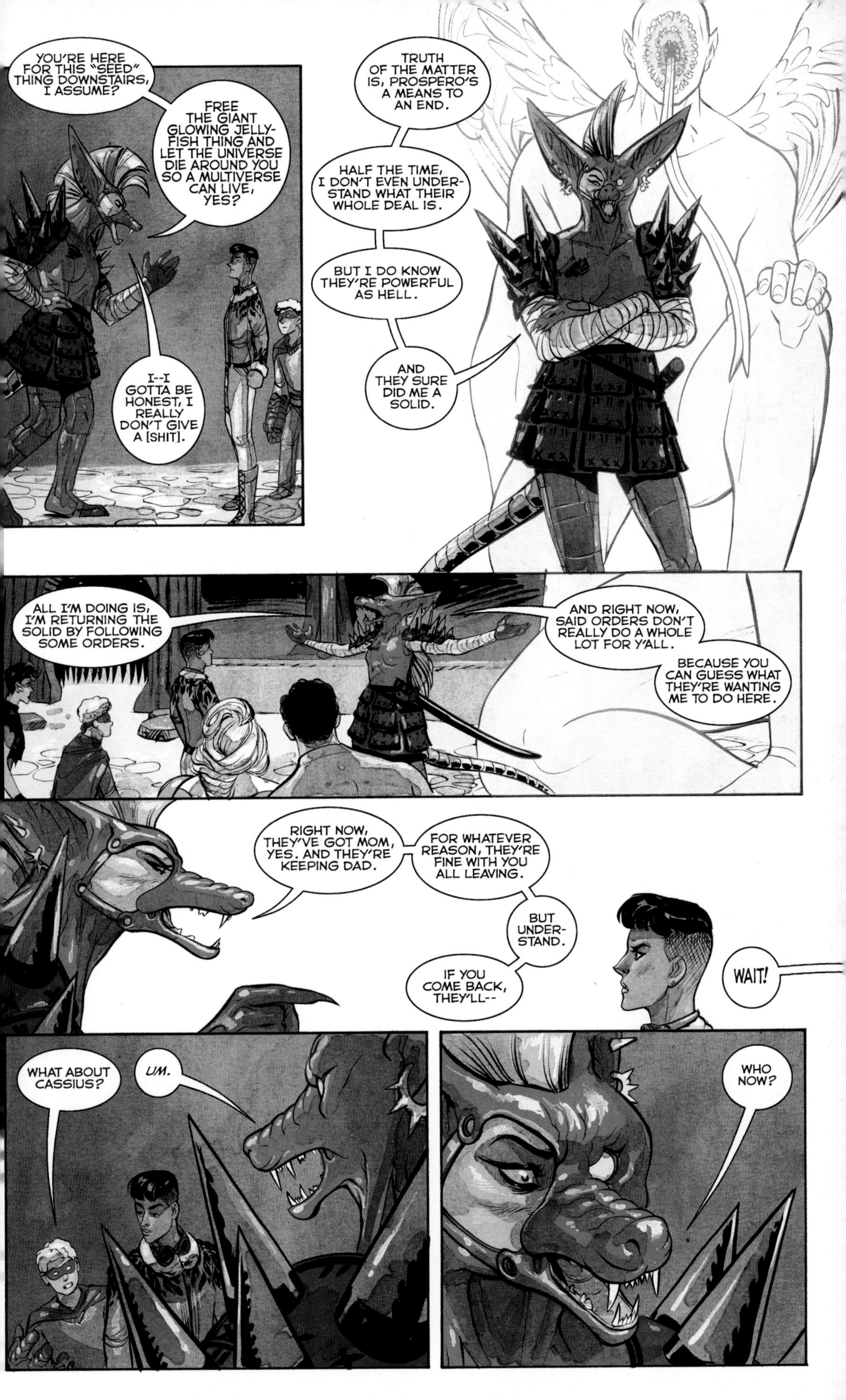
YOU'RE HERE FOR THIS "SEED" THING DOWNSTAIRS, I ASSUME?
FREE THE GIANT GLOWING JELLY-FISH THING AND LET THE UNIVERSE DIE AROUND YOU SO A MULTIVERSE CAN LIVE, YES?
I--I GOTTA BE HONEST, I REALLY DON'T GIVE A [SHIT].
TRUTH OF THE MATTER IS, PROSPERO'S A MEANS TO AN END.
HALF THE TIME, I DON'T EVEN UNDER-STAND WHAT THEIR WHOLE DEAL IS.
BUT I DO KNOW THEY'RE POWERFUL AS HELL.
AND THEY SURE DID ME A SOLID.
ALL I'M DOING IS, I'M RETURNING THE SOLID BY FOLLOWING SOME ORDERS.
AND RIGHT NOW, SAID ORDERS DON'T REALLY DO A WHOLE LOT FOR Y'ALL.
BECAUSE YOU CAN GUESS WHAT THEY'RE WANTING ME TO DO HERE.
RIGHT NOW, THEY'VE GOT MOM, YES. AND THEY'RE KEEPING DAD.
FOR WHATEVER REASON, THEY'RE FINE WITH YOU ALL LEAVING.
BUT UNDER-STAND.
IF YOU COME BACK, THEY'LL--
WAIT!
WHAT ABOUT CASSIUS?
UM.
WHO NOW?

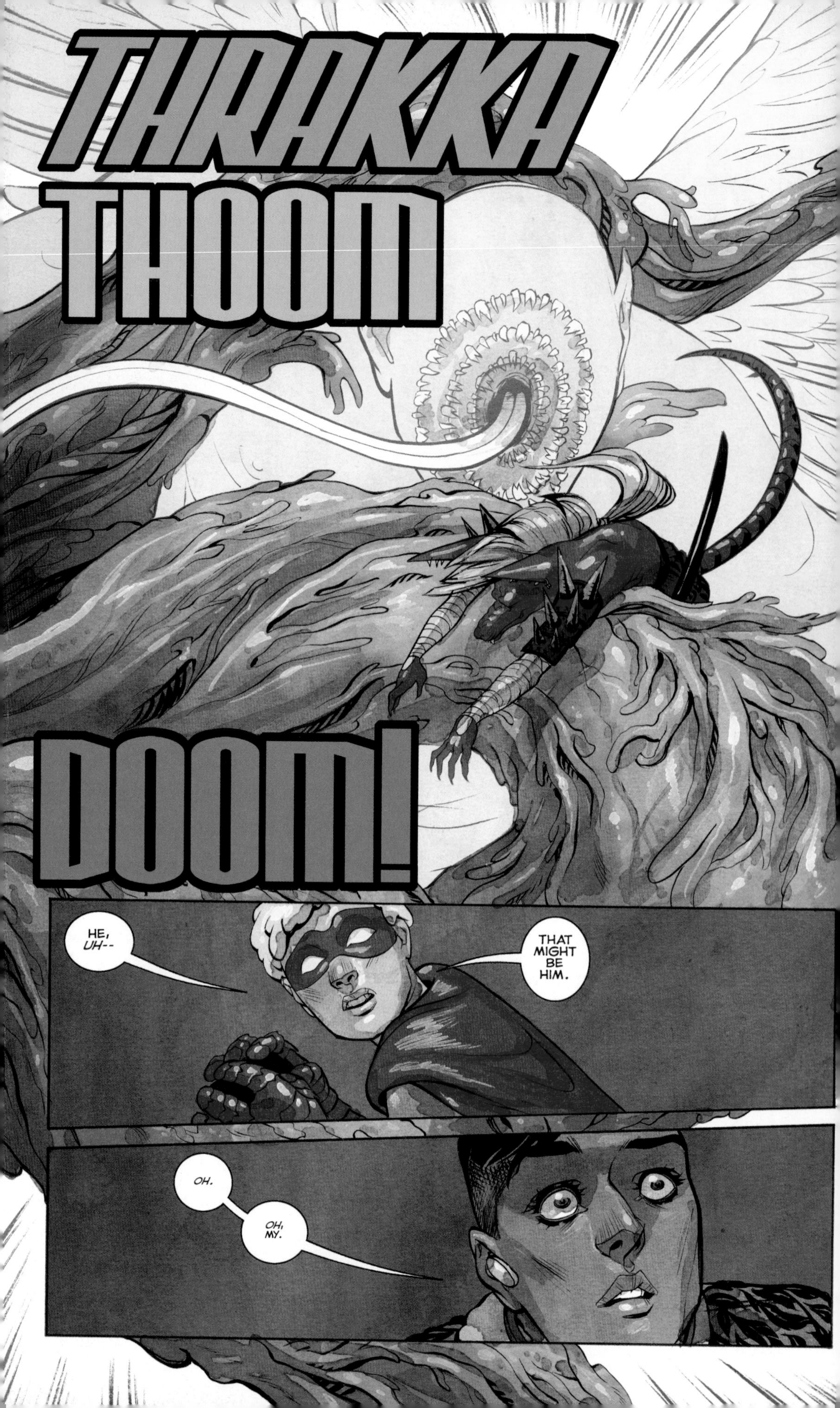
THRAKKA
THOOM
DOOM!
HE, UH--
THAT MIGHT BE HIM.
OH.
OH, MY.

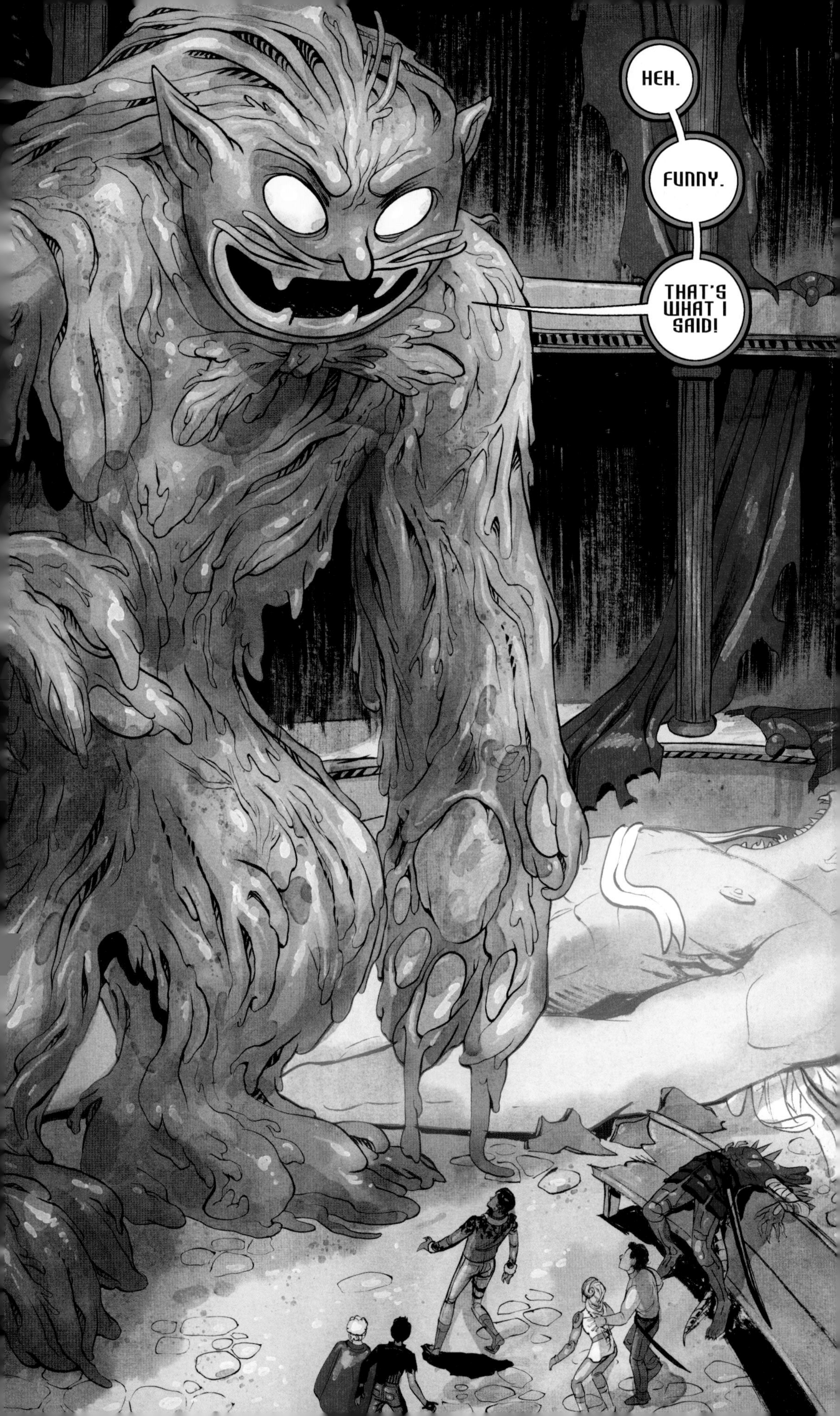
HEH.
FUNNY.
THAT'S WHAT I SAID!

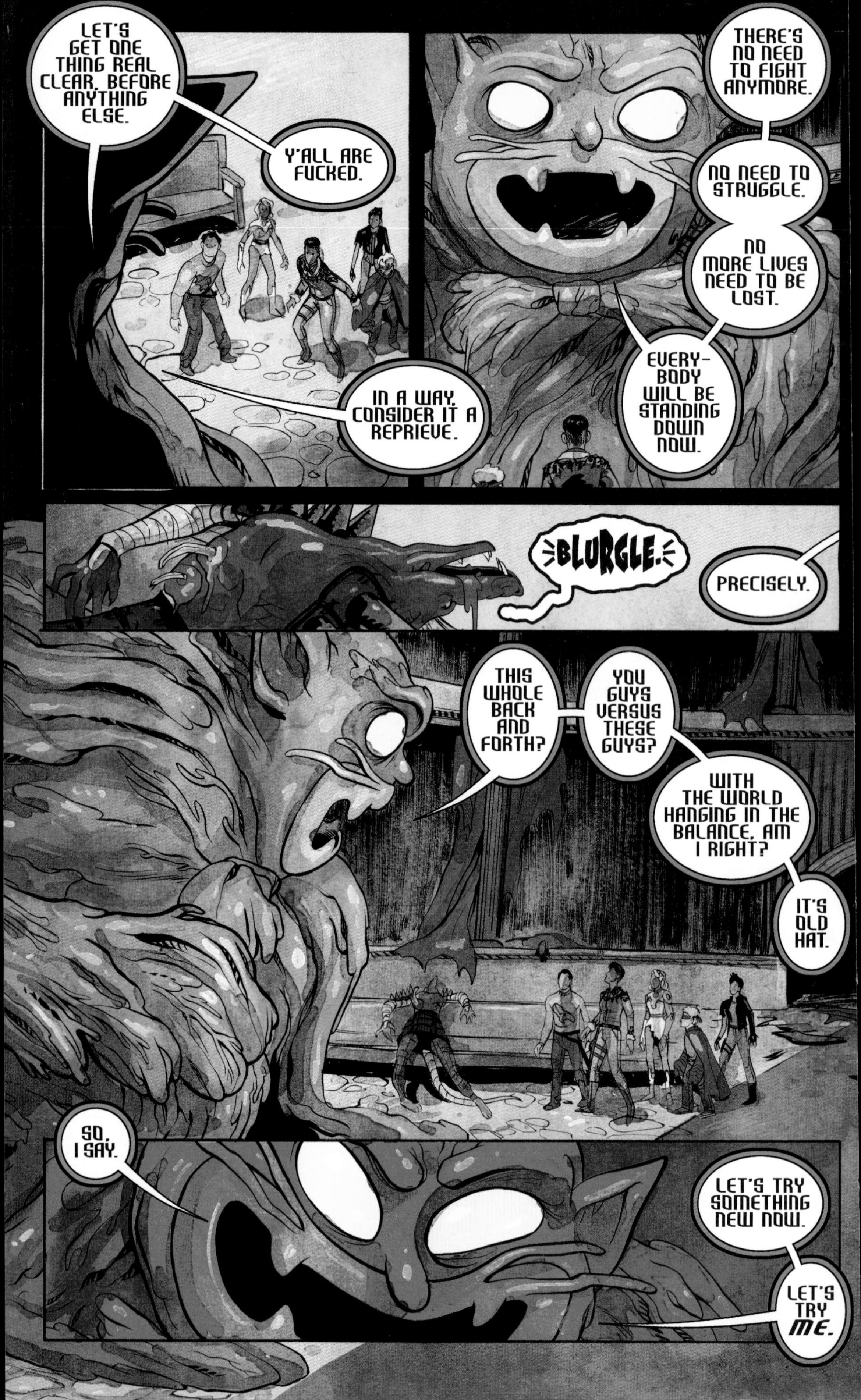
LET'S GET ONE THING REAL CLEAR, BEFORE ANYTHING ELSE.
Y'ALL ARE FUCKED.
IN A WAY, CONSIDER IT A REPRIEVE.
THERE'S NO NEED TO FIGHT ANYMORE.
NO NEED TO STRUGGLE.
NO MORE LIVES NEED TO BE LOST.
EVERY-BODY WILL BE STANDING DOWN NOW.
BLURGLE.
PRECISELY.
THIS WHOLE BACK AND FORTH?
YOU GUYS VERSUS THESE GUYS?
WITH THE WORLD HANGING IN THE BALANCE, AM I RIGHT?
IT'S OLD HAT.
SO, I SAY.
LET'S TRY SOMETHING NEW NOW.
LET'S TRY *ME*.

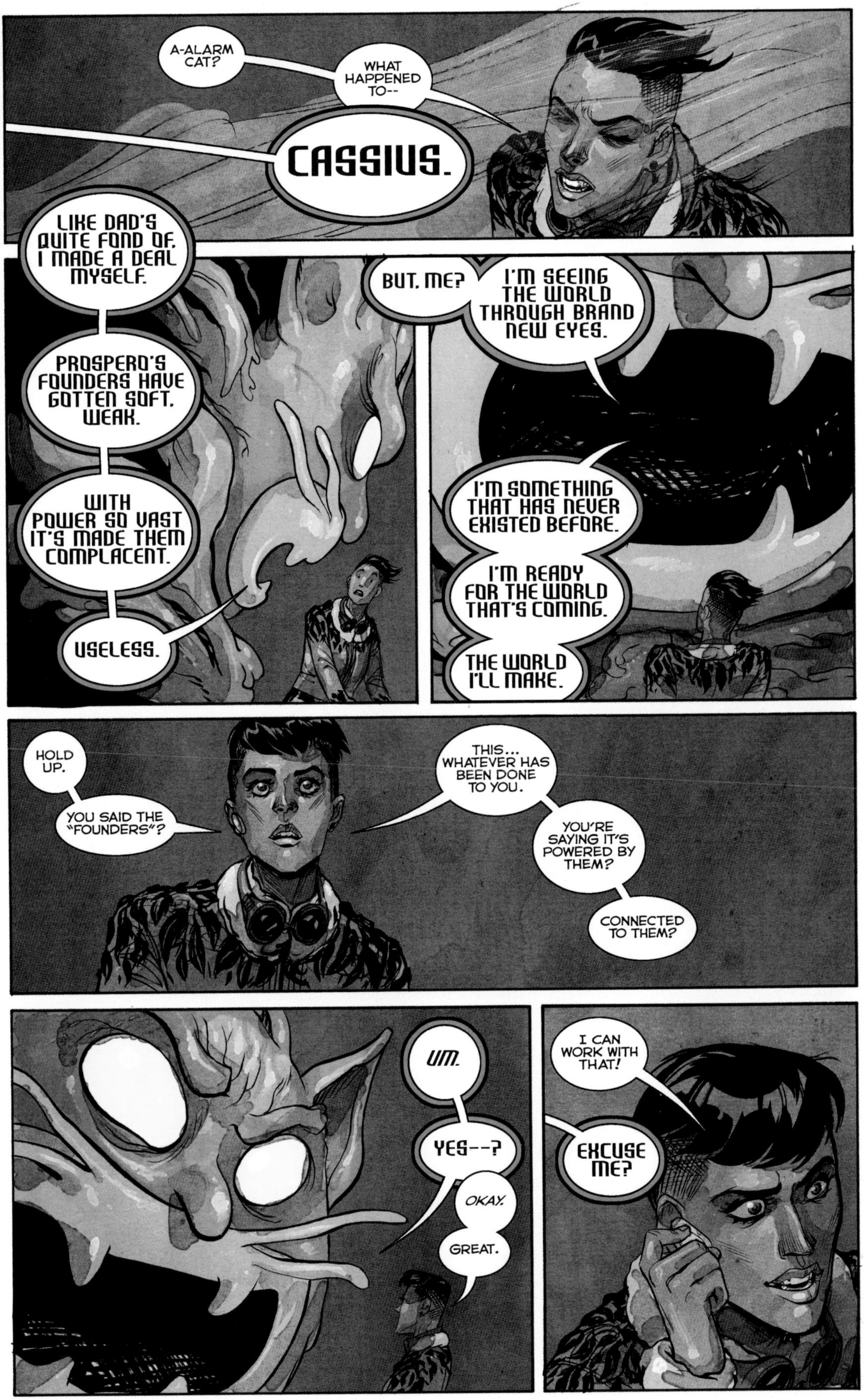
A-ALARM CAT?
WHAT HAPPENED TO--
CASSIUS.
LIKE DAD'S QUITE FOND OF. I MADE A DEAL MYSELF.
PROSPERO'S FOUNDERS HAVE GOTTEN SOFT. WEAK.
WITH POWER SO VAST IT'S MADE THEM COMPLACENT.
USELESS.
BUT, ME?
I'M SEEING THE WORLD THROUGH BRAND NEW EYES.
I'M SOMETHING THAT HAS NEVER EXISTED BEFORE.
I'M READY FOR THE WORLD THAT'S COMING.
THE WORLD I'LL MAKE.
HOLD UP.
YOU SAID THE "FOUNDERS"?
THIS... WHATEVER HAS BEEN DONE TO YOU.
YOU'RE SAYING IT'S POWERED BY THEM?
CONNECTED TO THEM?
UM.
YES--?
OKAY.
GREAT.
I CAN WORK WITH THAT!
EXCUSE ME?

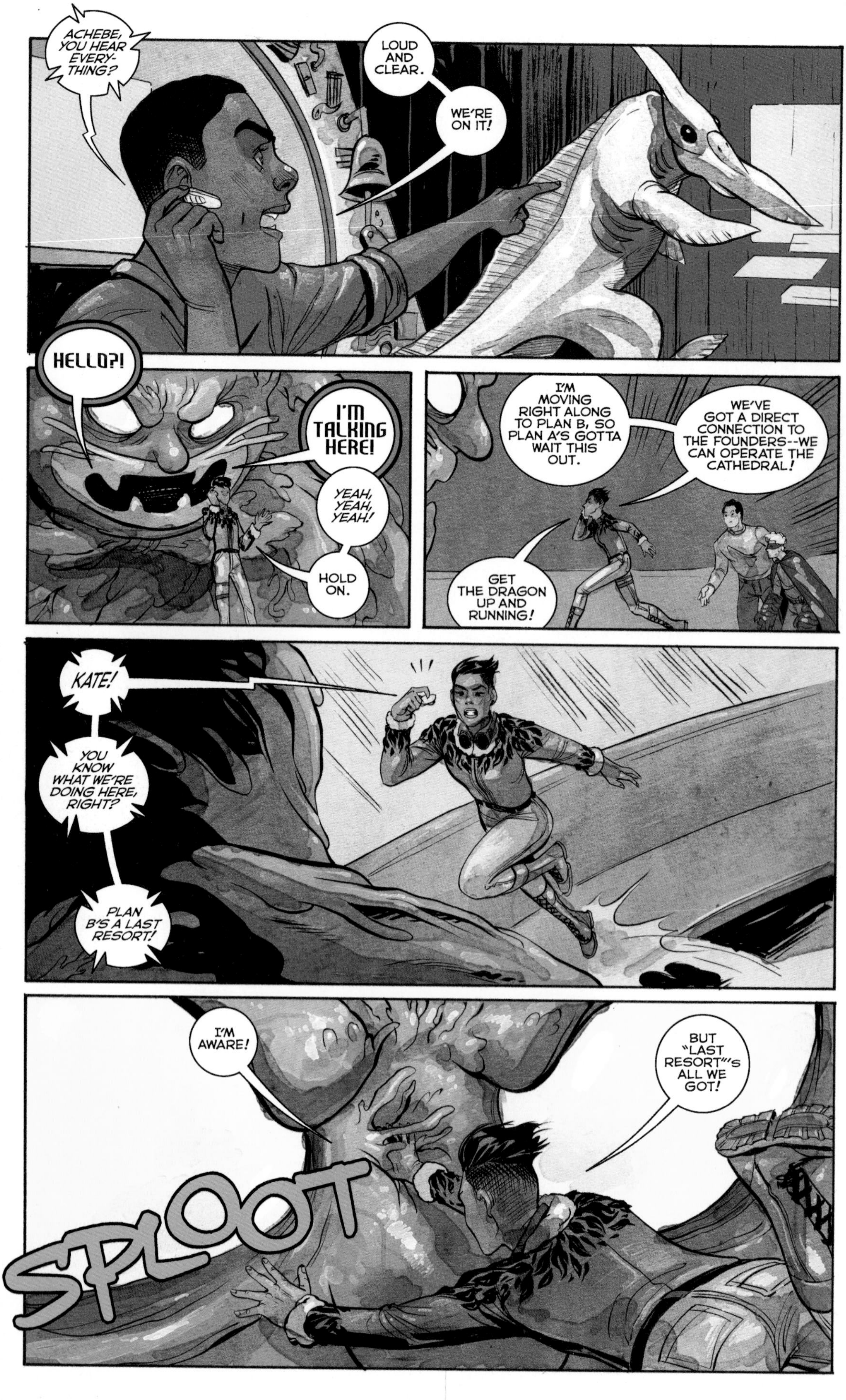

ACHEBE, YOU HEAR EVERYTHING?
LOUD AND CLEAR.
WE'RE ON IT!
HELLO?!
I'M TALKING HERE!
YEAH, YEAH, YEAH!
HOLD ON.
I'M MOVING RIGHT ALONG TO PLAN B, SO PLAN A'S GOTTA WAIT THIS OUT.
WE'VE GOT A DIRECT CONNECTION TO THE FOUNDERS--WE CAN OPERATE THE CATHEDRAL!
GET THE DRAGON UP AND RUNNING!
KATE!
YOU KNOW WHAT WE'RE DOING HERE, RIGHT?
PLAN B'S A LAST RESORT!
I'M AWARE!
BUT "LAST RESORT"'S ALL WE GOT!
SPLOOT

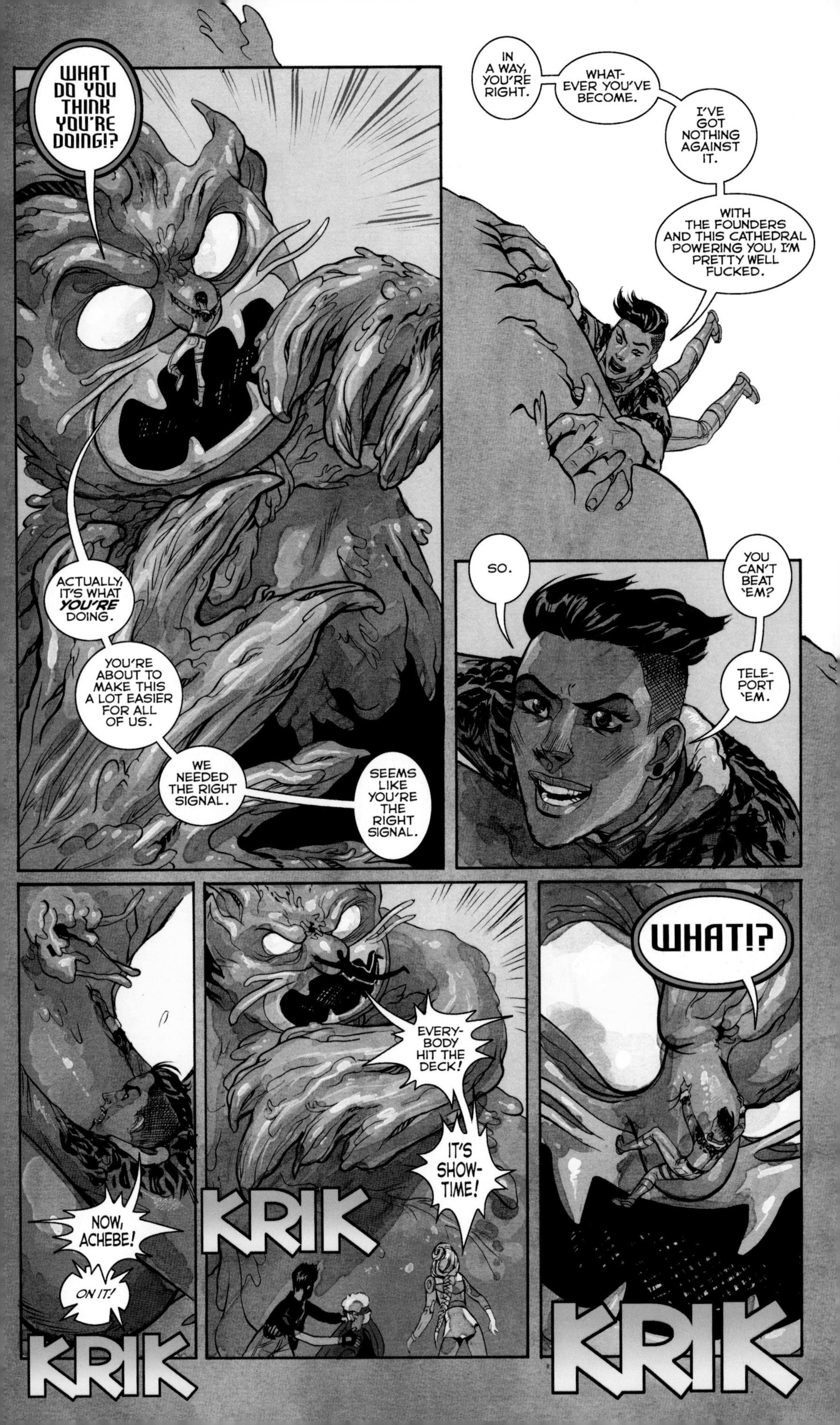
WHAT DO YOU THINK YOU'RE DOING!?
ACTUALLY, IT'S WHAT YOU'RE DOING.
YOU'RE ABOUT TO MAKE THIS A LOT EASIER FOR ALL OF US.
WE NEEDED THE RIGHT SIGNAL.
SEEMS LIKE YOU'RE THE RIGHT SIGNAL.
IN A WAY, YOU'RE RIGHT.
WHAT-EVER YOU'VE BECOME.
I'VE GOT NOTHING AGAINST IT.
WITH THE FOUNDERS AND THIS CATHEDRAL POWERING YOU, I'M PRETTY WELL FUCKED.
SO.
YOU CAN'T BEAT 'EM?
TELE-PORT 'EM.
NOW, ACHEBE!
ON IT!
KRIK
EVERY-BODY HIT THE DECK!
IT'S SHOW-TIME!
KRIK
WHAT!?
KRIK

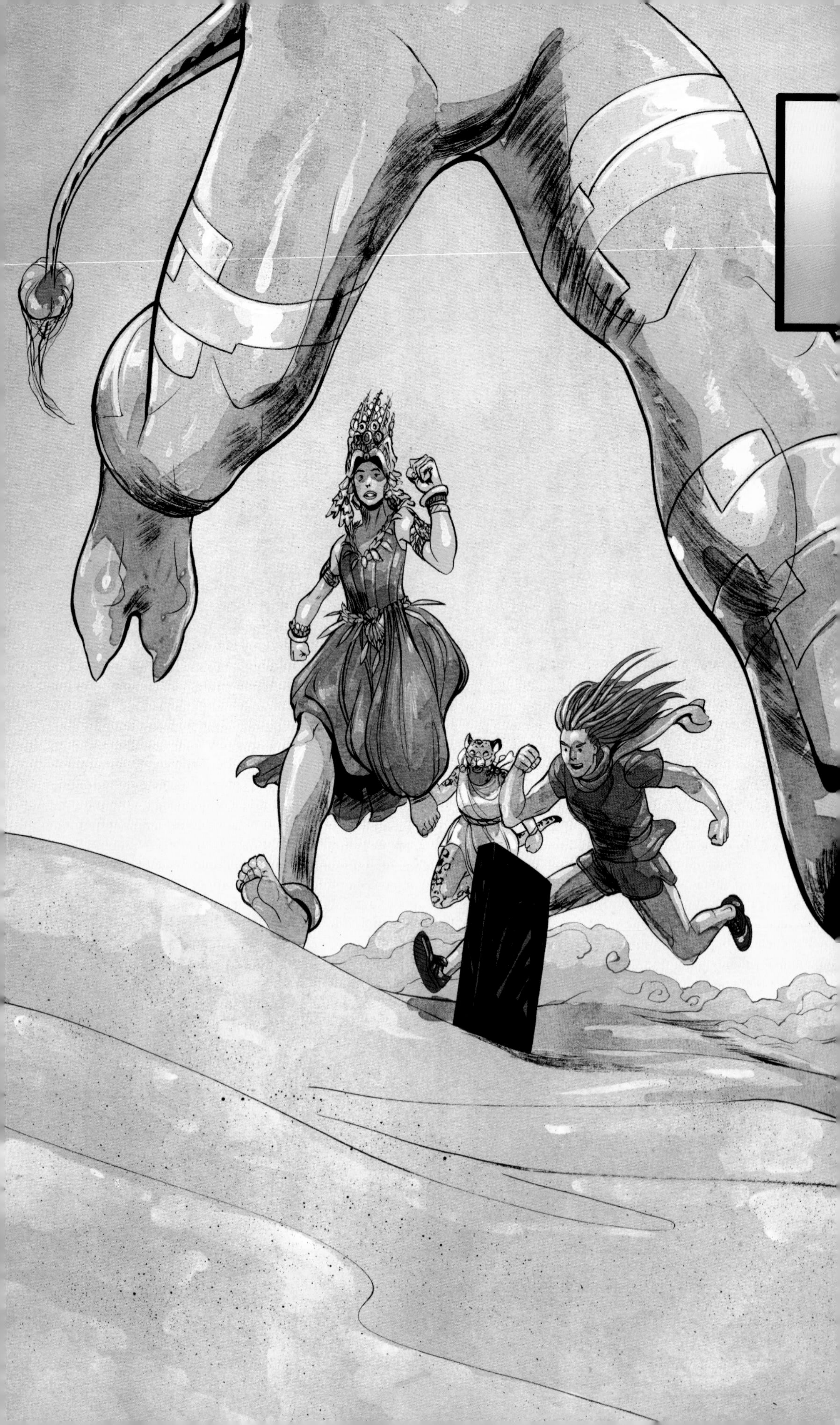

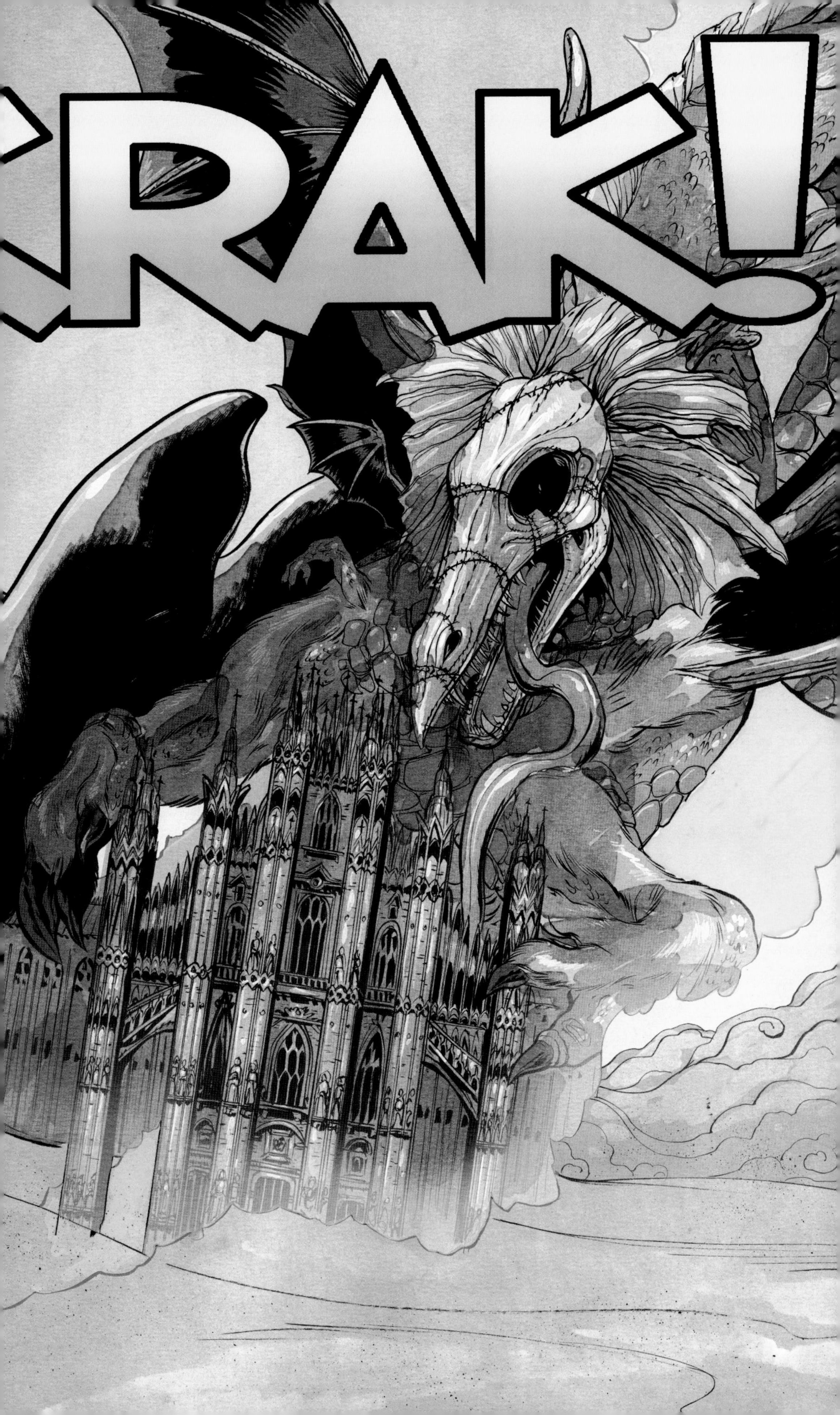
RAK!

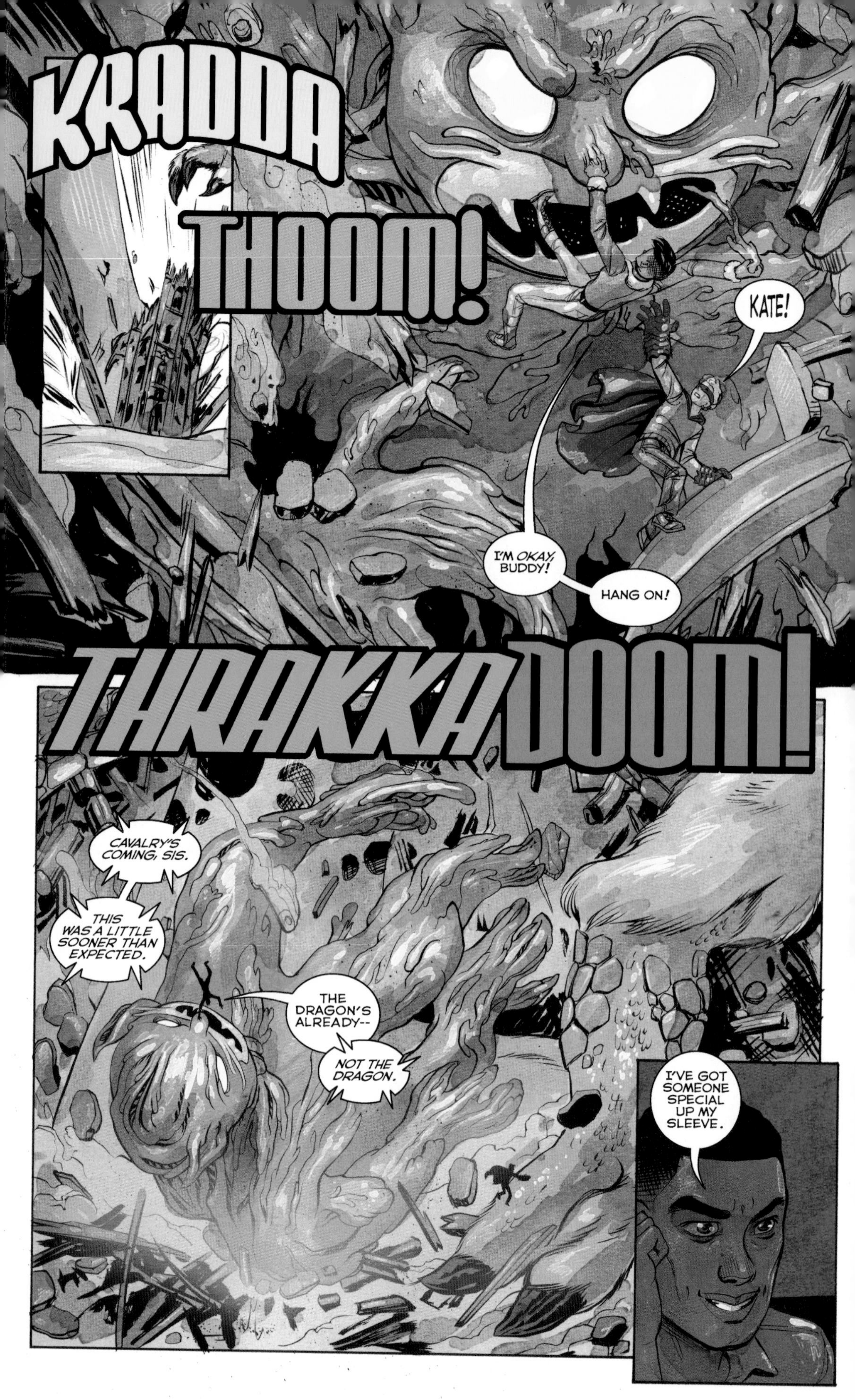

KRADDA
THOOM!
KATE!
I'M OKAY, BUDDY!
HANG ON!
THRAKKADOOM!
CAVALRY'S COMING, SIS.
THIS WAS A LITTLE SOONER THAN EXPECTED.
THE DRAGON'S ALREADY--
NOT THE DRAGON.
I'VE GOT SOMEONE SPECIAL UP MY SLEEVE.

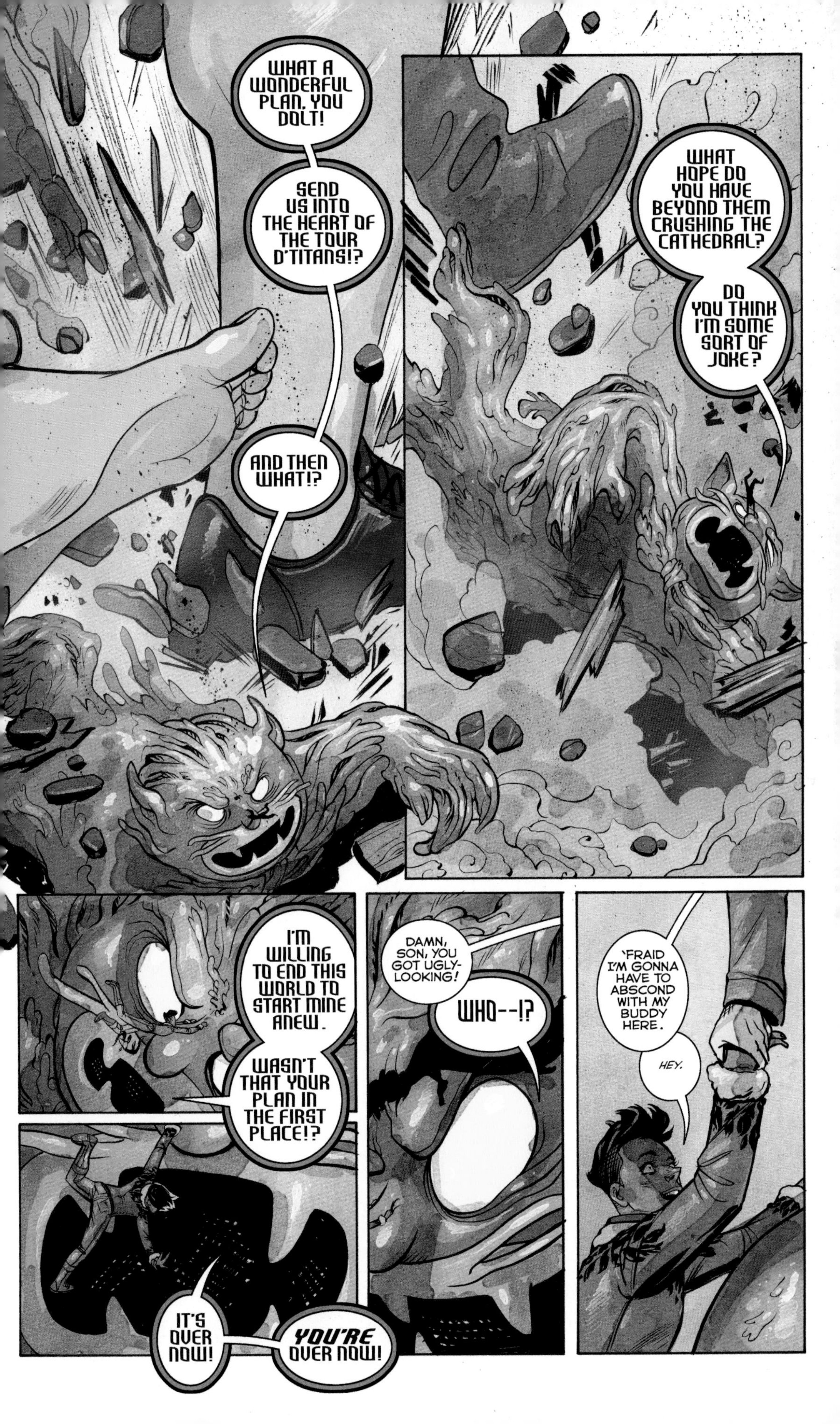
WHAT A WONDERFUL PLAN, YOU DOLT!
SEND US INTO THE HEART OF THE TOUR D'TITANS!?
AND THEN WHAT!?
WHAT HOPE DO YOU HAVE BEYOND THEM CRUSHING THE CATHEDRAL?
DO YOU THINK I'M SOME SORT OF JOKE?
I'M WILLING TO END THIS WORLD TO START MINE ANEW.
WASN'T THAT YOUR PLAN IN THE FIRST PLACE!?
IT'S OVER NOW!
YOU'RE OVER NOW!
DAMN, SON, YOU GOT UGLY-LOOKING!
WHO--!?
'FRAID I'M GONNA HAVE TO ABSCOND WITH MY BUDDY HERE.
HEY.

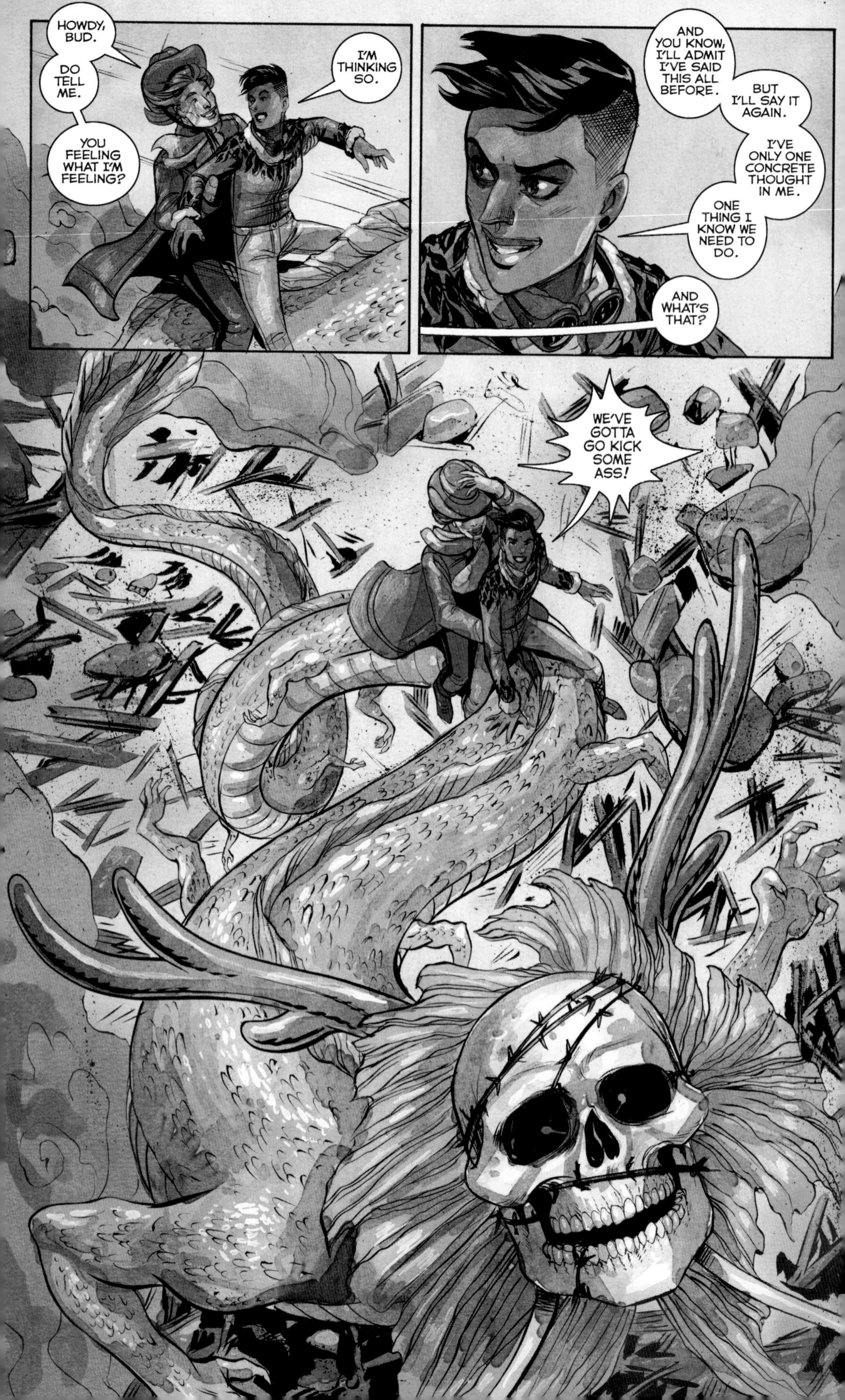
HOWDY, BUD.
DO TELL ME.
YOU FEELING WHAT I'M FEELING?
I'M THINKING SO.
AND YOU KNOW, I'LL ADMIT I'VE SAID THIS ALL BEFORE.
BUT I'LL SAY IT AGAIN.
I'VE ONLY ONE CONCRETE THOUGHT IN ME.
ONE THING I KNOW WE NEED TO DO.
AND WHAT'S THAT?
WE'VE GOTTA GO KICK SOME ASS!

CHAPTER

28

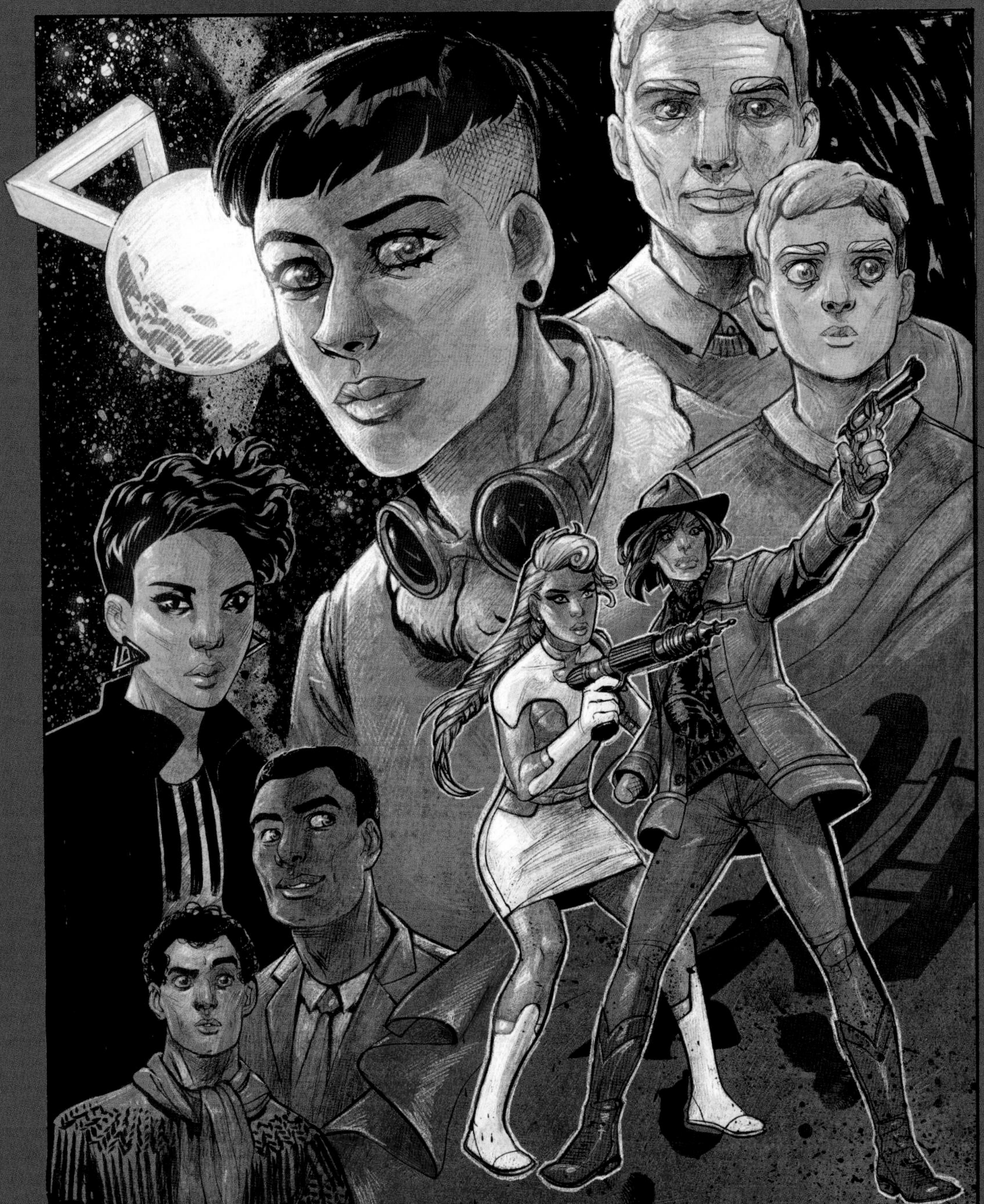

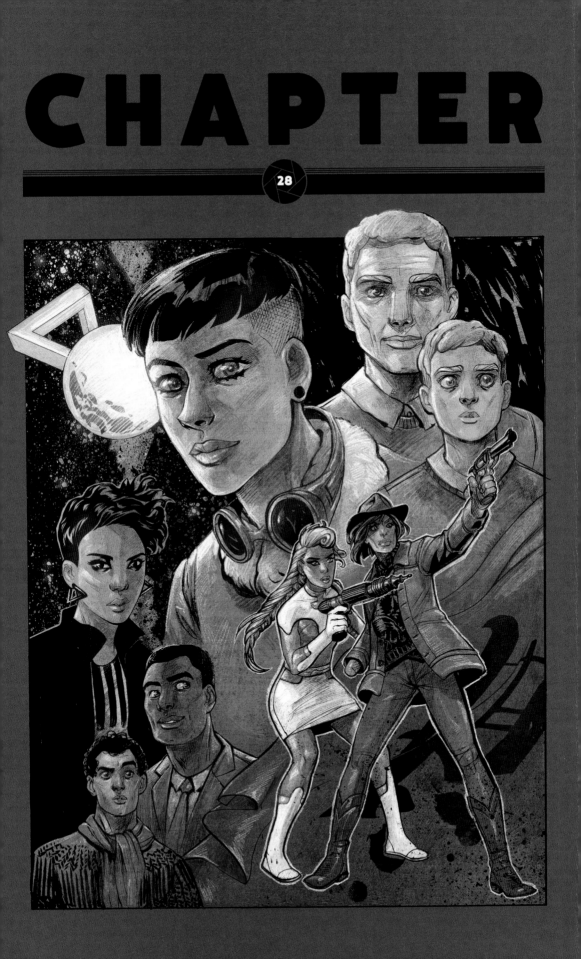

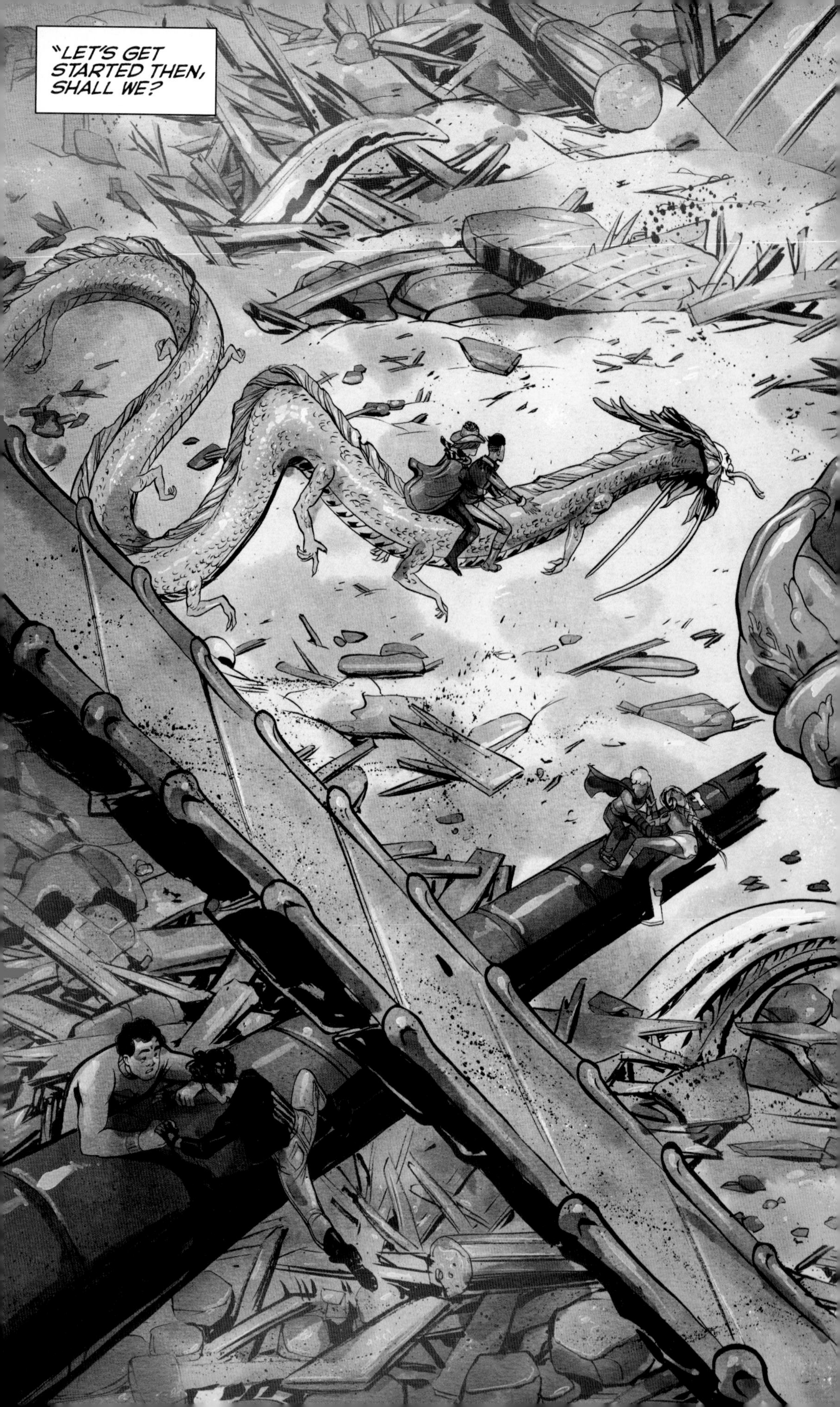
"LET'S GET STARTED THEN, SHALL WE?

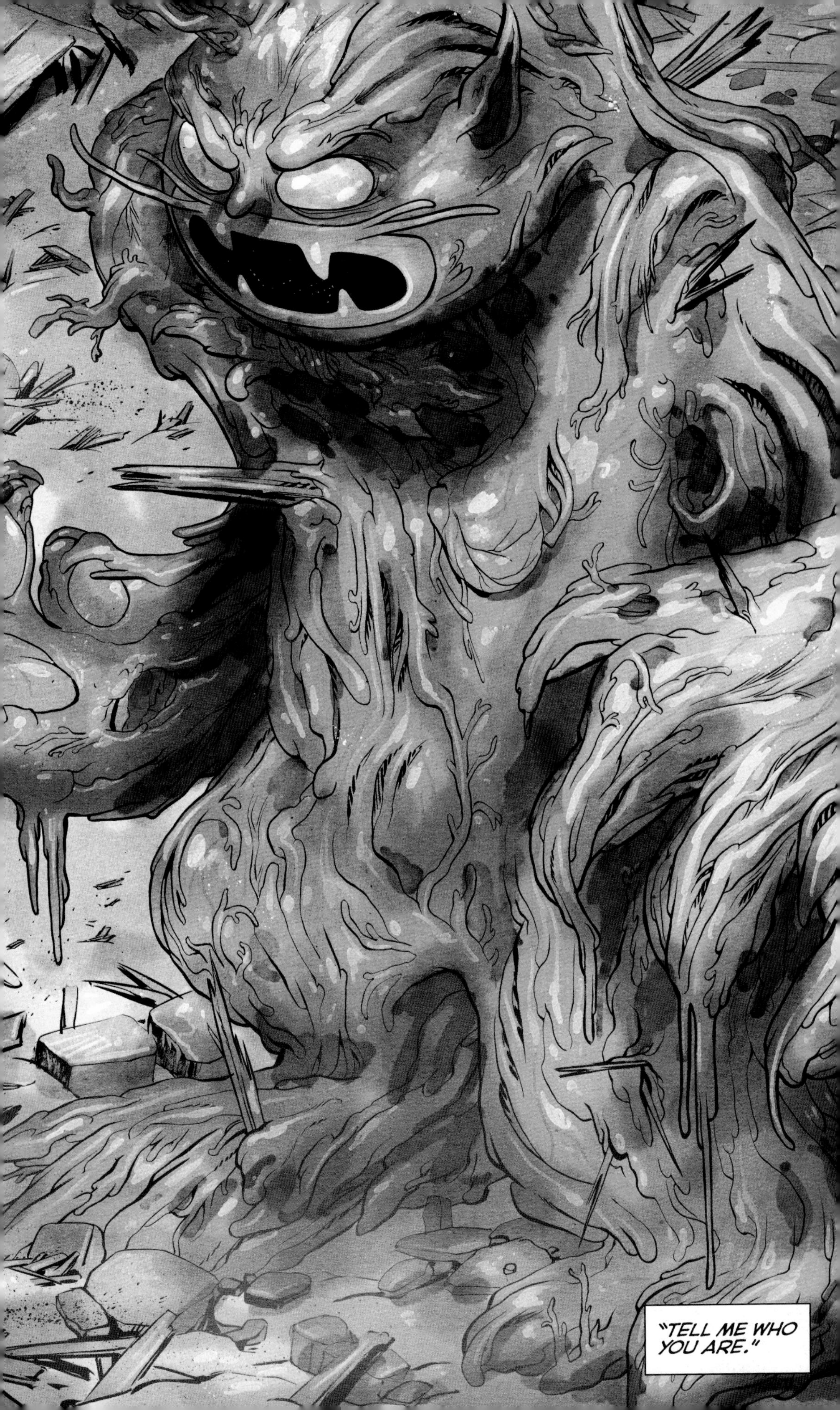
"TELL ME WHO YOU ARE."

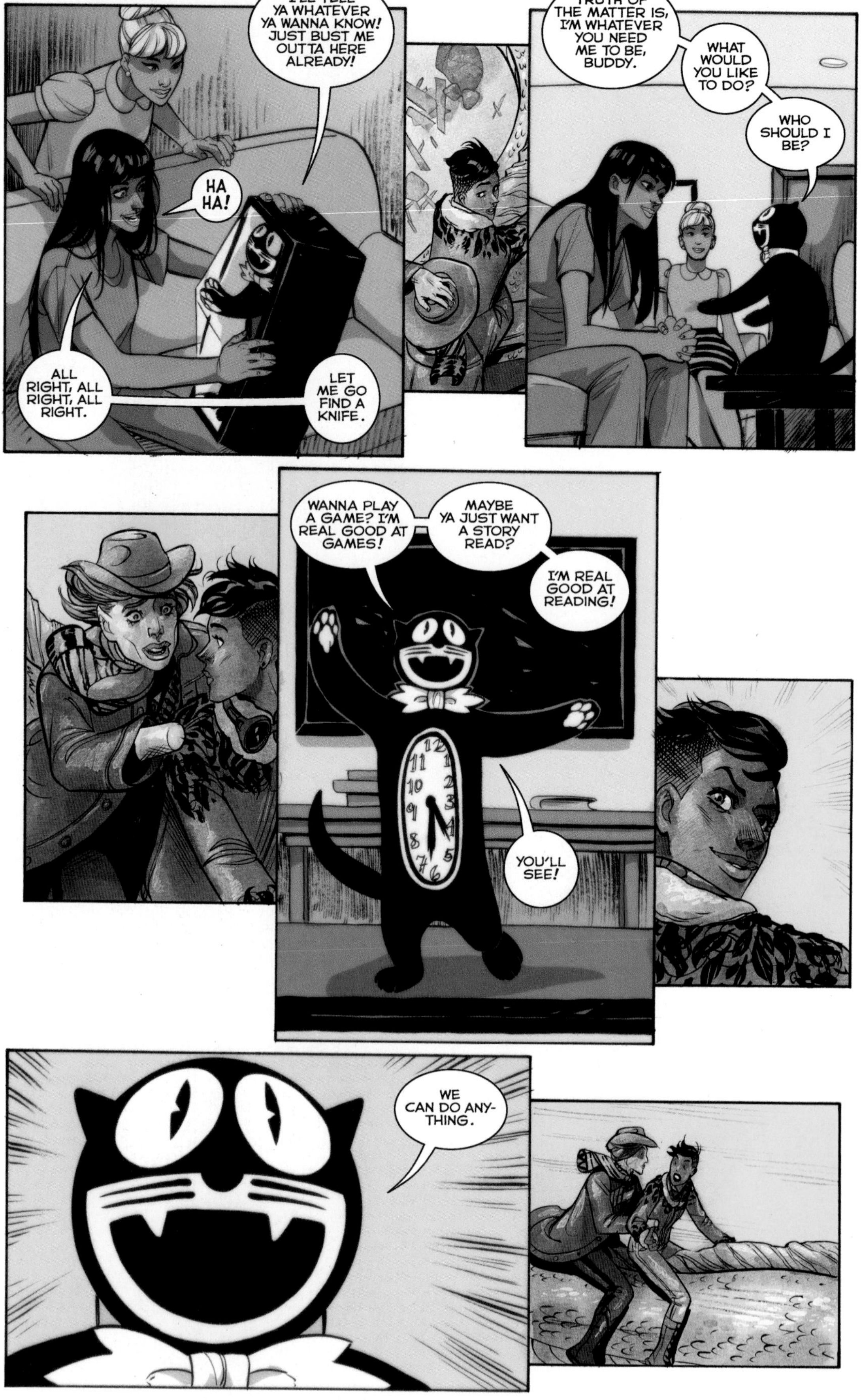
I'LL TELL YA WHATEVER YA WANNA KNOW! JUST BUST ME OUTTA HERE ALREADY!
HA HA!
ALL RIGHT, ALL RIGHT, ALL RIGHT.
LET ME GO FIND A KNIFE.
TRUTH OF THE MATTER IS, I'M WHATEVER YOU NEED ME TO BE, BUDDY.
WHAT WOULD YOU LIKE TO DO?
WHO SHOULD I BE?
WANNA PLAY A GAME? I'M REAL GOOD AT GAMES!
MAYBE YA JUST WANT A STORY READ?
I'M REAL GOOD AT READING!
YOU'LL SEE!
WE CAN DO ANY-THING.

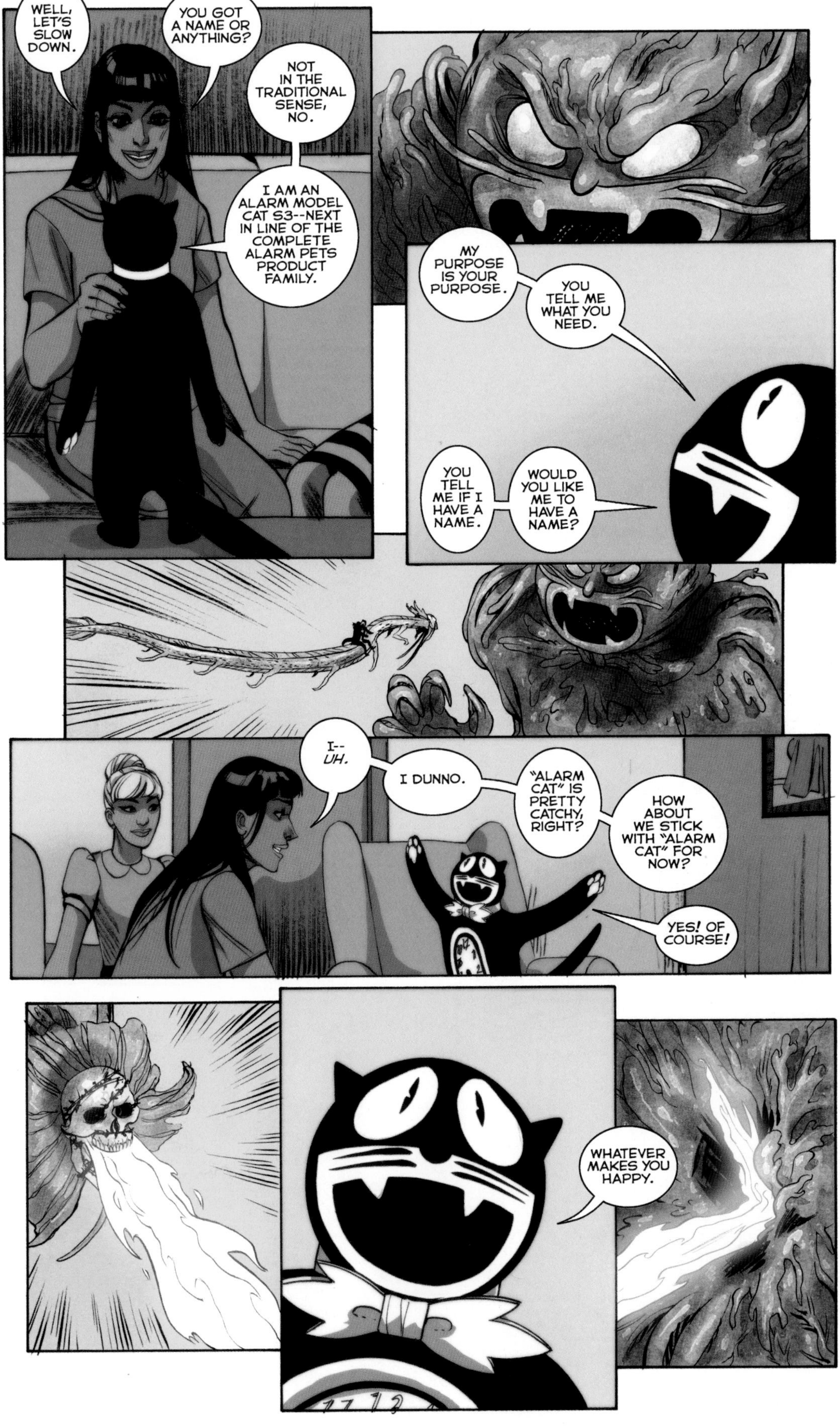
WELL, LET'S SLOW DOWN.
YOU GOT A NAME OR ANYTHING?
NOT IN THE TRADITIONAL SENSE, NO.
I AM AN ALARM MODEL CAT S3--NEXT IN LINE OF THE COMPLETE ALARM PETS PRODUCT FAMILY.
MY PURPOSE IS YOUR PURPOSE.
YOU TELL ME WHAT YOU NEED.
WOULD YOU LIKE ME TO HAVE A NAME?
YOU TELL ME IF I HAVE A NAME.
I-- UH.
I DUNNO.
"ALARM CAT" IS PRETTY CATCHY, RIGHT?
HOW ABOUT WE STICK WITH "ALARM CAT" FOR NOW?
YES! OF COURSE!
WHATEVER MAKES YOU HAPPY.

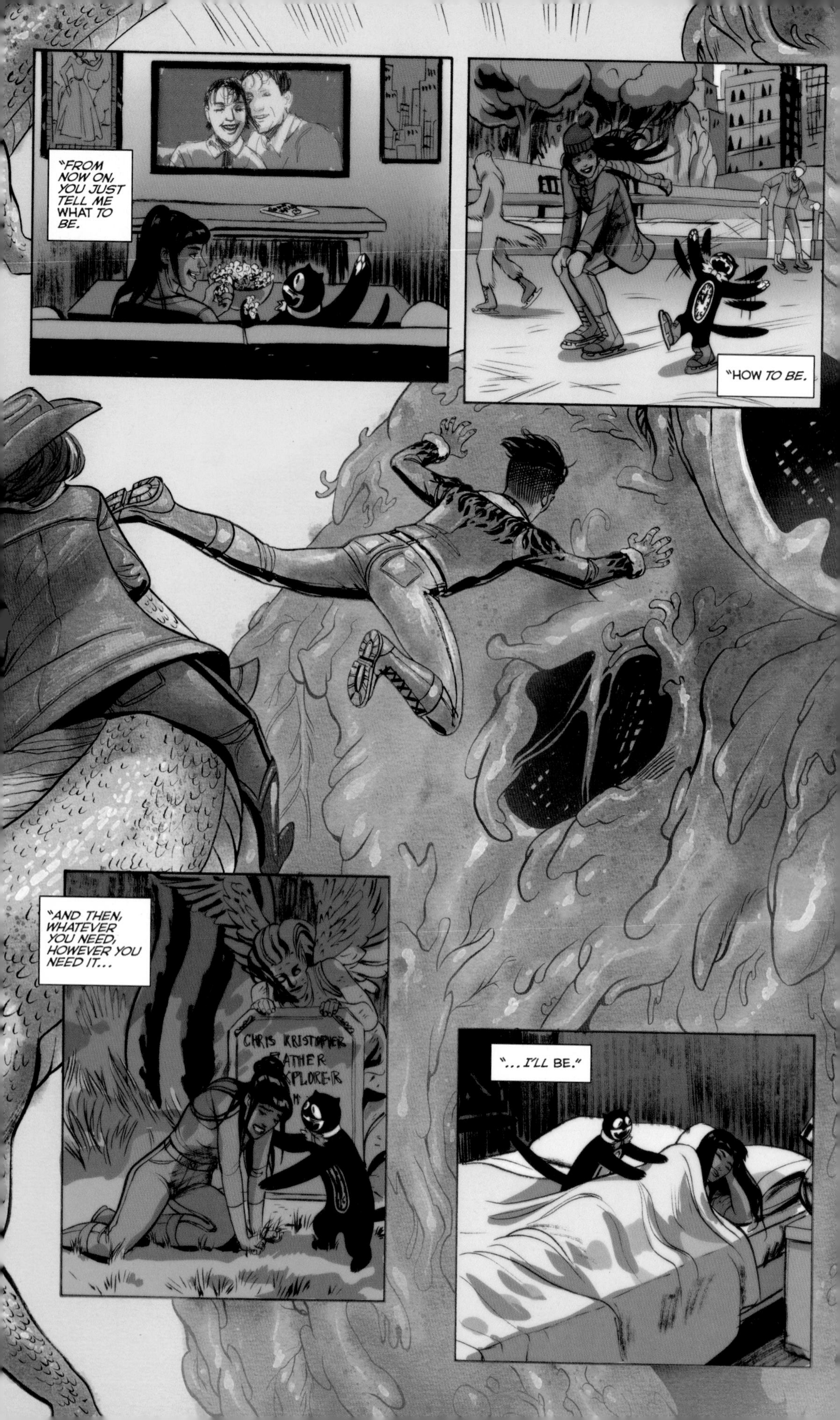
"FROM NOW ON, YOU JUST TELL ME WHAT TO BE.
"HOW TO BE.
"AND THEN, WHATEVER YOU NEED, HOWEVER YOU NEED IT...
"...I'LL BE."

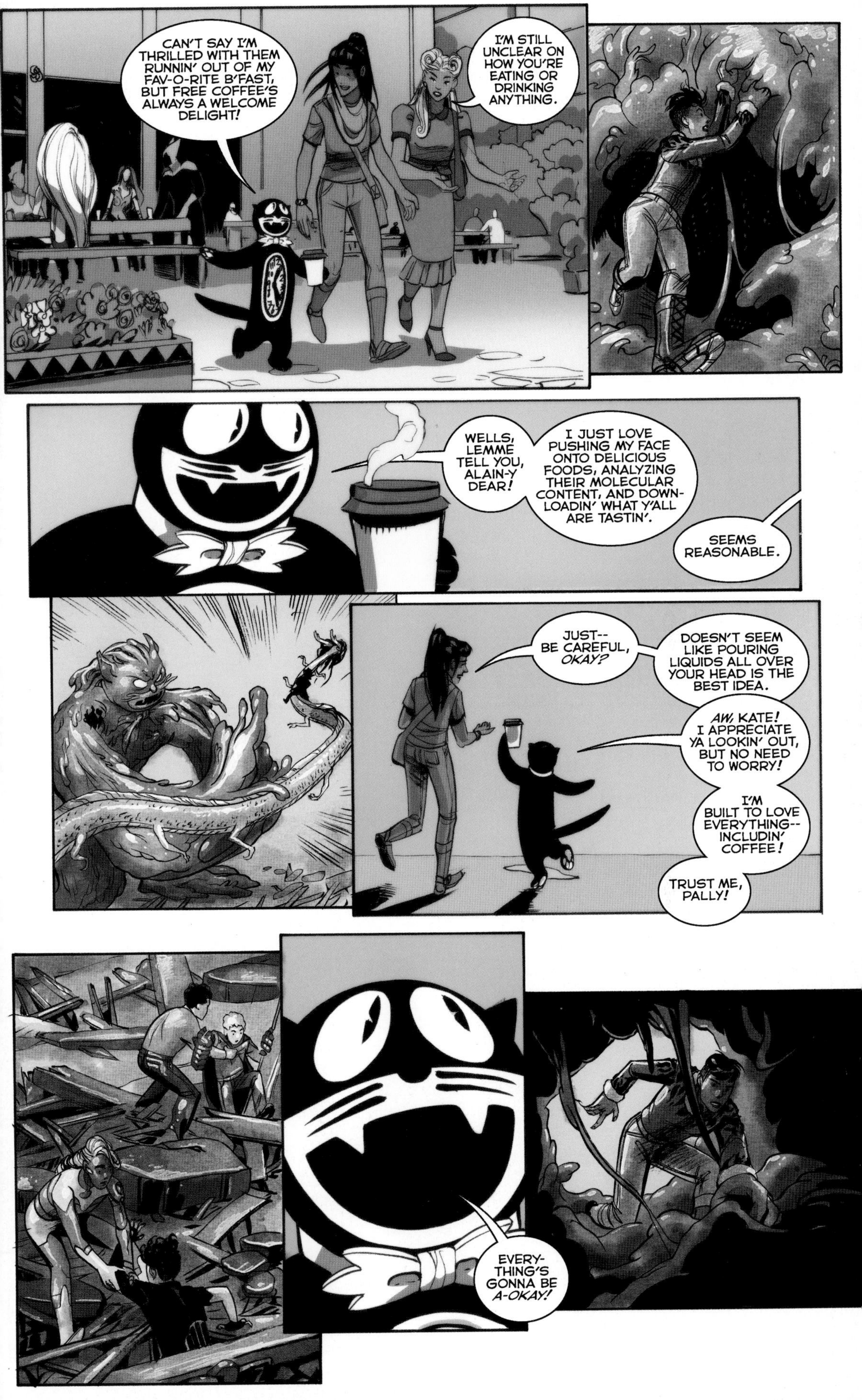
CAN'T SAY I'M THRILLED WITH THEM RUNNIN' OUT OF MY FAV-O-RITE B'FAST, BUT FREE COFFEE'S ALWAYS A WELCOME DELIGHT!
I'M STILL UNCLEAR ON HOW YOU'RE EATING OR DRINKING ANYTHING.
WELLS, LEMME TELL YOU, ALAIN-Y DEAR!
I JUST LOVE PUSHING MY FACE ONTO DELICIOUS FOODS, ANALYZING THEIR MOLECULAR CONTENT, AND DOWN-LOADIN' WHAT Y'ALL ARE TASTIN'.
SEEMS REASONABLE.
JUST-- BE CAREFUL, OKAY?
DOESN'T SEEM LIKE POURING LIQUIDS ALL OVER YOUR HEAD IS THE BEST IDEA.
AW, KATE! I APPRECIATE YA LOOKIN' OUT, BUT NO NEED TO WORRY!
I'M BUILT TO LOVE EVERYTHING-- INCLUDIN' COFFEE!
TRUST ME, PALLY!
EVERY-THING'S GONNA BE A-OKAY!

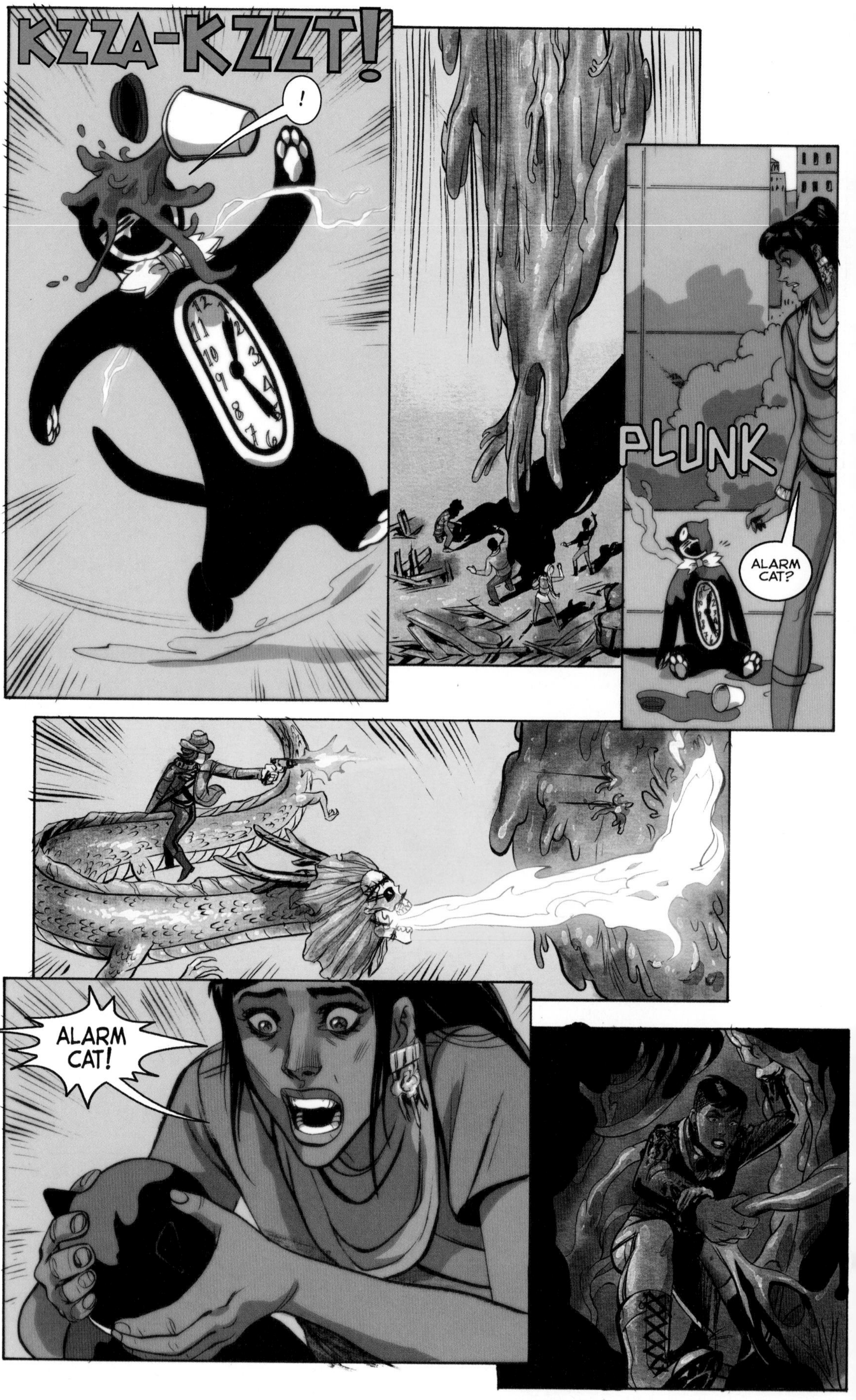
KZZA-KZZT!
!
PLUNK
ALARM CAT?
ALARM CAT!

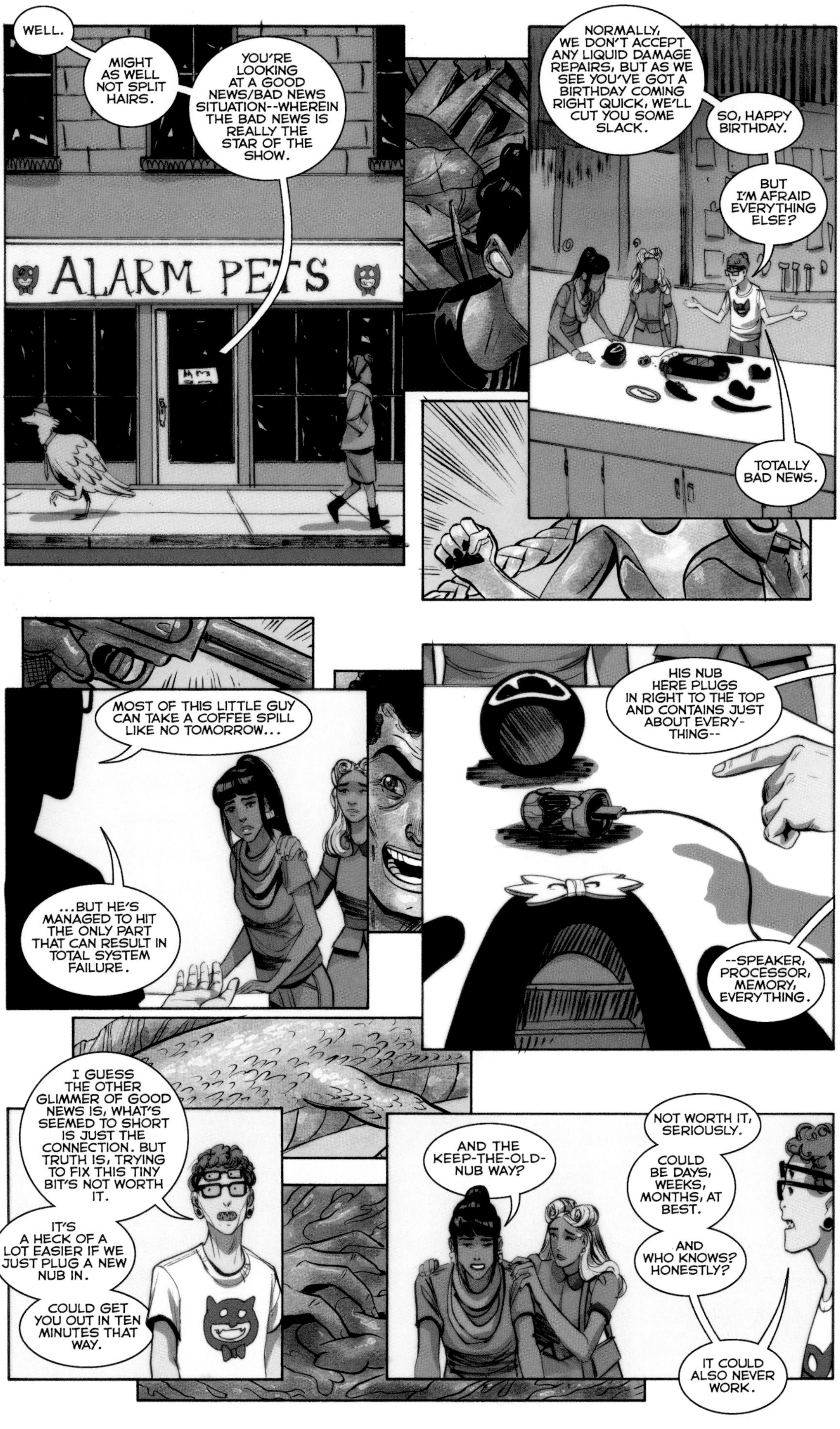
WELL.
MIGHT AS WELL NOT SPLIT HAIRS.
YOU'RE LOOKING AT A GOOD NEWS/BAD NEWS SITUATION--WHEREIN THE BAD NEWS IS REALLY THE STAR OF THE SHOW.
ALARM PETS
NORMALLY, WE DON'T ACCEPT ANY LIQUID DAMAGE REPAIRS, BUT AS WE SEE YOU'VE GOT A BIRTHDAY COMING RIGHT QUICK, WE'LL CUT YOU SOME SLACK.
SO, HAPPY BIRTHDAY.
BUT I'M AFRAID EVERYTHING ELSE?
TOTALLY BAD NEWS.
MOST OF THIS LITTLE GUY CAN TAKE A COFFEE SPILL LIKE NO TOMORROW...
...BUT HE'S MANAGED TO HIT THE ONLY PART THAT CAN RESULT IN TOTAL SYSTEM FAILURE.
HIS NUB HERE PLUGS IN RIGHT TO THE TOP AND CONTAINS JUST ABOUT EVERY-THING--
--SPEAKER, PROCESSOR, MEMORY, EVERYTHING.
I GUESS THE OTHER GLIMMER OF GOOD NEWS IS, WHAT'S SEEMED TO SHORT IS JUST THE CONNECTION. BUT TRUTH IS, TRYING TO FIX THIS TINY BIT'S NOT WORTH IT.
IT'S A HECK OF A LOT EASIER IF WE JUST PLUG A NEW NUB IN.
COULD GET YOU OUT IN TEN MINUTES THAT WAY.
AND THE KEEP-THE-OLD-NUB WAY?
NOT WORTH IT, SERIOUSLY.
COULD BE DAYS, WEEKS, MONTHS, AT BEST.
AND WHO KNOWS? HONESTLY?
IT COULD ALSO NEVER WORK.

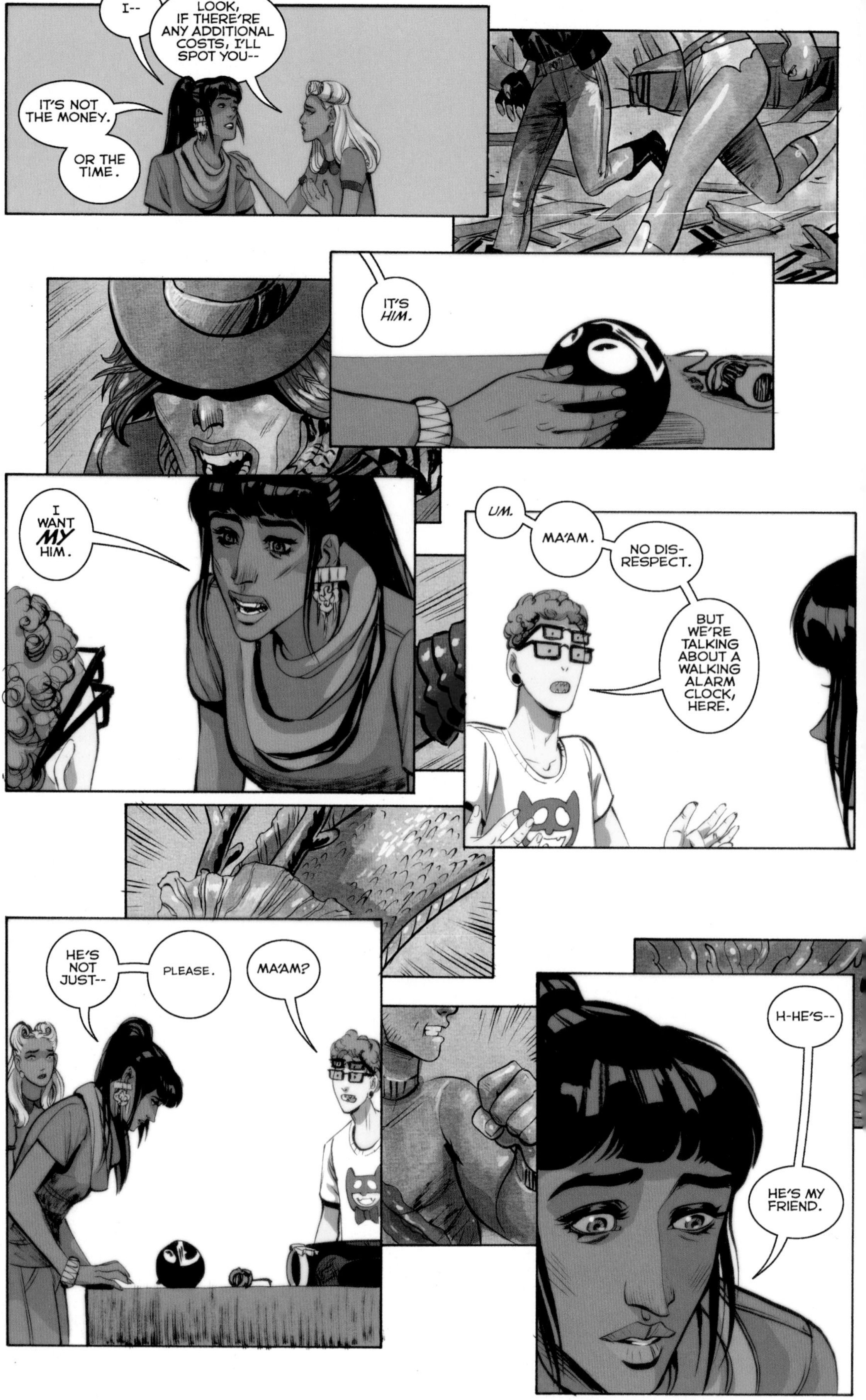
I--
LOOK, IF THERE'RE ANY ADDITIONAL COSTS, I'LL SPOT YOU--
IT'S NOT THE MONEY.
OR THE TIME.
IT'S *HIM.*
I WANT ***MY*** HIM.
UM.
MA'AM.
NO DIS-RESPECT.
BUT WE'RE TALKING ABOUT A WALKING ALARM CLOCK, HERE.
HE'S NOT JUST--
PLEASE.
MA'AM?
H-HE'S--
HE'S MY FRIEND.

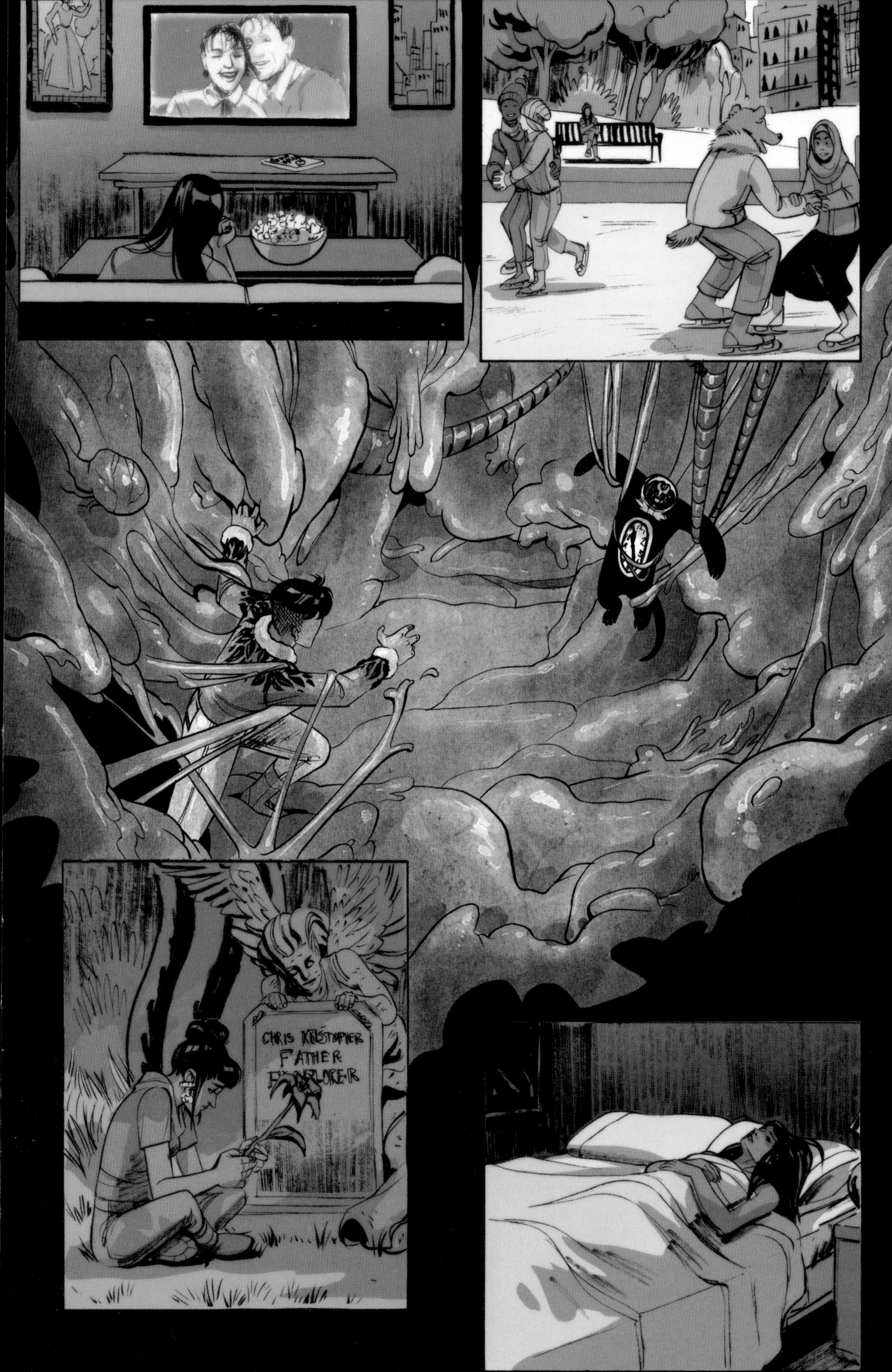
CHRIS KRISTOPHER
FATHER

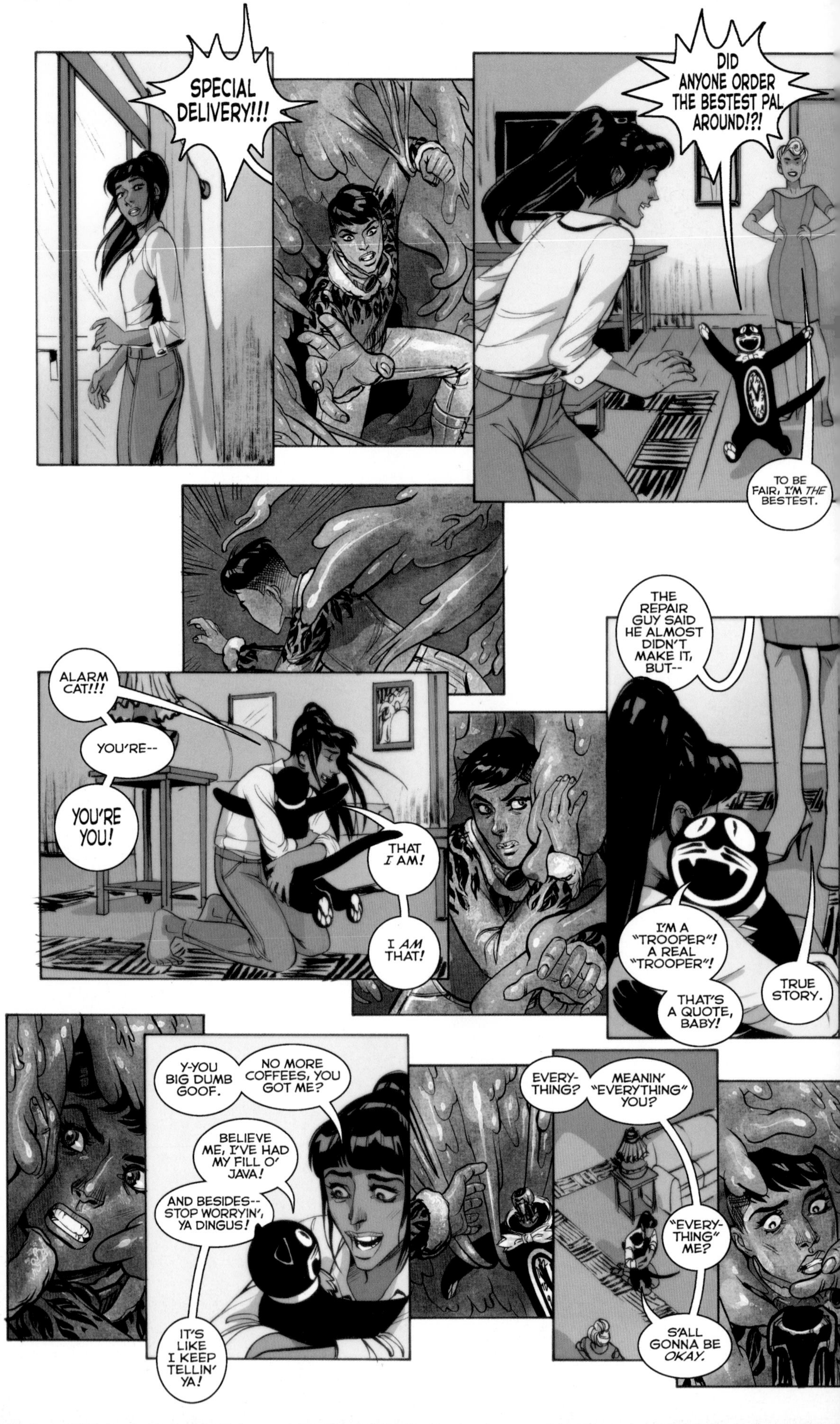
SPECIAL DELIVERY!!!
DID ANYONE ORDER THE BESTEST PAL AROUND!?!
TO BE FAIR, I'M *THE* BESTEST.
ALARM CAT!!!
YOU'RE--
YOU'RE YOU!
THAT *I* AM!
I *AM* THAT!
THE REPAIR GUY SAID HE ALMOST DIDN'T MAKE IT, BUT--
I'M A "TROOPER"! A REAL "TROOPER"!
THAT'S A QUOTE, BABY!
TRUE STORY.
Y-YOU BIG DUMB GOOF.
NO MORE COFFEES, YOU GOT ME?
BELIEVE ME, I'VE HAD MY FILL O' JAVA!
AND BESIDES-- STOP WORRYIN', YA DINGUS!
IT'S LIKE I KEEP TELLIN' YA!
EVERY-THING?
MEANIN' "EVERYTHING" YOU?
"EVERY-THING" ME?
S'ALL GONNA BE *OKAY*.

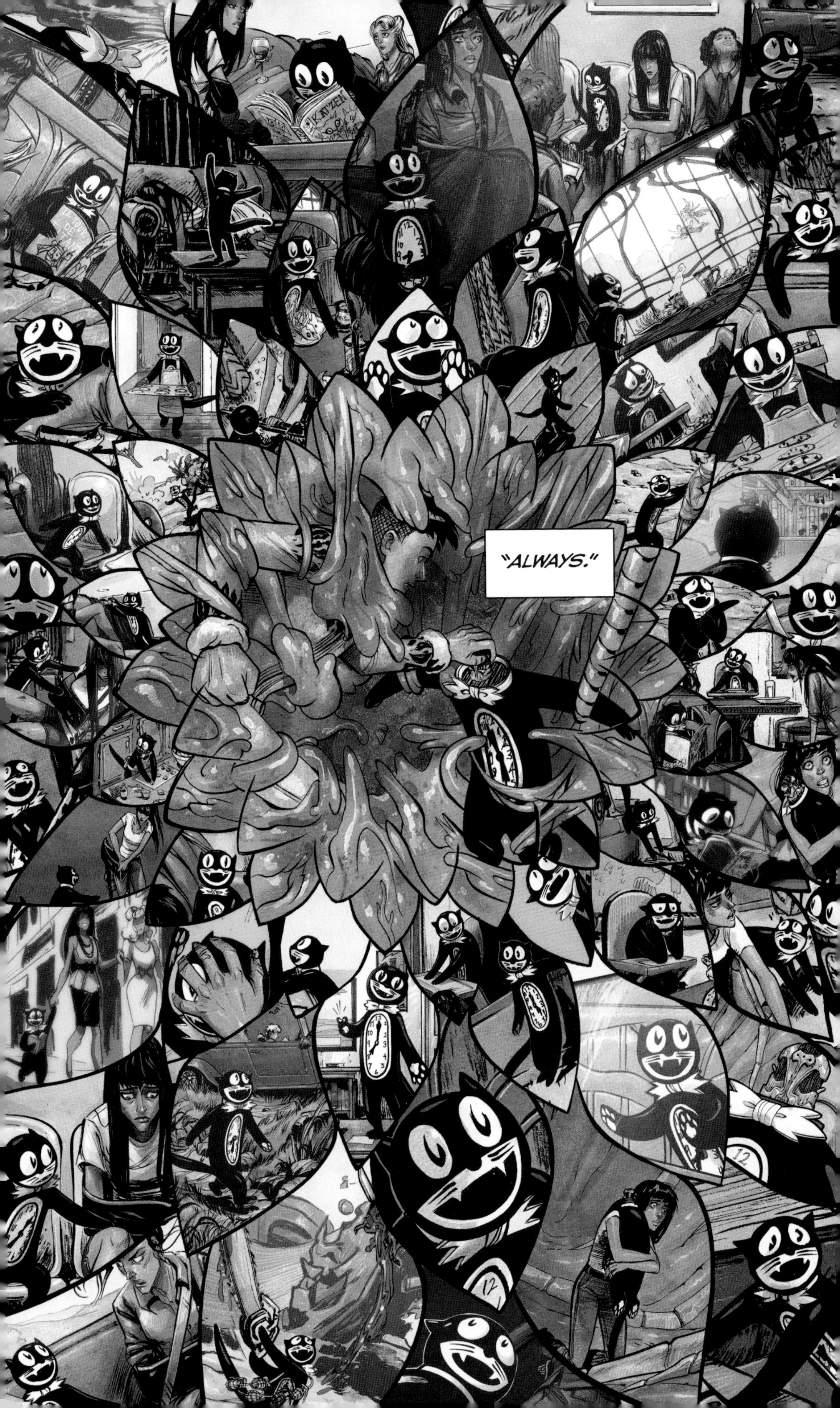
"ALWAYS."

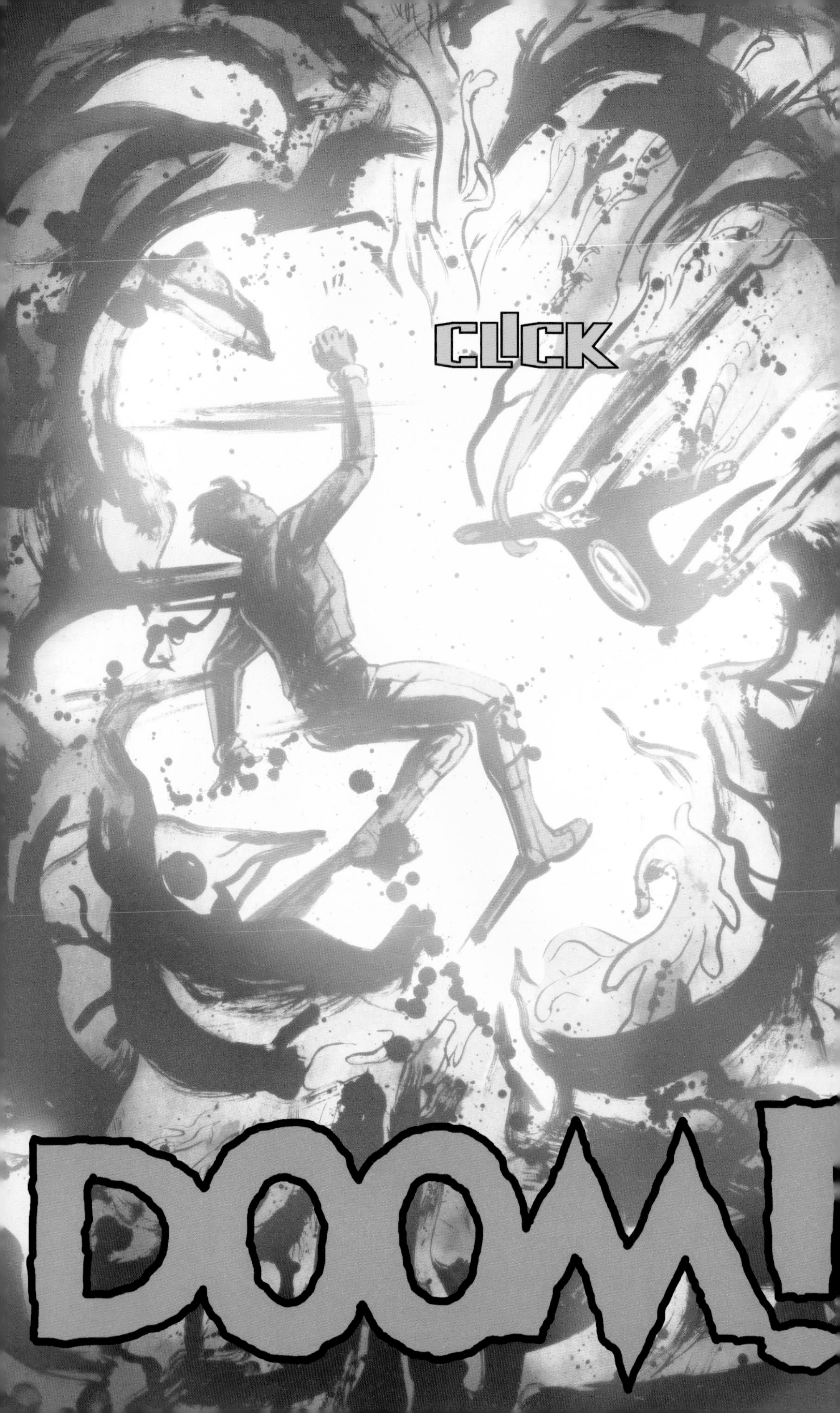
CLICK
DOOM!

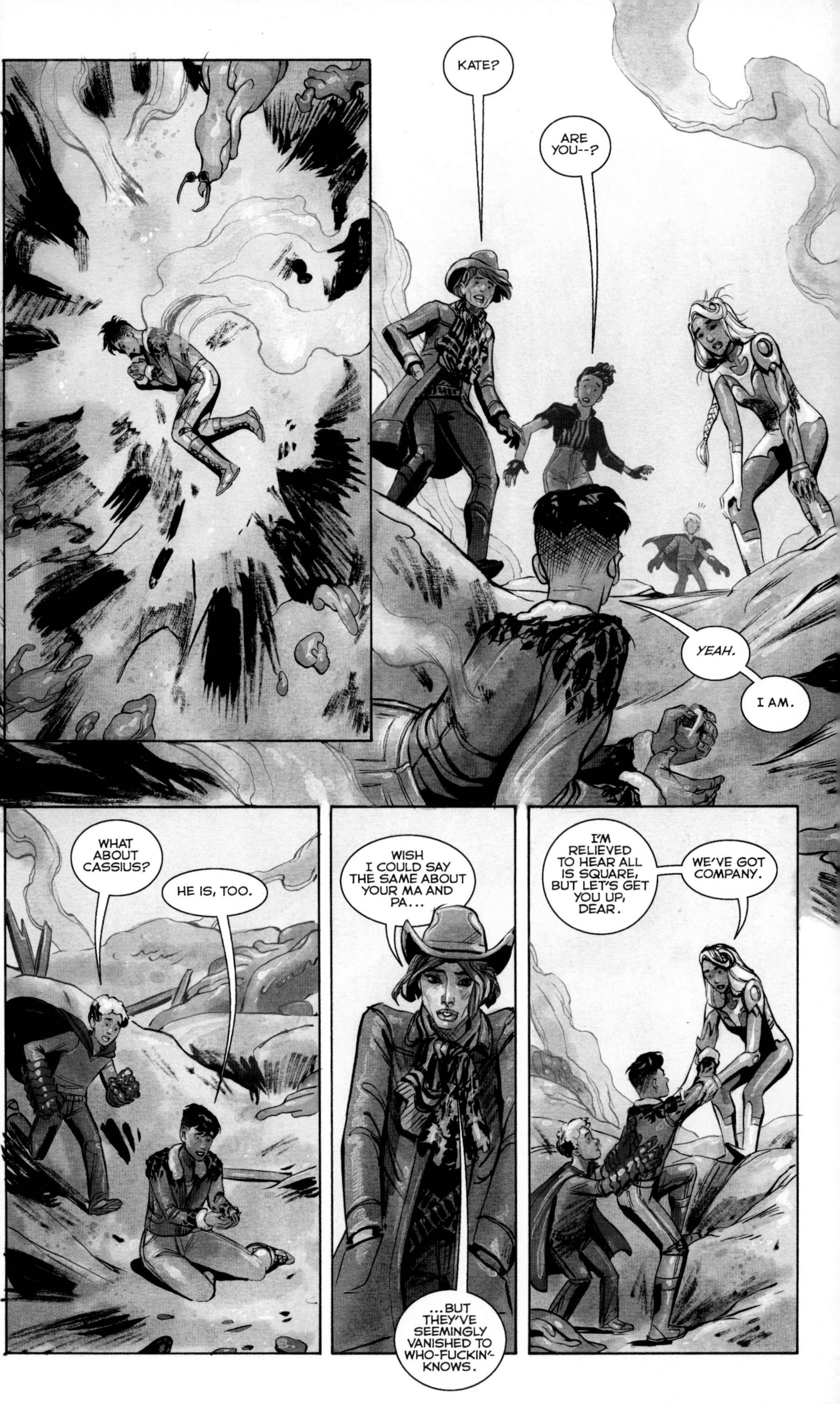
KATE?
ARE YOU--?
YEAH.
I AM.
WHAT ABOUT CASSIUS?
HE IS, TOO.
WISH I COULD SAY THE SAME ABOUT YOUR MA AND PA...
...BUT THEY'VE SEEMINGLY VANISHED TO WHO-FUCKIN'-KNOWS.
I'M RELIEVED TO HEAR ALL IS SQUARE, BUT LET'S GET YOU UP, DEAR.
WE'VE GOT COMPANY.

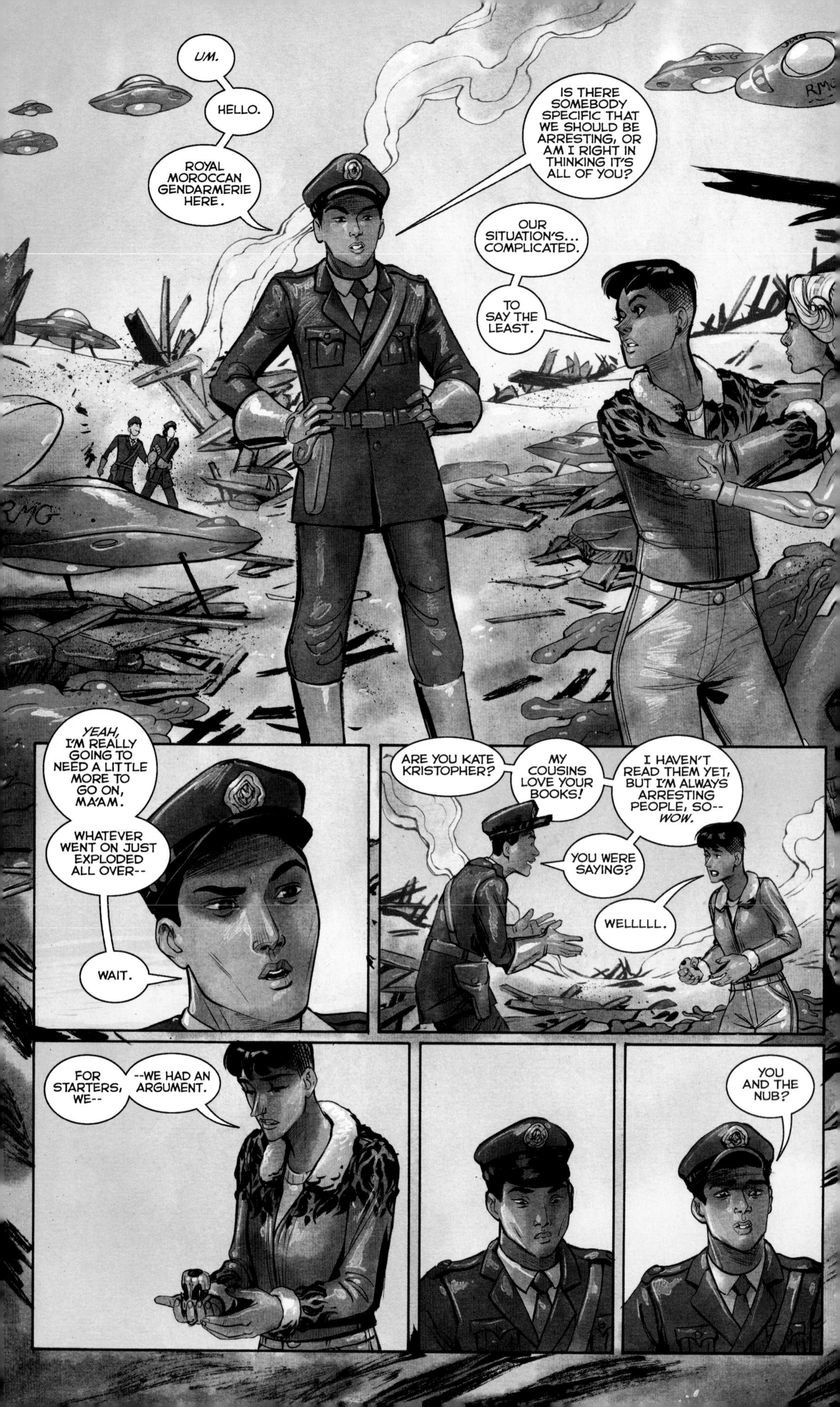
UM.
HELLO.
ROYAL MOROCCAN GENDARMERIE HERE.
IS THERE SOMEBODY SPECIFIC THAT WE SHOULD BE ARRESTING, OR AM I RIGHT IN THINKING IT'S ALL OF YOU?
OUR SITUATION'S... COMPLICATED.
TO SAY THE LEAST.
YEAH, I'M REALLY GOING TO NEED A LITTLE MORE TO GO ON, MA'AM.
WHATEVER WENT ON JUST EXPLODED ALL OVER--
WAIT.
ARE YOU KATE KRISTOPHER?
MY COUSINS LOVE YOUR BOOKS!
I HAVEN'T READ THEM YET, BUT I'M ALWAYS ARRESTING PEOPLE, SO-- WOW.
YOU WERE SAYING?
WELLLLL.
FOR STARTERS, WE--
--WE HAD AN ARGUMENT.
YOU AND THE NUB?

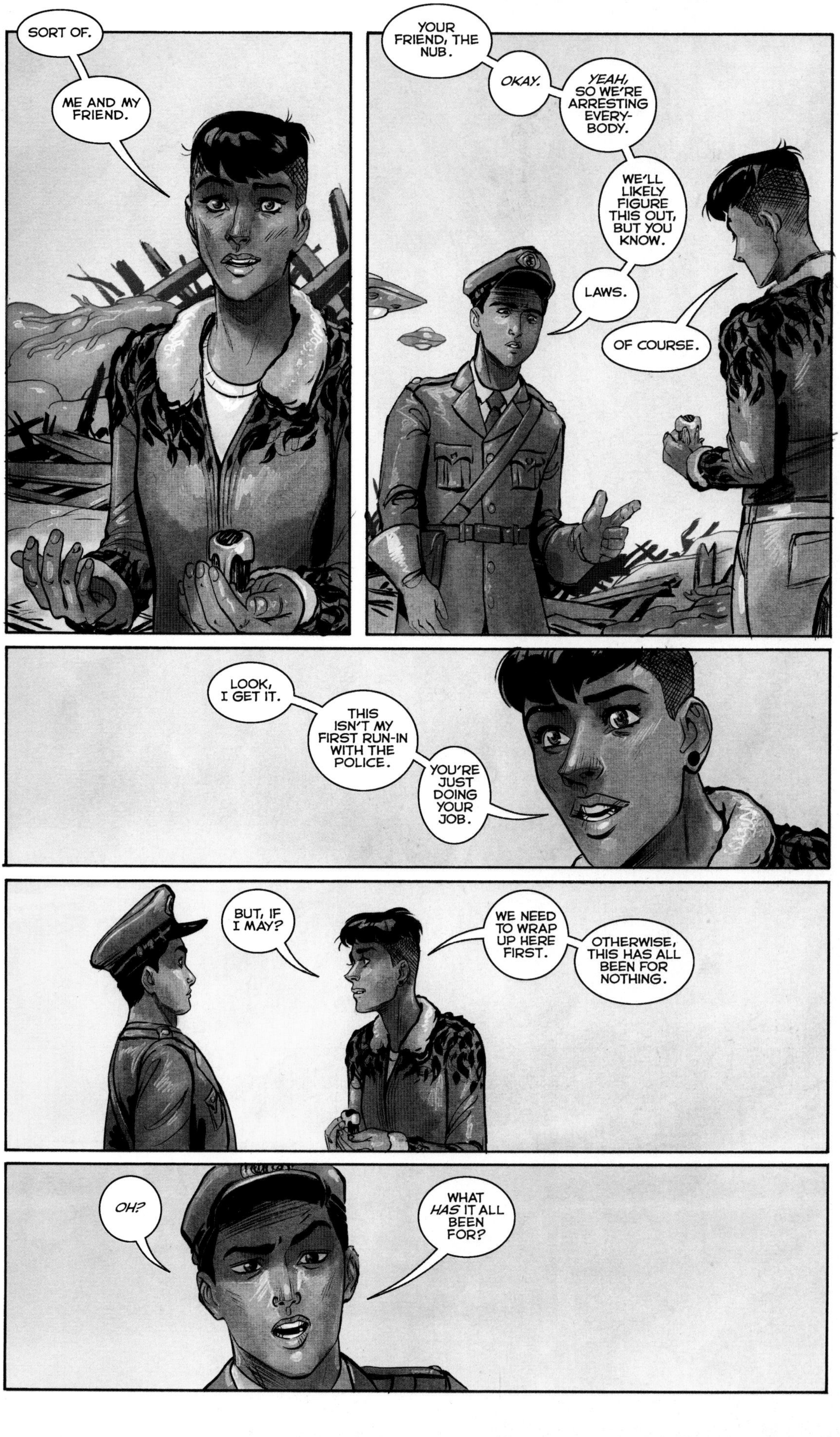
SORT OF.
ME AND MY FRIEND.
YOUR FRIEND, THE NUB.
OKAY.
YEAH, SO WE'RE ARRESTING EVERY-BODY.
WE'LL LIKELY FIGURE THIS OUT, BUT YOU KNOW.
LAWS.
OF COURSE.
LOOK, I GET IT.
THIS ISN'T MY FIRST RUN-IN WITH THE POLICE.
YOU'RE JUST DOING YOUR JOB.
BUT, IF I MAY?
WE NEED TO WRAP UP HERE FIRST.
OTHERWISE, THIS HAS ALL BEEN FOR NOTHING.
OH?
WHAT *HAS* IT ALL BEEN FOR?

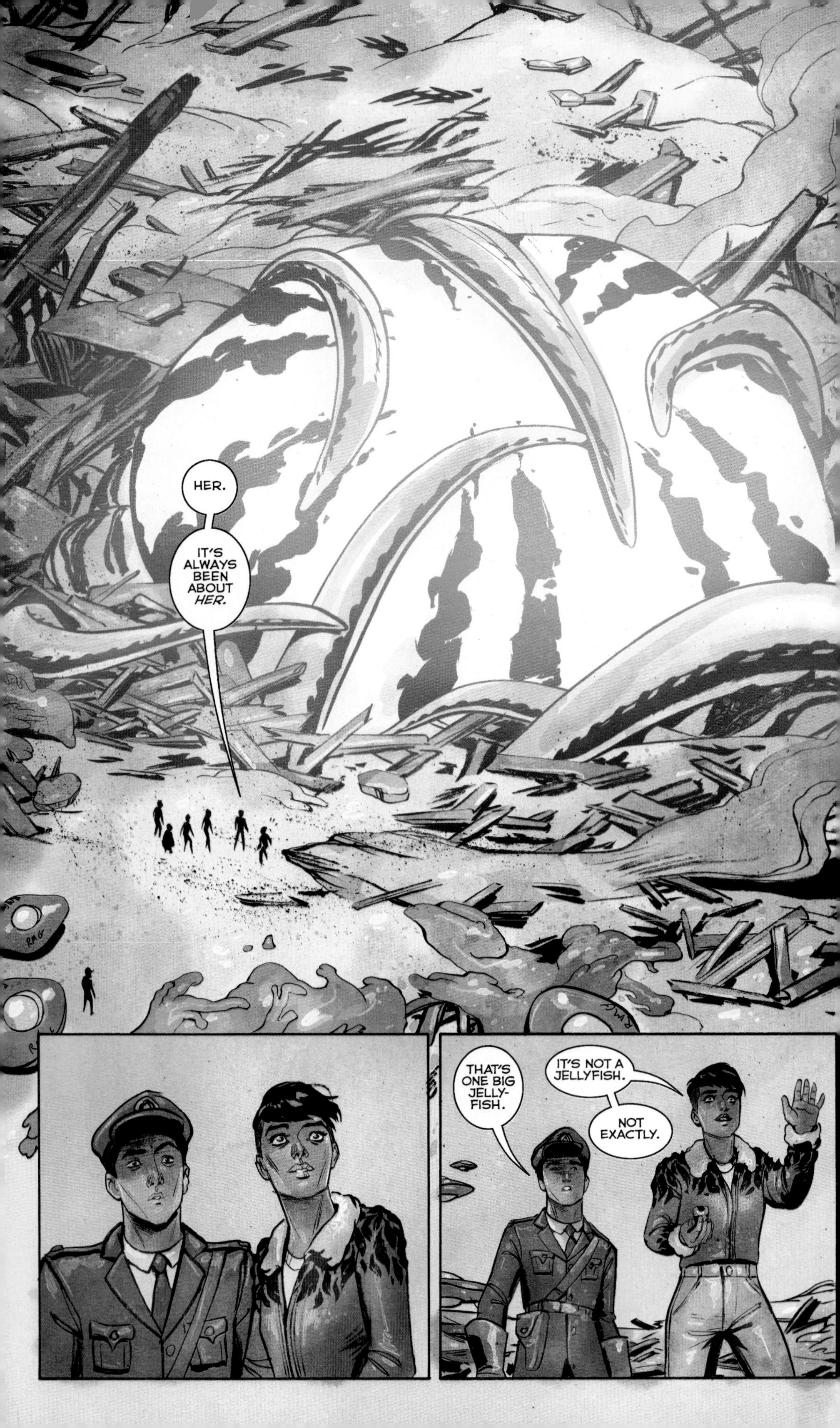
HER.
IT'S ALWAYS BEEN ABOUT *HER.*
THAT'S ONE BIG JELLY-FISH.
IT'S NOT A JELLYFISH.
NOT EXACTLY.

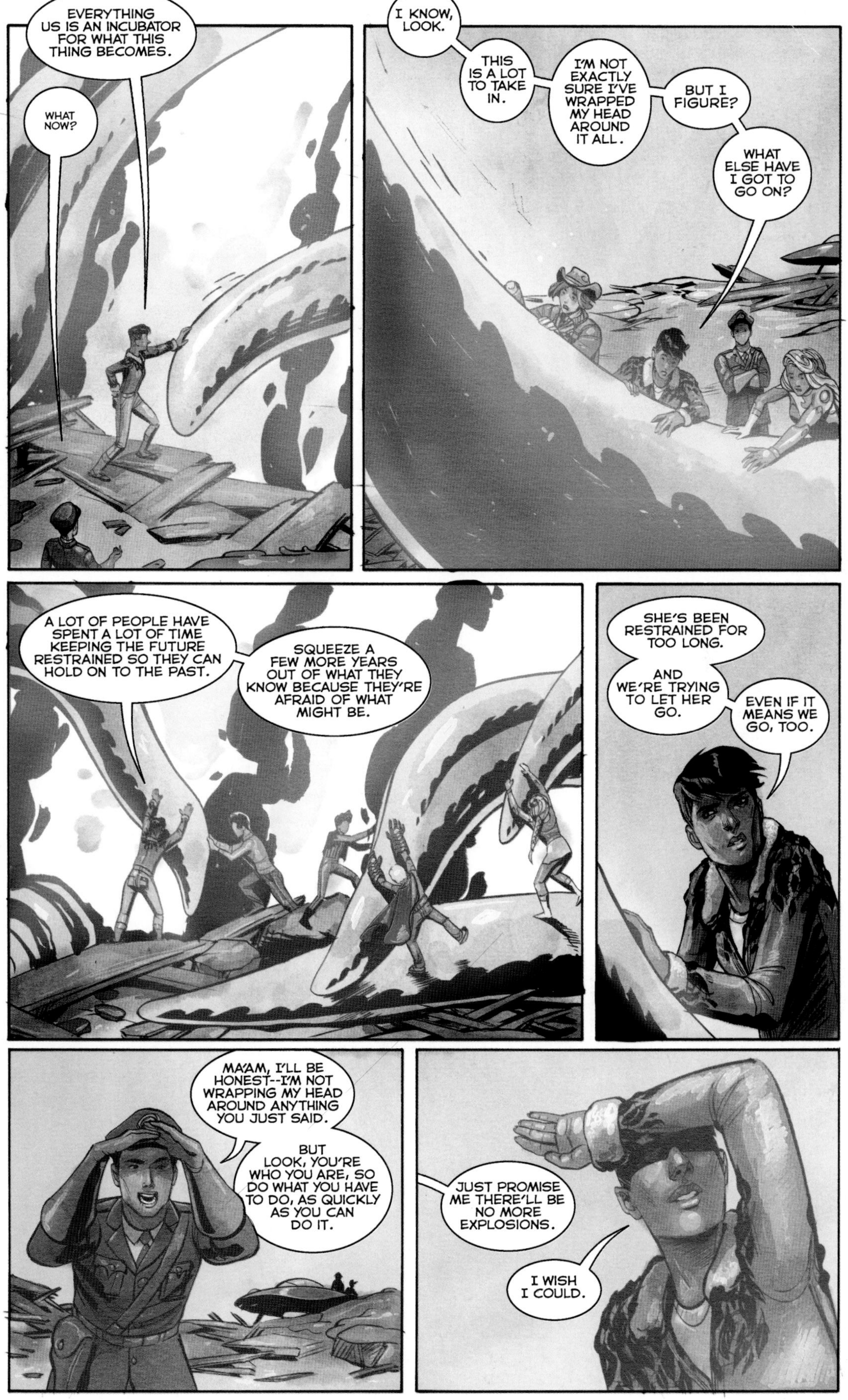
EVERYTHING US IS AN INCUBATOR FOR WHAT THIS THING BECOMES.
WHAT NOW?
I KNOW, LOOK.
THIS IS A LOT TO TAKE IN.
I'M NOT EXACTLY SURE I'VE WRAPPED MY HEAD AROUND IT ALL.
BUT I FIGURE?
WHAT ELSE HAVE I GOT TO GO ON?
A LOT OF PEOPLE HAVE SPENT A LOT OF TIME KEEPING THE FUTURE RESTRAINED SO THEY CAN HOLD ON TO THE PAST.
SQUEEZE A FEW MORE YEARS OUT OF WHAT THEY KNOW BECAUSE THEY'RE AFRAID OF WHAT MIGHT BE.
SHE'S BEEN RESTRAINED FOR TOO LONG.
AND WE'RE TRYING TO LET HER GO.
EVEN IF IT MEANS WE GO, TOO.
MA'AM, I'LL BE HONEST--I'M NOT WRAPPING MY HEAD AROUND ANYTHING YOU JUST SAID.
BUT LOOK, YOU'RE WHO YOU ARE, SO DO WHAT YOU HAVE TO DO, AS QUICKLY AS YOU CAN DO IT.
JUST PROMISE ME THERE'LL BE NO MORE EXPLOSIONS.
I WISH I COULD.

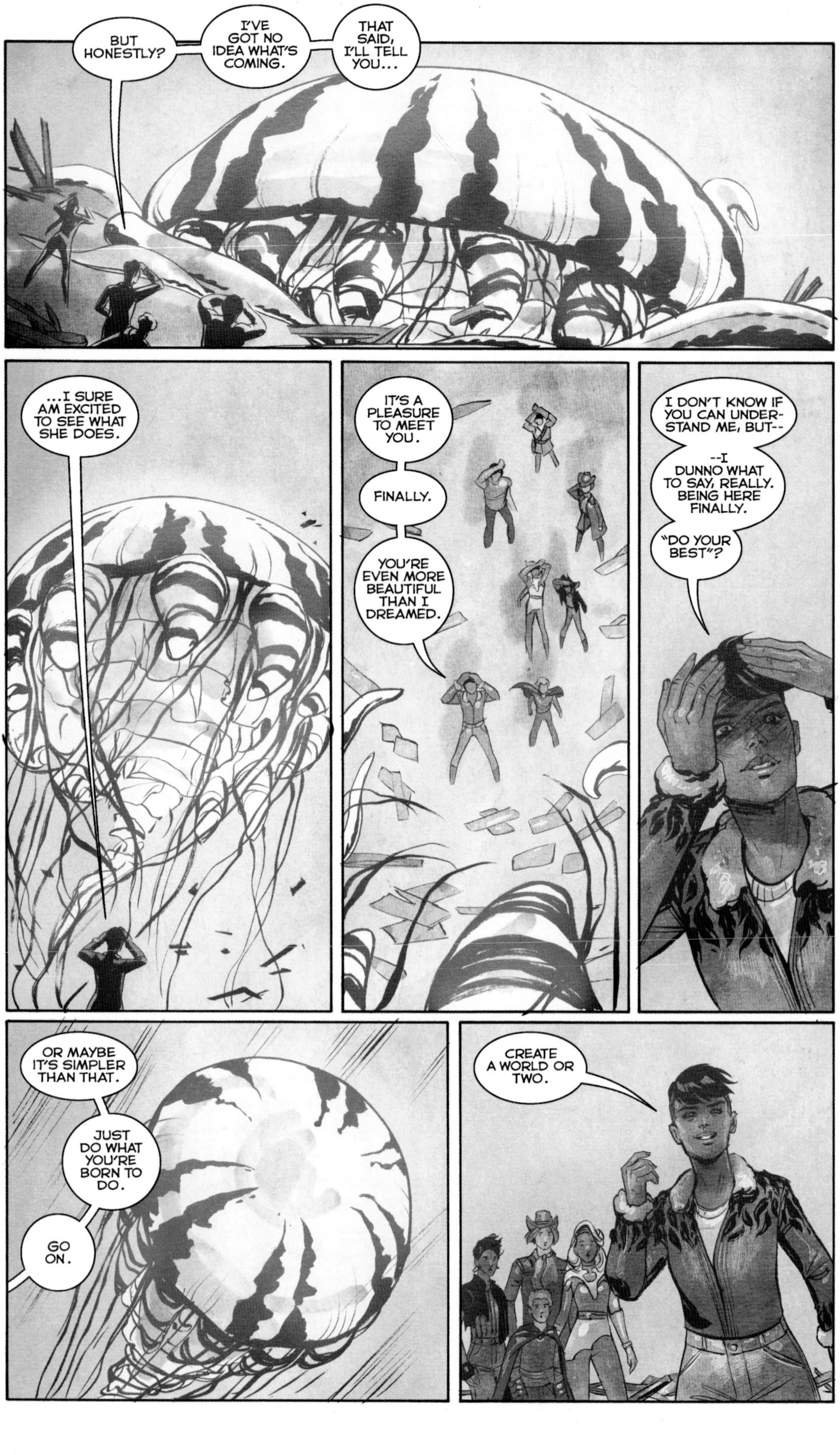
BUT HONESTLY?
I'VE GOT NO IDEA WHAT'S COMING.
THAT SAID, I'LL TELL YOU...
...I SURE AM EXCITED TO SEE WHAT SHE DOES.
IT'S A PLEASURE TO MEET YOU.
FINALLY.
YOU'RE EVEN MORE BEAUTIFUL THAN I DREAMED.
I DON'T KNOW IF YOU CAN UNDER-STAND ME, BUT--
--I DUNNO WHAT TO SAY, REALLY. BEING HERE FINALLY.
"DO YOUR BEST"?
OR MAYBE IT'S SIMPLER THAN THAT.
JUST DO WHAT YOU'RE BORN TO DO.
GO ON.
CREATE A WORLD OR TWO.

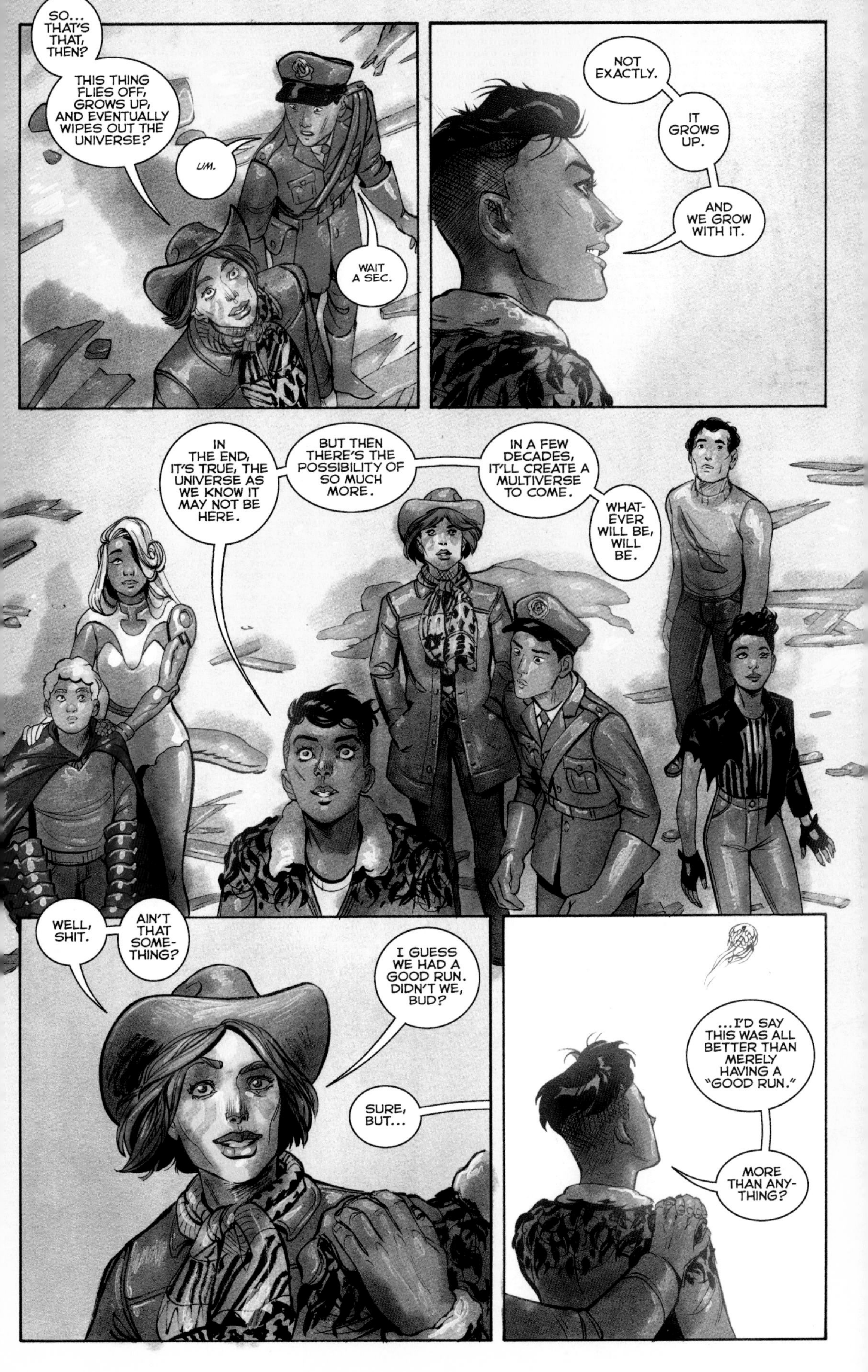
SO... THAT'S THAT, THEN?
THIS THING FLIES OFF, GROWS UP, AND EVENTUALLY WIPES OUT THE UNIVERSE?
UM.
WAIT A SEC.
NOT EXACTLY.
IT GROWS UP.
AND WE GROW WITH IT.
IN THE END, IT'S TRUE, THE UNIVERSE AS WE KNOW IT MAY NOT BE HERE.
BUT THEN THERE'S THE POSSIBILITY OF SO MUCH MORE.
IN A FEW DECADES, IT'LL CREATE A MULTIVERSE TO COME.
WHAT-EVER WILL BE, WILL BE.
WELL, SHIT.
AIN'T THAT SOME-THING?
I GUESS WE HAD A GOOD RUN. DIDN'T WE, BUD?
SURE, BUT...
...I'D SAY THIS WAS ALL BETTER THAN MERELY HAVING A "GOOD RUN."
MORE THAN ANY-THING?

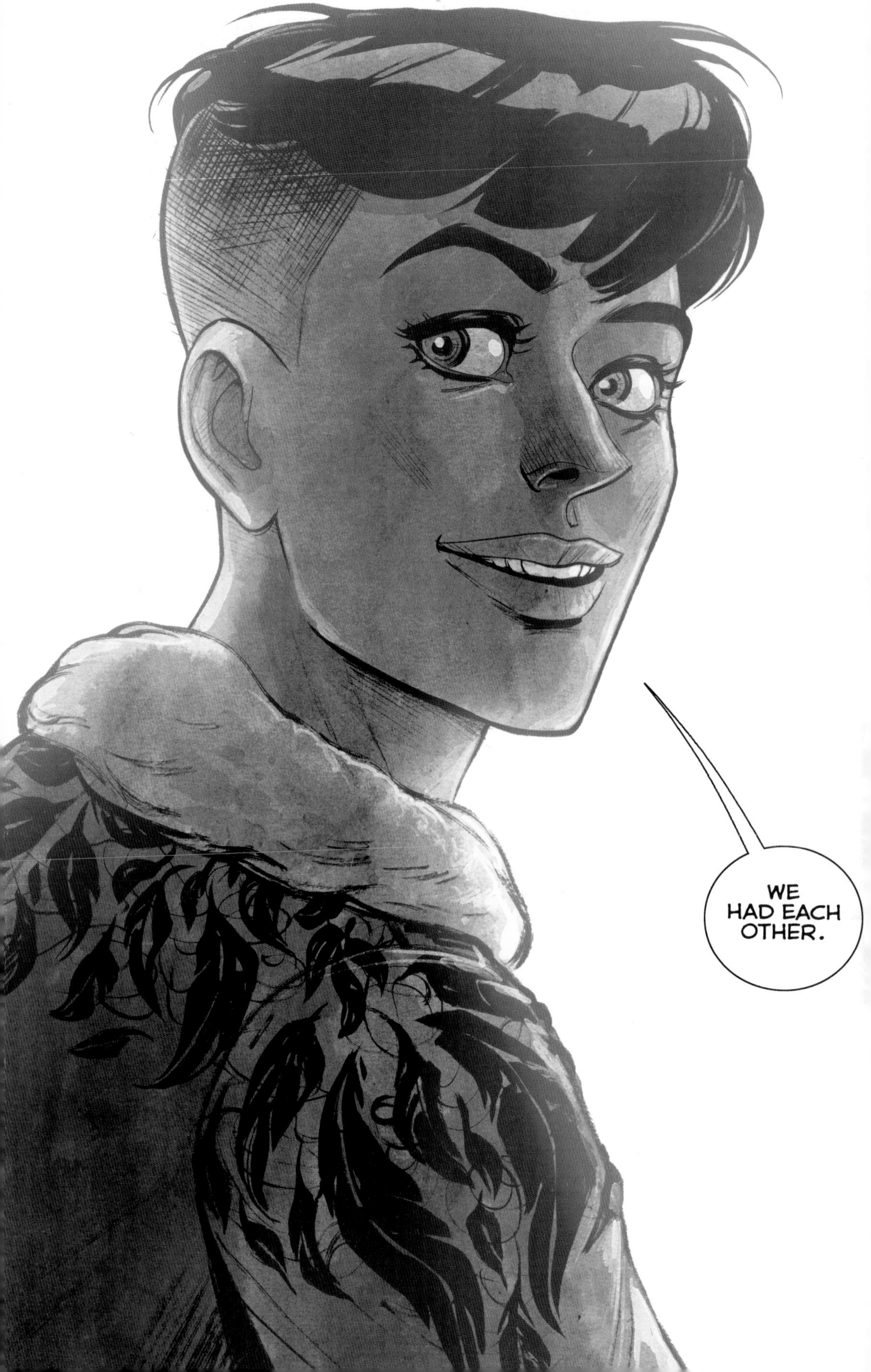
WE HAD EACH OTHER.

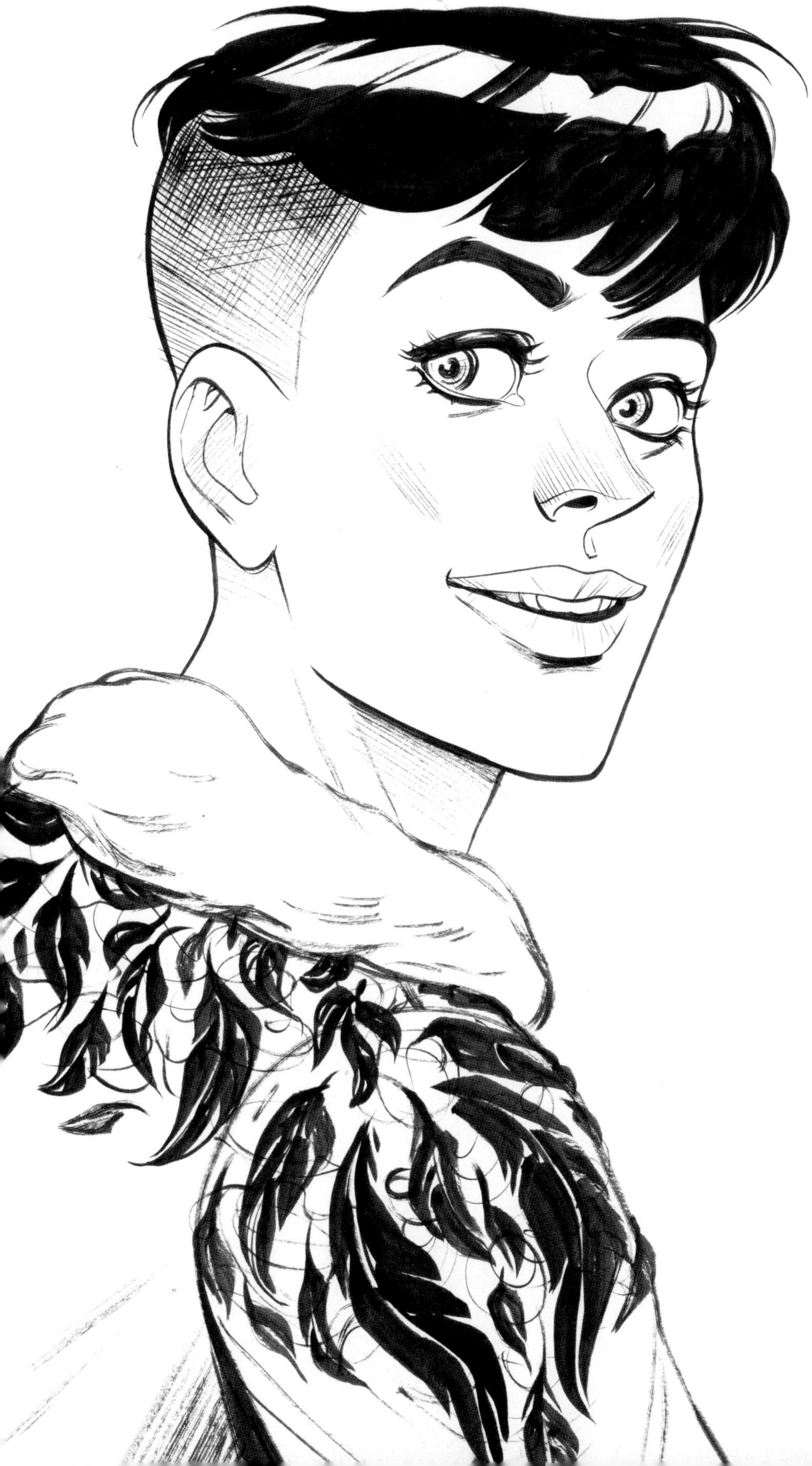

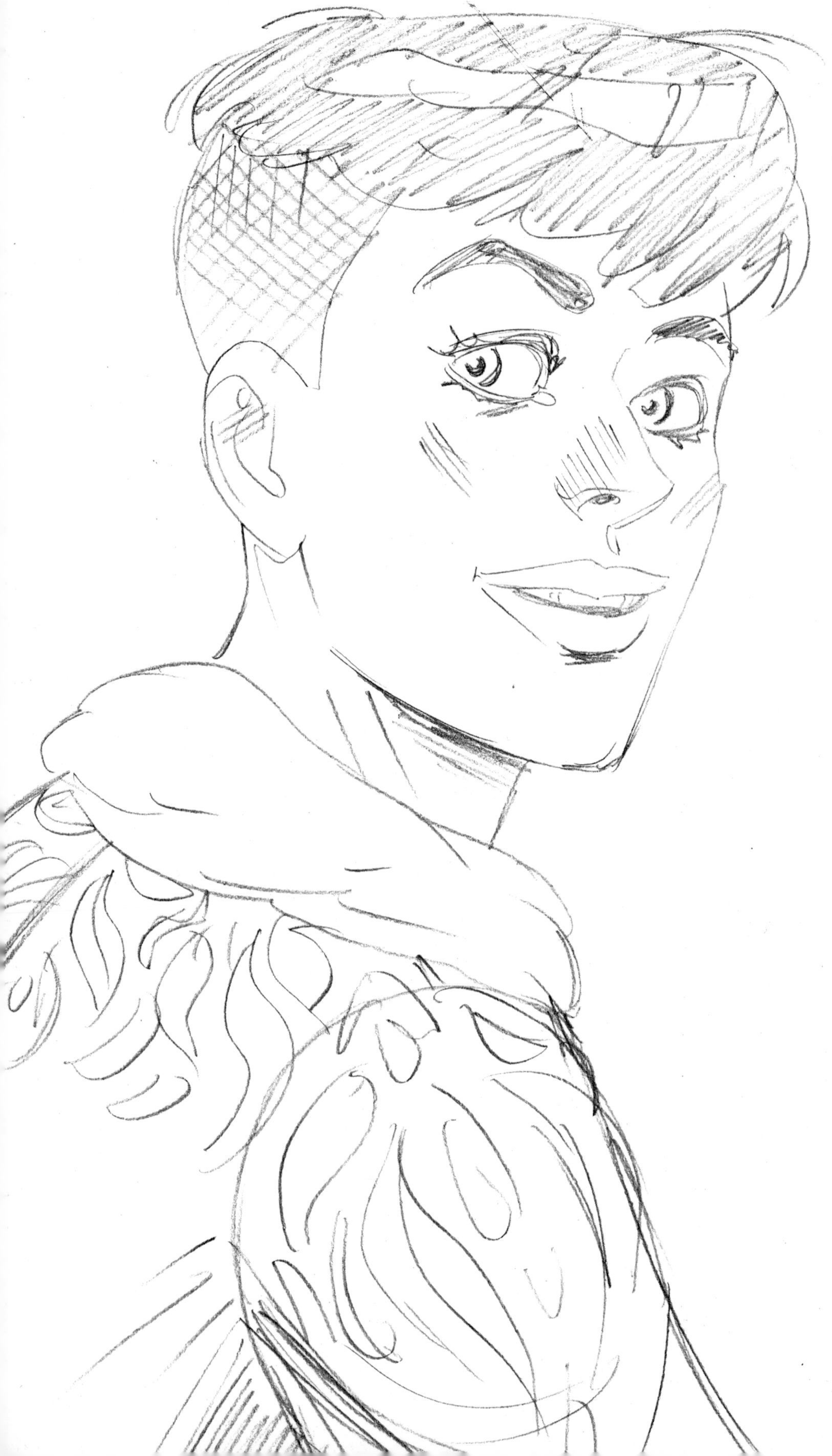

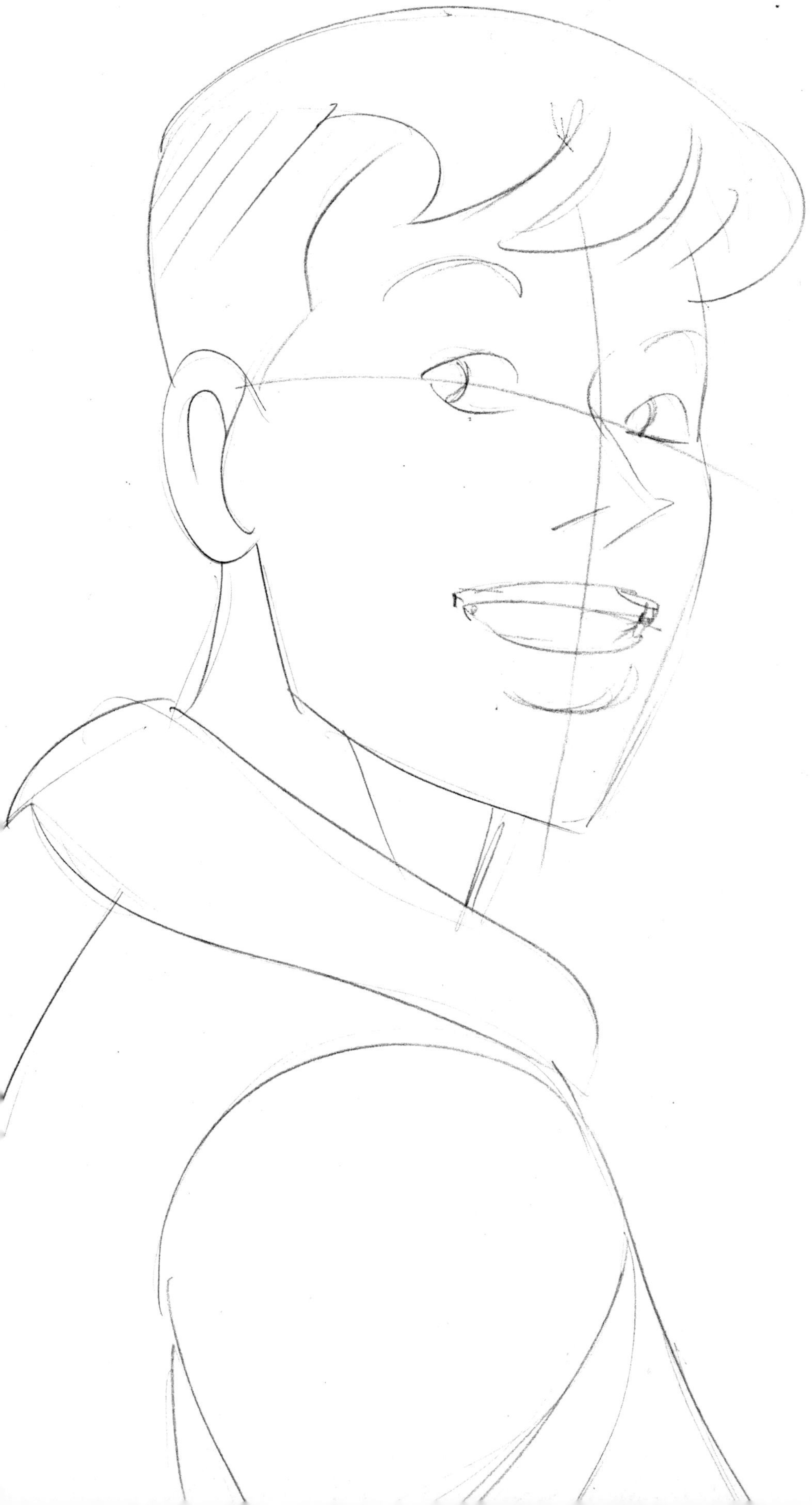

CHAPTER 29

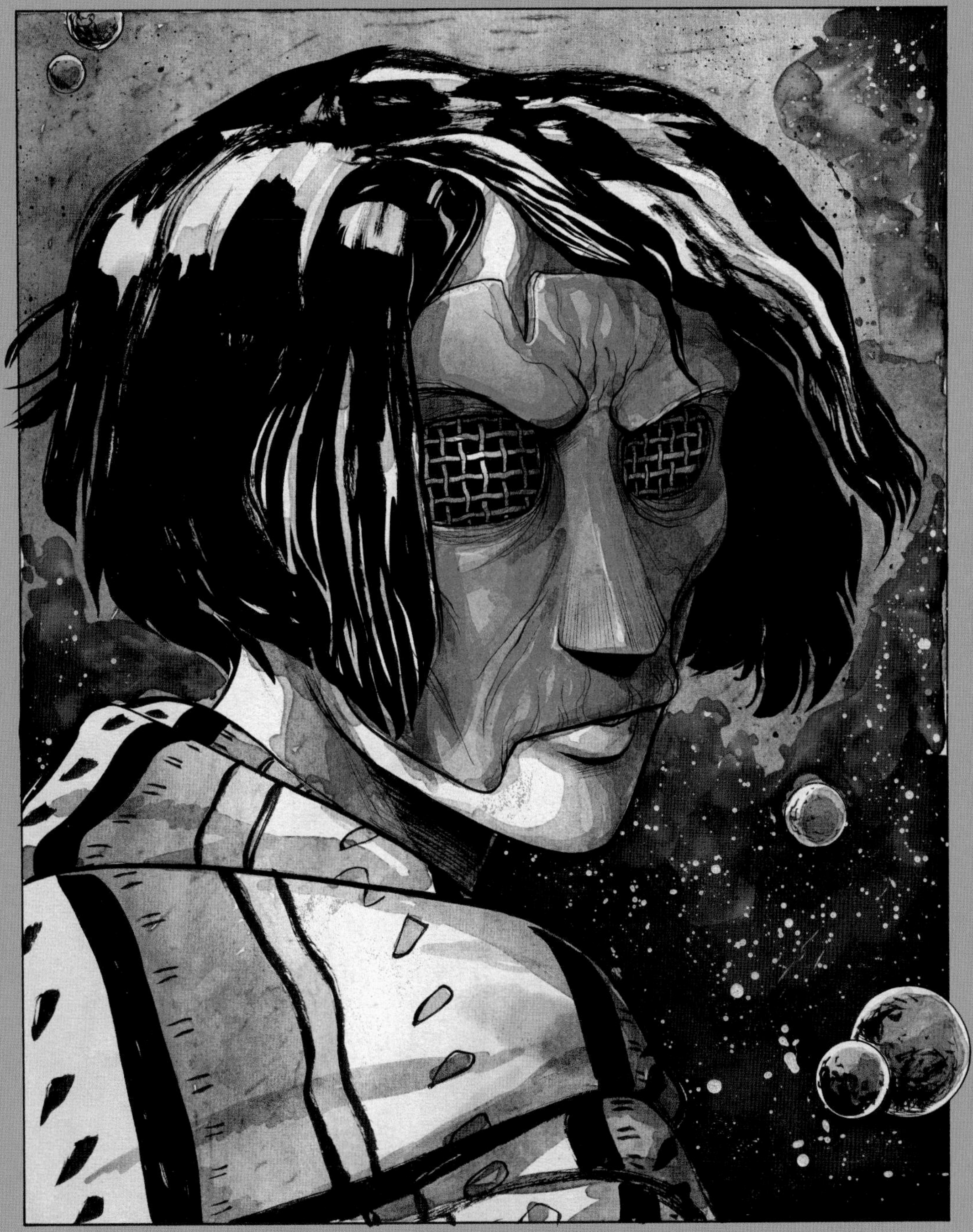

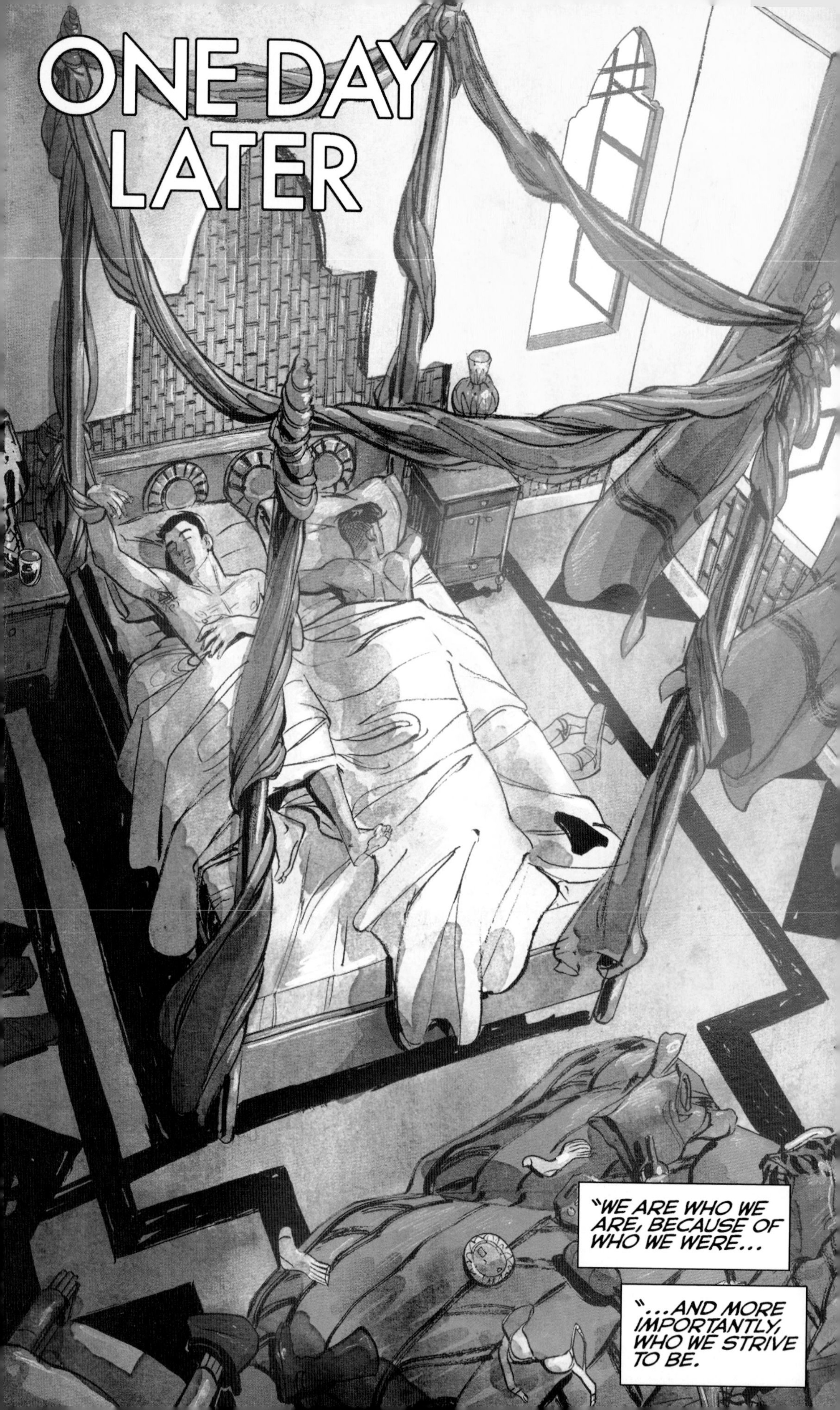
ONE DAY LATER
"WE ARE WHO WE ARE, BECAUSE OF WHO WE WERE...
"...AND MORE IMPORTANTLY, WHO WE STRIVE TO BE.

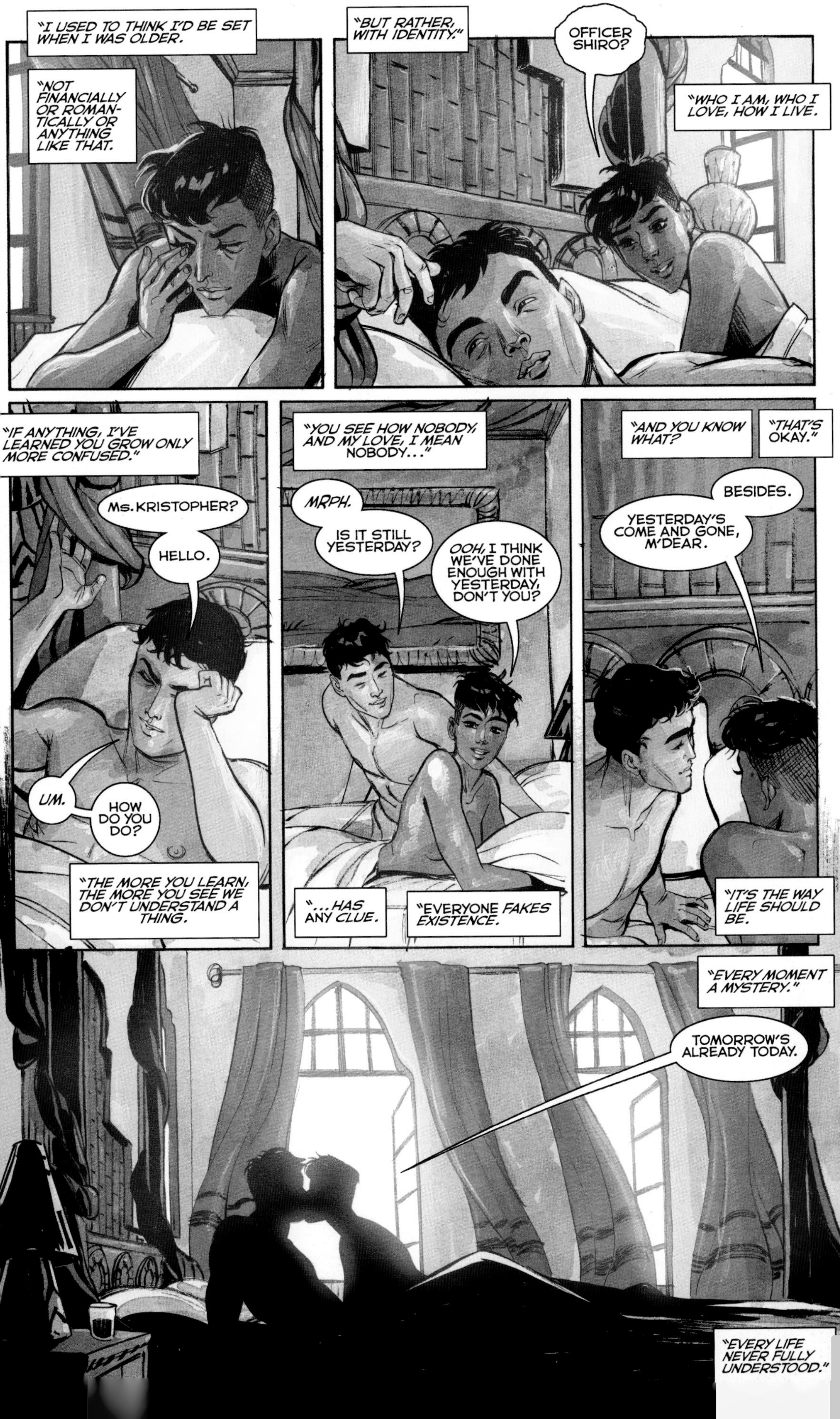
"I USED TO THINK I'D BE SET WHEN I WAS OLDER.
"NOT FINANCIALLY OR ROMANTICALLY OR ANYTHING LIKE THAT.
"BUT RATHER, WITH IDENTITY."
OFFICER SHIRO?
"WHO I AM, WHO I LOVE, HOW I LIVE.
"IF ANYTHING, I'VE LEARNED YOU GROW ONLY MORE CONFUSED."
Ms. KRISTOPHER?
HELLO.
UM.
HOW DO YOU DO?
"THE MORE YOU LEARN, THE MORE YOU SEE WE DON'T UNDERSTAND A THING.
"YOU SEE HOW NOBODY, AND MY LOVE, I MEAN NOBODY..."
MRPH.
IS IT STILL YESTERDAY?
OOH, I THINK WE'VE DONE ENOUGH WITH YESTERDAY, DON'T YOU?
"...HAS ANY CLUE.
"EVERYONE FAKES EXISTENCE.
"AND YOU KNOW WHAT?
"THAT'S OKAY."
BESIDES.
YESTERDAY'S COME AND GONE, M'DEAR.
"IT'S THE WAY LIFE SHOULD BE.
"EVERY MOMENT A MYSTERY."
TOMORROW'S ALREADY TODAY.
"EVERY LIFE NEVER FULLY UNDERSTOOD."

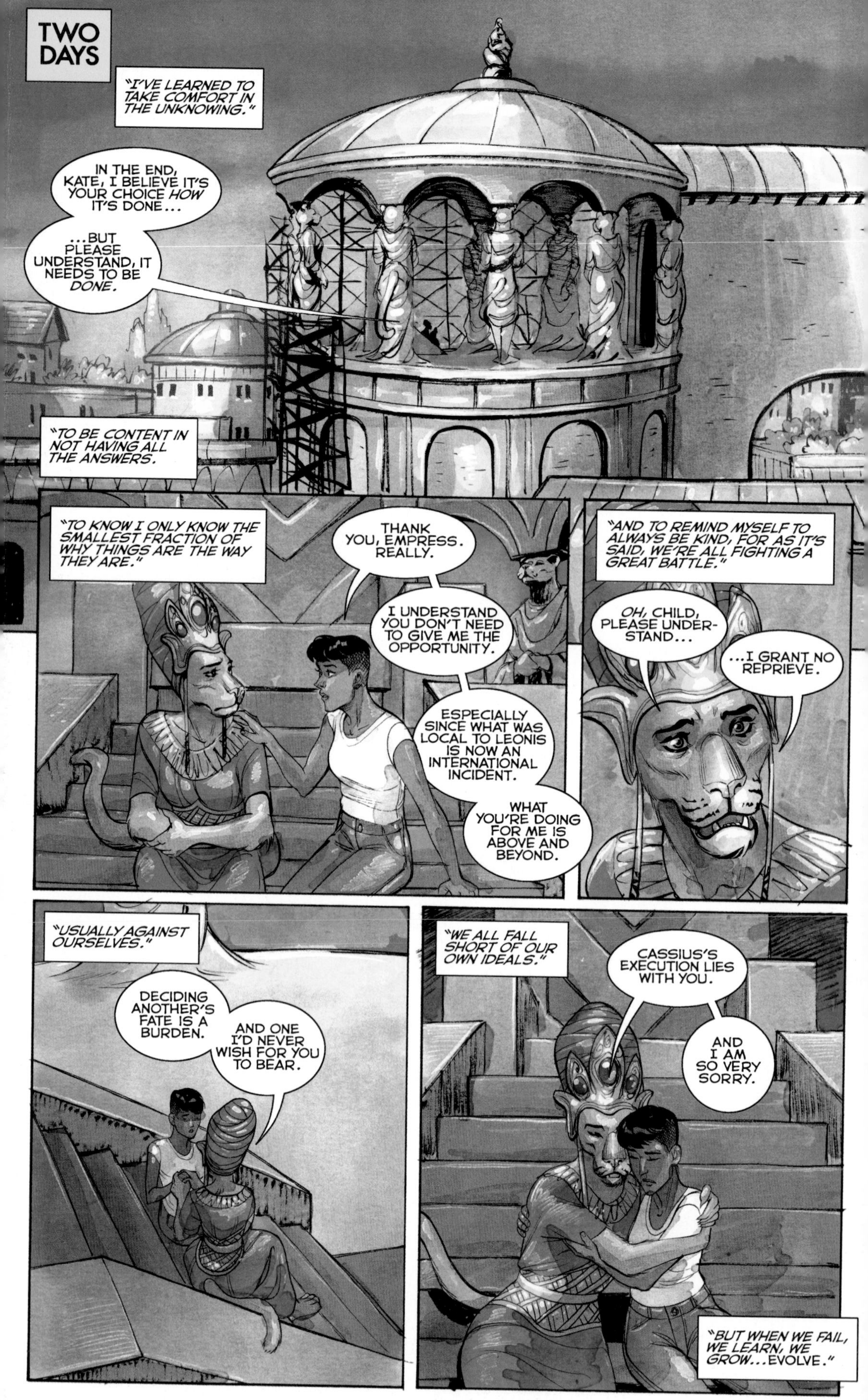

TWO DAYS
"I'VE LEARNED TO TAKE COMFORT IN THE UNKNOWING."
IN THE END, KATE, I BELIEVE IT'S YOUR CHOICE HOW IT'S DONE...
...BUT PLEASE UNDERSTAND, IT NEEDS TO BE DONE.
"TO BE CONTENT IN NOT HAVING ALL THE ANSWERS.
"TO KNOW I ONLY KNOW THE SMALLEST FRACTION OF WHY THINGS ARE THE WAY THEY ARE."
THANK YOU, EMPRESS. REALLY.
I UNDERSTAND YOU DON'T NEED TO GIVE ME THE OPPORTUNITY.
ESPECIALLY SINCE WHAT WAS LOCAL TO LEONIS IS NOW AN INTERNATIONAL INCIDENT.
WHAT YOU'RE DOING FOR ME IS ABOVE AND BEYOND.
"AND TO REMIND MYSELF TO ALWAYS BE KIND, FOR AS IT'S SAID, WE'RE ALL FIGHTING A GREAT BATTLE."
OH, CHILD, PLEASE UNDERSTAND...
...I GRANT NO REPRIEVE.
"USUALLY AGAINST OURSELVES."
DECIDING ANOTHER'S FATE IS A BURDEN.
AND ONE I'D NEVER WISH FOR YOU TO BEAR.
"WE ALL FALL SHORT OF OUR OWN IDEALS."
CASSIUS'S EXECUTION LIES WITH YOU.
AND I AM SO VERY SORRY.
"BUT WHEN WE FAIL, WE LEARN, WE GROW...EVOLVE."

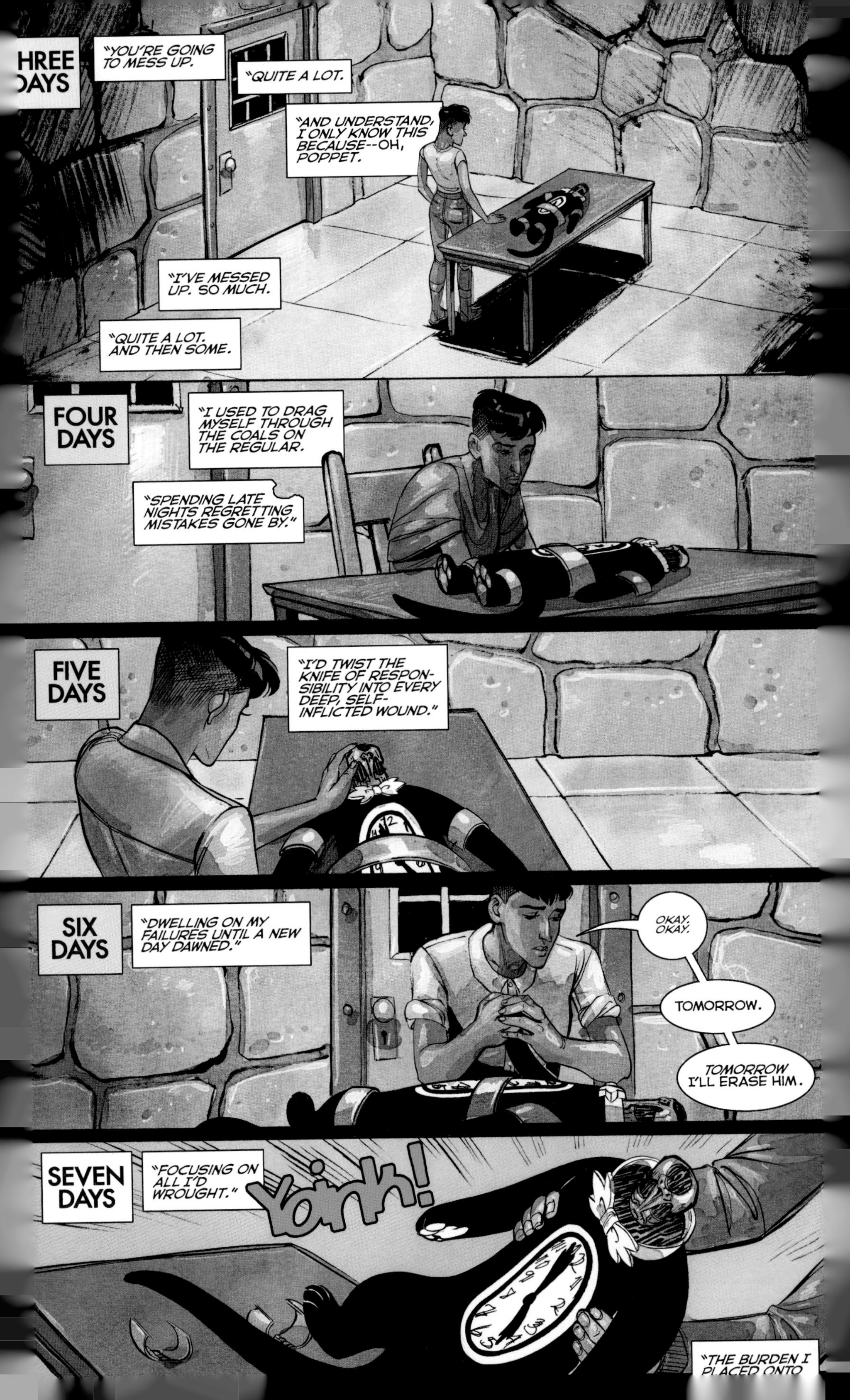

HREE DAYS
"YOU'RE GOING TO MESS UP.
"QUITE A LOT.
"AND UNDERSTAND, I ONLY KNOW THIS BECAUSE--OH, POPPET.
"I'VE MESSED UP. SO MUCH.
"QUITE A LOT. AND THEN SOME.
FOUR DAYS
"I USED TO DRAG MYSELF THROUGH THE COALS ON THE REGULAR.
"SPENDING LATE NIGHTS REGRETTING MISTAKES GONE BY."
FIVE DAYS
"I'D TWIST THE KNIFE OF RESPON-SIBILITY INTO EVERY DEEP, SELF-INFLICTED WOUND."
SIX DAYS
"DWELLING ON MY FAILURES UNTIL A NEW DAY DAWNED."
OKAY. OKAY.
TOMORROW.
TOMORROW I'LL ERASE HIM.
SEVEN DAYS
"FOCUSING ON ALL I'D WROUGHT."
Yoink!
"THE BURDEN I PLACED ONTO

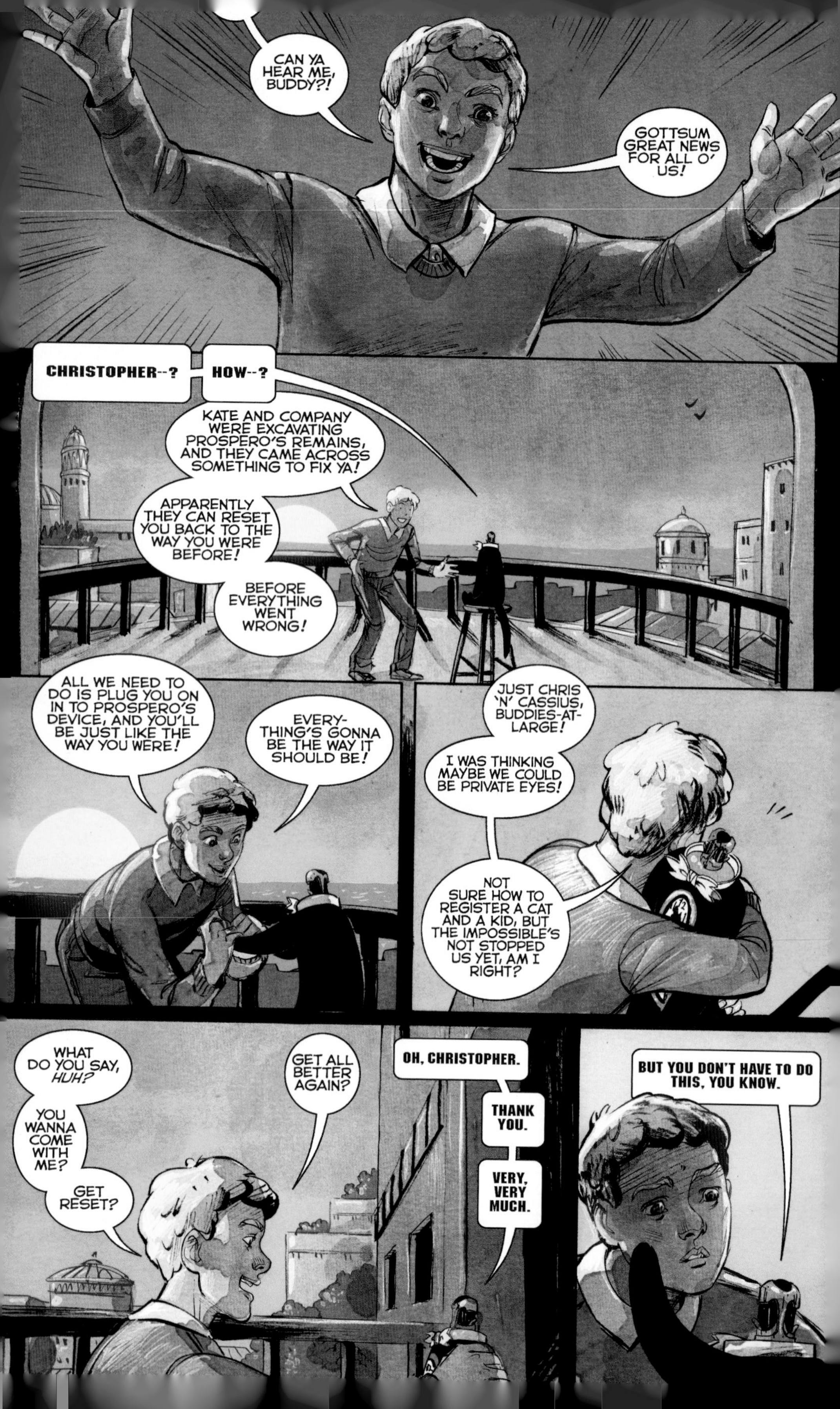
CAN YA HEAR ME, BUDDY?!
GOTTSUM GREAT NEWS FOR ALL O' US!
CHRISTOPHER--?
HOW--?
KATE AND COMPANY WERE EXCAVATING PROSPERO'S REMAINS, AND THEY CAME ACROSS SOMETHING TO FIX YA!
APPARENTLY THEY CAN RESET YOU BACK TO THE WAY YOU WERE BEFORE!
BEFORE EVERYTHING WENT WRONG!
ALL WE NEED TO DO IS PLUG YOU ON IN TO PROSPERO'S DEVICE, AND YOU'LL BE JUST LIKE THE WAY YOU WERE!
EVERY-THING'S GONNA BE THE WAY IT SHOULD BE!
JUST CHRIS 'N' CASSIUS, BUDDIES-AT-LARGE!
I WAS THINKING MAYBE WE COULD BE PRIVATE EYES!
NOT SURE HOW TO REGISTER A CAT AND A KID, BUT THE IMPOSSIBLE'S NOT STOPPED US YET, AM I RIGHT?
WHAT DO YOU SAY, HUH?
YOU WANNA COME WITH ME?
GET RESET?
GET ALL BETTER AGAIN?
OH, CHRISTOPHER.
THANK YOU.
VERY, VERY MUCH.
BUT YOU DON'T HAVE TO DO THIS, YOU KNOW.

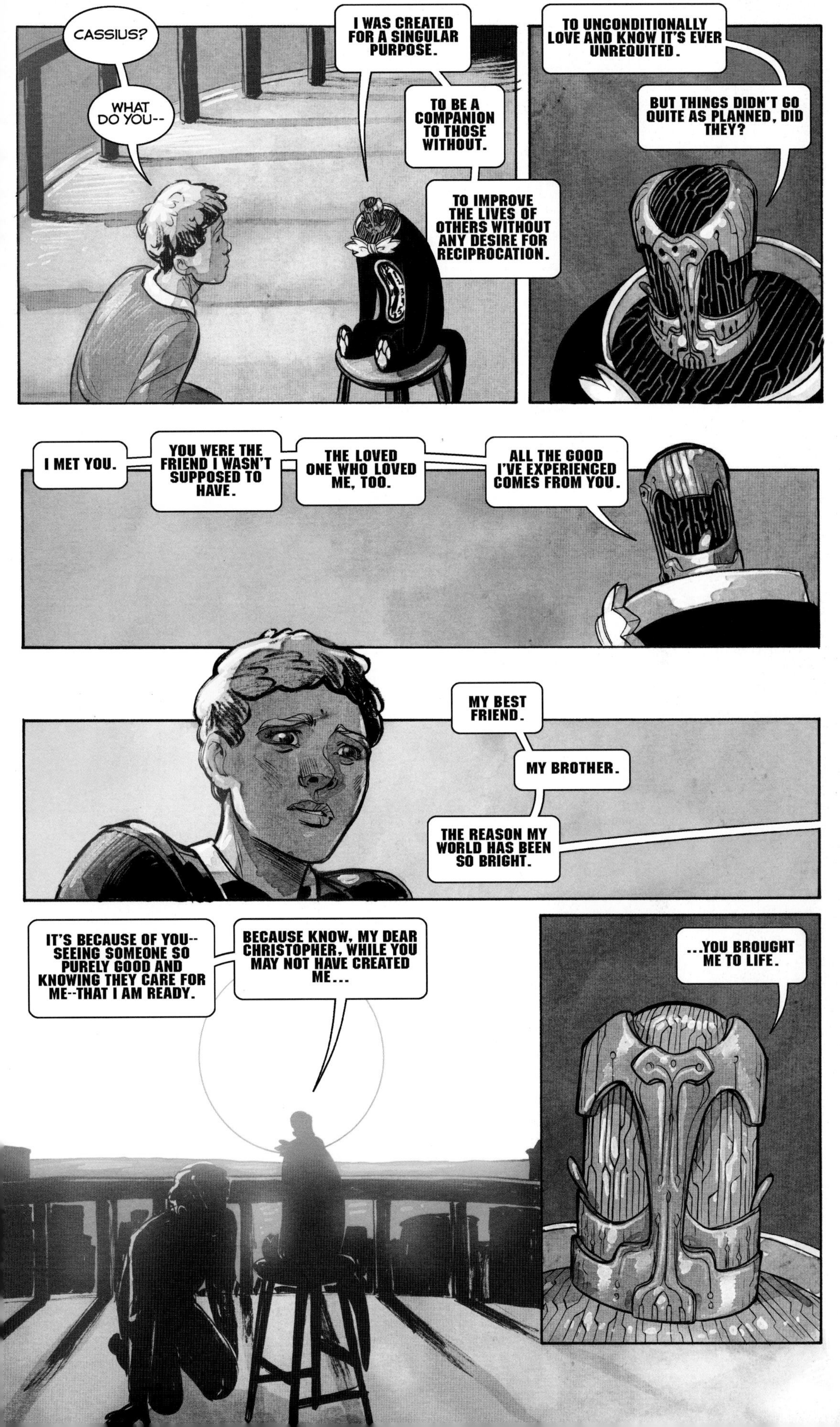
CASSIUS?
WHAT DO YOU--
I WAS CREATED FOR A SINGULAR PURPOSE.
TO BE A COMPANION TO THOSE WITHOUT.
TO IMPROVE THE LIVES OF OTHERS WITHOUT ANY DESIRE FOR RECIPROCATION.
TO UNCONDITIONALLY LOVE AND KNOW IT'S EVER UNREQUITED.
BUT THINGS DIDN'T GO QUITE AS PLANNED, DID THEY?
I MET YOU.
YOU WERE THE FRIEND I WASN'T SUPPOSED TO HAVE.
THE LOVED ONE WHO LOVED ME, TOO.
ALL THE GOOD I'VE EXPERIENCED COMES FROM YOU.
MY BEST FRIEND.
MY BROTHER.
THE REASON MY WORLD HAS BEEN SO BRIGHT.
IT'S BECAUSE OF YOU--SEEING SOMEONE SO PURELY GOOD AND KNOWING THEY CARE FOR ME--THAT I AM READY.
BECAUSE KNOW, MY DEAR CHRISTOPHER, WHILE YOU MAY NOT HAVE CREATED ME...
...YOU BROUGHT ME TO LIFE.

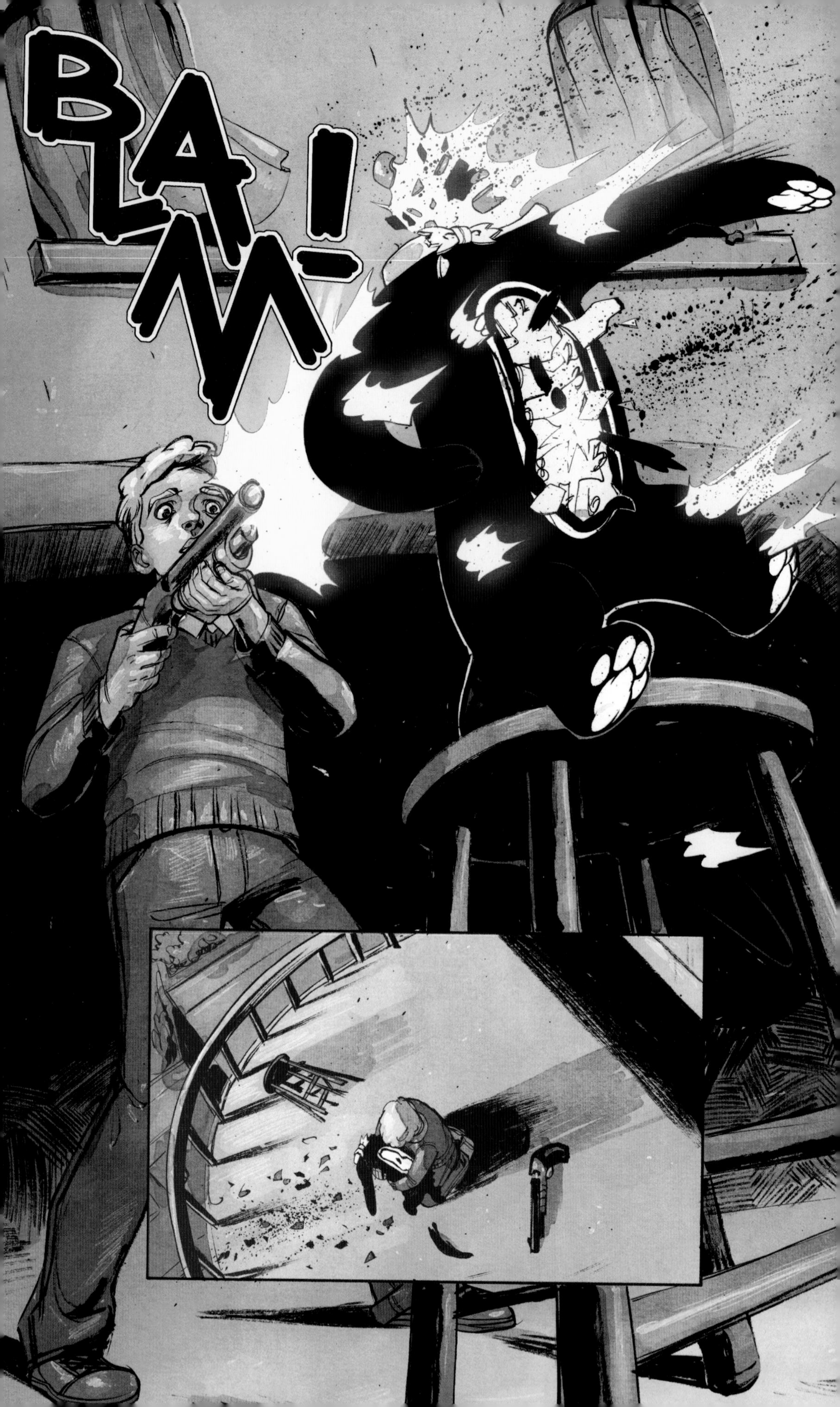
BLAM!

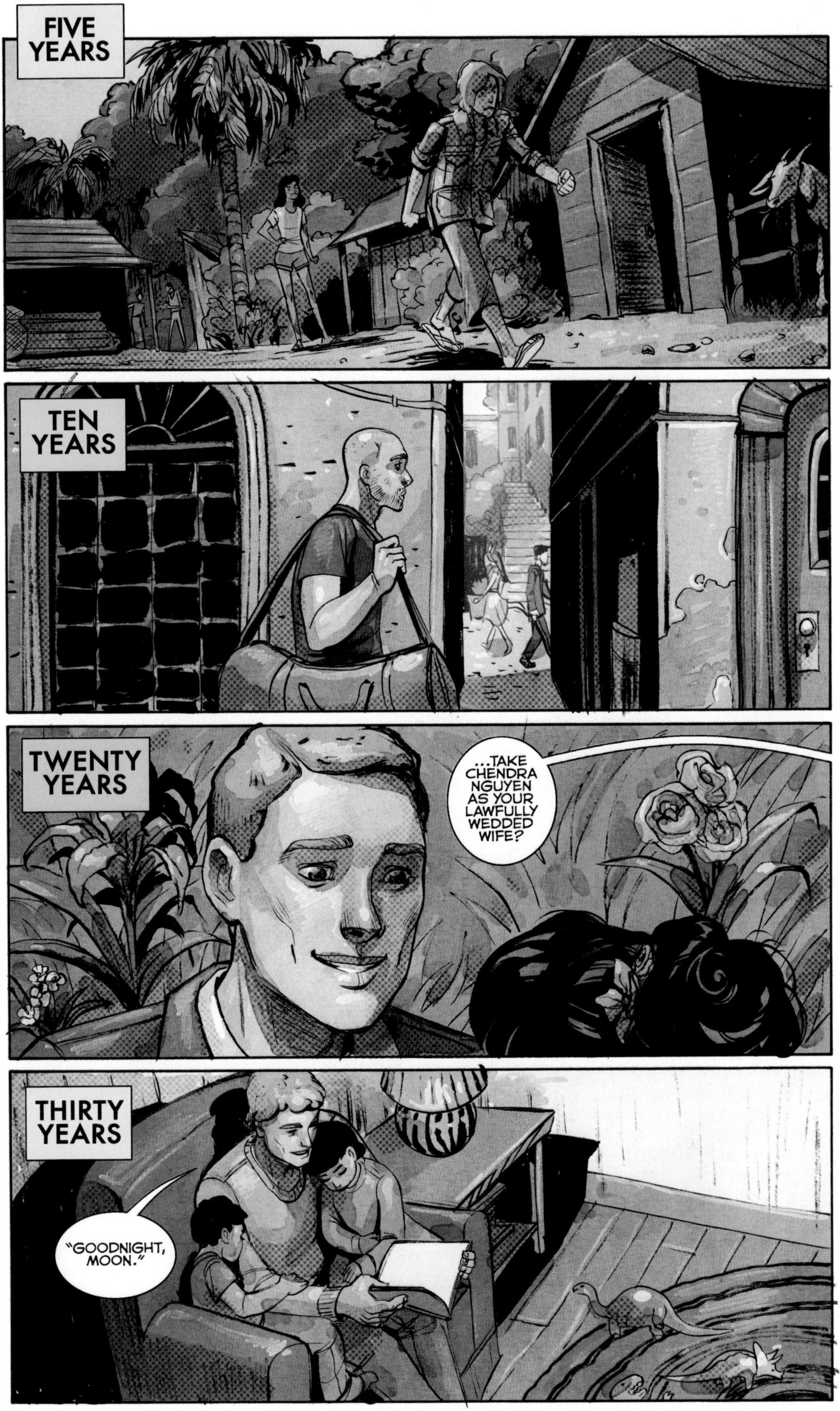
FIVE YEARS
TEN YEARS
TWENTY YEARS
...TAKE CHENDRA NGUYEN AS YOUR LAWFULLY WEDDED WIFE?
THIRTY YEARS
"GOODNIGHT, MOON."

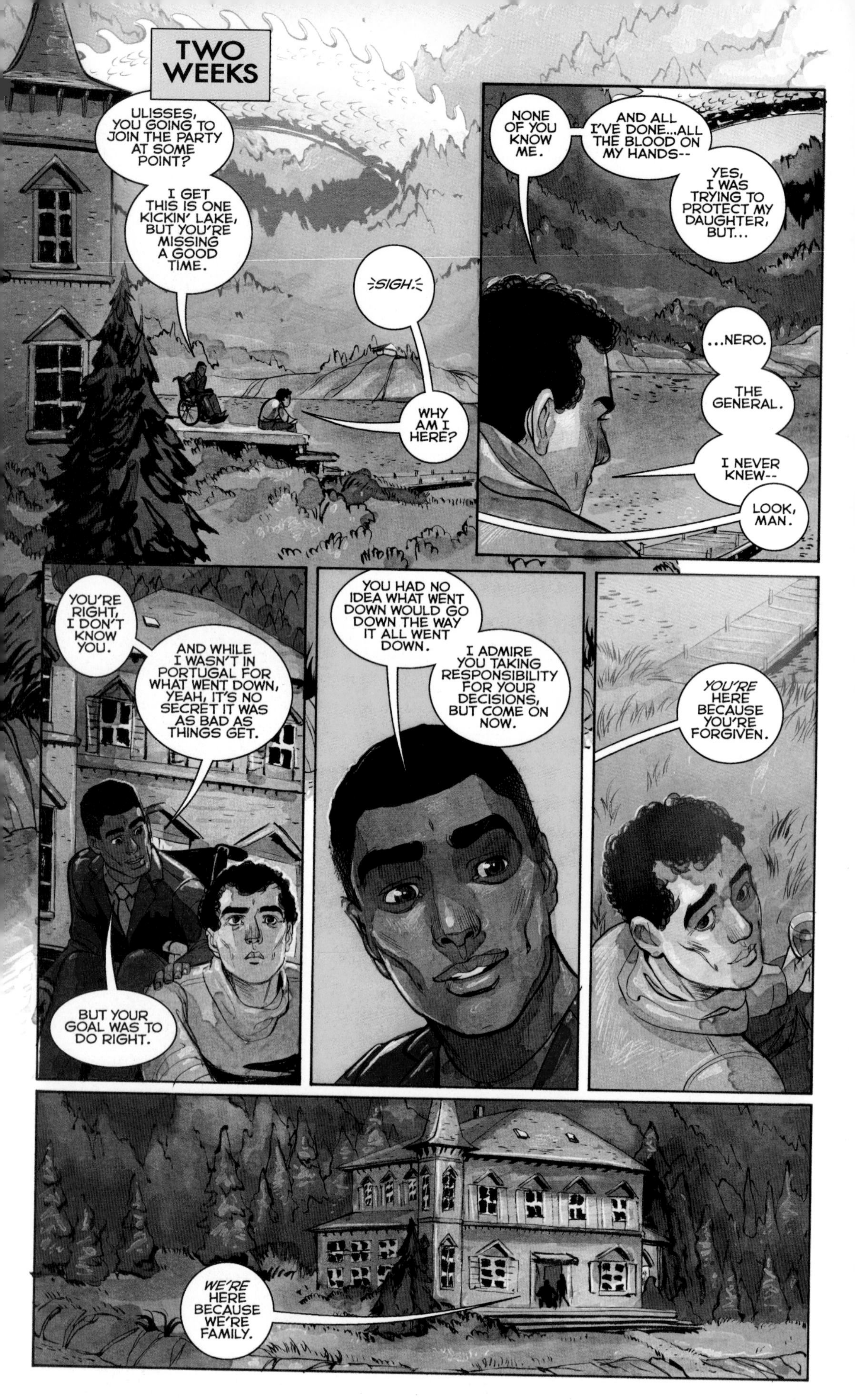
TWO WEEKS
ULISSES, YOU GOING TO JOIN THE PARTY AT SOME POINT?
I GET THIS IS ONE KICKIN' LAKE, BUT YOU'RE MISSING A GOOD TIME.
SIGH.
WHY AM I HERE?
NONE OF YOU KNOW ME.
AND ALL I'VE DONE...ALL THE BLOOD ON MY HANDS--
YES, I WAS TRYING TO PROTECT MY DAUGHTER, BUT...
...NERO.
THE GENERAL.
I NEVER KNEW--
LOOK, MAN.
YOU'RE RIGHT, I DON'T KNOW YOU.
AND WHILE I WASN'T IN PORTUGAL FOR WHAT WENT DOWN, YEAH, IT'S NO SECRET IT WAS AS BAD AS THINGS GET.
BUT YOUR GOAL WAS TO DO RIGHT.
YOU HAD NO IDEA WHAT WENT DOWN WOULD GO DOWN THE WAY IT ALL WENT DOWN.
I ADMIRE YOU TAKING RESPONSIBILITY FOR YOUR DECISIONS, BUT COME ON NOW.
YOU'RE HERE BECAUSE YOU'RE FORGIVEN.
WE'RE HERE BECAUSE WE'RE FAMILY.

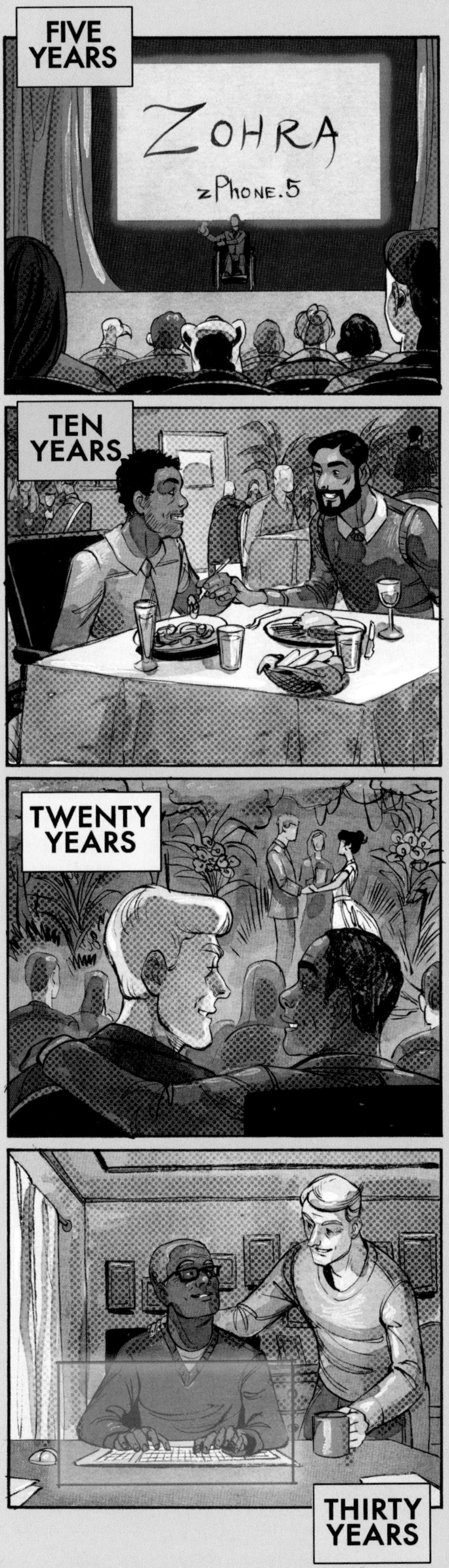
FIVE YEARS
ZOHRA
zPhone.5
TEN YEARS
TWENTY YEARS
THIRTY YEARS

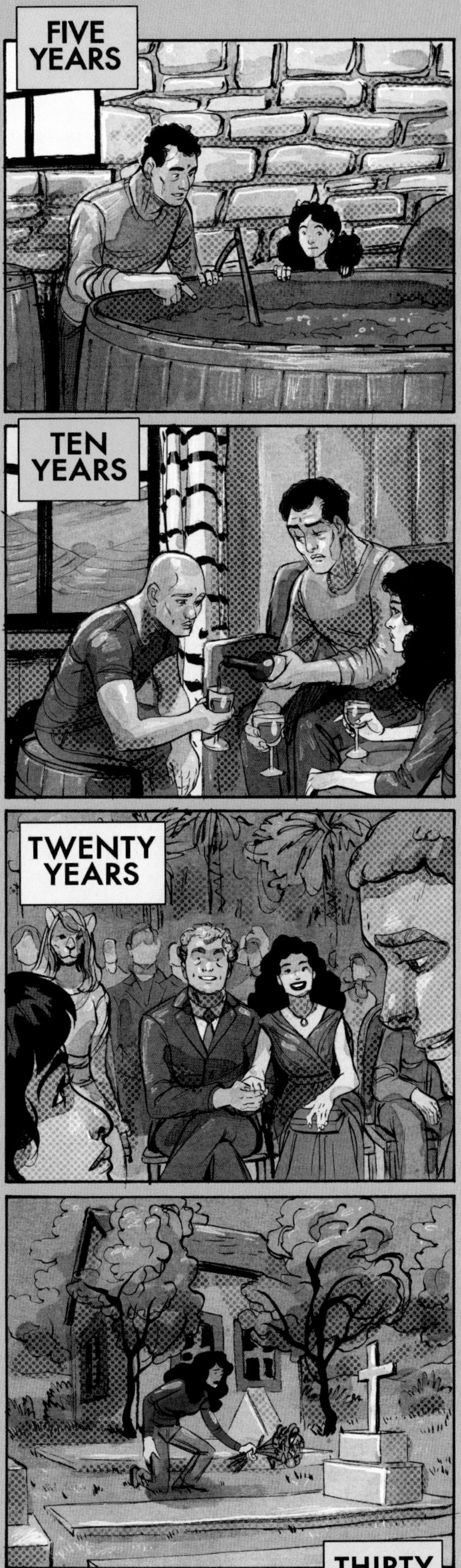
FIVE YEARS
TEN YEARS
TWENTY YEARS
THIRTY YEARS

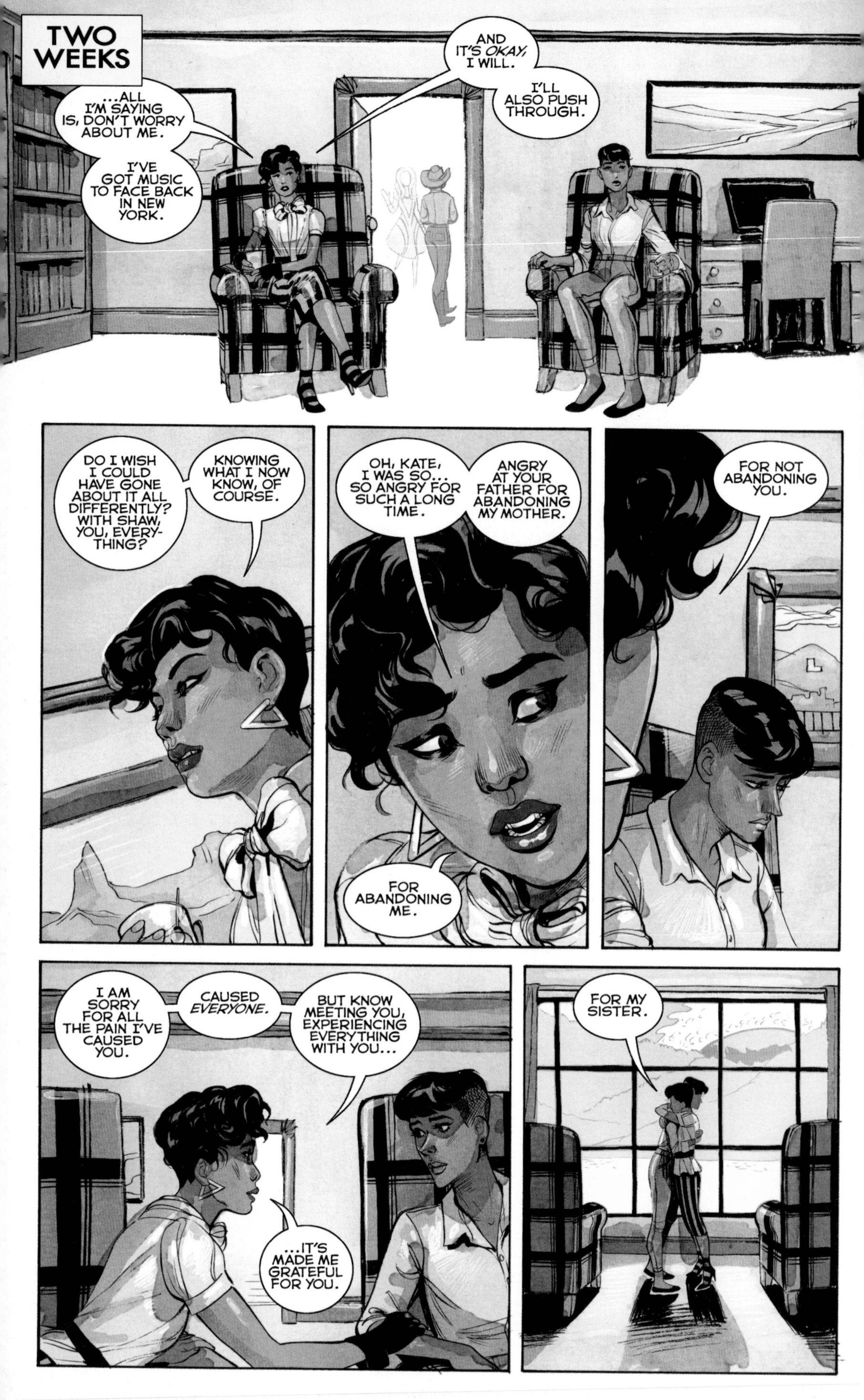
TWO WEEKS
...ALL I'M SAYING IS, DON'T WORRY ABOUT ME.
I'VE GOT MUSIC TO FACE BACK IN NEW YORK.
AND IT'S *OKAY,* I WILL.
I'LL ALSO PUSH THROUGH.
DO I WISH I COULD HAVE GONE ABOUT IT ALL DIFFERENTLY? WITH SHAW, YOU, EVERYTHING?
KNOWING WHAT I NOW KNOW, OF COURSE.
OH, KATE, I WAS SO... SO ANGRY FOR SUCH A LONG TIME.
ANGRY AT YOUR FATHER FOR ABANDONING MY MOTHER.
FOR ABANDONING ME.
FOR NOT ABANDONING YOU.
I AM SORRY FOR ALL THE PAIN I'VE CAUSED YOU.
CAUSED *EVERYONE.*
BUT KNOW MEETING YOU, EXPERIENCING EVERYTHING WITH YOU...
...IT'S MADE ME GRATEFUL FOR YOU.
FOR MY SISTER.

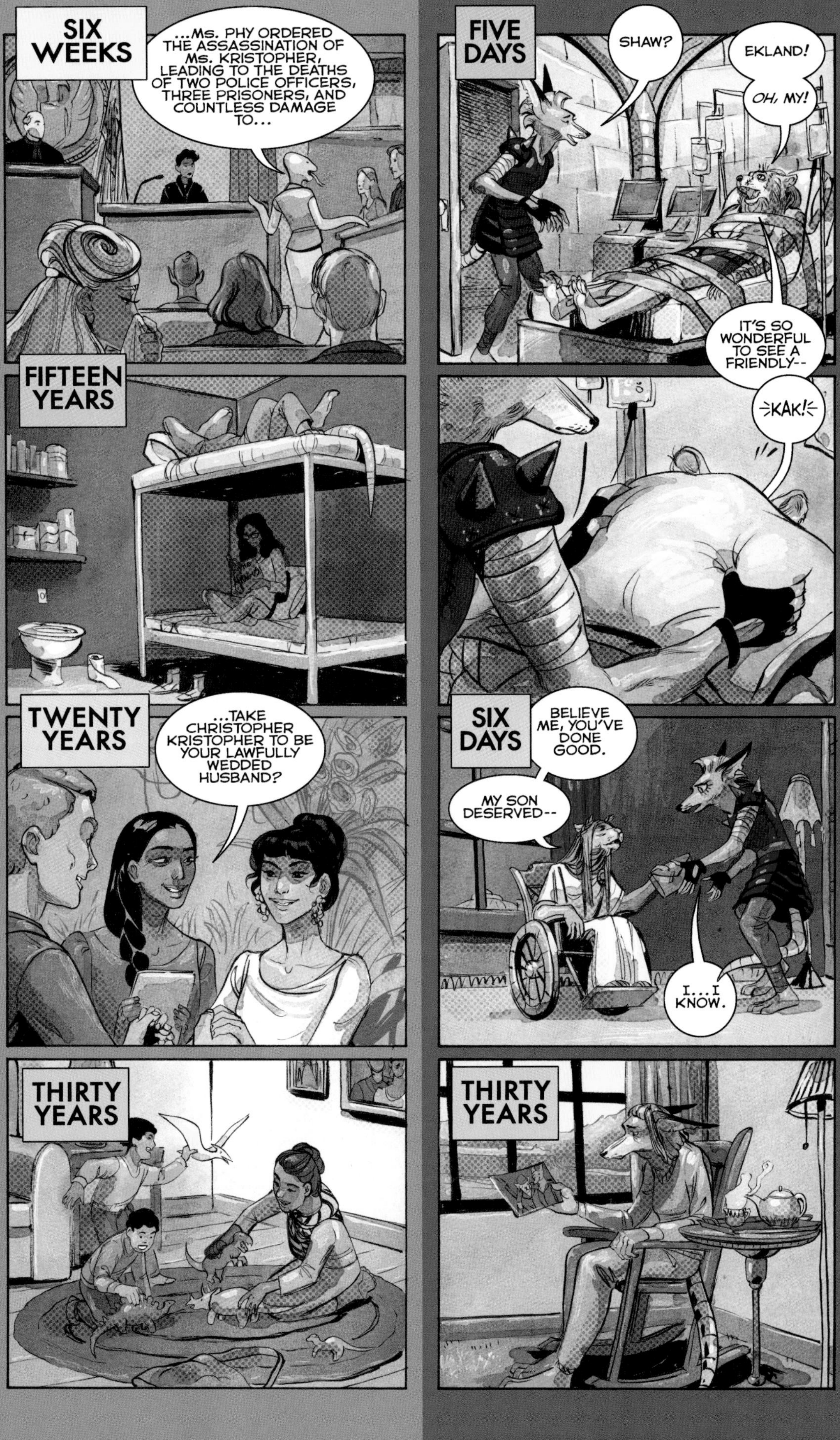
SIX WEEKS
...Ms. PHY ORDERED THE ASSASSINATION OF Ms. KRISTOPHER, LEADING TO THE DEATHS OF TWO POLICE OFFICERS, THREE PRISONERS, AND COUNTLESS DAMAGE TO...
FIFTEEN YEARS
TWENTY YEARS
...TAKE CHRISTOPHER KRISTOPHER TO BE YOUR LAWFULLY WEDDED HUSBAND?
THIRTY YEARS
FIVE DAYS
SHAW?
EKLAND!
OH, MY!
IT'S SO WONDERFUL TO SEE A FRIENDLY--
KAK!
SIX DAYS
BELIEVE ME, YOU'VE DONE GOOD.
MY SON DESERVED--
I...I KNOW.
THIRTY YEARS

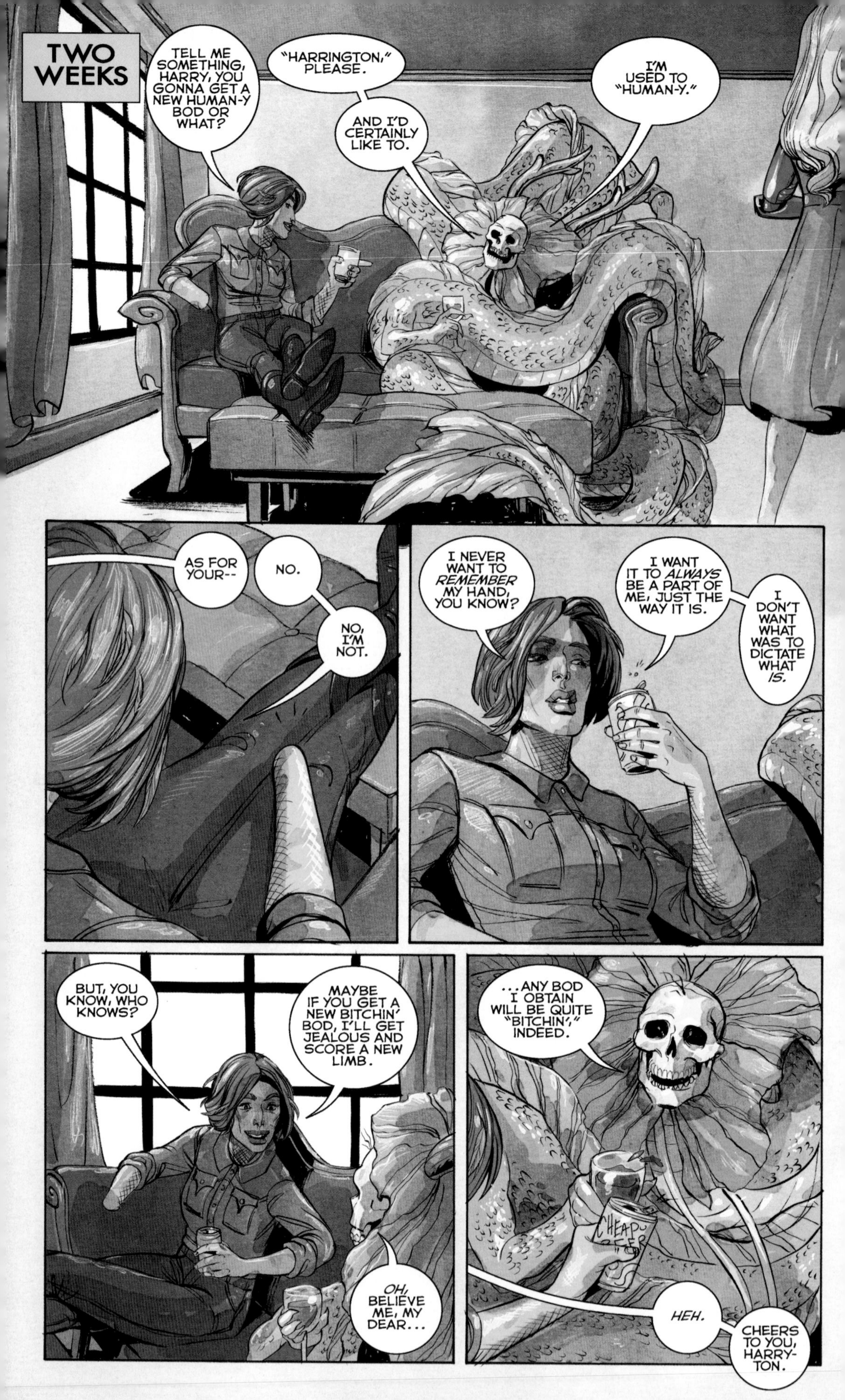
TWO WEEKS
TELL ME SOMETHING, HARRY, YOU GONNA GET A NEW HUMAN-Y BOD OR WHAT?
"HARRINGTON," PLEASE.
AND I'D CERTAINLY LIKE TO.
I'M USED TO "HUMAN-Y."
AS FOR YOUR--
NO.
NO, I'M NOT.
I NEVER WANT TO *REMEMBER* MY HAND, YOU KNOW?
I WANT IT TO *ALWAYS* BE A PART OF ME, JUST THE WAY IT IS.
I DON'T WANT WHAT WAS TO DICTATE WHAT *IS.*
BUT, YOU KNOW, WHO KNOWS?
MAYBE IF YOU GET A NEW BITCHIN' BOD, I'LL GET JEALOUS AND SCORE A NEW LIMB.
OH, BELIEVE ME, MY DEAR...
...ANY BOD I OBTAIN WILL BE QUITE "BITCHIN'," INDEED.
CHEAP BEER
HEH.
CHEERS TO YOU, HARRY-TON.

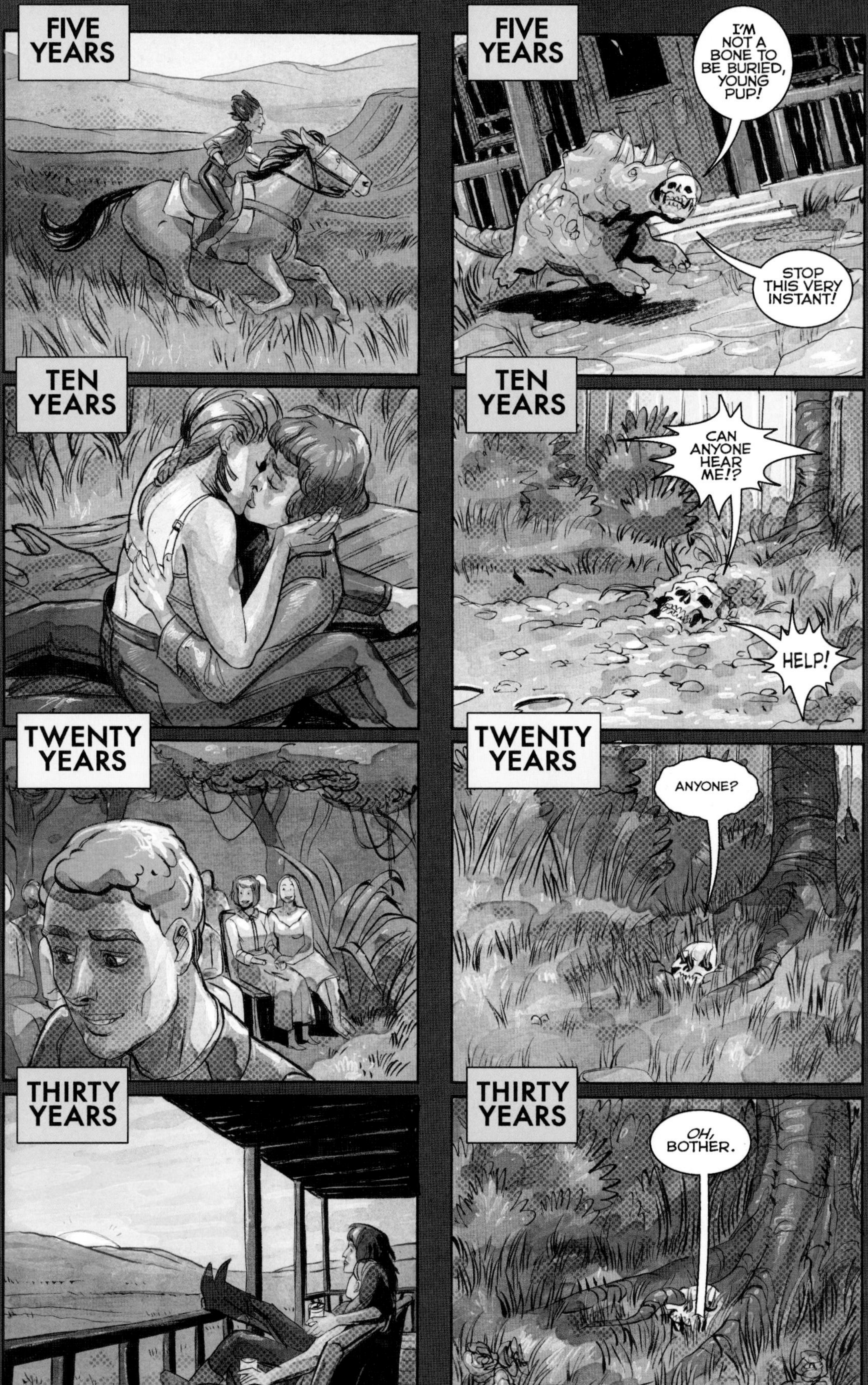
FIVE YEARS
FIVE YEARS
I'M NOT A BONE TO BE BURIED, YOUNG PUP!
STOP THIS VERY INSTANT!
TEN YEARS
TEN YEARS
CAN ANYONE HEAR ME!?
HELP!
TWENTY YEARS
TWENTY YEARS
ANYONE?
THIRTY YEARS
THIRTY YEARS
OH, BOTHER.

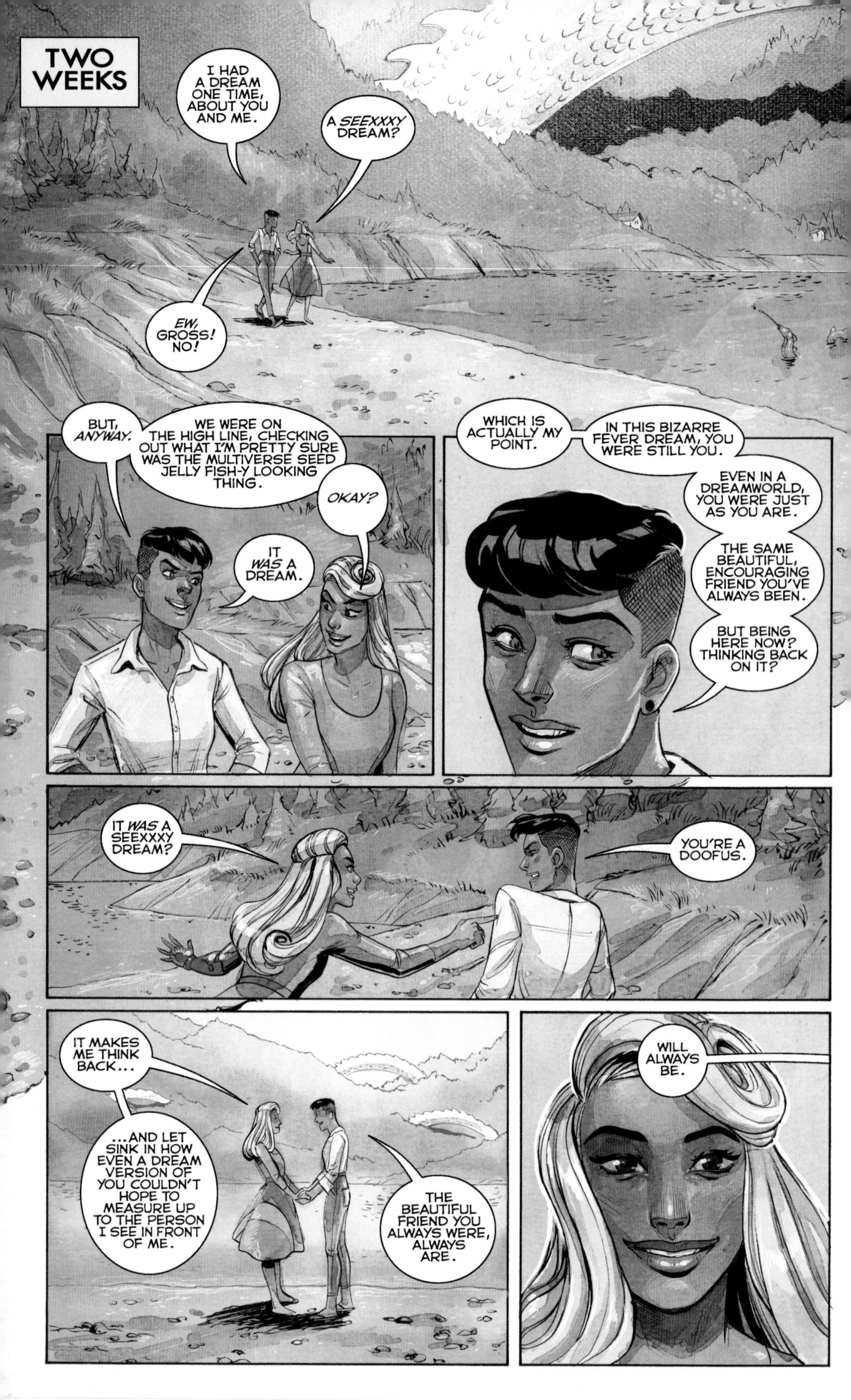
TWO WEEKS
I HAD A DREAM ONE TIME, ABOUT YOU AND ME.
A *SEEXXXY* DREAM?
EW, GROSS! NO!
BUT, *ANYWAY.*
WE WERE ON THE HIGH LINE, CHECKING OUT WHAT I'M PRETTY SURE WAS THE MULTIVERSE SEED JELLY FISH-Y LOOKING THING.
OKAY?
IT *WAS* A DREAM.
WHICH IS ACTUALLY MY POINT.
IN THIS BIZARRE FEVER DREAM, YOU WERE STILL YOU.
EVEN IN A DREAMWORLD, YOU WERE JUST AS YOU ARE.
THE SAME BEAUTIFUL, ENCOURAGING FRIEND YOU'VE ALWAYS BEEN.
BUT BEING HERE NOW? THINKING BACK ON IT?
IT *WAS* A SEEXXXY DREAM?
YOU'RE A DOOFUS.
IT MAKES ME THINK BACK...
...AND LET SINK IN HOW EVEN A DREAM VERSION OF YOU COULDN'T HOPE TO MEASURE UP TO THE PERSON I SEE IN FRONT OF ME.
THE BEAUTIFUL FRIEND YOU ALWAYS WERE, ALWAYS ARE.
WILL ALWAYS BE.

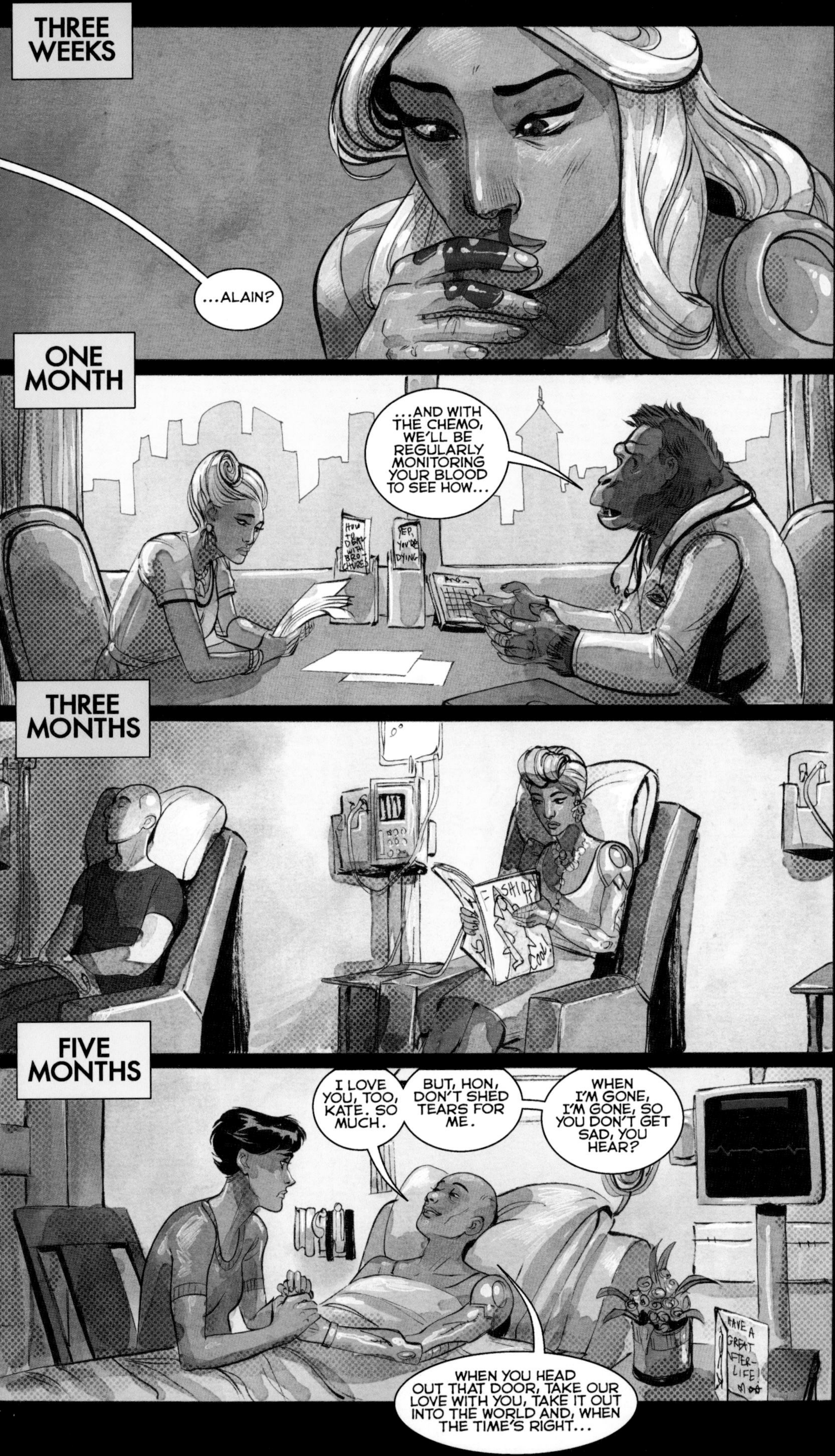
THREE WEEKS
...ALAIN?
ONE MONTH
...AND WITH THE CHEMO, WE'LL BE REGULARLY MONITORING YOUR BLOOD TO SEE HOW...
HOW TO DEAL WITH BRO-CHURES
YEP, YOU'RE DYING
THREE MONTHS
FASHION
Cool!
FIVE MONTHS
I LOVE YOU, TOO, KATE. SO MUCH.
BUT, HON, DON'T SHED TEARS FOR ME.
WHEN I'M GONE, I'M GONE, SO YOU DON'T GET SAD, YOU HEAR?
HAVE A GREAT AFTER-LIFE!
WHEN YOU HEAD OUT THAT DOOR, TAKE OUR LOVE WITH YOU, TAKE IT OUT INTO THE WORLD AND, WHEN THE TIME'S RIGHT...

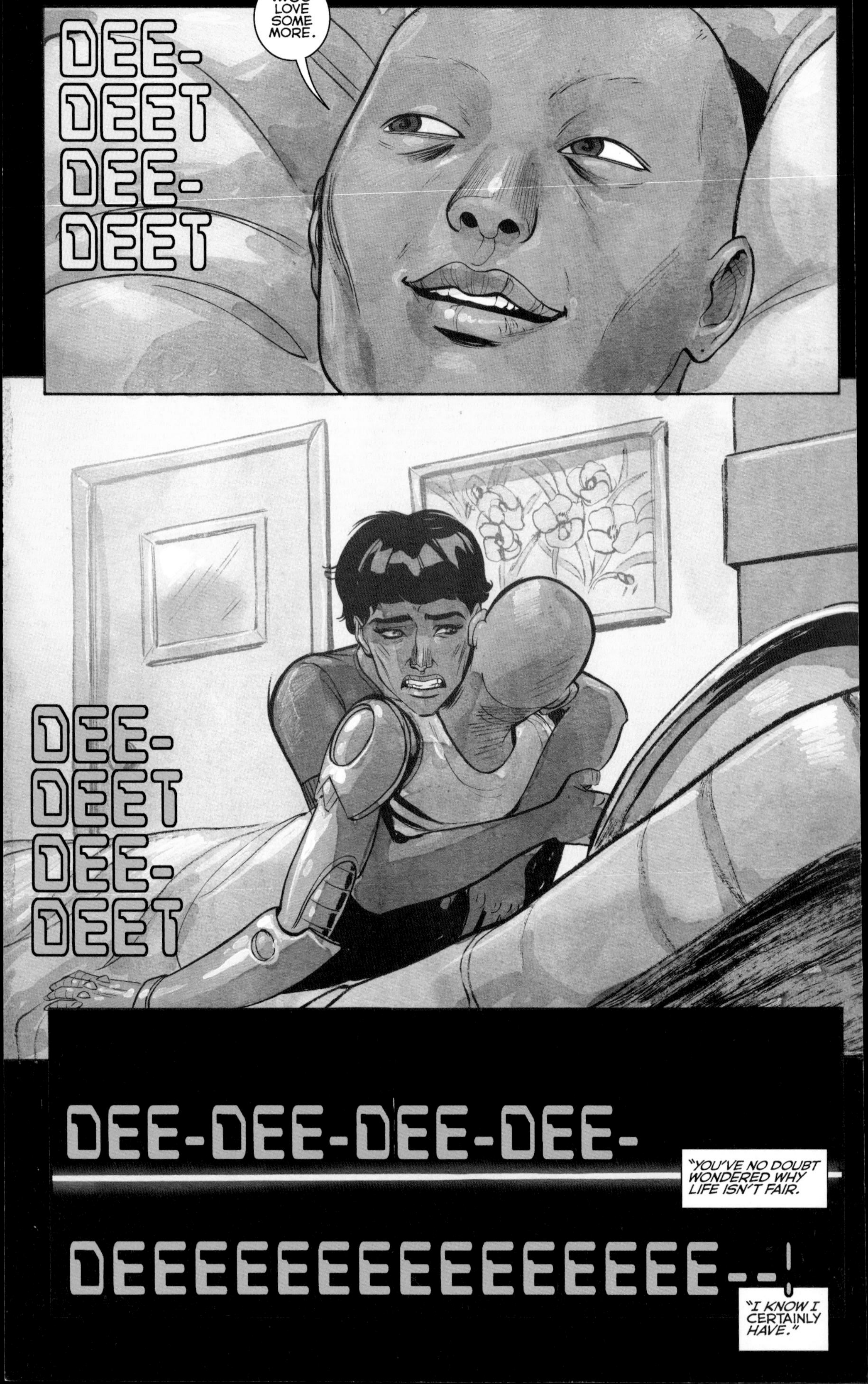

DEE-DEET DEE-DEET
...GO LOVE SOME MORE.
DEE-DEET DEE-DEET
DEE-DEE-DEE-DEE-
"YOU'VE NO DOUBT WONDERED WHY LIFE ISN'T FAIR.
DEEEEEEEEEEEEEEEEE--!
"I KNOW I CERTAINLY HAVE."

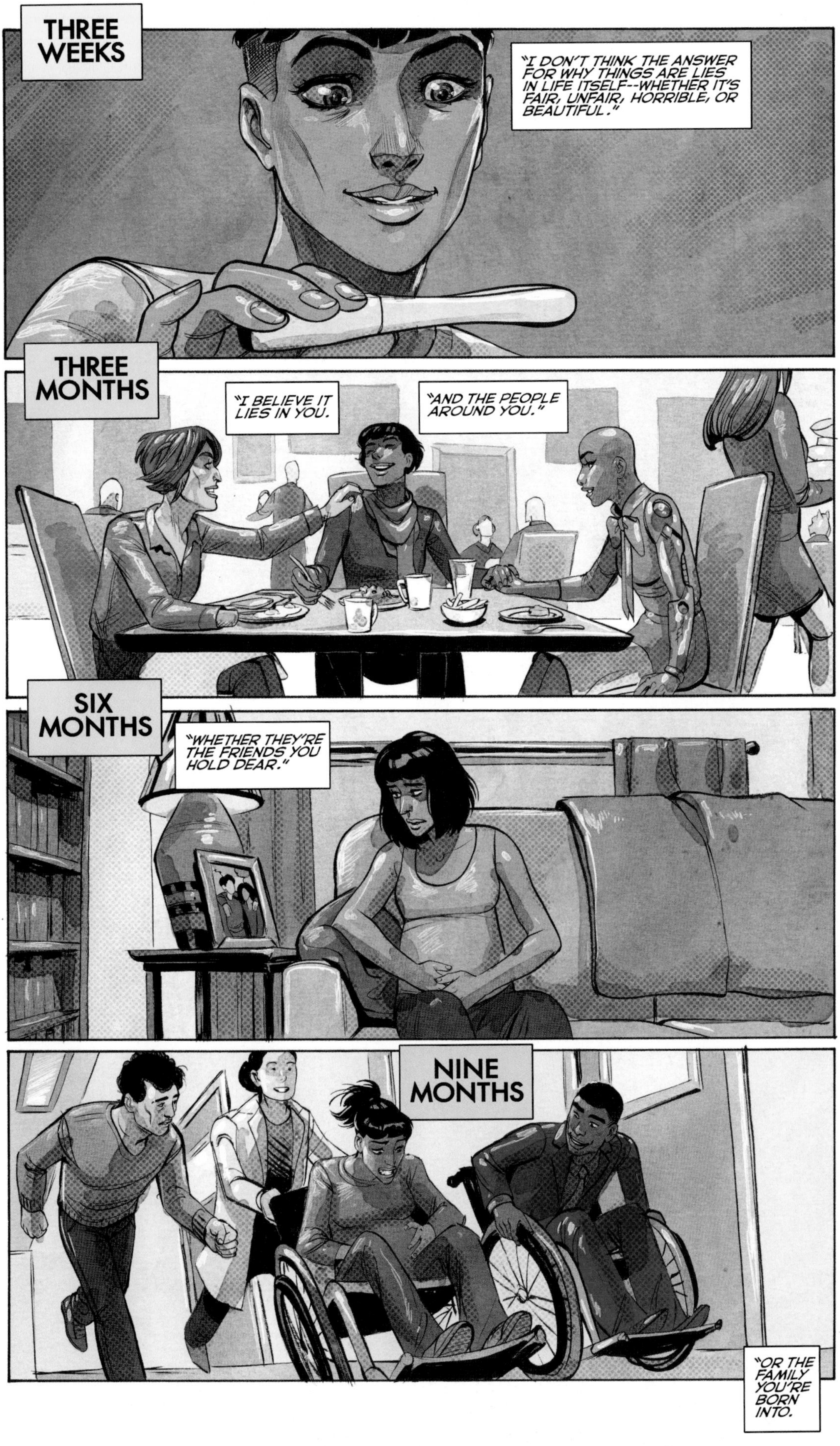
THREE WEEKS
"I DON'T THINK THE ANSWER FOR WHY THINGS ARE LIES IN LIFE ITSELF--WHETHER IT'S FAIR, UNFAIR, HORRIBLE, OR BEAUTIFUL."
THREE MONTHS
"I BELIEVE IT LIES IN YOU.
"AND THE PEOPLE AROUND YOU."
SIX MONTHS
"WHETHER THEY'RE THE FRIENDS YOU HOLD DEAR."
NINE MONTHS
"OR THE FAMILY YOU'RE BORN INTO.

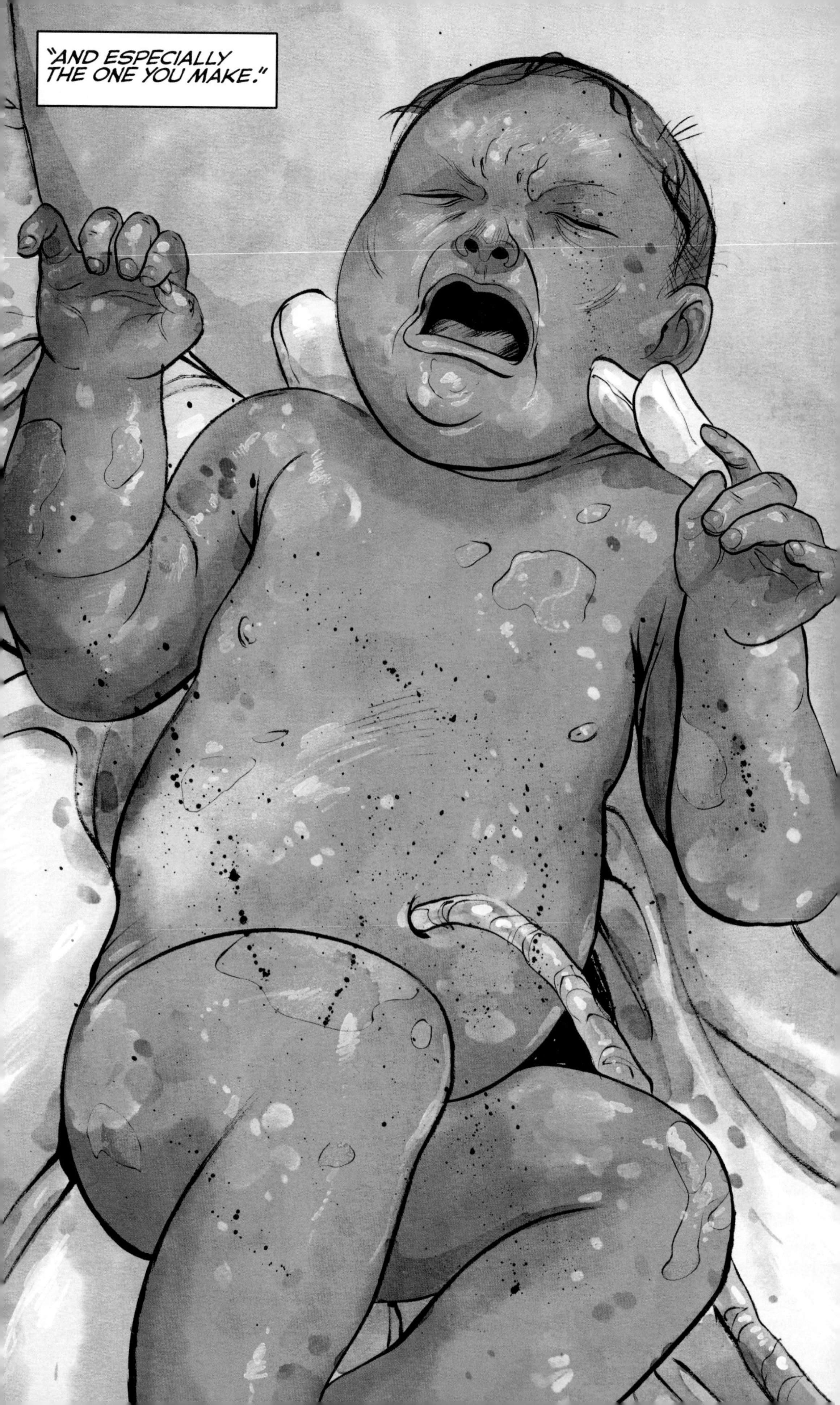
"AND ESPECIALLY THE ONE YOU MAKE."

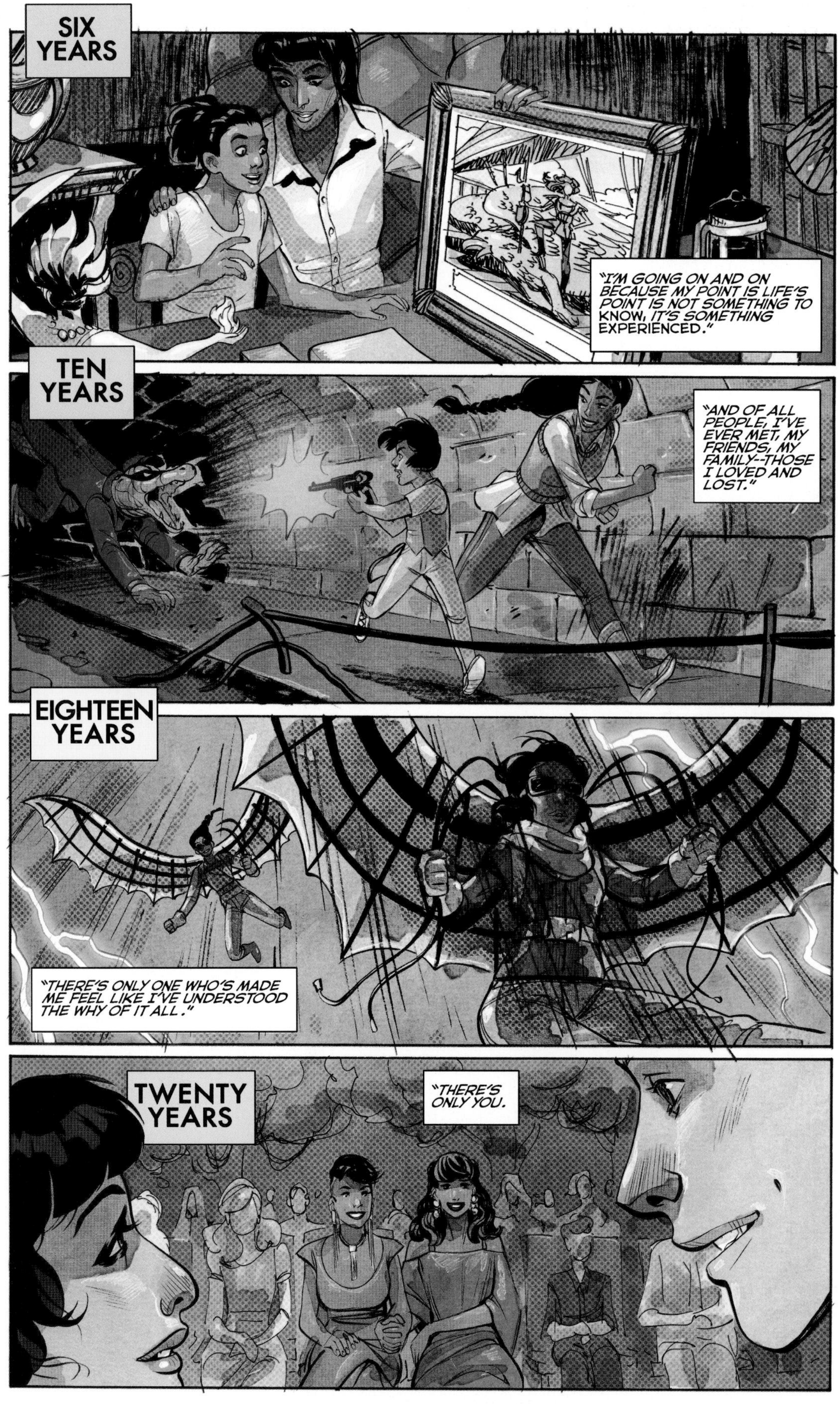
SIX YEARS
"I'M GOING ON AND ON BECAUSE MY POINT IS LIFE'S POINT IS NOT SOMETHING TO KNOW, IT'S SOMETHING EXPERIENCED."
TEN YEARS
"AND OF ALL PEOPLE, I'VE EVER MET, MY FRIENDS, MY FAMILY--THOSE I LOVED AND LOST."
EIGHTEEN YEARS
"THERE'S ONLY ONE WHO'S MADE ME FEEL LIKE I'VE UNDERSTOOD THE WHY OF IT ALL."
TWENTY YEARS
"THERE'S ONLY YOU.

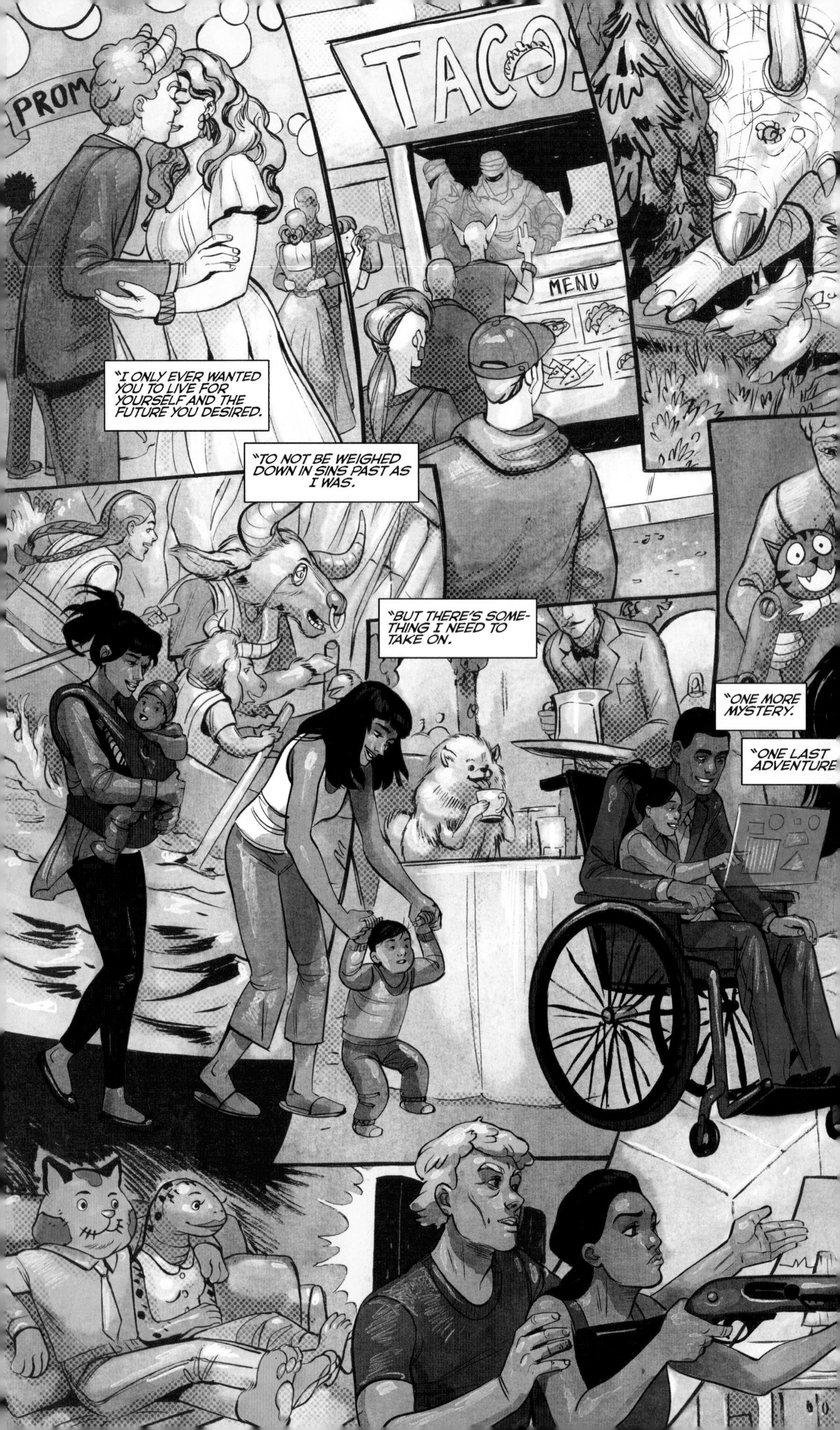
PROM
TACO
"I ONLY EVER WANTED YOU TO LIVE FOR YOURSELF AND THE FUTURE YOU DESIRED.
MENU
"TO NOT BE WEIGHED DOWN IN SINS PAST AS I WAS.
"BUT THERE'S SOMETHING I NEED TO TAKE ON.
"ONE MORE MYSTERY.
"ONE LAST ADVENTURE

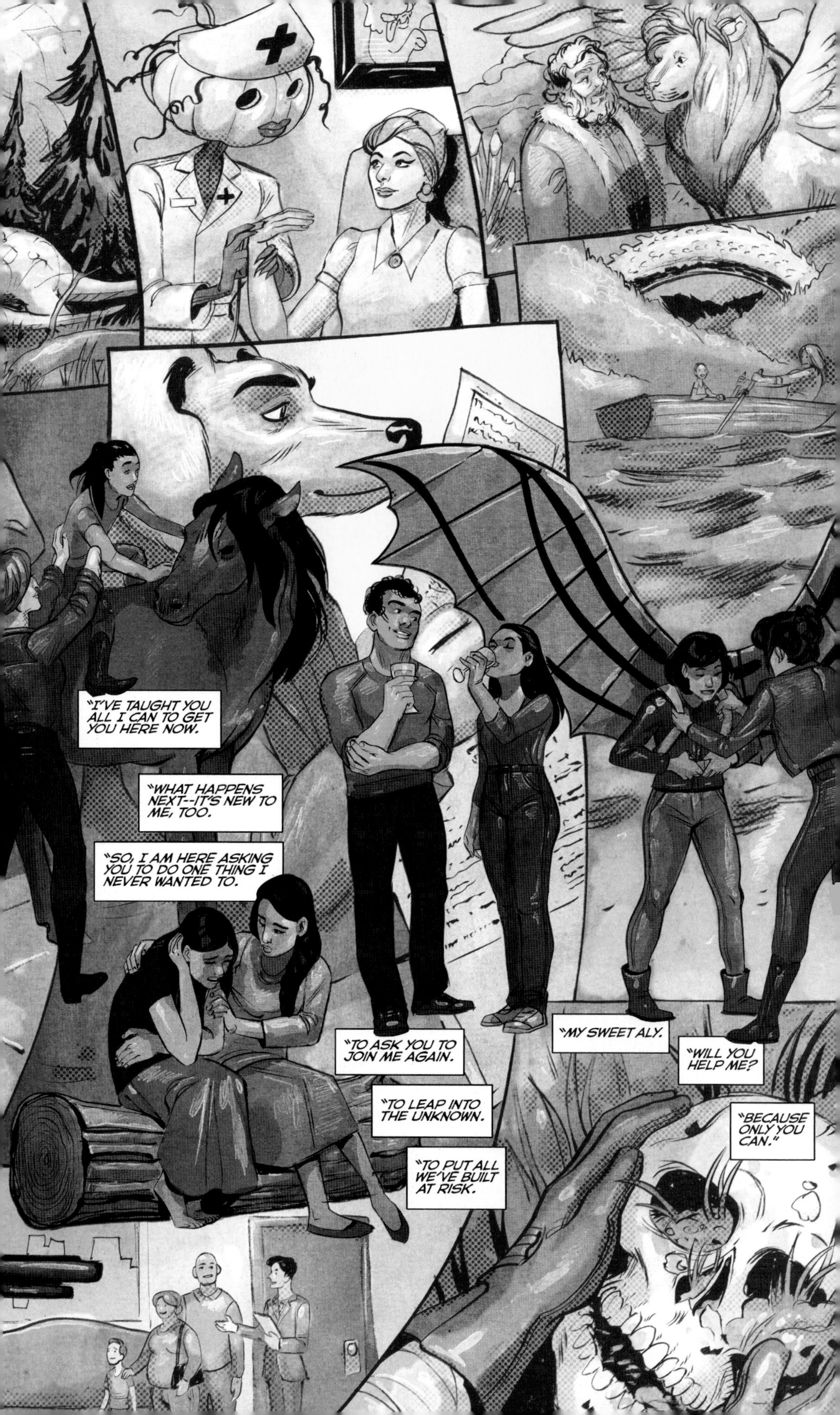
"I'VE TAUGHT YOU ALL I CAN TO GET YOU HERE NOW.
"WHAT HAPPENS NEXT--IT'S NEW TO ME, TOO.
"SO, I AM HERE ASKING YOU TO DO ONE THING I NEVER WANTED TO.
"TO ASK YOU TO JOIN ME AGAIN.
"TO LEAP INTO THE UNKNOWN.
"TO PUT ALL WE'VE BUILT AT RISK.
"MY SWEET ALY.
"WILL YOU HELP ME?
"BECAUSE ONLY YOU CAN."

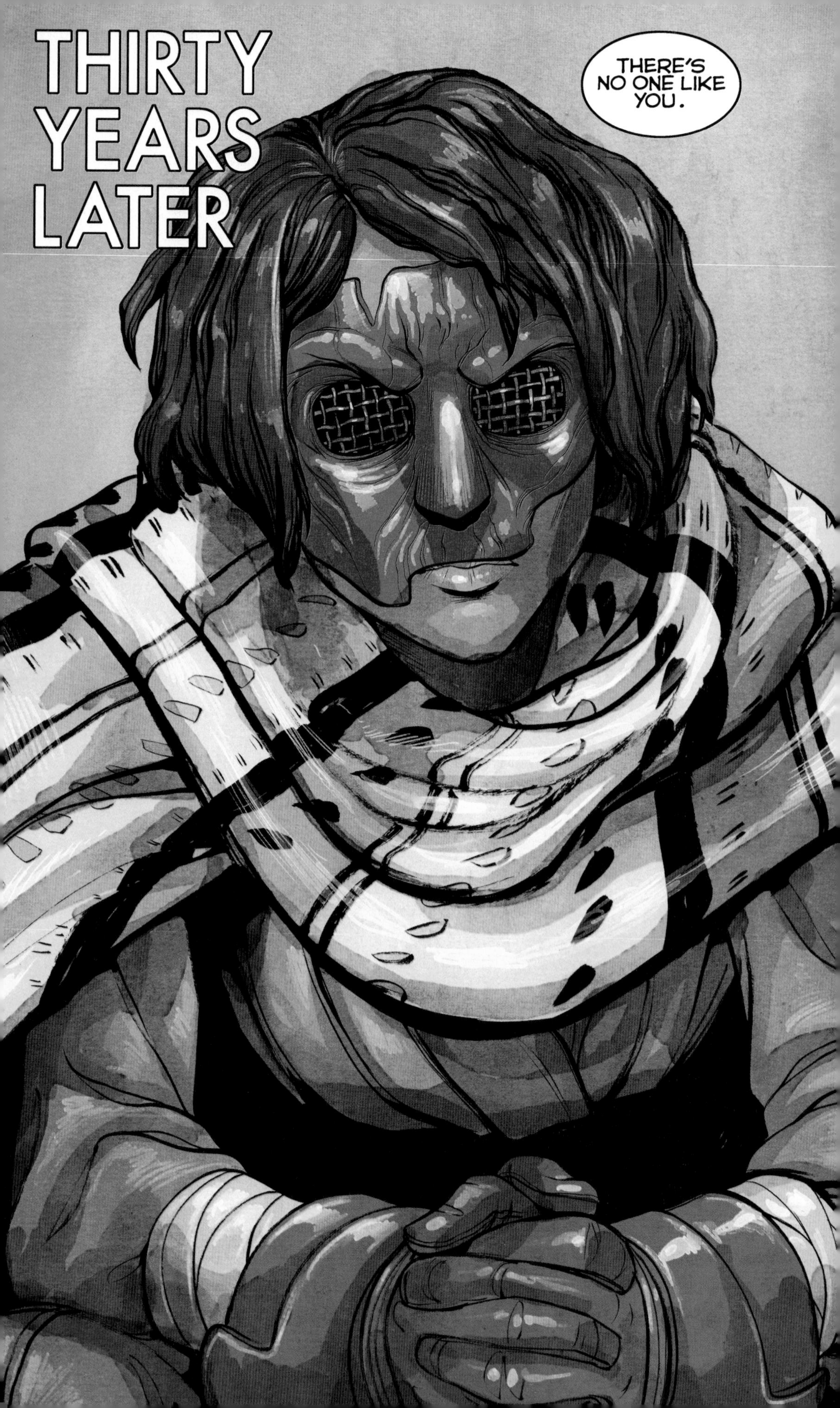
THIRTY YEARS LATER
THERE'S NO ONE LIKE YOU.

CHAPTER 30

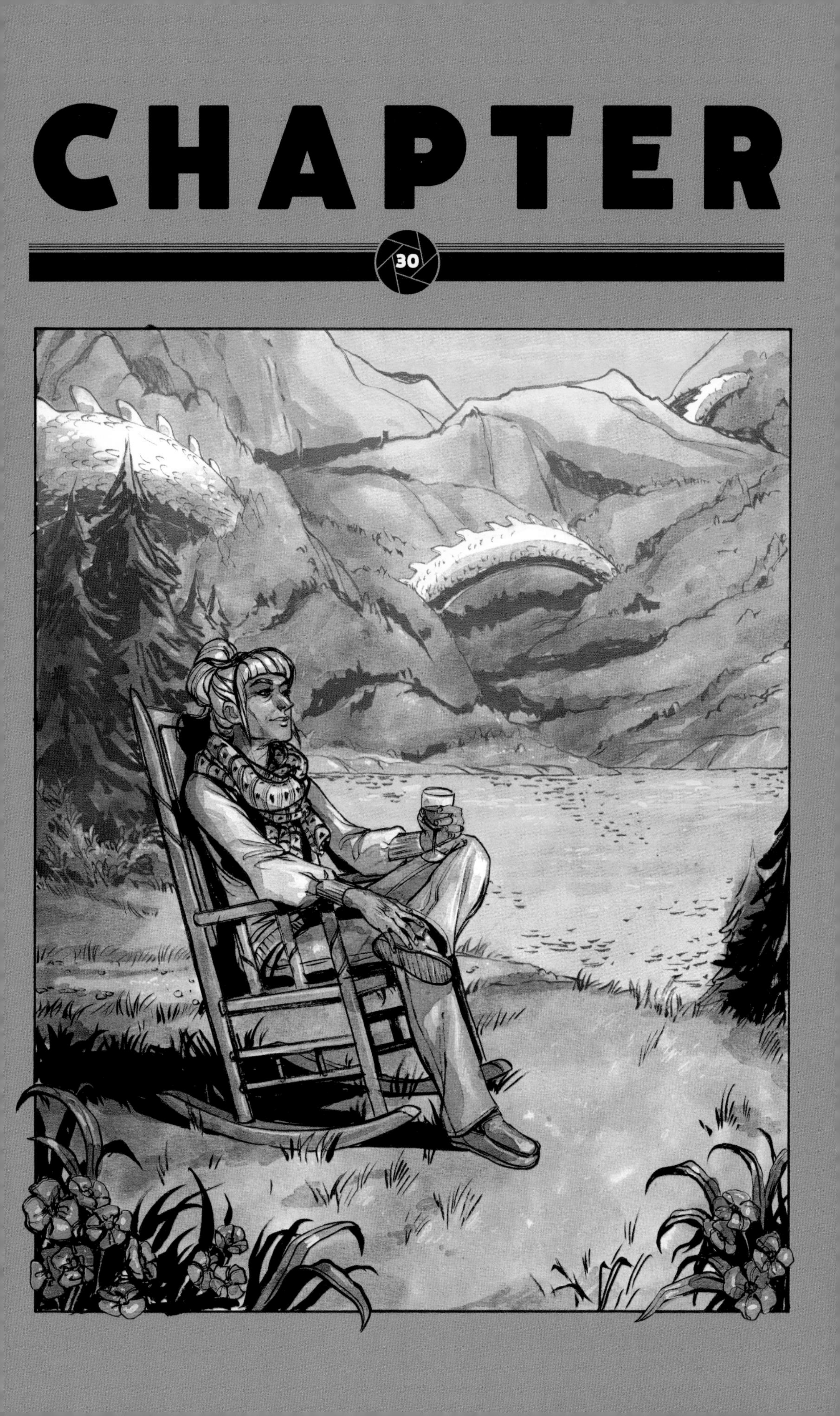

"THIS ALL STARTED BEFORE WE EVER BEGAN.

"FOR AS MUCH AS PROSPERO TOUTED THEMSELVES AS RULERS OF AN UNFREE WORLD, THEY WERE ALSO SLAVES TO A FUTILE SYSTEM.

"REALITY'S ULTIMATE PLAN NEVER CONCERNED ITSELF WITH HUMANITY.

"AND WHY WOULD IT?

"WE HAVEN'T DONE A GREAT JOB OF DESERVING ITS ATTENTION AND CARE.

"HERE WE ARE NOW. A SPECIES BILLIONS STRONG LOOKING DOWN THE BARREL OF A UNIVERSE SET TO MOVE ON WITHOUT US.

"PROSPERO'S SOLUTION?

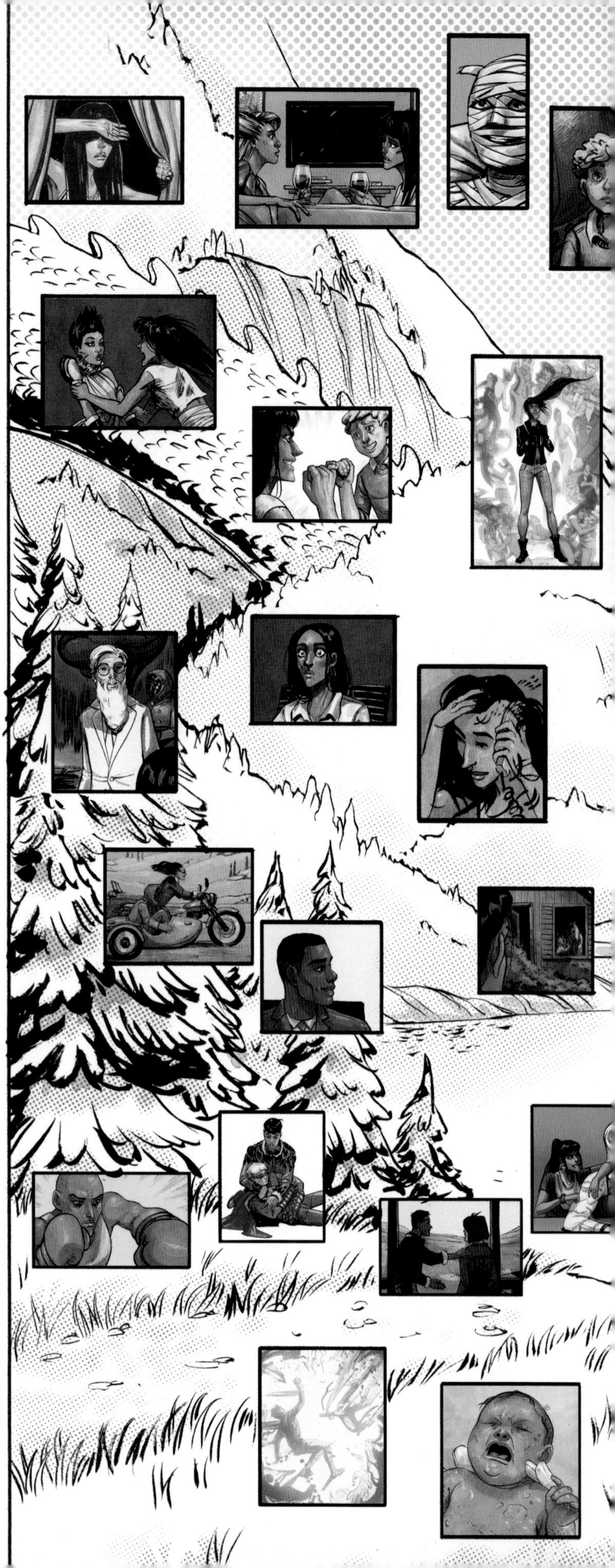

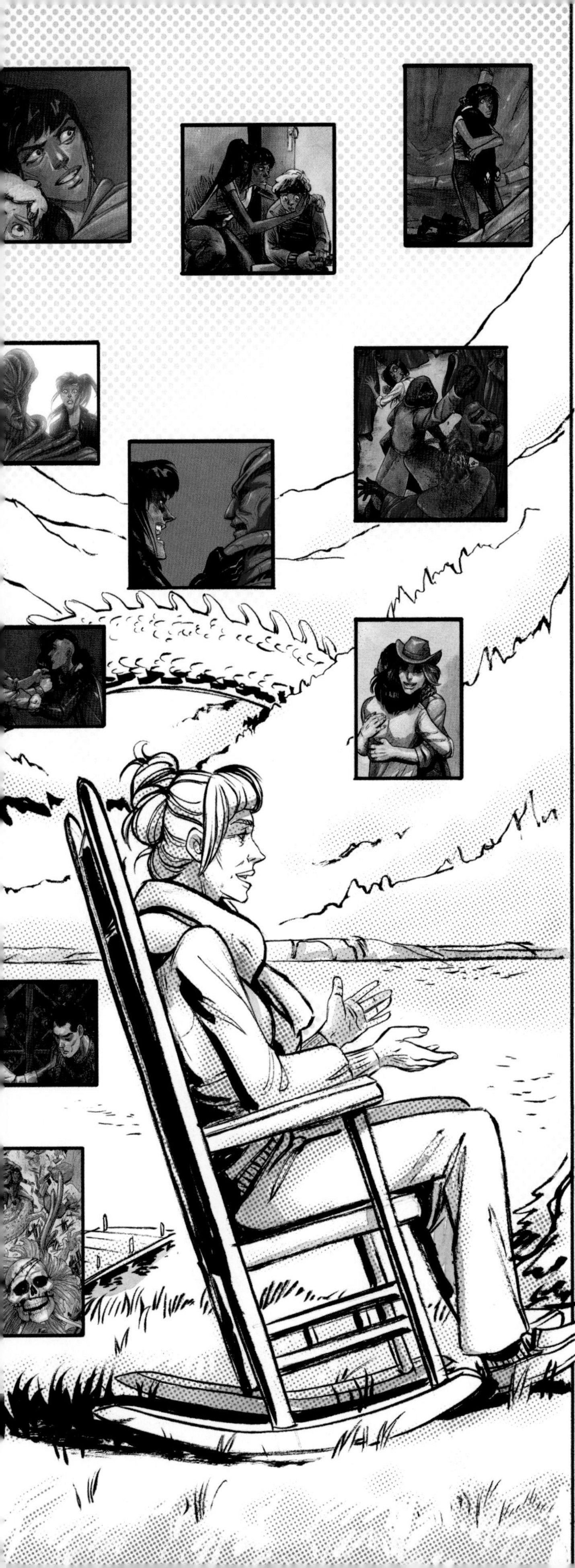

"SPEND CENTURIES--MILLENNIA--CONCOCTING ANY WAY THEY COULD TO PREVENT OUR UNIVERSE FROM ENDING ALL WE KNOW TO START SO MANY NEW WORLDS.

"THEY TRIED IMPRISONMENT; IT DIDN'T WORK. THEY TRIED A SPACE PROGRAM; IT ONLY CONFIRMED THEIR GREATEST FEARS.

"THEIR CURRENT SOLUTION? BUILD A WEAPON SO POWERFUL IT MIGHT--JUST MIGHT--HALT THE UNIVERSE'S PROLONGED DEATH RATTLE.

"THEY'LL DESTROY MORE, KILL MORE--THEY'LL DO WHATEVER IT TAKES TO SURVIVE AS LONG AS THEY CAN.

"THEY'LL MURDER THE NEW TO PRESERVE THEIR OLD.

"I CAN'T *ALLOW* THIS.

"MY HOPE IS, *WE* WON'T ALLOW THIS.

"SO, WHAT I'M ASKING YOU IS... IMPLORING YOU, REALLY..."

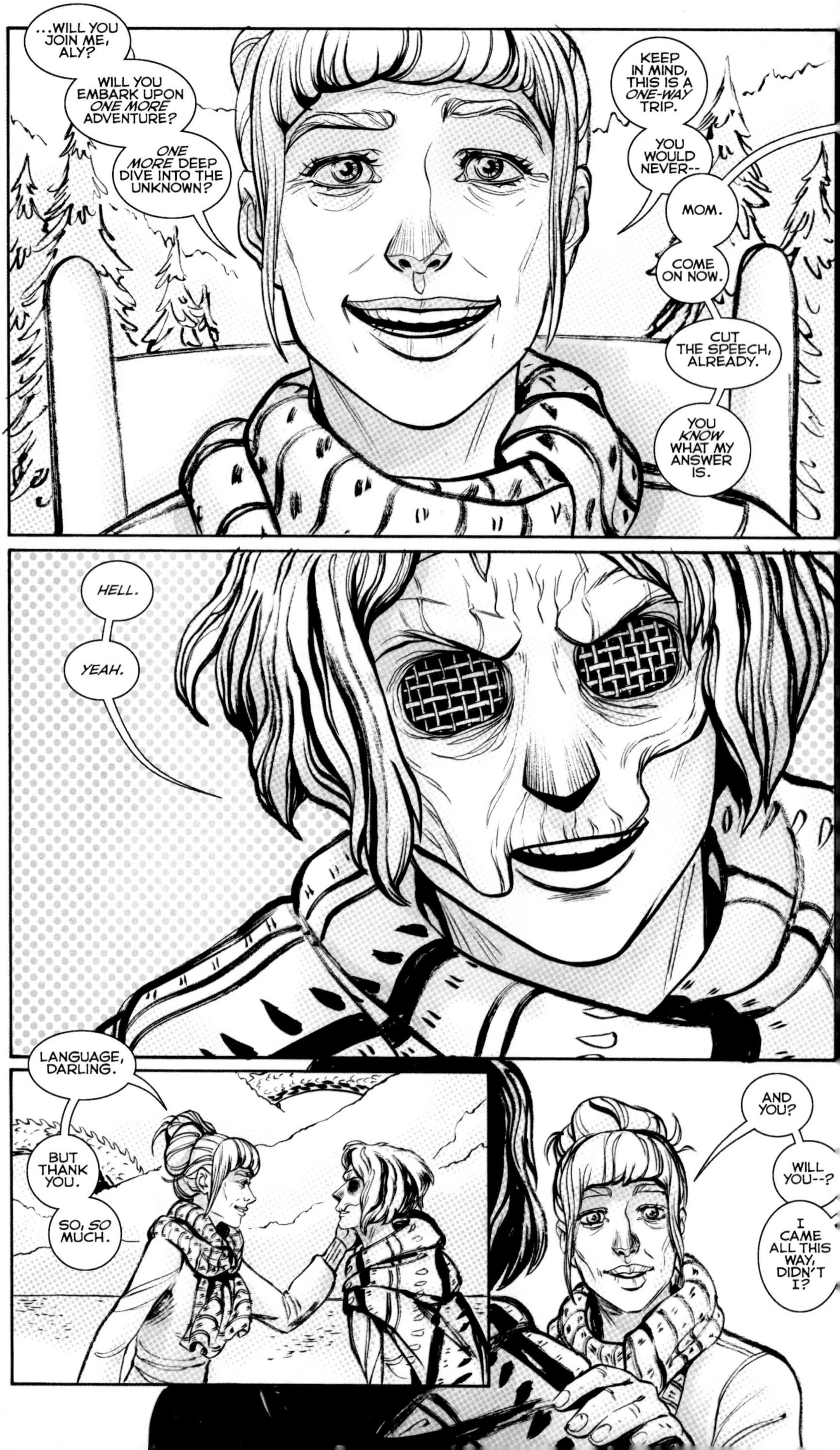
...WILL YOU JOIN ME, ALY?
WILL YOU EMBARK UPON *ONE MORE* ADVENTURE?
ONE MORE DEEP DIVE INTO THE UNKNOWN?
KEEP IN MIND, THIS IS A *ONE-WAY* TRIP.
YOU WOULD NEVER--
MOM.
COME ON NOW.
CUT THE SPEECH, ALREADY.
YOU *KNOW* WHAT MY ANSWER IS.
HELL.
YEAH.
LANGUAGE, DARLING.
BUT THANK YOU.
SO, *SO* MUCH.
AND YOU?
WILL YOU--?
I CAME ALL THIS WAY, DIDN'T I?

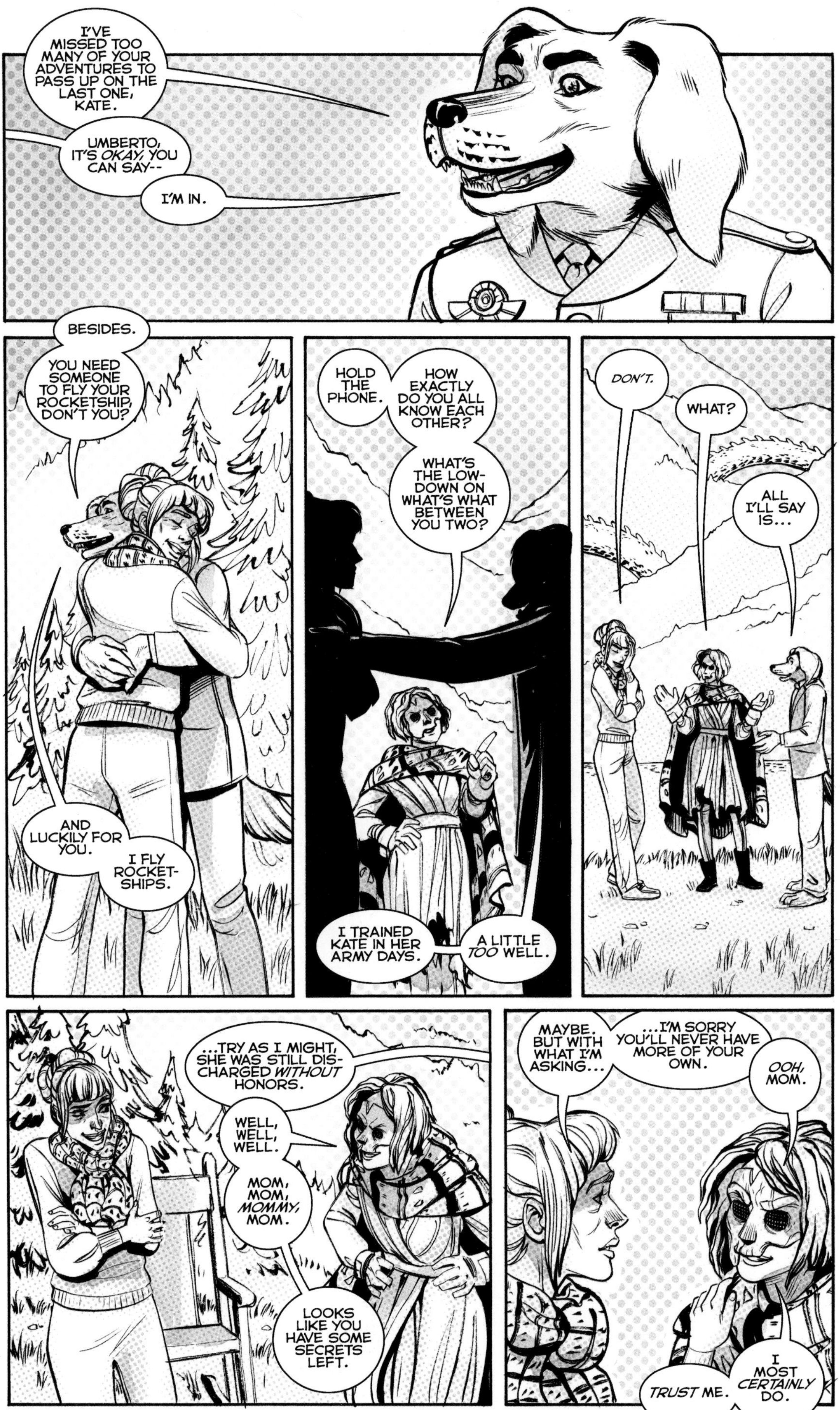
I'VE MISSED TOO MANY OF YOUR ADVENTURES TO PASS UP ON THE LAST ONE, KATE.
UMBERTO, IT'S *OKAY*, YOU CAN SAY--
I'M IN.
BESIDES.
YOU NEED SOMEONE TO FLY YOUR ROCKETSHIP, DON'T YOU?
AND LUCKILY FOR YOU.
I FLY ROCKET-SHIPS.
HOLD THE PHONE.
HOW EXACTLY DO YOU ALL KNOW EACH OTHER?
WHAT'S THE LOW-DOWN ON WHAT'S WHAT BETWEEN YOU TWO?
I TRAINED KATE IN HER ARMY DAYS.
A LITTLE *TOO* WELL.
DON'T.
WHAT?
ALL I'LL SAY IS...
...TRY AS I MIGHT, SHE WAS STILL DIS-CHARGED *WITHOUT* HONORS.
WELL, WELL, WELL.
MOM, MOM, *MOMMY,* MOM.
LOOKS LIKE YOU HAVE SOME SECRETS LEFT.
MAYBE. BUT WITH WHAT I'M ASKING...
...I'M SORRY YOU'LL NEVER HAVE MORE OF YOUR OWN.
OOH, MOM.
TRUST ME.
I MOST *CERTAINLY* DO.

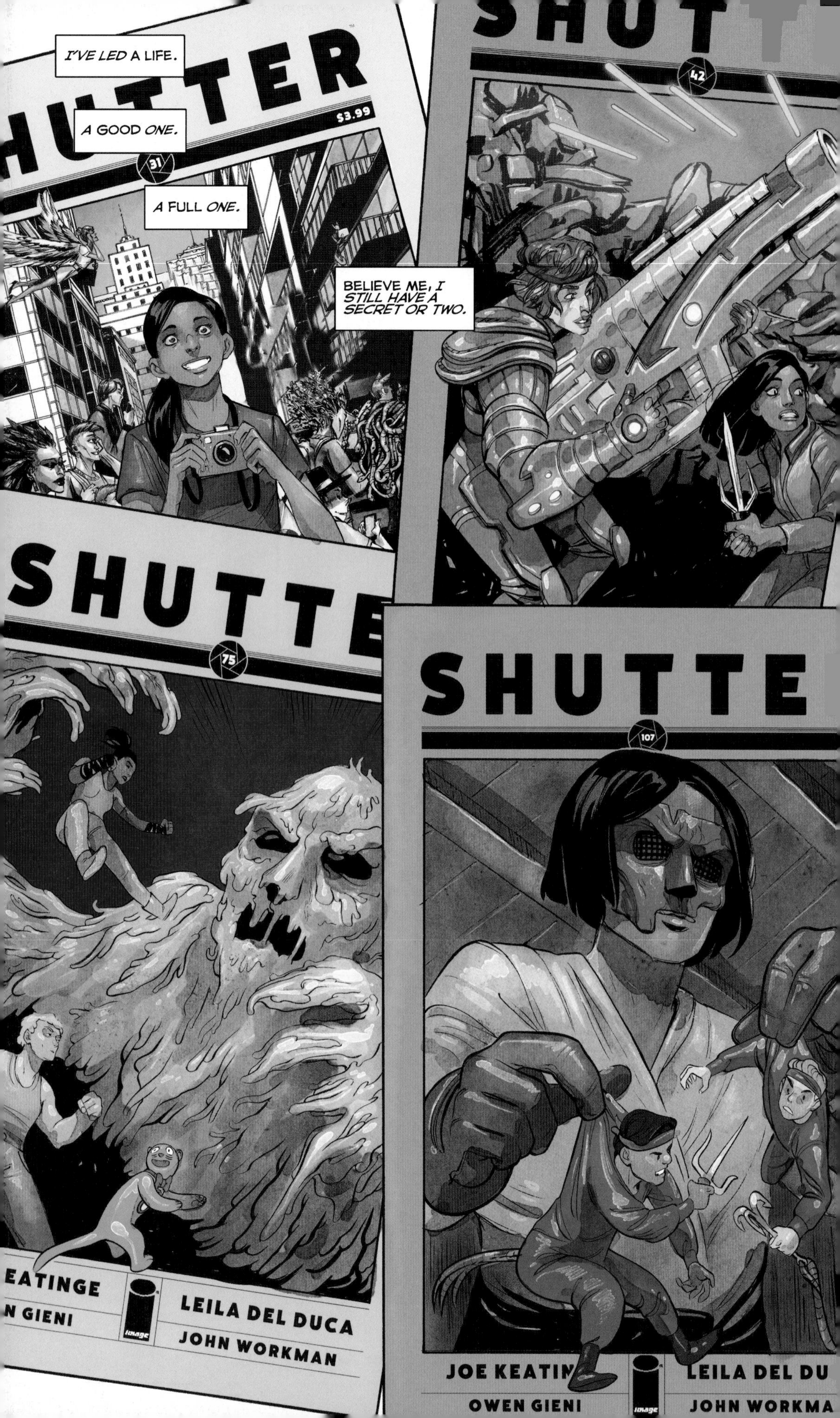
SHUTTER
I'VE LED A LIFE.
A GOOD ONE.
$3.99
31
A FULL ONE.
BELIEVE ME, I STILL HAVE A SECRET OR TWO.
SHUT
42
SHUTTE
75
EATINGE
N GIENI
LEILA DEL DUCA
JOHN WORKMAN
SHUTTE
107
JOE KEATIN
OWEN GIENI
LEILA DEL DU
JOHN WORKMA

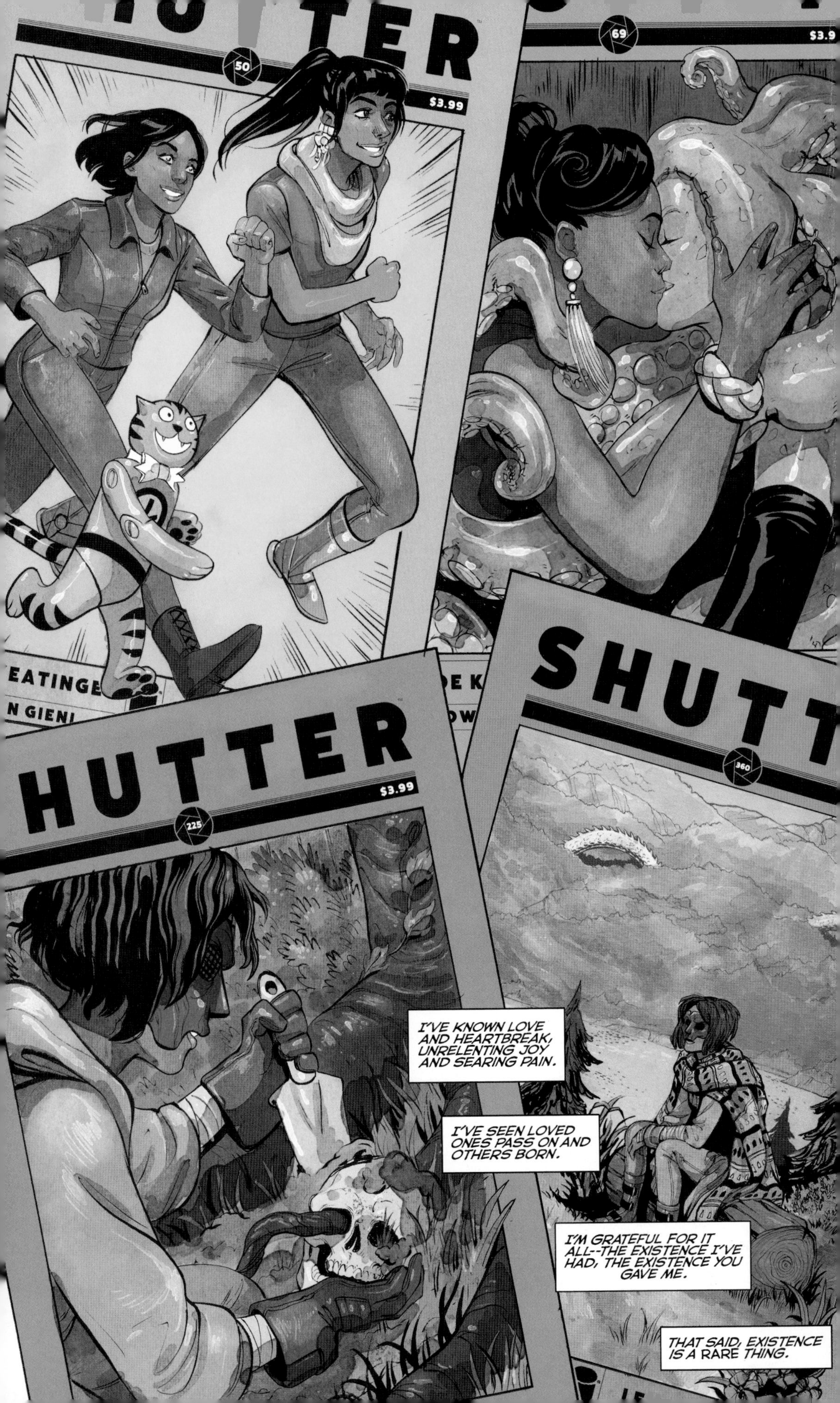

SHUTTER
50
$3.99
69
$3.9
EATINGE
N GIENI
DE K
OW
SHUTTER
$3.99
225
SHUTT
360
I'VE KNOWN LOVE AND HEARTBREAK, UNRELENTING JOY AND SEARING PAIN.
I'VE SEEN LOVED ONES PASS ON AND OTHERS BORN.
I'M GRATEFUL FOR IT ALL--THE EXISTENCE I'VE HAD, THE EXISTENCE YOU GAVE ME.
THAT SAID, EXISTENCE IS A RARE THING.

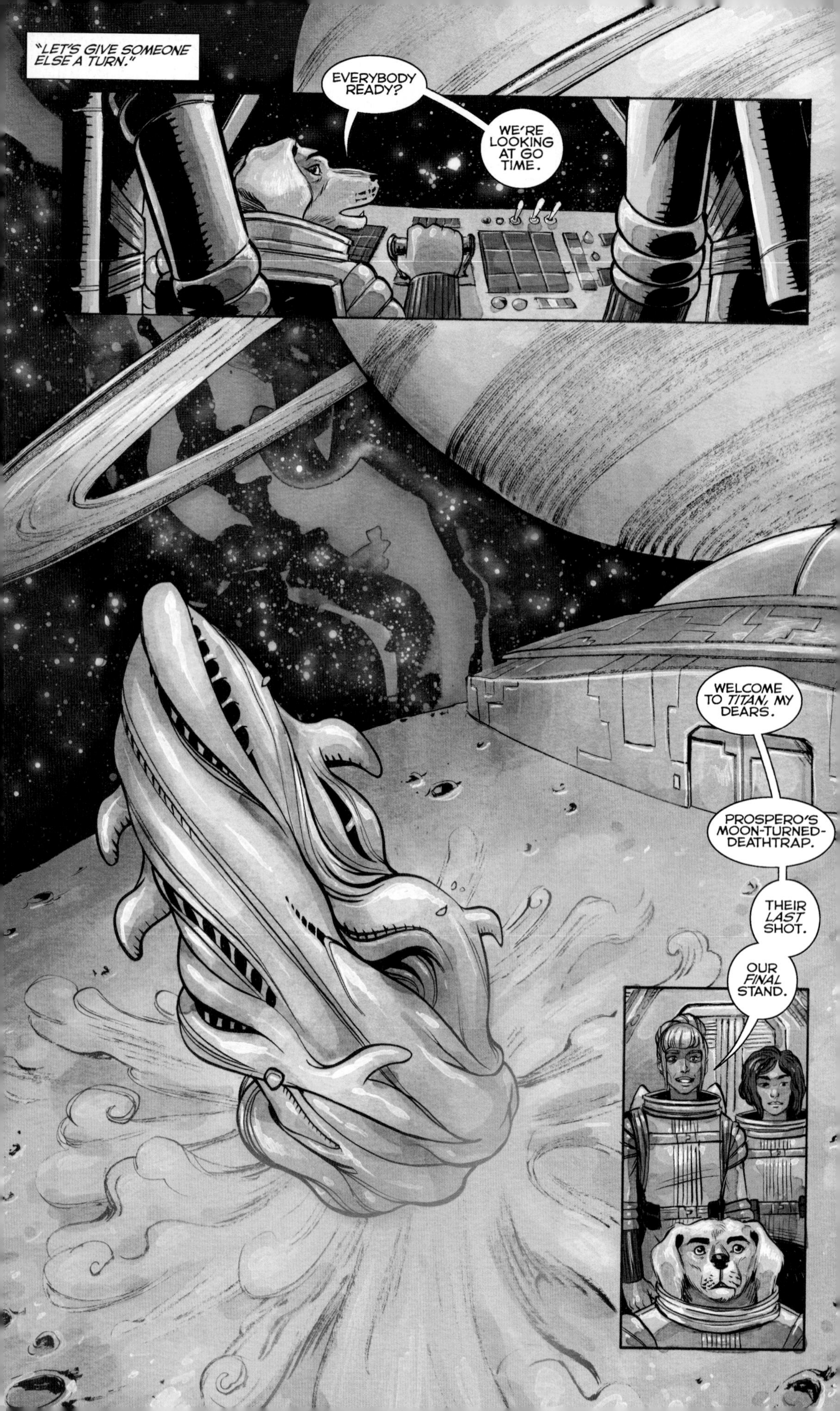
"LET'S GIVE SOMEONE ELSE A TURN."
EVERYBODY READY?
WE'RE LOOKING AT GO TIME.
WELCOME TO *TITAN*, MY DEARS.
PROSPERO'S MOON-TURNED-DEATHTRAP.
THEIR *LAST* SHOT.
OUR *FINAL* STAND.

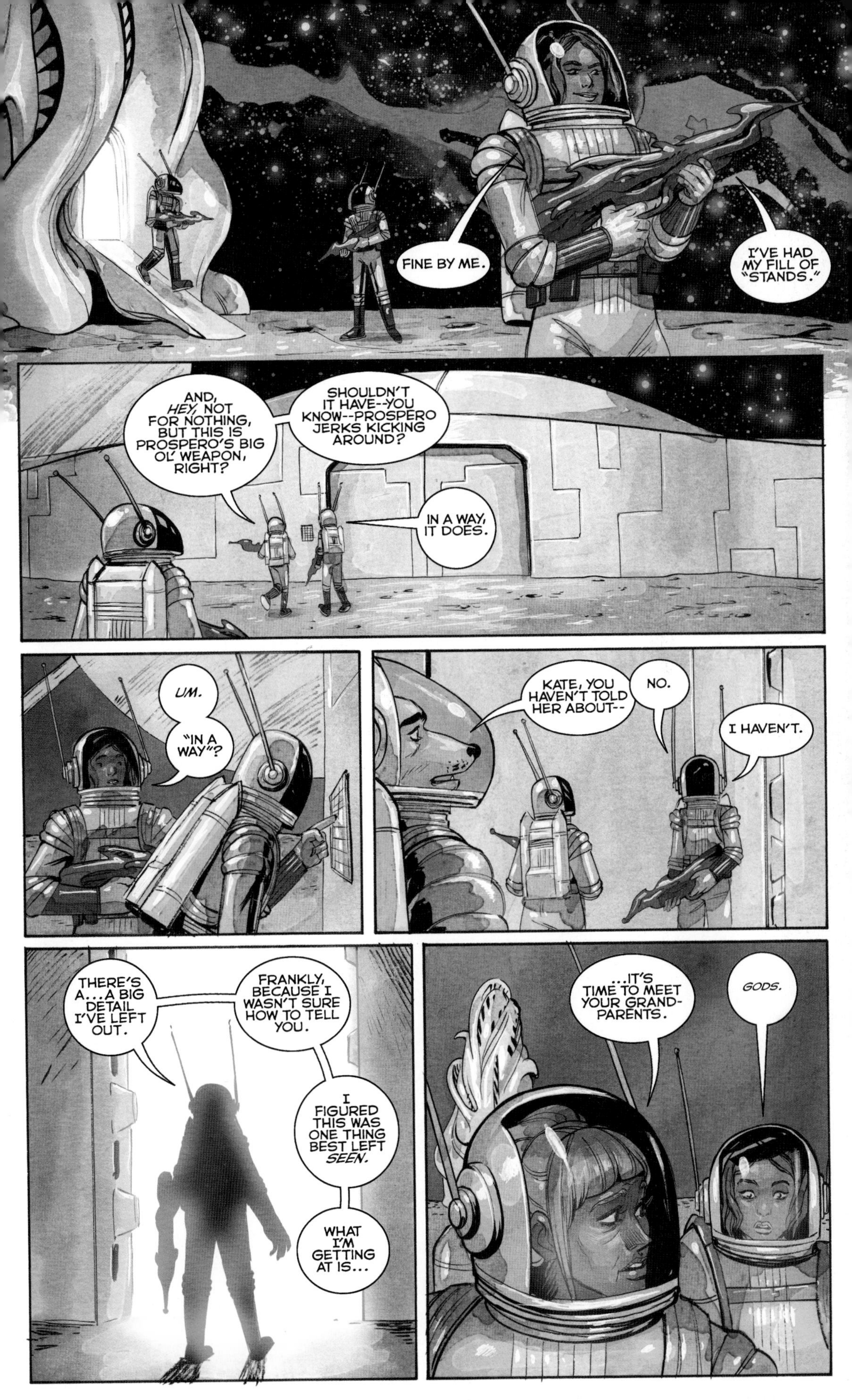
FINE BY ME.
I'VE HAD MY FILL OF "STANDS."
AND, *HEY,* NOT FOR NOTHING, BUT THIS IS PROSPERO'S BIG OL' WEAPON, RIGHT?
SHOULDN'T IT HAVE--YOU KNOW--PROSPERO JERKS KICKING AROUND?
IN A WAY, IT DOES.
UM.
"IN A WAY"?
KATE, YOU HAVEN'T TOLD HER ABOUT--
NO.
I HAVEN'T.
THERE'S A...A BIG DETAIL I'VE LEFT OUT.
FRANKLY, BECAUSE I WASN'T SURE HOW TO TELL YOU.
I FIGURED THIS WAS ONE THING BEST LEFT *SEEN.*
WHAT I'M GETTING AT IS...
...IT'S TIME TO MEET YOUR GRAND-PARENTS.
GODS.

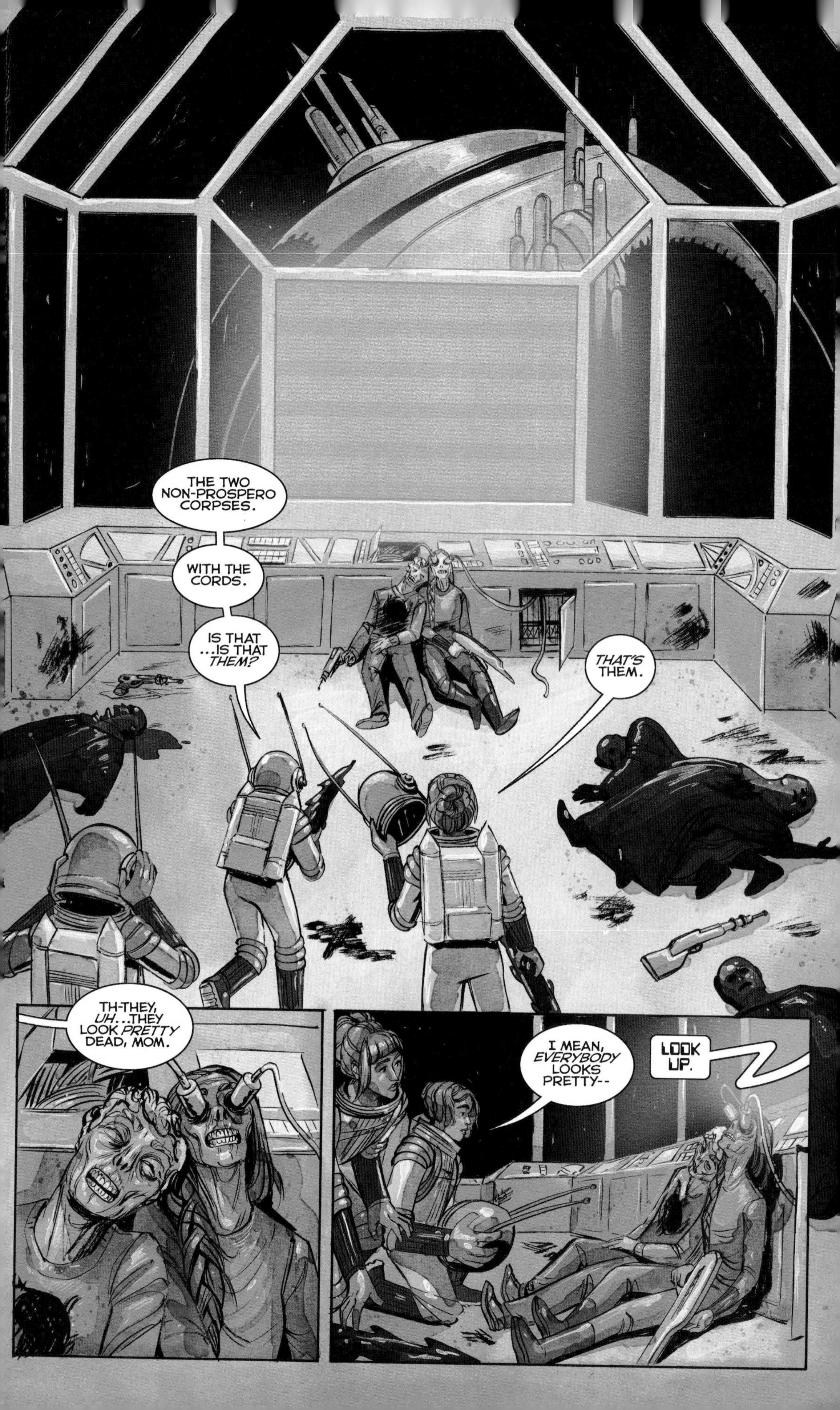
THE TWO NON-PROSPERO CORPSES.
WITH THE CORDS.
IS THAT ...IS THAT *THEM?*
THAT'S THEM.
TH-THEY, *UH*...THEY LOOK *PRETTY* DEAD, MOM.
I MEAN, *EVERYBODY* LOOKS PRETTY--
LOOK UP.

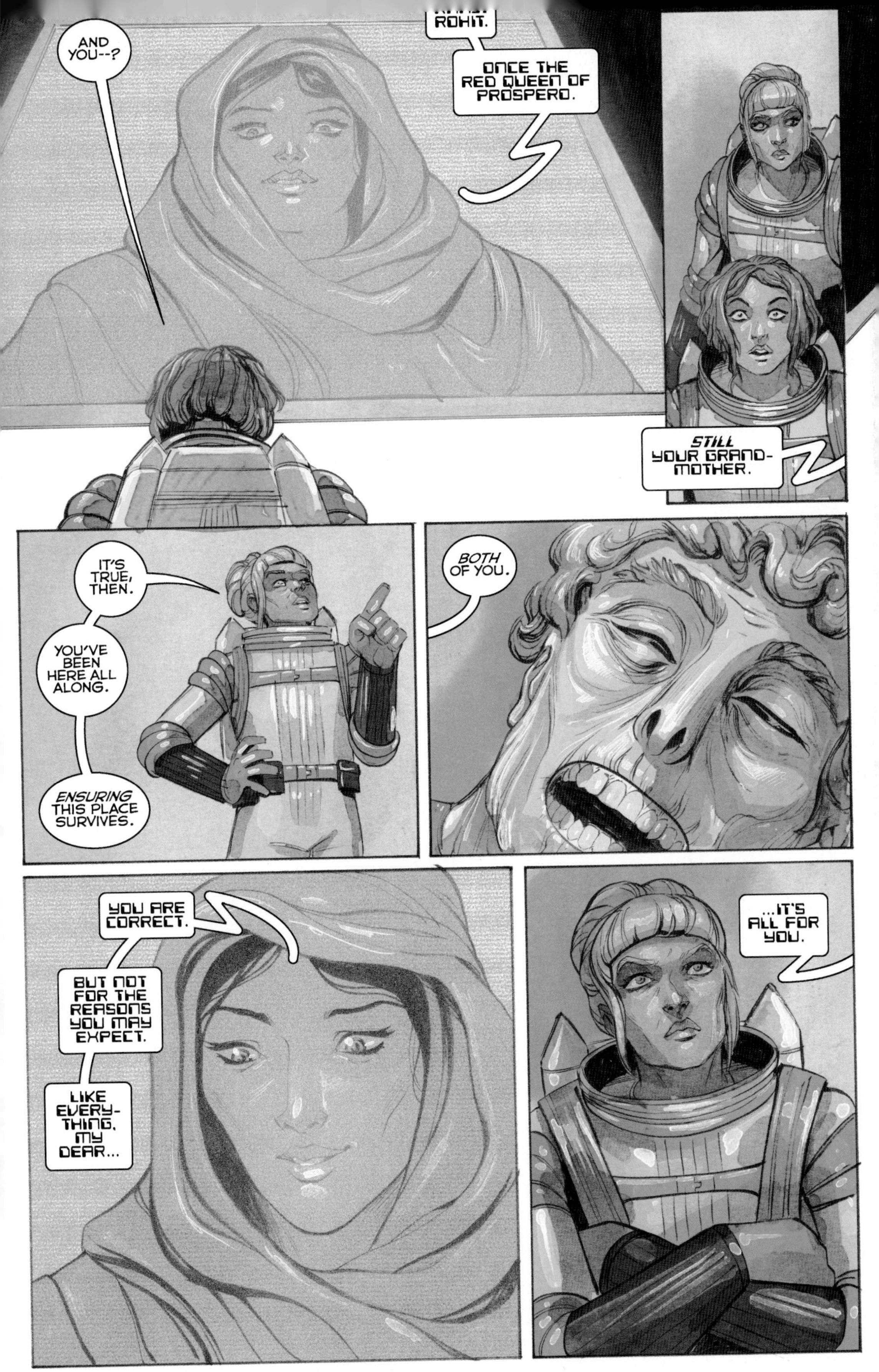

AND YOU--?
ROHIT.
ONCE THE RED QUEEN OF PROSPERO.
STILL YOUR GRAND-MOTHER.
IT'S TRUE, THEN.
YOU'VE BEEN HERE ALL ALONG.
ENSURING THIS PLACE SURVIVES.
BOTH OF YOU.
YOU ARE CORRECT.
BUT NOT FOR THE REASONS YOU MAY EXPECT.
LIKE EVERY-THING, MY DEAR...
...IT'S ALL FOR YOU.

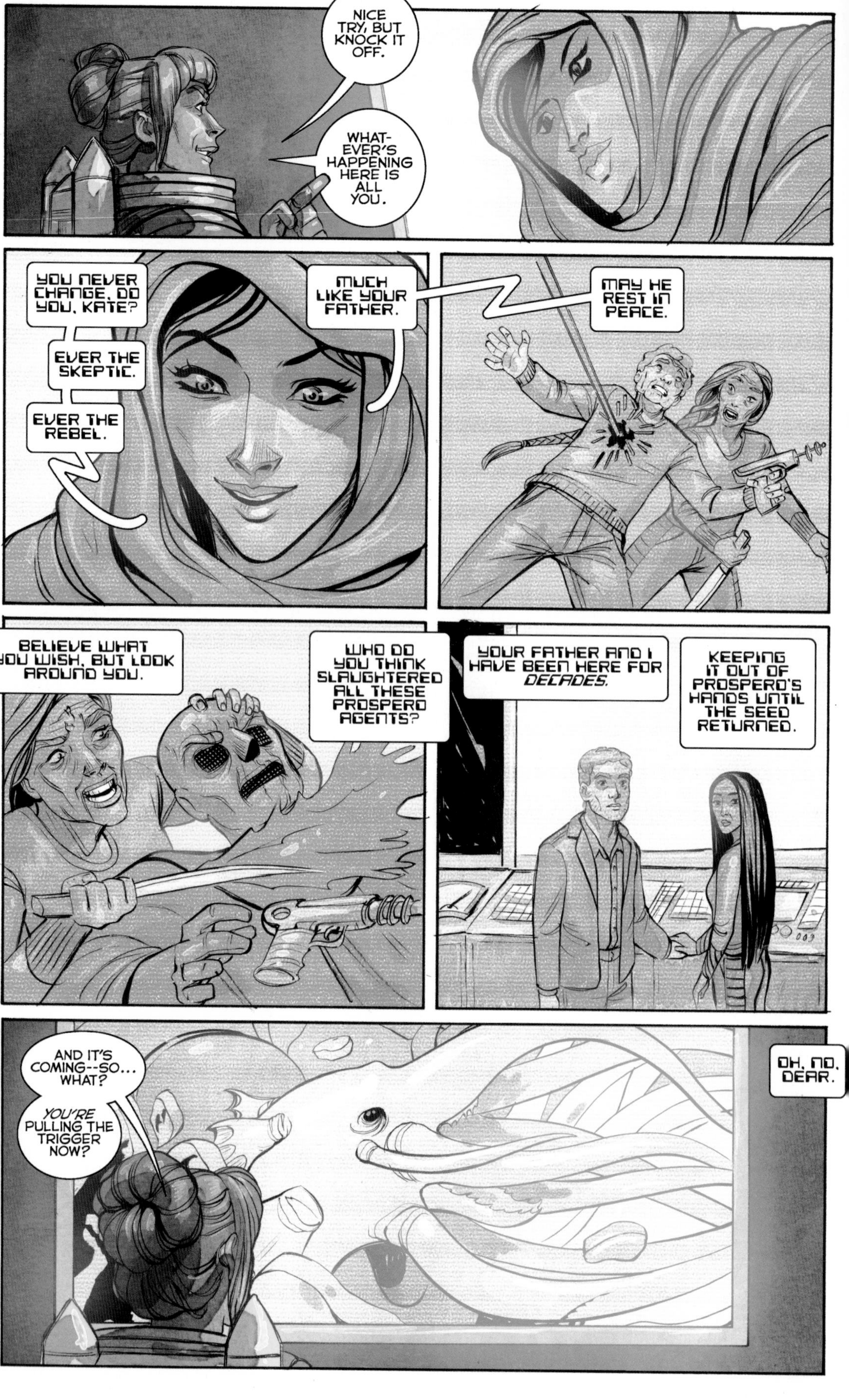
NICE TRY, BUT KNOCK IT OFF.
WHAT-EVER'S HAPPENING HERE IS ALL YOU.
YOU NEVER CHANGE, DO YOU, KATE?
EVER THE SKEPTIC.
EVER THE REBEL.
MUCH LIKE YOUR FATHER.
MAY HE REST IN PEACE.
BELIEVE WHAT YOU WISH, BUT LOOK AROUND YOU.
WHO DO YOU THINK SLAUGHTERED ALL THESE PROSPERO AGENTS?
YOUR FATHER AND I HAVE BEEN HERE FOR *DECADES.*
KEEPING IT OUT OF PROSPERO'S HANDS UNTIL THE SEED RETURNED.
AND IT'S COMING--SO... WHAT?
YOU'RE PULLING THE TRIGGER NOW?
OH, NO, DEAR.

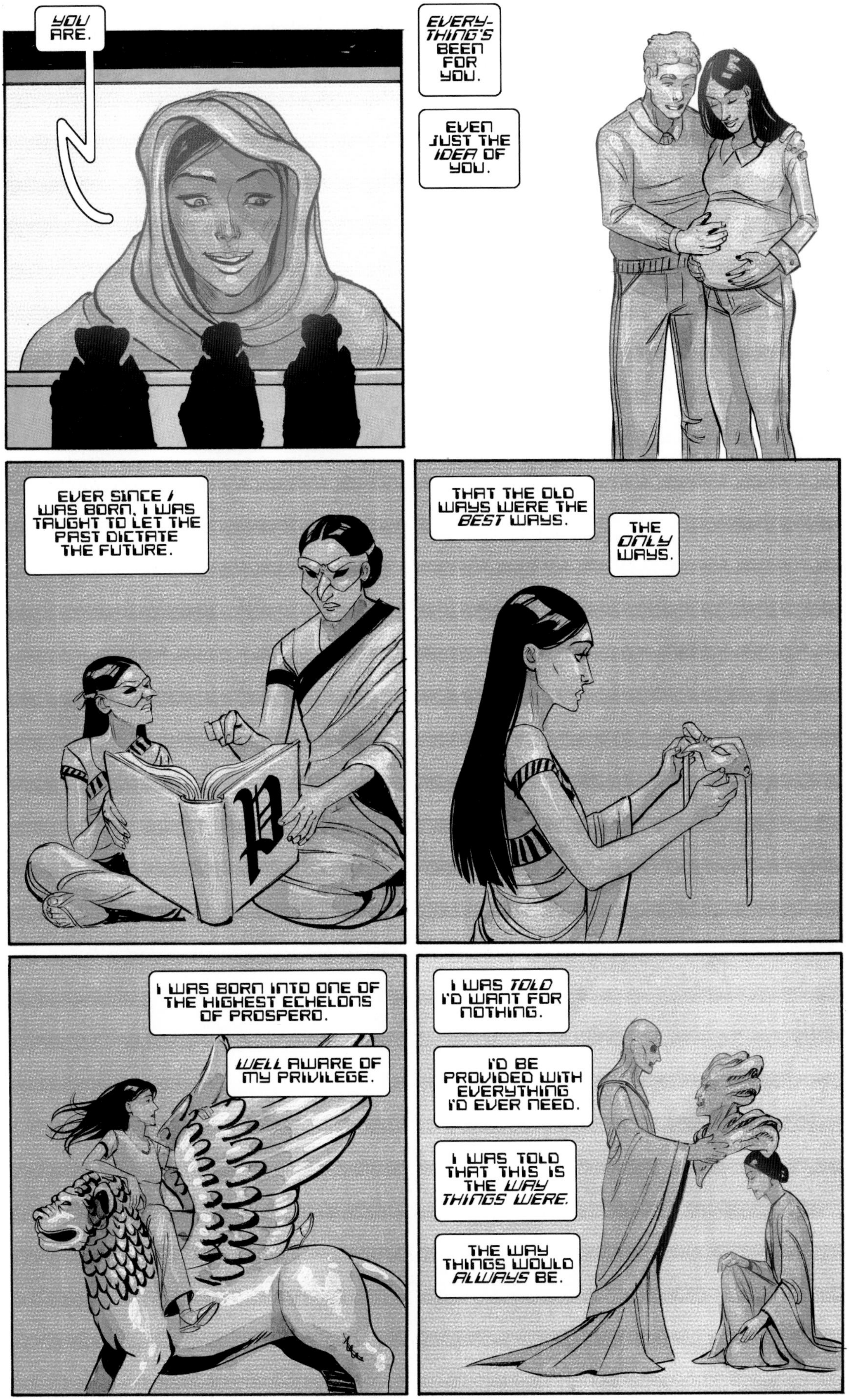
YOU ARE.
EVERYTHING'S BEEN FOR YOU.
EVEN JUST THE IDEA OF YOU.
EVER SINCE I WAS BORN, I WAS TAUGHT TO LET THE PAST DICTATE THE FUTURE.
THAT THE OLD WAYS WERE THE BEST WAYS.
THE ONLY WAYS.
I WAS BORN INTO ONE OF THE HIGHEST ECHELONS OF PROSPERO.
WELL AWARE OF MY PRIVILEGE.
I WAS TOLD I'D WANT FOR NOTHING.
I'D BE PROVIDED WITH EVERYTHING I'D EVER NEED.
I WAS TOLD THAT THIS IS THE WAY THINGS WERE.
THE WAY THINGS WOULD ALWAYS BE.

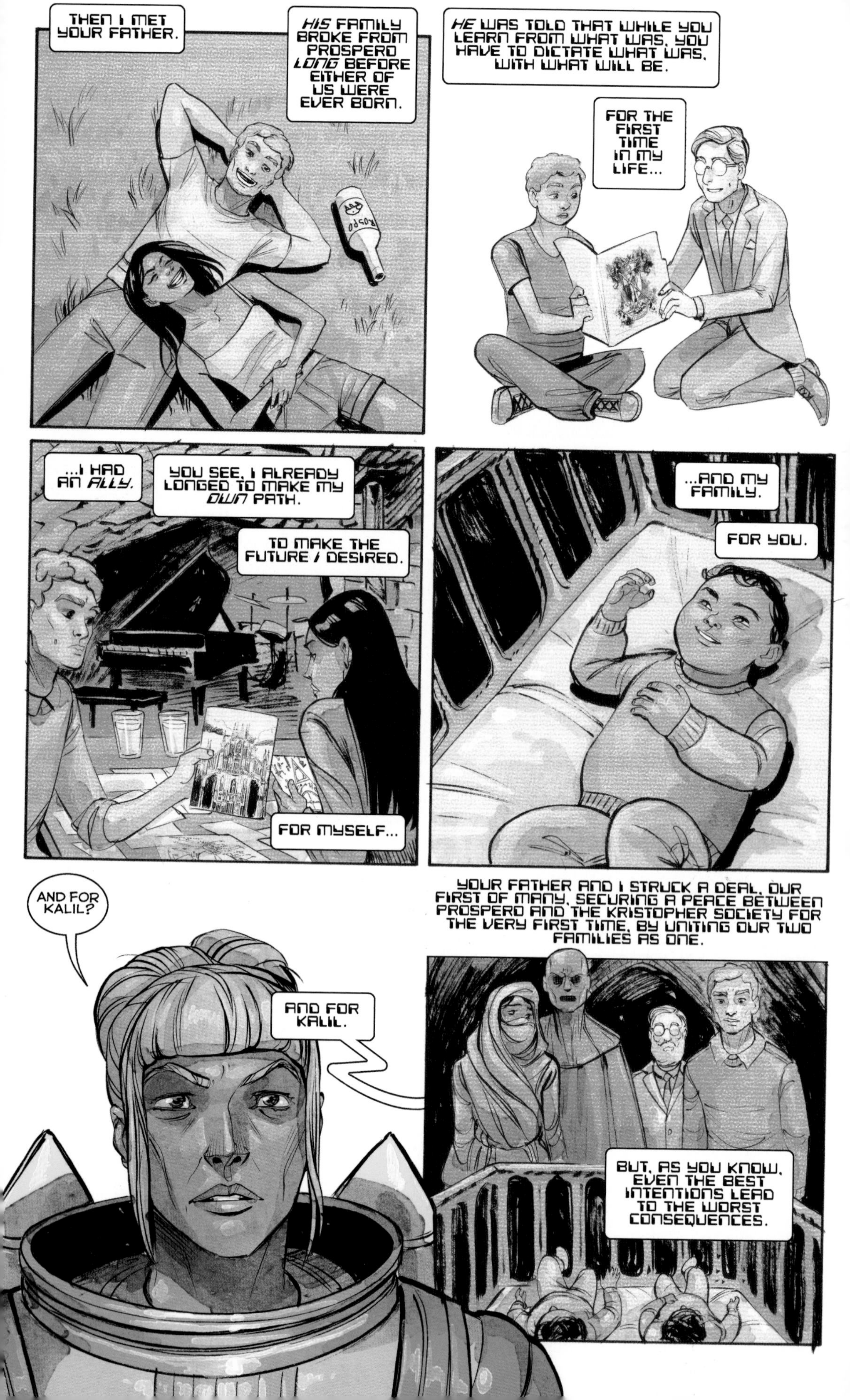
THEN I MET YOUR FATHER.
HIS FAMILY BROKE FROM PROSPERO LONG BEFORE EITHER OF US WERE EVER BORN.
ROSPO
HE WAS TOLD THAT WHILE YOU LEARN FROM WHAT WAS, YOU HAVE TO DICTATE WHAT WAS, WITH WHAT WILL BE.
FOR THE FIRST TIME IN MY LIFE...
...I HAD AN ALLY.
YOU SEE, I ALREADY LONGED TO MAKE MY OWN PATH.
TO MAKE THE FUTURE I DESIRED.
FOR MYSELF...
...AND MY FAMILY.
FOR YOU.
AND FOR KALIL?
AND FOR KALIL.
YOUR FATHER AND I STRUCK A DEAL, OUR FIRST OF MANY, SECURING A PEACE BETWEEN PROSPERO AND THE KRISTOPHER SOCIETY FOR THE VERY FIRST TIME, BY UNITING OUR TWO FAMILIES AS ONE.
BUT, AS YOU KNOW, EVEN THE BEST INTENTIONS LEAD TO THE WORST CONSEQUENCES.

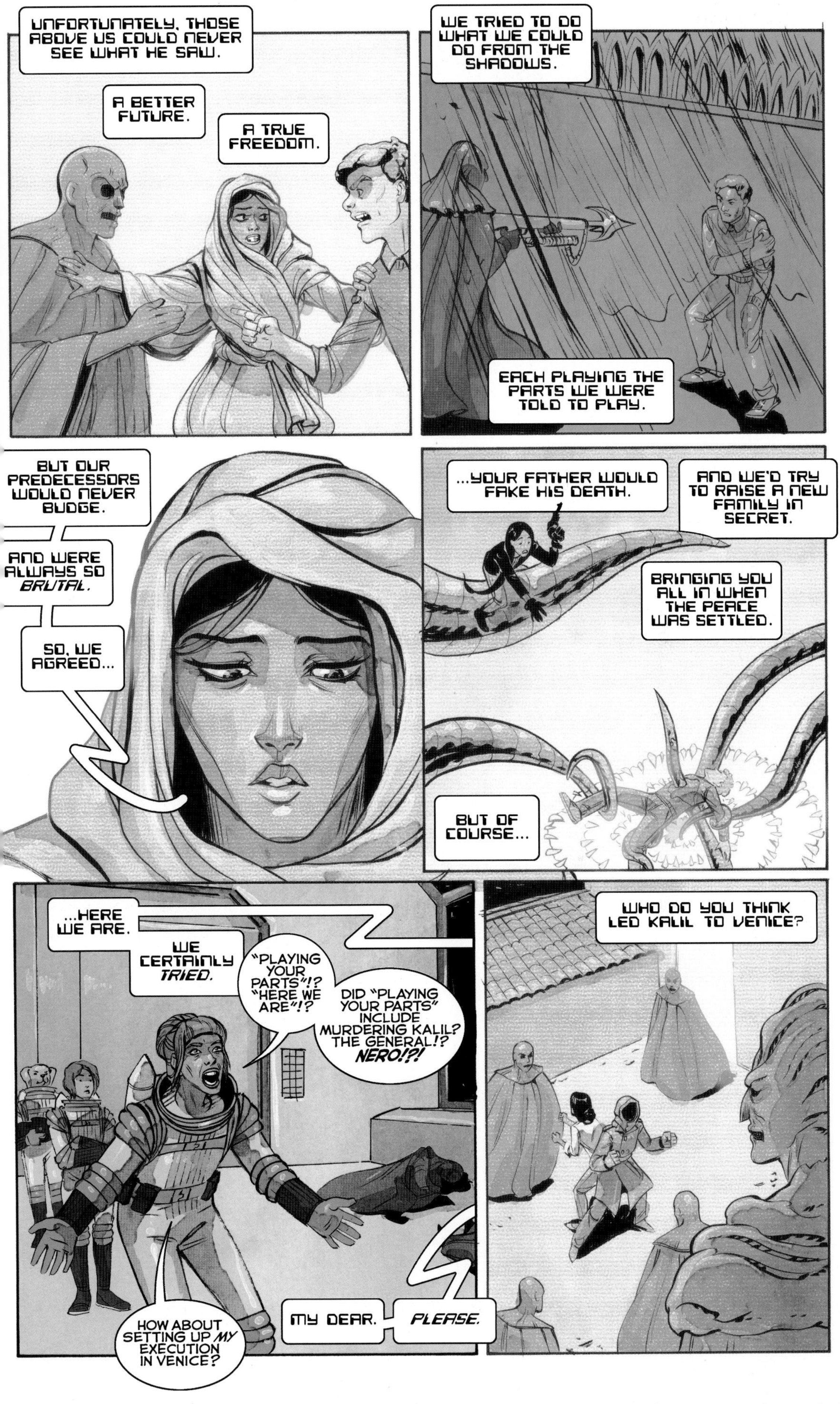
UNFORTUNATELY, THOSE ABOVE US COULD NEVER SEE WHAT HE SAW.
A BETTER FUTURE.
A TRUE FREEDOM.
WE TRIED TO DO WHAT WE COULD DO FROM THE SHADOWS.
EACH PLAYING THE PARTS WE WERE TOLD TO PLAY.
BUT OUR PREDECESSORS WOULD NEVER BUDGE.
AND WERE ALWAYS SO *BRUTAL*.
SO, WE AGREED...
...YOUR FATHER WOULD FAKE HIS DEATH.
AND WE'D TRY TO RAISE A NEW FAMILY IN SECRET.
BRINGING YOU ALL IN WHEN THE PEACE WAS SETTLED.
BUT OF COURSE...
...HERE WE ARE.
WE CERTAINLY *TRIED*.
"PLAYING YOUR PARTS"!? "HERE WE ARE"!?
DID "PLAYING YOUR PARTS" INCLUDE MURDERING KALIL? THE GENERAL!? ***NERO!?!***
HOW ABOUT SETTING UP *MY* EXECUTION IN VENICE?
MY DEAR.
PLEASE.
WHO DO YOU THINK LED KALIL TO VENICE?

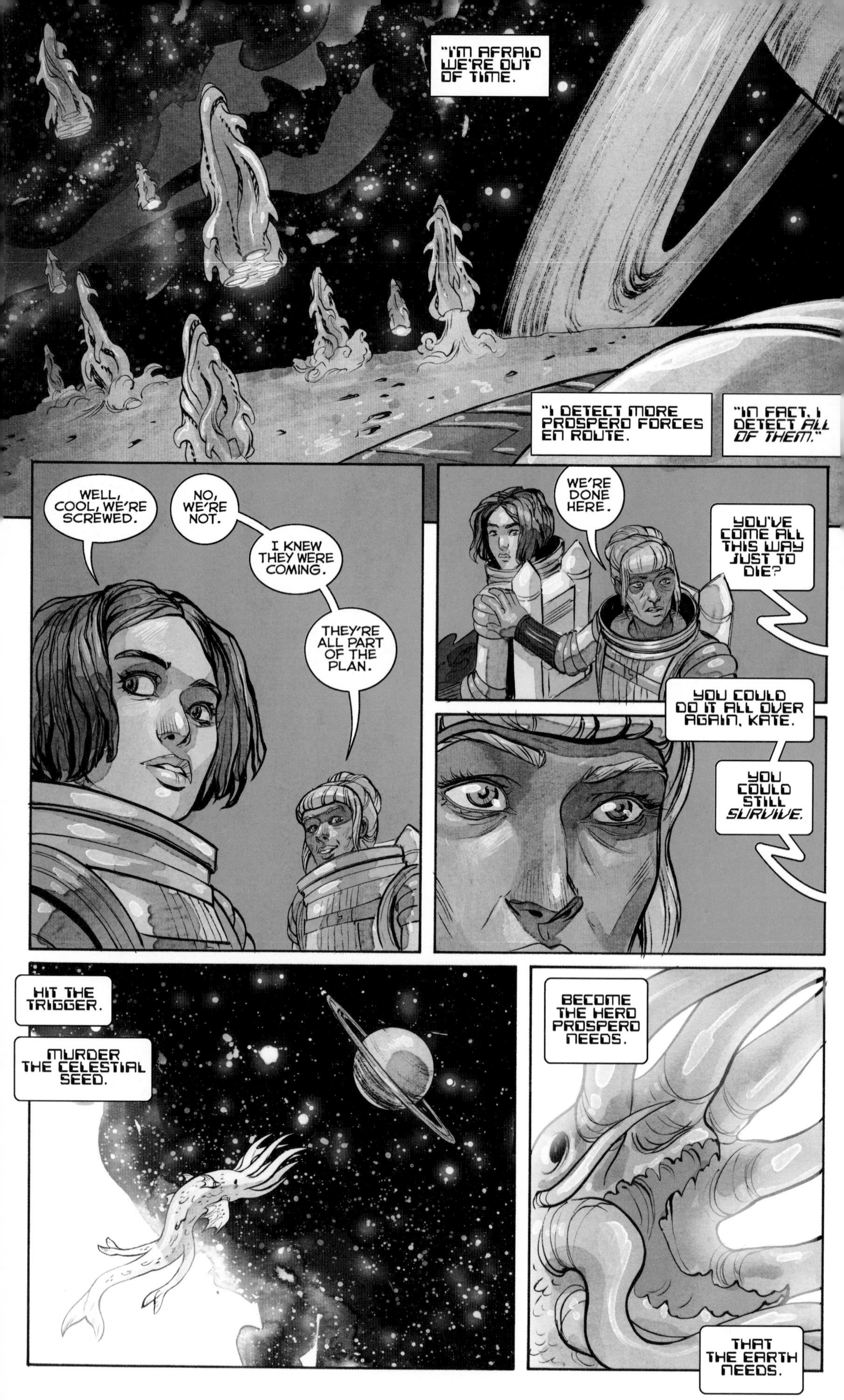
"I'M AFRAID WE'RE OUT OF TIME.
"I DETECT MORE PROSPERO FORCES EN ROUTE.
"IN FACT, I DETECT *ALL OF THEM.*"
WELL, COOL, WE'RE SCREWED.
NO, WE'RE NOT.
I KNEW THEY WERE COMING.
THEY'RE ALL PART OF THE PLAN.
WE'RE DONE HERE.
YOU'VE COME ALL THIS WAY JUST TO DIE?
YOU COULD DO IT ALL OVER AGAIN, KATE.
YOU COULD STILL *SURVIVE.*
HIT THE TRIGGER.
MURDER THE CELESTIAL SEED.
BECOME THE HERO PROSPERO NEEDS.
THAT THE EARTH NEEDS.

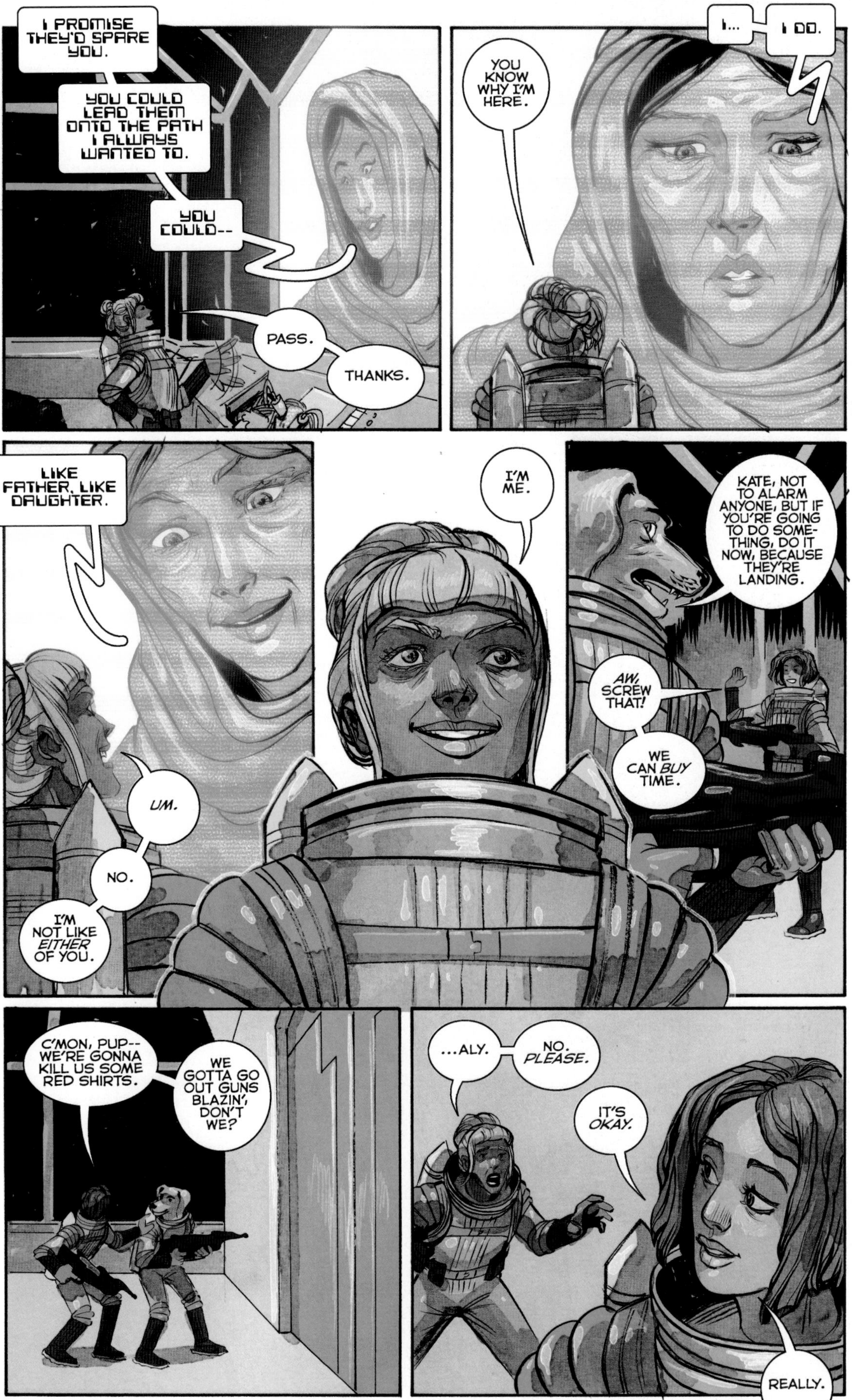
I PROMISE THEY'D SPARE YOU.
YOU COULD LEAD THEM ONTO THE PATH I ALWAYS WANTED TO.
YOU COULD--
PASS.
THANKS.
YOU KNOW WHY I'M HERE.
I...
I DO.
LIKE FATHER, LIKE DAUGHTER.
UM.
NO.
I'M NOT LIKE *EITHER* OF YOU.
I'M ME.
KATE, NOT TO ALARM ANYONE, BUT IF YOU'RE GOING TO DO SOME-THING, DO IT NOW, BECAUSE THEY'RE LANDING.
AW, SCREW THAT!
WE CAN *BUY* TIME.
C'MON, PUP-- WE'RE GONNA KILL US SOME RED SHIRTS.
WE GOTTA GO OUT GUNS BLAZIN', DON'T WE?
...ALY.
NO. *PLEASE.*
IT'S *OKAY.*
REALLY.

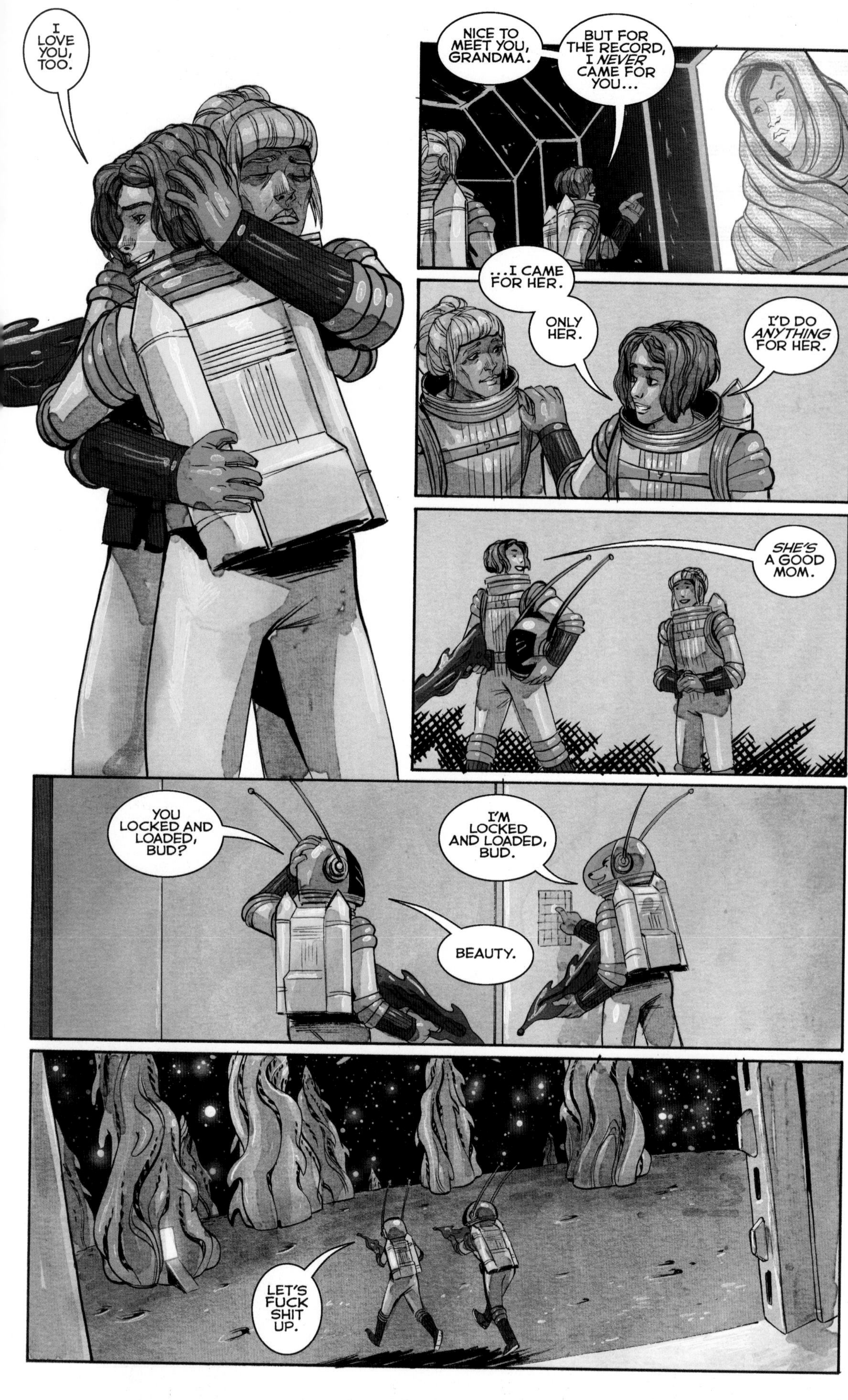
I LOVE YOU, TOO.
NICE TO MEET YOU, GRANDMA.
BUT FOR THE RECORD, I *NEVER* CAME FOR YOU...
...I CAME FOR HER.
ONLY HER.
I'D DO *ANYTHING* FOR HER.
SHE'S A GOOD MOM.
YOU LOCKED AND LOADED, BUD?
I'M LOCKED AND LOADED, BUD.
BEAUTY.
LET'S FUCK SHIT UP.

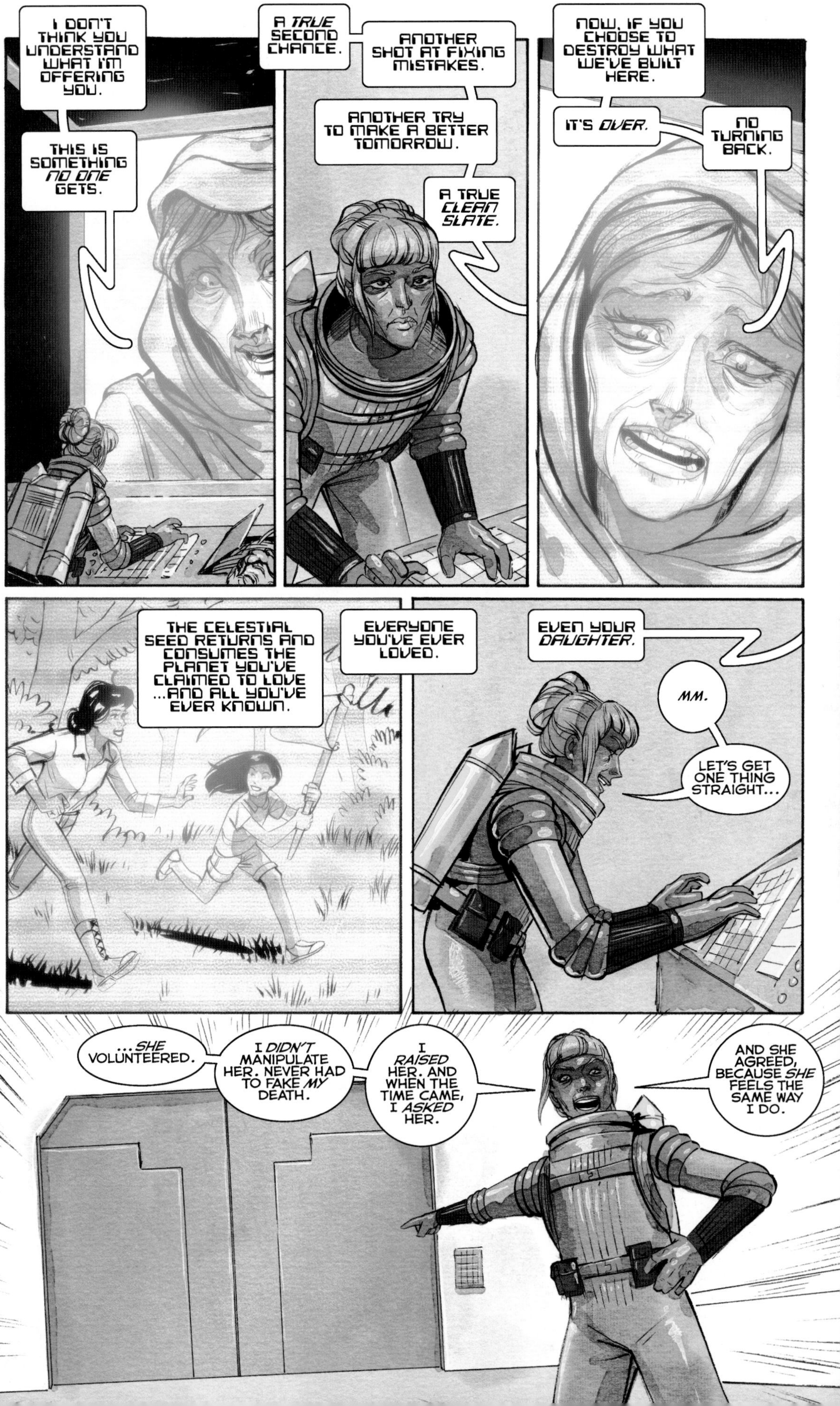
I DON'T THINK YOU UNDERSTAND WHAT I'M OFFERING YOU.
THIS IS SOMETHING *NO ONE* GETS.
A *TRUE* SECOND CHANCE.
ANOTHER SHOT AT FIXING MISTAKES.
ANOTHER TRY TO MAKE A BETTER TOMORROW.
A TRUE *CLEAN SLATE.*
NOW, IF YOU CHOOSE TO DESTROY WHAT WE'VE BUILT HERE.
IT'S *OVER.*
NO TURNING BACK.
THE CELESTIAL SEED RETURNS AND CONSUMES THE PLANET YOU'VE CLAIMED TO LOVE ...AND ALL YOU'VE EVER KNOWN.
EVERYONE YOU'VE EVER LOVED.
EVEN YOUR *DAUGHTER.*
MM.
LET'S GET ONE THING STRAIGHT...
...*SHE* VOLUNTEERED.
I *DIDN'T* MANIPULATE HER. NEVER HAD TO FAKE *MY* DEATH.
I *RAISED* HER. AND WHEN THE TIME CAME, I *ASKED* HER.
AND SHE AGREED, BECAUSE *SHE* FEELS THE SAME WAY I DO.

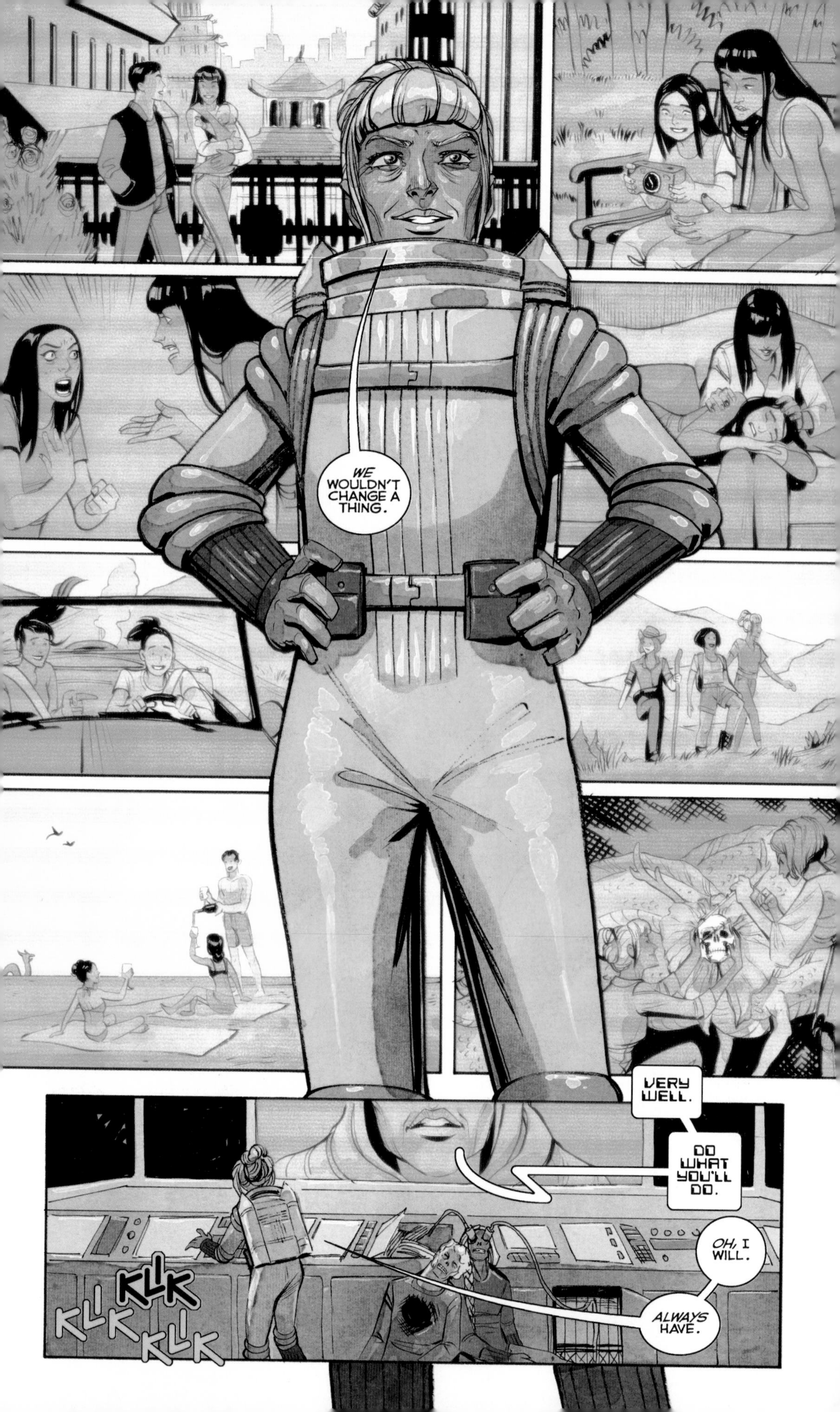
WE WOULDN'T CHANGE A THING.
VERY WELL.
DO WHAT YOU'LL DO.
OH, I WILL.
ALWAYS HAVE.
KLIK KLIK KLIK KLIK

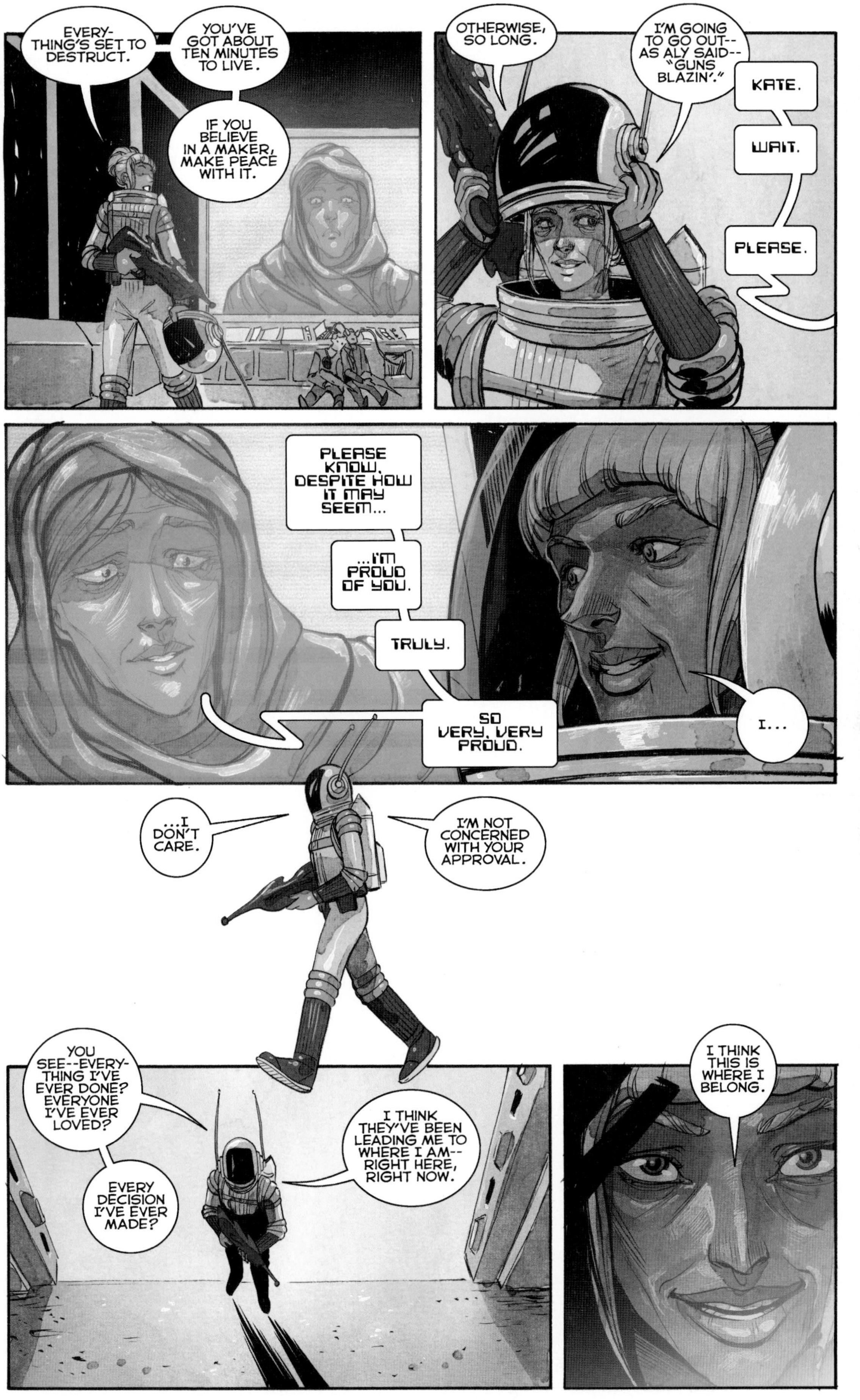
EVERY-THING'S SET TO DESTRUCT.
YOU'VE GOT ABOUT TEN MINUTES TO LIVE.
IF YOU BELIEVE IN A MAKER, MAKE PEACE WITH IT.
OTHERWISE, SO LONG.
I'M GOING TO GO OUT-- AS ALY SAID-- "GUNS BLAZIN'."
KATE.
WAIT.
PLEASE.
PLEASE KNOW, DESPITE HOW IT MAY SEEM...
...I'M PROUD OF YOU.
TRULY.
SO VERY, VERY PROUD.
I...
...I DON'T CARE.
I'M NOT CONCERNED WITH YOUR APPROVAL.
YOU SEE--EVERY-THING I'VE EVER DONE? EVERYONE I'VE EVER LOVED?
EVERY DECISION I'VE EVER MADE?
I THINK THEY'VE BEEN LEADING ME TO WHERE I AM-- RIGHT HERE, RIGHT NOW.
I THINK THIS IS WHERE I BELONG.

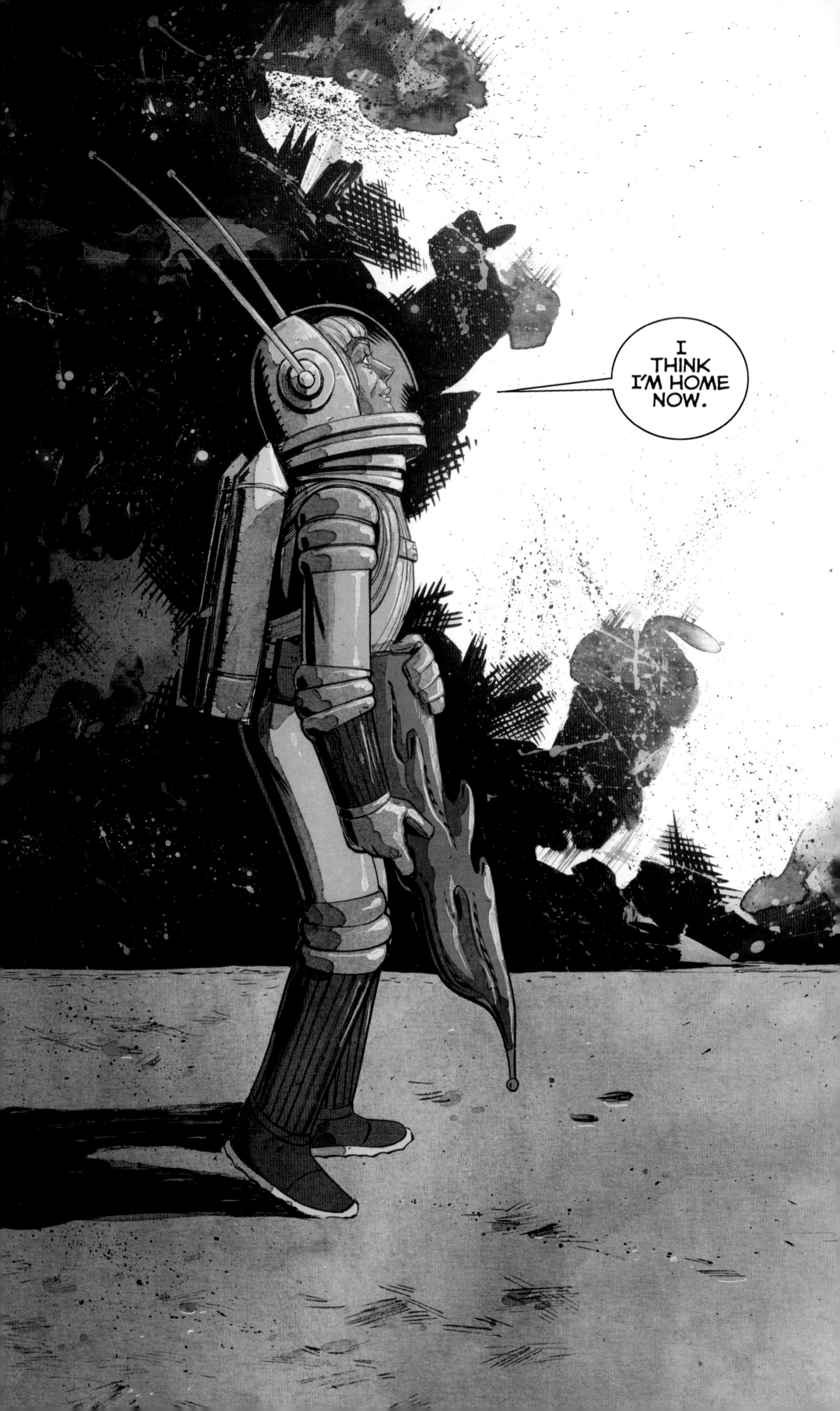
I THINK I'M HOME NOW.

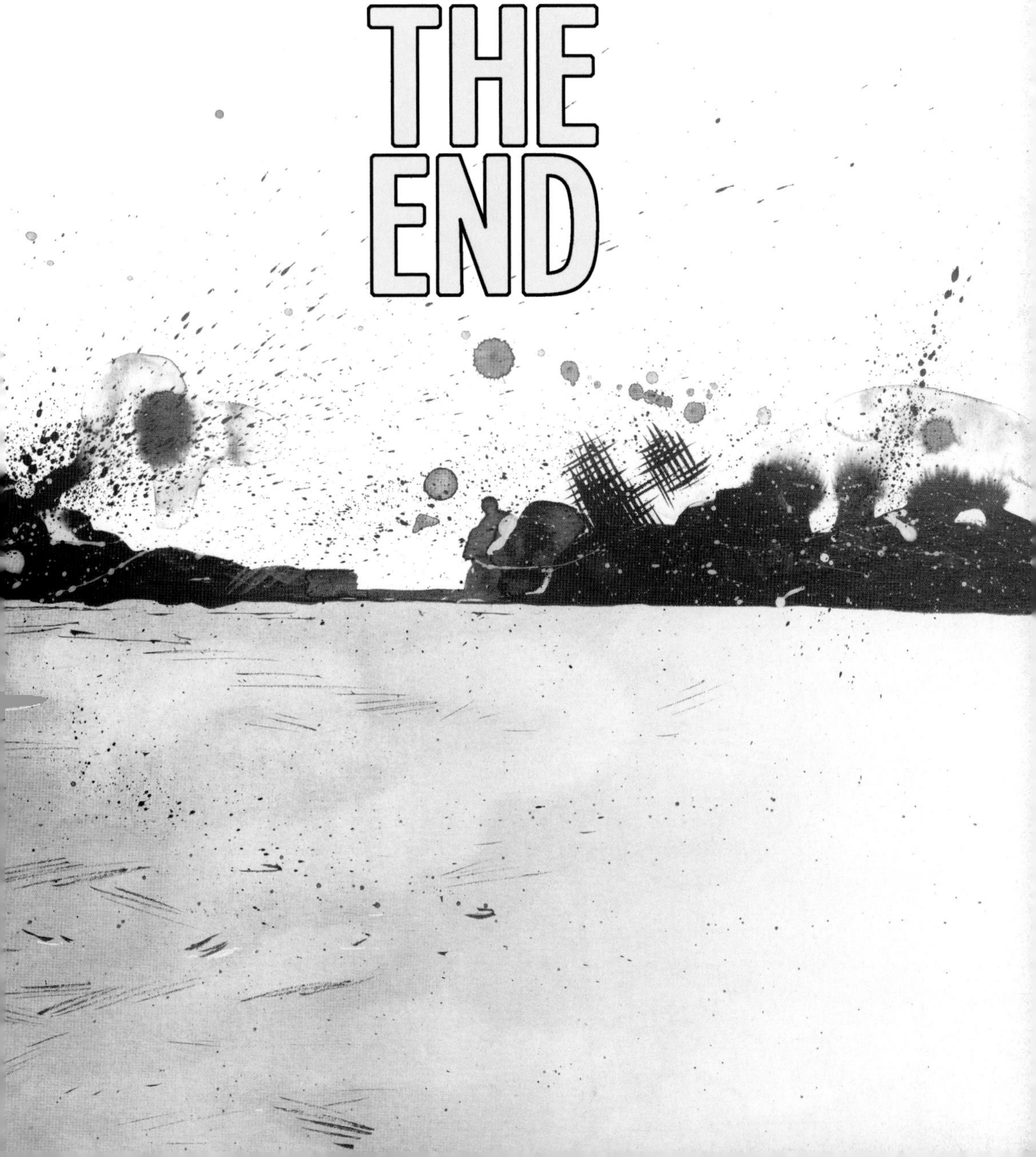
THE END

SKETCHBOOK

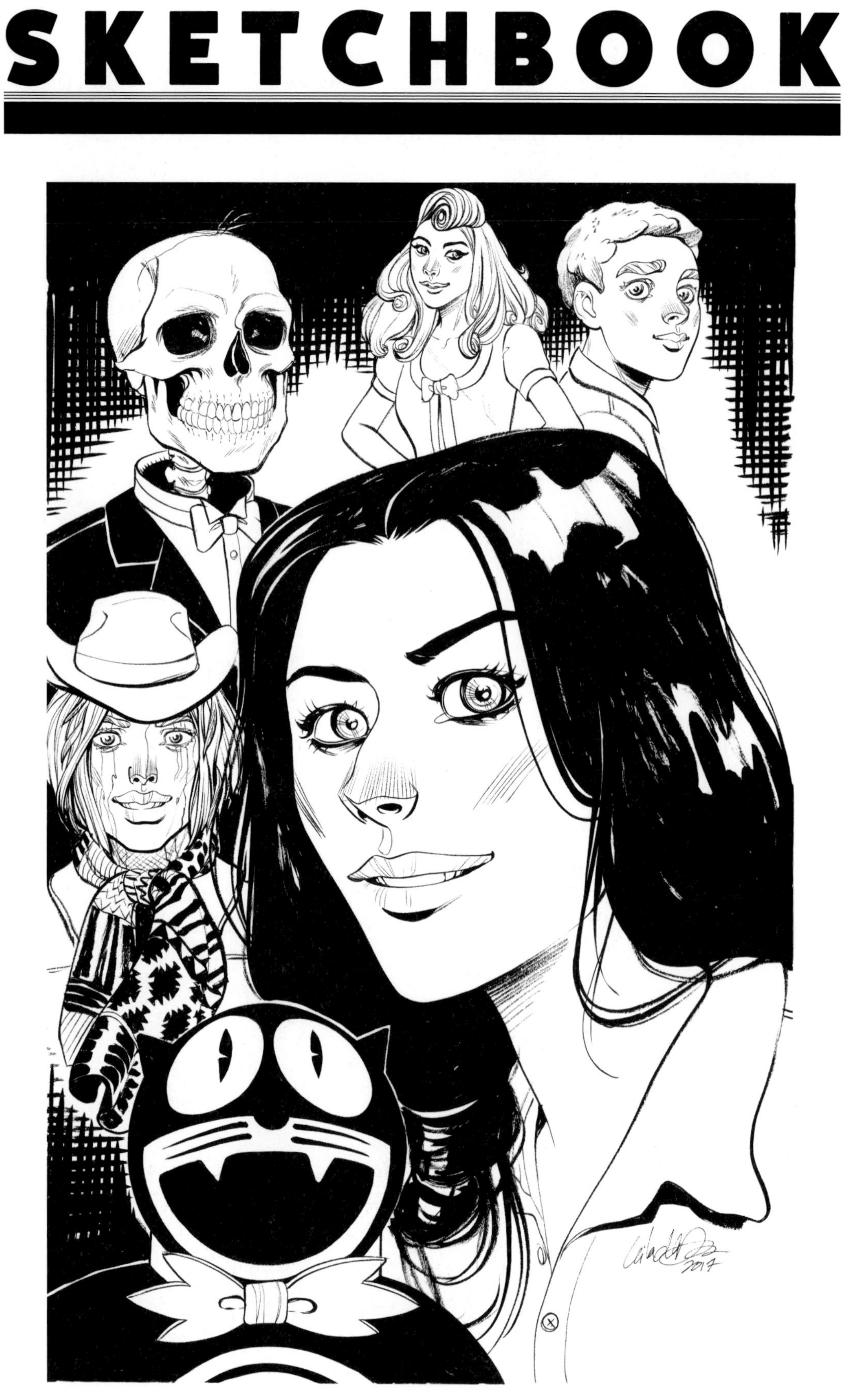

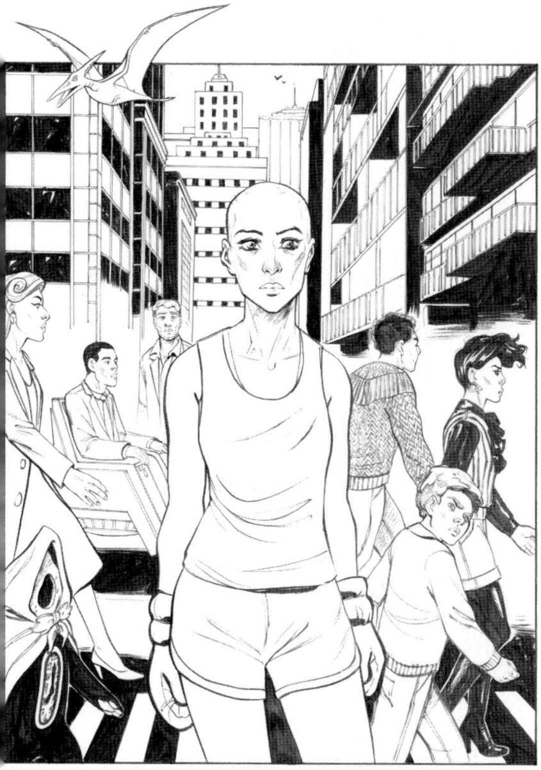

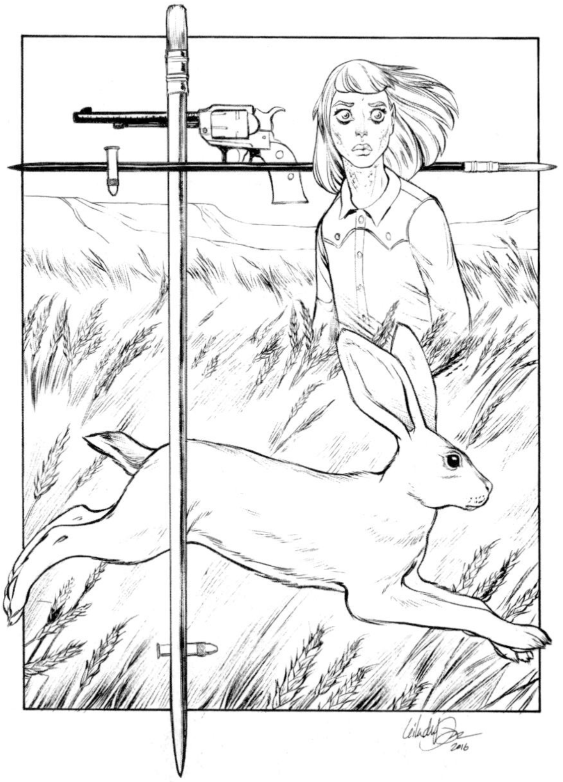

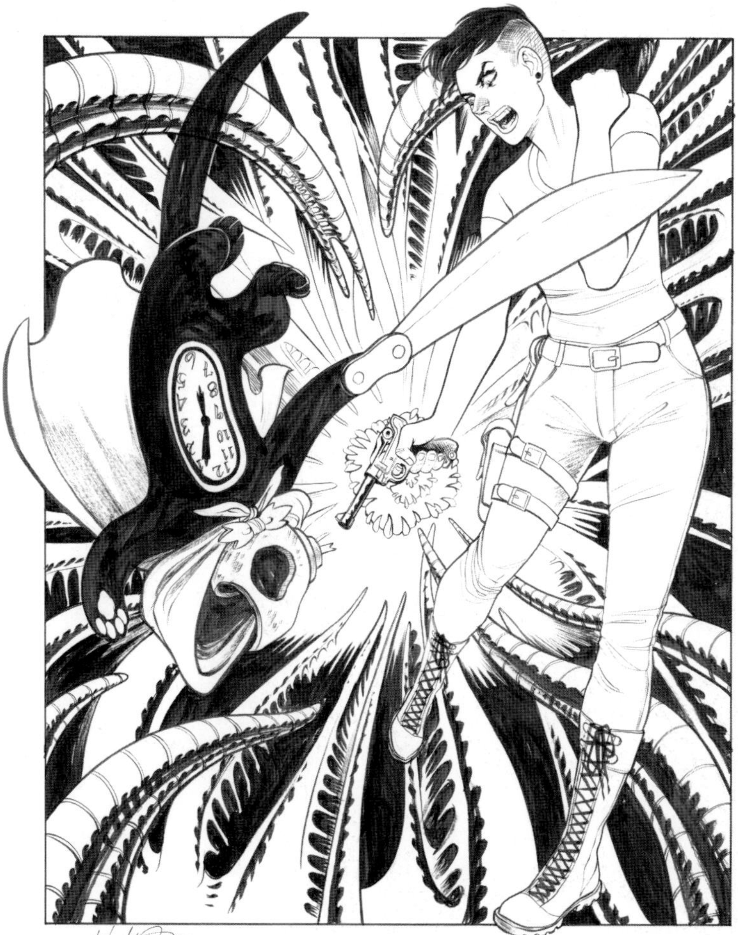

COVER INKS FOR ISSUES 23, 24 & 26

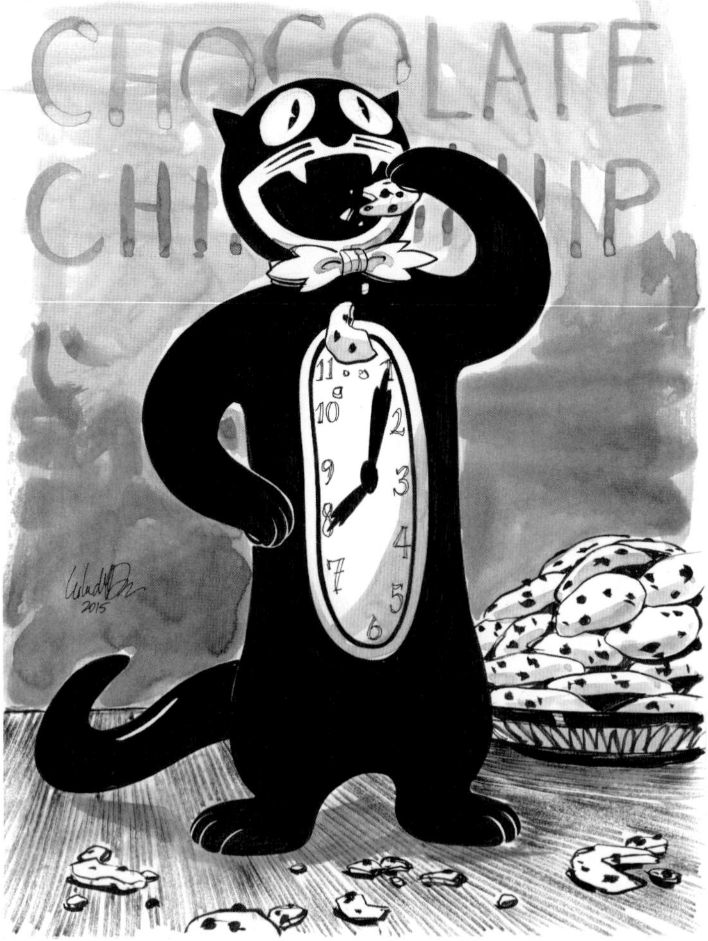
CHOCOLATE
CHIP

CONVENTION SKETCHES

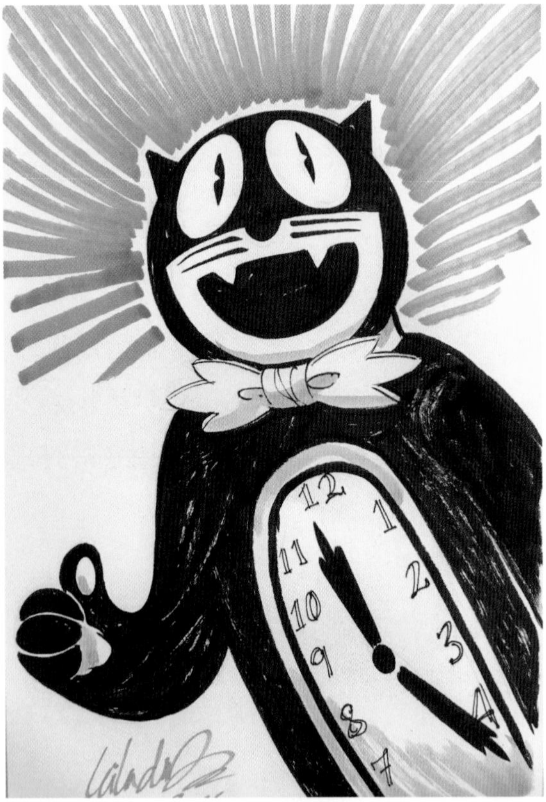

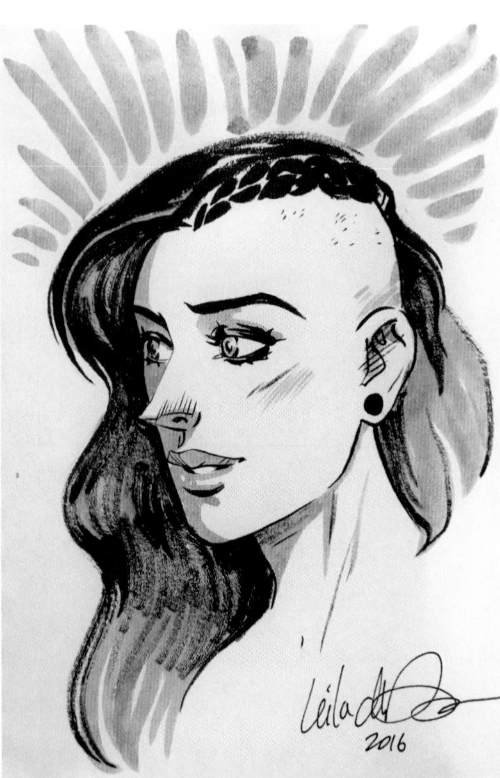

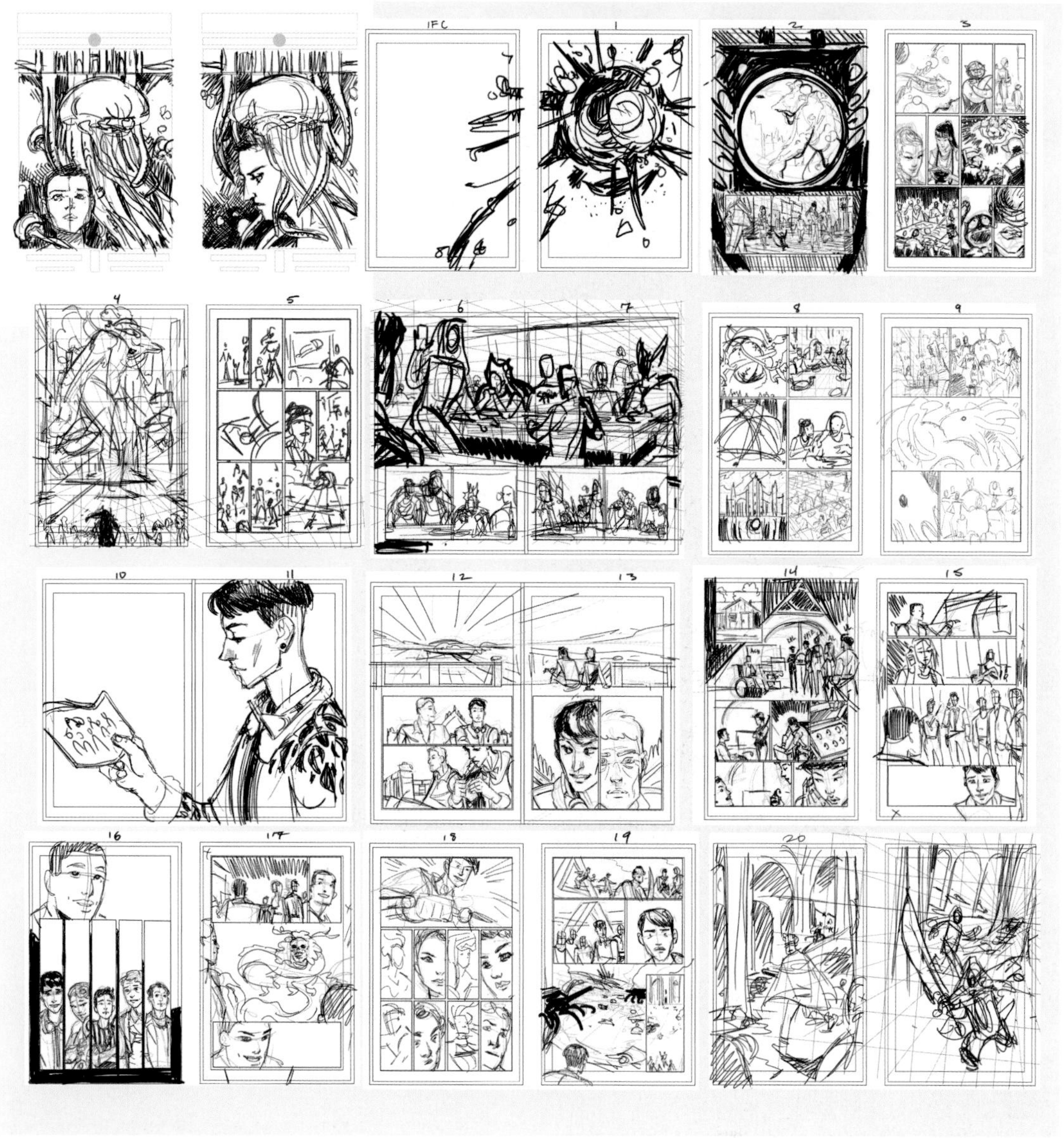
IFC
1
2
3
4
5
6
7
8
9
10
11
12
13
14
15
16
17
18
19
20

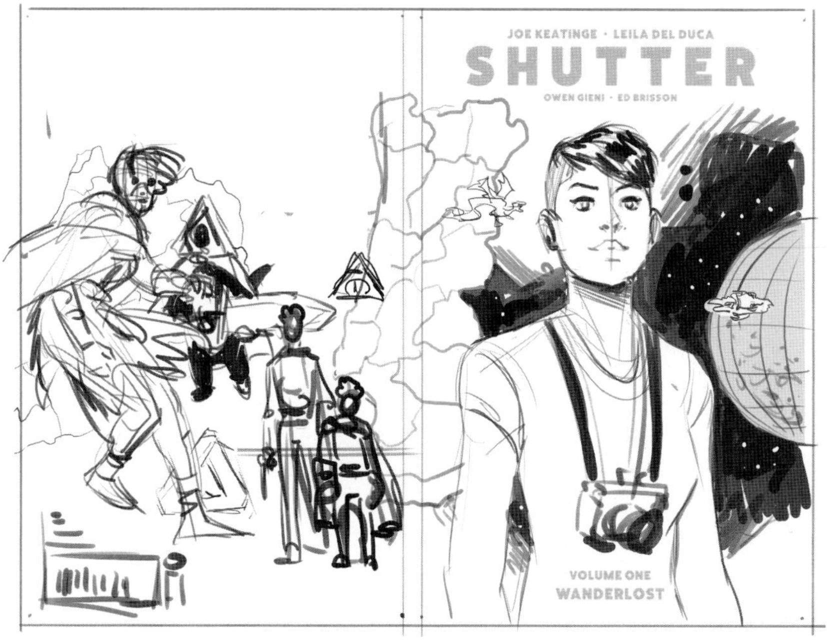
JOE KEATINGE · LEILA DEL DUCA
SHUTTER
OWEN GIENI · ED BRISSON
VOLUME ONE
WANDERLOST

SHUTTER 25 LAYOUTS & VOLUME 5 COVER SKETCH

SHUTTER

JOE KEATINGE is the writer of Image, Skybound, Marvel, and DC Comics titles including SHUTTER, RINGSIDE, GLORY, TECH JACKET, MARVEL KNIGHTS: HULK, and ADVENTURES OF SUPERMAN as well as the Executive Editor of Eisner & Harvey award-winning Image Comics anthology, POPGUN, and the Courtney Taylor-Taylor penned ONE MODEL NATION.

LEILA DEL DUCA is a comic book artist and writer currently living in Portland, OR. Since co-creating SHUTTER with Joe Keatinge in 2014, Leila has worked on other titles including THE WICKED + THE DIVINE, SCARLET WITCH, and AMERICAN VAMPIRE. She also wrote AFAR, the young adult graphic novel drawn by Kit Seaton, published by Image Comics. In 2015 and 2016, Leila was nominated for the Russ Manning Promising Newcomer Award for her work on SHUTTER. She enjoys reading, making food, and staring off into space during her free time.

TEAM BIOS

OWEN GIENI is the artist of RAT QUEENS from Shadowline, colourist of MANIFEST DESTINY from Skybound, and colourist of SHUTTER from Image central. He is also the artist of NEGATIVE SPACE from Dark Horse Comics.

JOHN WORKMAN

In 1967...after six years of drawing and writing comics stories, creating comics characters, and learning all that he could about doing those things, John Workman made his first money from putting pencil to paper. The next five decades would take him from a small town in Washington State to

JOHN WORKMAN, CATHY WORKMAN, SERGIO ARAGONES, AND WALTER SIMONSON. PHOTO BY LOUISE SIMONSON.

New York and to working for multiple publishers in the US and in other parts of the world. His years at HEAVY METAL MAGAZINE were his happiest time spent in the world of comics. In addition to his production, editorial, and design work, he wrote, drew, lettered, and colored stories for HM that, for a while, reached an average of one million diverse readers. He very much misses those days and the even larger audience that saw various aspects of his abilities demonstrated in PLAYBOY, SPORTS ILLUSTRATED, and TV GUIDE. Workman has lettered 24 issues of SHUTTER, and...thanks to the faith in his abilities demonstrated by Joe Keatinge and Leila Del Duca...also did a bit of drawing and writing for the book. He, in turn, has a lot of faith in the continuing possibilities of SHUTTER on both a domestic and an international level. It's been an interesting time, working in the comics form from 1967 to the present, and there will always exist the amazing promise of the future.

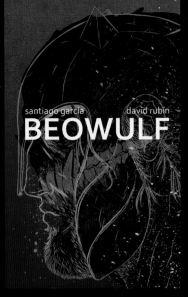

Written by Joe Keatinge

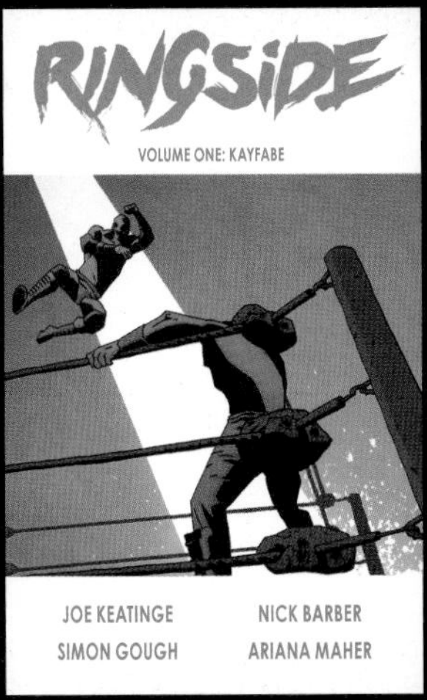
RINGSIDE
VOLUME ONE: KAYFABE
JOE KEATINGE
NICK BARBER
SIMON GOUGH
ARIANA MAHER

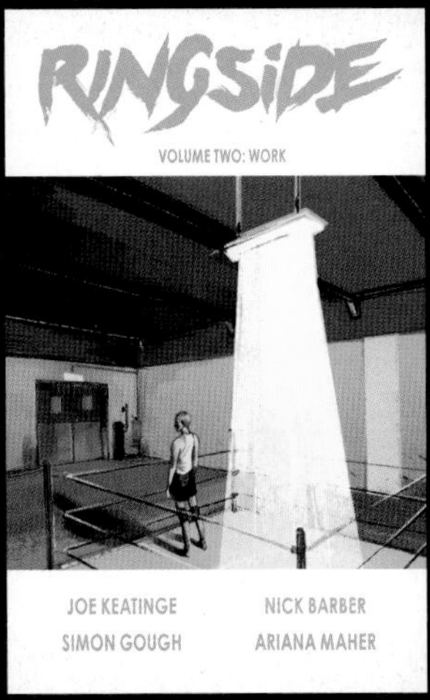
RINGSIDE
VOLUME TWO: WORK
JOE KEATINGE
NICK BARBER
SIMON GOUGH
ARIANA MAHER

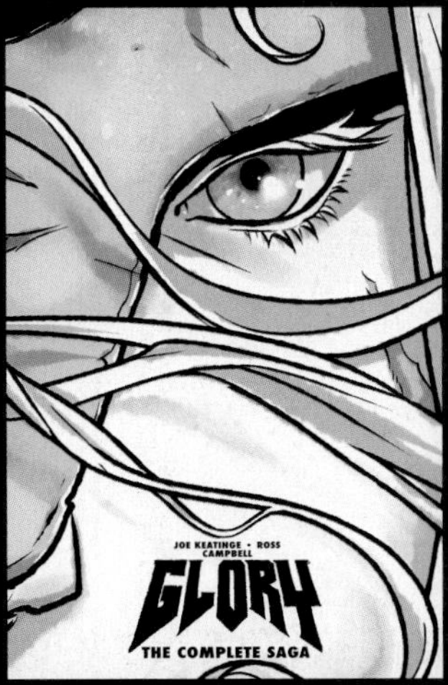
JOE KEATINGE • ROSS CAMPBELL
GLORY
THE COMPLETE SAGA

"RINGSIDE is essentially an ensemble drama about a group of struggling professional wrestlers. And while that may sound like the sort of thing that would only appeal to dedicated WWE viewers, this book has plenty to offer readers of all tastes."

- IGN

"It will stand the test of time as being one of the boldest, bravest, and most wonderfully bizarre superhero books — a superhero book that is utterly un-superhero in the best of ways."

- Comic Book Resources

Edited by Joe Keatinge

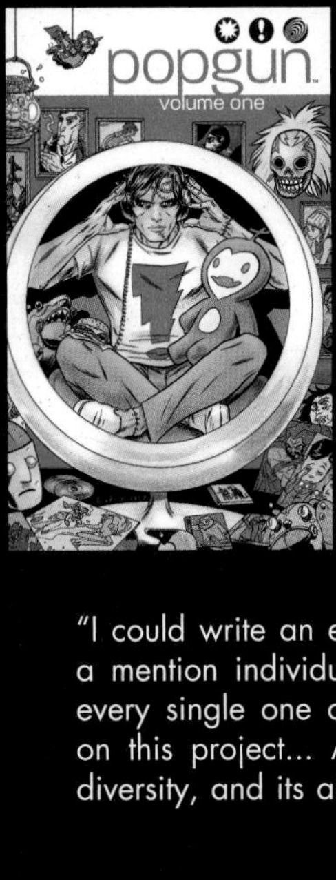
popgun
volume one

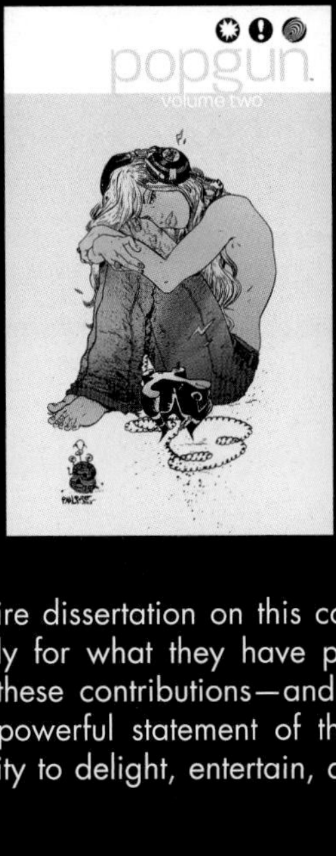
popgun
volume two

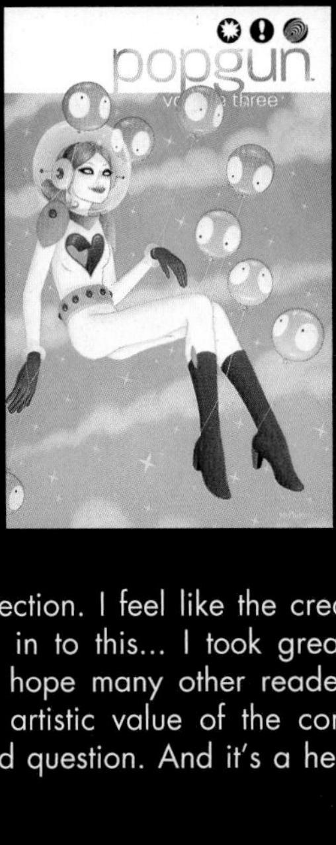
popgun

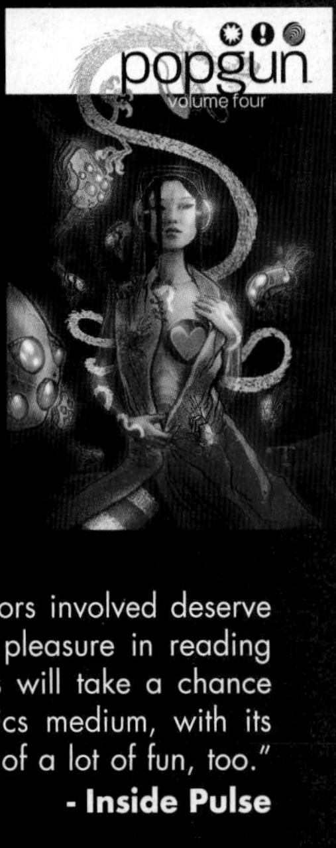
popgun
volume four

"I could write an entire dissertation on this collection. I feel like the creators involved deserve a mention individually for what they have put in to this... I took great pleasure in reading every single one of these contributions—and I hope many other readers will take a chance on this project... A powerful statement of the artistic value of the comics medium, with its diversity, and its ability to delight, entertain, and question. And it's a hell of a lot of fun, too."

- Inside Pulse

JOE KEATINGE - WRITER

LEILA DEL DUCA - ARTIST

OWEN GIENI - COLORIST

JOHN WORKMAN - LETTERER

COVER DESIGN BY
LEILA DEL DUCA

EDITED BY
SHANNA MATUSZAK

IMAGE COMICS, INC.

Robert Kirkman - chief operating officer
Erik Larsen - chief financial officer
Todd McFarlane - president
Marc Silvestri - chief executive officer
Jim Valentino - vice president
Eric Stephenson - publisher
Corey Murphy - director of sales
Jeff Boison - director of publishing planning
& book trade sales

Chris Ross - director of digital sales
Jeff Stang - director of specialty sales
Kat Salazar - director of pr & marketing
Branwyn Bigglestone - controller
Kali Dugan - senior accounts manager
Sue Korpela - accounting & HR manager
Drew Gill - art director
Heather Doornink - production director
Leigh Thomas - print manager

Tricia Ramos - traffic manager
Briah Skelly - publicist
Aly Hoffman - conventions & events coordinator
Sasha Head - sales & marketing production designer
David Brothers - branding manager
Melissa Gifford - content manager
Drew Fitzgerald - publicity assistant
Vincent Kukua - production artist
Erika Schnatz - production artist

Ryan Brewer - production artist
Shanna Matuszak - production artist
Carey Hall - production artist
Esther Kim - direct market sales representative
Emilio Bautista - digital sales representative
Leanna Caunter - accounting analyst
Chloe Ramos-Peterson - library market sales representative
Marla Eizik - administrative assistant
IMAGECOMICS.COM